THE BALINTOL CYCLE II

The Dray Prescot Series

THE BALINTOL CYCLE II

Kenneth Bulmer

writing as
Alan Burt Akers

Published by
Bladud Books

First published in 2015 by Bladud Books

Originally published separately in German by Heyne Verlag in 1994-6.

Published separately by Mushroom eBooks as:
Scourge of Antares (2014)
Challenge of Antares (2014)
Wrath of Antares (2014)

This paperback omnibus edition published in 2015 by Bladud Books, an imprint of Mushroom Publishing, Bath, BA1 4EB, United Kingdom

www.bladudbooks.com

ISBN 978-1-84319-924-3

Contents

Scourge of Antares

Dray Prescot

If you are prepared to hurl yourself into adventure, to face peril with a brave heart, to risk all, then the marvelous world of Kregen offers you everything you have ever dreamed.

For Dray Prescot the challenges are enormous. Snatched up to Kregen, four hundred light years from Earth, by the giant Scorpion of the Star Lords, his task is to unite the sub-continent of Balintol to resist the reiving fish-headed Shanks from around the curve of the world. The trouble is—due to the megalomaniac striving for power of various factions within the countries of Balintol, the whole place looks set to go up in the flames of both Civil and Foreign Wars.

Dray Prescot, as described by one who has seen him on this Earth, is a man above middle height with brown hair and level brown eyes, with enormously broad shoulders and superbly muscled physique. He moves like a savage hunting cat, silent and lethal. There is about him an abrasive honesty and an indomitable courage. Reared in the harsh conditions of Nelson's Navy he is a man who considered himself a failure on Earth, but who has found himself and destiny upon the terrible and beautiful world of Kregen.

He has uncovered some of the details of a plot by the cultists of the religion of Dokerty in the country of Caneldrin. They have successfully contrived to turn ordinary men and women into receptacles for demons, who then destroy wantonly until the frail human body can no longer support the intolerable demonic forces. This horrific power will be turned upon the other countries of the subcontinent when Dray Prescot has the task of uniting Balintol.

Thoughts of Delia, Delia of Delphond, Delia of the Blue Mountains, sustain him in his darkest hours. Now he has escaped from the Dokerty temple with a mysterious young woman, Veda. They are fleeing for their lives as the Suns of Scorpio descend into night.

Alan Burt Akers

One

One intriguing fact about young Veda was her incredible ability to discard her clothing at the slightest opportunity. Here we were, fleeing for our lives through the twilight streets of Prebaya. She'd put on the clothes we'd borrowed during our escape from the temple. Now she ripped off and flung the skirt aside impatiently.

"Run better." She spoke curtly, sensibly saving her breath for running.

A few steps abaft, I bent and snatched the skirt up as I ran. Her long bare legs looked splendid in the last of the suns' radiance; skirts to cover them might not be so easily found later on.

The mob baying at our heels by this time had attracted all manner of riff-raff. The Katakis leading the pursuit might be hated and abhorred by most folk; the mob could sense blood and fun and so joined in the chase. Unless we outdistanced them or found a safe refuge we'd be done for.

We'd crossed the river by one of the many bridges and were now entering the aracloins where deviltry was a way of life among the narrow crooked streets. The smells of sour wine, of ancient cooking, of the sewers that were mostly above ground, assaulted our nostrils. The twin suns slanted down the sky and the mingled ruby and emerald shadows lay long. The evening's entertainments were beginning.

Leaping a festering gutter, Veda sprinted on and then at the junction of three alleyways halted. Grimy buildings leaned each side, lamps already throwing pools of yellow radiance into the red and green tinged shadows. Noise spurted up from a tavern on one side, and music sounded across the alley.

Veda, poised, looked about.

Well, she knew this city far better than did I. She must know where she intended to go. From our rear the dull roaring of the mob neared.

The tavern door swung open spilling orange light. A fellow reeled out, checked himself, straightened up, saw Veda.

Already this early in the evening his breath reeked of the devil drink dopa. His bulbous nose glowed, hair sprouted from under a flat leather cap, his clothes were grease-stained. He lurched towards Veda.

"My lovely!" he croaked. "You're mine. Come here!"

What he must have thought, seeing a superlatively beautiful girl just standing, poised, as though waiting for him, is anybody's guess. Those legs of Veda's, alone, must have dizzied him with lust.

He reached for her.

Oh, well, I said to myself, you might feel sorry for the idiot drunk; but we can't hang about here. We've a mob chasing us. I took a step forward ready to drag him off.

I needn't have bothered.

Veda's toes were very hard. Her legs were long and muscled. She kicked. She put those pretty iron-hard toes where they would do the most good.

Myself, I think the drunk felt more surprise than any other emotion. He just let out a: "Zhunk!" stood for a moment like a gate hit by a battering ram, and then he quietly doubled up and rolled over onto his side.

Here in Balintol we were nearer to the equator than was Vallia and so the Suns of Scorpio descended rapidly and the twilight did not last too long. Down our back trail the sparks of fire from torches showed where the Kataki-led mob thirsted for our blood. We could hear them yelling, a chilling sound, a sound, in truth, that should never issue from human throats. But it did.

I grabbed Veda's hand and pulled her on. Furiously she snatched her hand away. She ran on ahead, lithe and lovely in the erratic illumination. Abruptly, I felt the agonizing ache sweep over me. Ah! Delia! How much more wonderful was my Delia, Delia of Delphond, Delia of the Blue Mountains, even than this lovely girl!

Not for the first time I wondered what on Kregen I thought I was doing, running about in foreign lands, when I should be breaking all speed records back to Esser Rarioch where I could take Delia into my arms again. By Vox! I knew why. The Star Lords constrained me. Even now much of my destiny lay in their superhuman hands.

Running along through the nighted streets of Prebaya, I knew I could not leave here until the task was finished. Those damned demons, those horrific ibmanzies, would flood over Balintol destroying everything in their path. The regent, C'Chermina, would gloat in her triumph. Balintol would run with blood. And my task to unite the subcontinent against the Shanks would have failed.

That outcome, of course, was not to be contemplated.

The mob kept doggedly following our route.

We twisted and turned through dolorous alleys, dodged up side streets, kept going at a good speed.

Persistently, the pursuit clung on.

The destination that I wished to attain with Veda in Prebaya could not be visited with that chase on our tails. The hunt bayed on remorselessly. We were unable to shake them off.

There was, by Krun, only one reasonable explanation for that!

Giving the fleeting form of Veda a shrewd look among the blurred lights and shadows I fancied she'd have to use her special trick and throw off the rest of her borrowed clothing.

By now numbers of people were moving in the more open streets. From alley to alley as we fled we had, necessarily, from time to time, to cross or traverse one of the streets where the evening's pleasures could be found. Puppet shows, fire eaters, food stalls, balladeers, thronged the torch-lit scene. Beggars called out ceaselessly. Here we slowed to a brisk walk. Although Veda attracted admiring glances she did not stand out because of her attire. There were many women scantily-clad laughing with painted faces.

We came out onto a kyro which was far better lit than most of the plazas in this area. Folk were moving towards a large structure, festooned with lamps, from which came the strains of popular music.

Veda rapped out: "We'll have to cross. There's no other way."

About to agree and follow her lead, I paused.

"Hold on, Veda. This might just be the place."

She gave me a look. Now I'd had a long day in which much had occurred. I was entitled to be tired. Tiredness, as you know, is a sin and must be ignored. But Veda? She'd been through some fraught experiences and was by now probably thoroughly tired out. A decision had to be made.

I made it. "In we go," I said. "And smile!"

"You—!" she started. Then: "Yes, all right. I see."

We joined the couples entering and paid over the admission charge, a silver apiece. Mind you, I reflected as we went in, there was something very different about this whole atmosphere and place of Balintol from other countries of Kregen. Balintol had always been spoken of as a land of mystery. True, I'd encountered some highly unhealthy mysteries here. At one time I'd been foolish enough to think Balintol not very different from anywhere else, as I'd once thought the same of Loh, until events showed otherwise. The truth probably lay somewhere between, halfway between the familiar and the unknown.

The foyer was decorated in a vulgarly ostentatious fashion. Beyond that the dancing area was flanked by chairs and tables and drinks were being served. This establishment clearly aped its betters in the more refined parts of the city.

There was no doubt that we'd have done better to have found a Baths of the Nine; nothing so grand was likely to last here. We'd just have to make the best of it, do what we had to do, and then get to hell out of it.

Veda glanced around, chin up. She knew exactly what she was about. Whilst this establishment stood absolutely no comparison with places like The Dancing Rostrum in Ruathytu, it had a style far higher than the dens of iniquity past which we had fled. Veda told me to make my way to the far end.

"We'll go out that far door. More respectable avenues there."

I nodded. Evidently we'd cut across a neck of the poor section and this place, called Nalgre Froi's Deren, stood at the line of juncture. Meetings could take place here, and liaisons begun. This was an interesting slant on the mores of the Prebayans.

Veda went off and I began slowly to edge around past the drinkers. There had been no weapons check at the doors, although bouncers stood in strategic spots to jump on trouble the moment it began. Because of those two facts, a certain decorum prevailed.

All the same, being the kind of dump it was, I was not at all surprised to detect the furtive fingers at my belt and purse.

Putting my brown fist over the hand after my purse, I squeezed reasonably hard—reasonably hard. No more, I swear, by Krun!

A gasp of shock as much of pain blasted up, so I looked down into the narrow anguished face of the polsim who writhed about like a fish on a hook.

"Master! Master!" he managed to stutter out. "Please! I meant no harm—please!"

I let him go.

He scuttled off into the crowd of drinkers, a flurry of narrow legs and raggedy clothes and a hand tucked up under the other armpit. I felt quite sorry for the little fellow.

A broad hand clapped me on the shoulder. A voice boomed: "Poor old Larghos Deft-fingers! He caught a right woflo in you, dom."

The speaker, an olumai all white and black, clutched a tankard, smiling widely. He was dressed in the finery that a farmer would don going off to his weekly treat in the big city.

"I suppose you have to feel sorry for 'em."

His use of woflo here was an intriguing linguistic affectation, after the fashion of The Savage Woflo as a name for a tavern.

"Sorry? Aye, by Tolaar, if they don't steal my silver."

He gave a hiccup, slopped some ale, and, smiling, wandered off. The sword he wore was a braxter, and there were two knives in his belt. There was no doubt that a pickpocket's trade here was difficult.

Shortly after that as I reached the far wall and saw the exit through a passageway, I understood that the thieves hereabouts well understood the difficulties of their profession and took steps accordingly.

Out on the floor dancers swayed and gyrated. The music blared selections of popular airs. The atmosphere reeked of cheap perfume and sweat and good humor and—thankfully—not a single solitary trace of tobacco smoke. People wanted to enjoy themselves. I wanted to grab Veda and get out of here just as fast as possible.

I fretted, standing just to the side of the exit passage. Where was the girl?

Larghos Deft-fingers clearly had decided that he was not finished with me. Not a chance, by Diproo the Nimble-Fingered!

Here he was, smirking, walking towards me with half a dozen of his cronies. They walled me off in the passageway from the main hall. They were a mixed bunch of diffs, but they all held wicked-looking knives in their fists.

They fancied they could overwhelm me in a single charge and sweeping me through the passageway finish me off outside. No one in the noise and uproar of the dancing hall would be any the wiser.

Just as they were about to launch themselves forward, knives first, a chorus of screams and shrieks burst up from the entrance.

Through the shrieks of panic a sound rose, a chilling, ominous sound that was joined by others. The thieves, wrapped up in their desire to finish me off, charged. And, over all, the deep baying of the bloodhounds that had followed us here mounted to a crescendo of anticipated final destruction.

Two

I, Dray Prescot, Vovedeer, Lord of Strombor and Krozair of Zy, faced by seven thieves brandishing knives would, in normal circumstances, have been merely inconvenienced. Now, though, there was young Veda to consider. Where was the girl?

The cut over her left breast which we'd staunched with underclothes continued to trouble me. I felt we'd been lucky the bleeding had not started again in all our exertions. Veda needed the attentions of a Puncture Lady, and the quicker the sooner, by Vox!

Larghos Deft-fingers in his cunning polsim way started off the attack bravely enough. Then he drew back slightly to allow a Rapa, all bristle greeny feathers, to get at me. At his side another Rapa who could have been the first's twin joined in. A third Rapa tried to edge around to stab me in the flank.

This, I felt, was no occasion for the Krozair brand. So I drew my drexer.

The first two Rapas looked most astonished not to say shocked when with a twinkle the blade lay flat alongside their beaks. What was going on in the dance hall must be highly entertaining, for the racket bloomed to the roof. The deep ominous baying continued, so I surmised the bloodhounds were still on their leashes and were snuffling their way through the crowds. The dancers must be flying off every which way, by Krun!

The third Rapa essayed his attack so I skipped aside, leaving him short, and hit a largish polsim over the head. This fellow fell down all tangled up with Larghos Deft-fingers. The two Rapas on the floor slumbered and their fellow, having missed his first onslaught, checked. There should be two polsims left to deal with.

There was only one standing. As I swung towards him he fell down. He tumbled down atop of the polsim who should have been helping him. I looked—and I gaped.

Veda held a bottle in each hand. Her face flushed rosy through her pale skin. She looked cross.

"Do you always get into scrapes, jikai?"

"Uh—" I started and then leaped and so brought down the hesitating Rapa.

Veda looked at Larghos Deft-fingers.

"This the blintz?"

Before I could answer Larghos fell to his knees and clasped his hands before his face in the attitude of prayer.

"Master! Mistress! Please—"

Well, yes, the recumbent bodies bore some resemblance to the aftermath of a battle. Veda gave him a smart kick. She wore new shoes. The rest of her outfit was new, a decorous deep blue tunic and skirt.

"The bloodhounds," she snapped out. "Come on!"

The bloodhounds had not yet started in to snarling, so there was time. In addition, as was to be expected, a flood of refugees from the ruined dance poured towards the exit. What they thought of the unconscious bodies scattered about I'd no idea. Veda and I were swept away in the rout.

I call these tracker dogs bloodhounds because that is what their name is in Kregish. They are not, however, a lot like Earthly bloodhounds having six legs and fangs rather longer than shorter. They'll track the scent of your clothes and when they grip their choppers into your rump, well, then, dom, you stay gripped.

When I'd grabbed the outfit for Veda from the temple dressing room I'd snatched up various garments from different pegs. Now I saw that had been a mistake. The owners had identified their missing clothes, the dogs had sniffed the rest of the outfit, and set off on our scent, baying. None of my clothes had been left. Now Veda was freshly dressed we had a chance to make good our escape.

So, together with the panic-stricken dancers, we fled.

Out in the street we all rushed. It was quite warm and so far the rain had not started. The girls in their fancy, scanty dancing costumes shouldn't suffer from the weather. Veda, of course, had picked an outdoor suit, and very fine she looked in it, too.

Every which way everybody ran and soon we were able to slip off into a side street and so free ourselves of the panic-stricken herd.

The Maiden with the Many Smiles rose about then and shone her pinkish light down refulgently. We walked quietly on through pink-tinged shadows.

"What did you do with the clothes?"

"Buried them in the vosk swill."

"Ah!"

So that piece of forward thinking had been what had delayed her. This Veda, of whom I knew nothing, was proving to be a lady of parts.

Mind you, there was no way of telling just how good the Dokerty bloodhounds were at following a scent. If Veda's blood was in their nostrils we were still in danger. Not for the first time in my hectic career on Kregen I wished for the impossible—like, for instance, right now, the ability to shed all betraying scents and possess the power of invisibility. Still, all that was for the fairy stories they told kiddies in the nursery.

In addition, and this may sound ridiculously backhanded, to have powers of that order would make adventuring remarkably dull, by Krun!

The costume Veda had borrowed from Nalgre Froi's Deren stood no comparison with the sumptuous outfit we'd liberated from the temple disrobing room. Mind you, she had put on a skirt which reached down to her knees. Instead of a voluminous cloak she'd flung a dark green cape about her shoulders on brass cords, and now she pushed the hood back so that the Maiden with the Many Smiles lit up her flaxen hair to smokey-gold. Oh, yes, a splendid woman, Veda!

She tilted her face up to me. "There is nowhere safe in the city I may go."

Like the onker I am, I blurted out: "But I thought you were running to friends—"

She shook her head. "No."

By the disgusting diseased liver and lights of Makki Grodno! My lips clamped shut. "Sink me!" I snarled to myself. "So that plan is shot into tiny little pieces."

Therefore, a fresh plan was called for, and needed in a hurry.

Obviously there was one place I could go and be perfectly safe. Veda would be safe there, too—unless the regent C'Chermina wanted to bring an overseas war to add to the wars she intended to foment in Balintol. Mind you, with these damned ibmanzies of her Dokerty-loving chief priest to call on, the crazed woman might not shrink from challenging a powerful empire.

If she did that, why, then, what of my obedience to the desires of the Star Lords to unite Balintol? Not only would I have failed in that, I'd have spread the conflagration over a much wider area. By the Black Chunkrah! What a moil for a simple sailorman!

A piquant thought struck me. My Val! Suppose I did!

After my recent highly unsavory interview with the lady Quensella when her passion had overwhelmed her sensibilities, suppose I turned up bringing with me a beautiful girl! What would be Quensella's reaction? Anger, resentment, the overpowering feeling of being rejected for another woman? Nothing I could say would convince her of anything other than that I had scorned her for another.

And, by Krun, we all know what hath no fury compared with that!

So therefore it seemed there was nothing else for it but to go and see Elten Naghan Vindo. My cover name was Varghan na Vernheim, and I did not particularly want young Veda to know that.

Veda asked just the once about our destination and I simply said that we were going to see a friend I'd recently made in the city and who, I hoped, would help us. We walked along more silent than not. When we arrived, even though we went in the back way she could quite plainly see this was the Vallian Embassy.

She gave me a quick upward glance. "You have—interesting—friends, Drajak the Sudden."

"I just hope he'll help us."

I was not going to tell her that Elten Naghan would jump through flaming hoops to assist me, for was I not Dray Prescot, once Emperor of Vallia, and now Emperor of Emperors, Emperor of All Paz?

That title and conception, which I continued to find ridiculous, was quite clearly not going to be easily accepted by quite a lot of people. Right now, it was not being accepted by the regent, the lady C'Chermina. Mind you, who could blame her? How would you like some foreigner strutting in and telling you he was going to become your overlord? Or her, for that matter. Oh, no, by the distended belly and swollen thighs of the Divine Madam of Belschutz! Tsleetha tsleethi, softly softly, as they say, to persuade great and puissant lords that for the good of Paz they had to unite.

Speaking the name of Varghan na Vernheim so that Veda could not hear, and then ushering her into the hall and through to the ambassador's private apartments, gave me the opportunity of putting my finger to my lips as the Elten received us, smiling. He understood at once.

"Lahal. I am glad to see you—Horter Drajak."

"Lahal. And I you, notor. May I introduce this lady, Veda, who is in immediate need of a Puncture Lady."

In very short order after that Veda was carted off into a bedroom where a Hytak woman of extreme competence, Suzy the Surcease, shooed we mere men out. "She'll be as bright as the celene in the morning," Suzy said in her brisk way. "Now let me stick some needles in her and clean up the cuts." Out, therefore, we trailed.

Closeted with Naghan Vindo and with a good wine in my fist I told him what I knew of Veda. Unlike many of the splendid young women I'd met in my adventures upon Kregen, she couldn't be affectionately called 'that young madam' or 'that little lady'. There was in her a core of seriousness, of gravity. She did smile—from time to time.

Naghan confirmed that she would be kept safely in the embassy until between us we sorted out what would be best for her future. Then I turned in, and, as always, my last thought before sleep was exceedingly sweet.

Because of my dip in the Sacred Pool in far Aphrasöe wounds healed with phenomenal speed without leaving the trace of a scar. The next morning, rested and bandaged up, Veda surprised me by her recovery rate. She ate an enormous first breakfast and we finished as ever with luscious palines. They, alone, revived the weary.

Gently, I put certain questions, and gradually her story came out. Her name began with a Double—V'Veda—and went on for a mouthful of syllables before ending in charran. She'd been born in Kildrin, where her father was a priest of Aaran and her mother a priestess. Aaran, I gathered, was a small and select religion of the utmost dedication. Her childhood had been severe, unpleasant, rigidly disciplined. She had eight brothers, four sets of twins, and she'd come along right in the middle. As a lone girl in a family of boys her upbringing had been a rough and tumble struggle to survive. Sitting quietly, slightly bent forward with her hands clasped between her knees, she spoke composedly. She had been beaten by her father far too frequently.

One day she suffered a beating far worse than anything she had experienced before and so she had run away.

"I wasn't even naughty. My brothers and I were working with the other boys and my dress fell off."

The fact was perfectly plain that as she grew up she had no idea her body was developing into dazzling beauty.

"So I ran away. I should have run away before. I was lucky enough to be taken under the wing of a lady going to join the Jikai Vuvushis of Kildrin."

Of course, other countries of Kregen besides Vallia had their sororities of War Women, Battle Maidens.

Veda had learned well, as I could testify by her spirited actions during our hectic if brief acquaintance. The trouble was, the disciplined lifestyle reminded her too much of her miserable childhood. Then she fell in with Dokerty.

As she told me, with a sigh, the revelation was magical. Here was a religion so vastly different from that in which she had been brought up, so libertarian in its beliefs, so free in its actions, that she had plunged in head over heels. She had become a devoted Dokerty disciple.

Caneldrin offered a place where she could start afresh. Her devotion and dedication had elevated her rapidly through the lower ranks and she had been selected for special training. She was recruited into what became the ibmanzy programme.

Then the man she referred to as His Highness turned lustful eyes upon her. The result of her scornful rejection brought her to the condition in which I'd met her—a victim of the ibmanzy programme.

Her lips twisted. "At home they called me Veda the Mazarnil." That is to say, Veda the Unruly. "I lived up to my name, to my great misfortune, until you came along, Drajak the Sudden."

"I am glad I was able," I said, uncomfortably.

"Very able." She essayed one of her rare smiles. "Oh, yes, you carry weapons like his, and ape his ways and sayings, and carry it off very well; but you're no Dray Prescot."

My harsh old wine spout remained very firmly shut.

By all the devils in a Herrelldrin Hell! The many books and plays and puppet shows and songs about Dray Prescot got everywhere in Paz these days! I scooped up a handful of palines and placed—not popped—the luscious yellow berries one at a time into my mouth, for I didn't trust myself to say anything at that precise moment.

How could a simple sailorman like me live up to the inflated legend of the Dray Prescot festering in the credulous minds of all the folk who believed implicitly in the fantastic stories of his prowess?

This line of conversation had to be terminated, and terminated at once. Far more importantly, the fascinating prospect of what young Veda could reveal of the ibmanzy project tantalized me with expectation. By Vox! She'd been at the heart of the damned business, assistant to this bastard called His Highness. He was marked down in what can euphemistically be dubbed my little black book.

Very little in the way of subtle questioning was needed to start the Mazarnil telling me what she knew.

As she began to speak the ambassador came in carrying a book. He sat quietly in a chair in the comfortable sitting room placed at our disposal, listening intently.

Religion is a relentless taskmaster. Many incredible acts have been performed in the service of one religion or another. Belief can move mountains. Here we had the case of belief in the existence of a pantheon of demons actually bringing them into existence. By whatever means they made the journey from their occult other realm to Kregen, make that awful leap they did.

Whilst remaining unconvinced they were real demons of the devilish persuasion within the occult, I had to accept that they did exist once they'd taken over the body of a human being. Let loose over Kregen they would become a scourge.

From what I'd already witnessed I knew the pathway was opened by inflicting intolerable pain upon the subject. His own ib, his spirit, was suffused by demonic forces from whatever dark realm they spawned, grew, bloated, became an ibmanzy.

When that bastard called His Highness leveled the symbol of the two upflung wings at the victim, and shouted: 'Dokomek!' in the voice of command, the ibmanzy took over.

What I wanted to know from Veda was how that command would reach the ibmanzies when they were scattered throughout Balintol.

"Dokerty," she told us in a tight, controlled voice, "is the great god. Oltomek is his hand upon the face of Kregen."

She hesitated, and then went on in so low a voice we leaned closer. "I have seen what I did not see, what I did not want to see. I now wish I had never met with Dokerty. I see clearly now, now it is too late. Regrets—"

"The thing now is, Veda the Unruly," I said, "regrets are useless baggage in life. We have to find a way to halt this monstrous project, and you're the only one who can help us."

"Yes."

She admitted she was not fully aware of all the processes. I felt alarmed dismay at this. The method once she explained it was mind-bogglingly obvious, logical, and dazzlingly simple—in hindsight.

Belief.

"There is concealed in the winged symbol, the Flutubium," she said in that small voice, "a thing sacred to Dokerty. It is said to have been sent down from Dokerty himself by the hand of Oltomek to the first high priest when Dokerty revealed himself to Kregen. These things are kept secret. They are known to few."

"What is it, Veda?"

"A Prism of Power."

Well, now. Belief in the powers of the god and his prophet channeled through the Prism of Power—that, then, was the answer. People of Kregen believed in their wizards, for they could see what marvels the sorcerers wrought. That was belief. Religious belief, too, could work miracles. Oltomek would carry the messages across the world to turn ordinary young men and women into monsters.

We all sat silent for some time. I could feel in the atmosphere in the room an oppressive closeness, an unpleasant reminder of the claustrophobic pressure within the temple to Dokerty.

Finally, Naghan Vindo stirred. He tugged his little goatee, and the book fell from his lap onto the carpet. He picked it up. The gaudy cover blazed the title *Dray Prescot and the Castle of Doom*. I winced.

"What, then," said the ambassador, "is to be done about these devilish ibmanzies?"

Veda looked up, and then pointed a rigid forefinger at the book.

"I do not know. But if he were here, Dray Prescot would know what to do, and go out and do it!"

Three

What I intended to do was go out and steal the Prism of Power.

Just how that desirable objective was to be achieved I didn't yet know. From what I knew of the temple to Dokerty I might be able to sneak in using the secret passageways. Veda could probably make a fair shot at mapping them for me. There were those damned Whiptails to consider. The Katakis presumably were no longer finding rich pickings for their slaving habits among prisoners of war. So they'd signed on as guards for the temple. Once the wars began they'd be at their despicable trade, like a flock of Rippasch, ripping flesh.

The silence in the room held after Veda's last remark. She'd spoken with more passion than at any other time during the whole talk. The pallor of her face was emphasized by the faintest of flushes along her cheekbones.

I said: "I may not be the fabled Dray Prescot. But I intend to steal this wonderful Prism of Power."

The Ambassador coughed, and put a delicate yellow lace kerchief to his mouth.

"Yes!" snapped Veda. "But—!" She checked.

I told her she was in no fit state to accompany me. She flared up at this, so I threatened her with Suzy the Surcease, whose word, I told the Unruly, was law.

The thought crossed my mind that I hoped she wouldn't regard me in the same light as her father.

From the story of her miserable upbringing anybody could see that she would inevitably not care for men, not particularly care at all. In fact, from what she had suffered she'd be bound to hate men. That fact that I'd rescued her from being turned into an ibmanzy, and she'd then given me the jikai, might—perhaps—cause her to look on some men with a little less disfavor.

She was looking at me now with a long calculating stare. "The Prism of Power is well guarded. Those disgusting Katakis—" Her shoulders shook briefly. Her head went up. "Yes, well. I need to serve Gralufon for what he did. And His Highness. You will need a guide through the temple."

Gralufon, therefore, was the name of Granumin's twin brother. If he ran security for the temple he'd be the tough nut I'd already assessed him to be. Of course, a guide would be useful.

"You're not fit," I said in my old gravel shifting voice.

So, naturally, a wrangle ensued.

The upshot of that little argument saw Veda with more color in her face than I'd ever seen before. She breathed deeply. Her nostrils pinched in. She worked herself up into a right old paddy.

She called me a few choicely ripe names, too. But, to my relief, she didn't say something to the effect that I was just like any other blintz of a man. I needed her friendship, for I needed her knowledge of the ibmanzy project if Balintol—and Paz—were to be saved.

In the event, as I'd threatened her with Suzy the Surcease when she'd first flared up in anger, I damned well had to come through on my word. Suzy stuck a few needles into the Unruly, who promptly went into a calm, deep sleep.

Staring down at her as she lay under a thin yellow sheet in the bed, with Suzy making sure she was comfortable, I reflected that during my hectic career upon Kregen a considerable number of headstrong women had bothered me. Quite apart from the queens and empresses and the grand ladies of that ilk, I recalled how Mevancy and Tiri, to name but two of the most recent, had bedeviled me. Rather glumly, I suppose, I fancied this willful young lady with her serious ways would give me a whole heap more trouble.

I shook myself. This was no way for a bold thrusting adventurer to behave, by Krun!

The ambassador swiftly provided me with the change of clothes I requested. A simple russet tunic, not a shamlak, with black bone fastenings. The trousers were russet too, and gathered in at the ankle in the style here. The cape was dark gray, covering my weapons. A red—or reddish—outfit has always, as you know, been my choice; now, though, with these cramphs of the Dokerty persuasion prancing around in their red robes, the color served a dual purpose.

Breaking into palaces and temples is so very often the proper business of your gallant adventurer. I'd done that a few times, by Vox! But, I never forgot that each time was different. What perils lurked in the temple to Dokerty only time would reveal. That they'd be unpleasant was a foregone conclusion.

"Well, Drajak," said Naghan Vindo, "you are set on this?"

I hitched up my sword. "Yep."

He let out a little sigh, and then tugged his goatee.

"My duty requires me to send a report to the Emperor."

There was no answer to that. I asked him to tell my lad Drak, the Emperor of Vallia, that his father might be a harebrained maniac but that there seemed no other way of resolving the problem of the ibmanzies. The regent C'Chermina had the young king, Yando, under her thumb. Should she succeed in her lunatic ambitions to conquer Tolindrin and then Winlan to the north west, she'd go after the other countries of Balintol. Then, why then, by Vox, she might cast megalomaniac eyes upon Vallia. Drak should start to make preparations.

Of course, by that time yours truly, Dray Prescot, would be cast away on the planet of his birth, four hundred light years from his home on Kregen. The Star Lords, the Everoinye, were not to be failed. Oh, no, by the pendulous bosom and bounteous bottom of the Divine Madam of Belschutz!

There was nothing else for it. I just had to go off and grab this infernal Prism of Power.

As you know, my comrade Wizard of Loh, Deb Lu Quienyin, had shown me how to alter my facial appearance, subtly changing the planes and angles. This deception could be kept up for some time, albeit at the cost of considerable discomfort. Every time I put on a new face the effect was as of a swarm of bumblebees all stinging like crazy. The more often I used this wizardly technique, the less it stung, to be sure. But, by Krun, sting it still did!

Naghan Vindo produced a wide-brimmed hat at my request. Black and without feathers, it would serve to shield my face until the time came for me to change my appearance.

The hat did not have the two slots in the front brim that are so distinctive of Vallian apparel. I put it on and tweaked the brim down so that shadows fell over my face.

"Very fetching," said the ambassador in his dry way.

I felt my lips twitch. Oh, yes, we Vallians—as I considered myself a Vallian among many other homelands—like the humor of a situation no matter how dark and ominous the surroundings.

The ambassador leaned across the table and picked up the sheet of paper on which Veda during those moments when she hadn't been shouting at me had sketched out a plan of what she knew of the temple. As she had indicated, the inner sanctum was well guarded. The whole place was a mazy labyrinth, like so many temples and palaces upon Kregen. Apart from the vulgarly imposing front entrance, I knew of two other doors. One stood in the blind wall at the back where I'd first ventured in, the other where Veda had led us out. Neither of those, I fancied, would prove suitable.

She had marked other entrances, with some idea of what lay beyond them. The quarters occupied by His Highness consisted, on Veda's map, of a blank square surrounded by porticoes and anterooms. This confounded winged symbol, the Flutubium, must be concealed somewhere there. Most probably it was stuck in some damned heathen shrine above an altar. If they sacrificed young virgins on that, I, for one, would not be surprised.

This whole enterprise looked more and more difficult the longer I looked at it. Well, I'd stop fretting and get on with it. There was one useful way of insinuating myself into the temple to Dokerty. Accordingly, that was exactly what I would do.

"This looks a right leem's nest." The ambassador tugged his goatee, frowning at Veda's map. "I'd better have some of my lads go with you."

"That's a sporting offer, Naghan. But—no thanks. I'll be slipperier on my own."

"As you wish." In his dry way he added: "I had, of course, intended to accompany you myself."

By Krun! Here it was again! This correct diplomat knew the stories of Dray Prescot, how he went haring off over Kregen clad in a scarlet breech-clout and wielding a Great Krozair longsword. So, like many another, he hungered for the chance to go along. With some carefully chosen words I soothed him down. He retained his dignity intact.

Now, as you know, many and many a time I've laid a pretty plan and many and many a time my clever scheme has gone hideously wrong.

There should be no insuperable difficulty in assuming the face of one of the people in the Dokerty pest-hole. So I'd be able to get in. The problem thereafter was obvious. No. Oh, no, by Vox. I had to find out something about this person, whoever it might be. Enough information had to be gathered to allow me to make sensible replies to simple questions.

I stood up.

"Right, Naghan, I'm off. I'm not breaking into the temple now. I want to find out more. You'll see me again when you do."

"Majister."

I gave a sort of half cough half grunt at this nicety and took myself off.

Selecting a suitable mark was not difficult. Positioning myself outside the temple in a shadowy alcove I assumed that guileless face, not quite stupid, more that of a simpleton, which has served me so well in the past. In addition, its very simpleness meant it did not sting like the deuce all the time.

When the fellow I wanted walked out—strutted out rather—in an affected, pompous way, I followed him and by bumping into him and apologizing profusely and buttering on the flattery, and buying him a drink, convinced him he had met a boon companion. I hung on his every word, oohing and aahing as appropriate. He was fleshy, with broken veins over his nose, and watery eyes. The broken veins would have to be painted on with cosmetics. He appeared to be slightly more bulky than I was. His might be mostly fat and mine muscle, but I could ape him well enough. I sucked up to him. He talked. He had a black-fanged winespout that loved to hear its own words. I learned enough, I fancied, for my purpose.

He said his name was Hyslop Nath ti Vernaloin. He told me this with such an air of pomposity, of grandness, that I guessed I was supposed to be mightily impressed.

Despite his name and his attitude he was still only a sub-priest, although with pretensions and, as he assured me with the gesture he had of rubbing that veinous nose, the certainty of achieving senior priesthood in the next couple of seasons.

This Hyslop struck me as being the perfect pompous nincompoop for my nefarious purposes.

The one great problem that still faced me was—where to stow the idiot?

The day wore on, it rained a trifle, we went for a meal, for which I paid, and then I decided it was time to act. At my suggestion we had taken a private room at The Harland Lifter, a middling tavern where, I recall, tensed up as I was for the murky deeds ahead, the ale was very fair. We sat eating palines from a pottery dish.

"Praise to Dokerty!" enunciated this fat Hyslop, popping a paline. I stood up, casually, and walked across so that I would pass beyond his chair. He did not turn around as he went on talking. "You're a very fine fellow, Logan." I'd told him my name was Logan Umpitor. "A very fine fellow. Now if you joined us in Dok—"

He stopped gabbling away by reason of the fact that he went to sleep. Admittedly, he went to sleep sitting instead of standing as more often than not happened. I took my pressing, cunning fingers away from his neck, and sighed. The things one did in the service of the Star Lords!

His clothes came off in a trice, he was bound hand and foot and gagged with the table cloth and the curtain cords and stuffed away in a cupboard among the crockery. I bundled up my own clothes and hid them in the upholstered bottom of a chair, thanking all the Names that I'd discovered this suitable hiding place. He wore a braxter and daggers.

The cape would cover my rapier and my drexer would pass as a braxter. Now you will well understand I was loath to part with the trusty Krozair brand. It was concealed well enough; there would be times, I felt sure, when some movement would reveal it about the person of Hyslop Nath ti Vernaloin. He did not carry a longsword.

There were plenty of the northern and local longswords in the city. I felt I could not risk abandoning the Krozair blade, particularly when at any moment I might be confronted by a damned great ibmanzy, a foaming maniacal monster out to destroy me utterly. Only the Krozair longsword had proved effective against one of these demons. No, by the Blade of Kurin! The weapon must be kept.

Well aware of the risks I was taking I went downstairs in the exaggeratedly important strut of Hyslop and told the landlord that my friend was sleeping it off, that I'd be back later. I paid over gold—Hyslop's gold, I might add, to my secret glee—retained the room for the night and requested my friend Logan Umpitor not be disturbed. Then I went off, wearing Hyslop's face as well as his clothes. The game, as they say in Clishdrin, was afoot.

One odd fact I noticed was that wearing red gave me quite a lift in spirits.

Entering the vulgar temple by the front stairways and giant doors, I found the obnoxious personality of Hyslop served me well. I stuck my nose in the air and stalked on.

From Veda's map committed to memory the various pathways and corridors proved easy to follow. The usual motley assemblage of people moved about their business in the temple. The air smelled unpleasantly close, of sweat and incense and—quite distinct to an old leem-hunter—of fear.

What went on between these grim walls was enough to induce outright terror in the stoutest of hearts.

Few guards showed themselves until some way into the structure. A party of mixed diffs marched past escorting a girl in the last stages of exhaustion. She was naked. Instinctively my hand gripped onto my sword hilt. Then I, Dray Prescot, had to harden my heart. There was nothing in reality I could do, and, in addition, I knew nothing of the case. If she was to be punished that would be a normal and accepted part of running the temple. By the time I'd reached that reluctant conclusion, the guards rounded a corner and were gone.

All the same, mind you! What had Dray Prescot become in these latter days upon Kregen! Still, in those early days when I'd gone raving into instant action, I'd not had the enormous burdens and responsibilities weighing me down now.

Of course, she was just one poor little naked girl being dragged off to some ghastly punishment. Nothing at all to do with me. She was nothing whatsoever to do with me, who was supposed to be the Emperor of Emperors, the Emperor of All Paz.

Was she?

Without really understanding, I found myself brisking up in that strutting, ridiculous walk of Hyslop's.

Around the corner after the party of guards I went.

They were just about to pass through a doorway smaller rather than larger than most of the portals in here. The door was black.

By the trailing infested entrails and mucus congested eyeballs of Makki Grodno! No! This was sheer lunacy. This would smash my plan to pieces! I had to get after the Prism of Power.

There was no escape.

I was still the maniacal Dray Prescot who'd been brought to Kregen and gone sailing down the River Aph with a Scorpion for crew. No, there was no escape from my destiny.

Turning my face to the wall I changed it, putting on the simple countenance that served me so well.

I hitched up my sword. I finished with Hyslop's stupid strut.

Cursing destiny, cursing my fate, cursing what you will, off I charged through the black doorway after the guards.

Four

The door opened onto a courtyard. The slanting rays of the twin suns fell in ruby and emerald across the northern wall. Shadows bathed the rest, the courtyard was not overlarge and the walls were three storeys tall, pierced with small dormitory-like windows. The impression I had, from this place and from Veda's map, was that it formed a wing of the main building.

The party ahead were just about to enter a door opposite, and a girl coming out shrank away. She was a Fristle and she wore a neat yellow apron over her simple clothes. I followed.

There were eight guardsmen in the audo, the section being commanded by a dwa-Deldar. They went into the building. The Fristle serving girl gave me a little half-bow of the head, half-curtsey as we passed. Having some knowledge of the way these places were run and disciplined, I felt it prudent to give no friendly acknowledgement.

Inside the door a blackwood staircase led up. The walls were lath and plaster, daubed here and there with an ochre paint. Among the mingled odors of dust and polish there lingered the strong after-scent of cheap perfume.

These rooms, then, were the living quarters of the female servants of Dokerty's temple.

So—what would a sub priest be doing here?

Hyslop's clothes proclaimed his rank. Bluff—yes, that was the way of it. A few hints, a haughty mien, and I might just get away with it. If I didn't—well, eight guardsmen, none of whom was from any of the more renowned warrior races of diffs, would have to be disposed of—sharpish, by Krun, very sharpish!

At the next landing I peered cautiously around to see the dwa-Deldar pushing open a door along the near side of the corridor. His men took the girl in and, shortly, came out again. The door was closed, a man posted to stand guard, and the audo began to march back again towards me. I marked the door. Then I ran silently back down the stairs and out into the courtyard.

Spinning about, I stood for a moment, and began slowly to walk towards the open door. The Deldar came out first, saw me, and for a fraction of a second a tiny smile moved his lips. So it was going to be all right, thank Zair!

"Notor!" he barked in true Deldar fashion. So these jumped up priests of Dokerty gave themselves the name of lord, did they? I half-lifted a hand.

"Deldar!"

He went off with his men and without looking back I sprinted up the blackwood stairs.

By this time I felt totally committed to this foolish and harebrained behavior of mine. Now I'd have to see the hand played through to the end.

Mind you, I could quite clearly see how ridiculous all this was. There might be any number of explanations for the girl's condition. She might have fainted at work. Yes; but why should the soldiers have dragged her along so callously? Anyway, she was a Hytak, and the Hytak women are known as being tough as well as nice-looking.

Very often I know in this my narrative I fail to give the race of a person among the splendid array of Kregen's diffs. But people are people, and do not assume everyone I mention is apim, Homo sapiens sapiens like me.

The guard on duty looked up as I approached. Again, that small, secret smile fleeted across his face. I went to walk past boldly, not deigning to notice him. He continued to look at me, and barked: "Notor!" in a swod's imitation of a Deldar's bull roar.

This made my attempt to press the vital spot under his ear difficult. He jerked back from my hand. His face showed shock; but all the same he snatched at his sword hilt. So I had to hit him.

This I did, and he pitched over. I caught him as he fell and eased him to the floor. He'd be out for long enough, I hoped, for me to complete this hazardous, stupid, completely nonsensical mission with which I'd saddled myself.

The door opened easily. The room was a bedroom cum sitting room, cheaply furnished. The girl lay on the bed. They hadn't even bothered to throw a coverlet over her naked body.

Her eyes opened as I approached.

"Who—? What—?"

"It's all right," I said in a voice I tried to make calm and reasonable. She scrabbled up and huddled back, her hands to her breast. "I'm not going to hurt you. You are in trouble, I can see."

"Go away!" She husked it out, and she began to tremble.

Opaz knew what she was imagining. Something dreadful, of that I could be sure. I tried to smile. "I've come to help you."

Hoping that some normal action might calm her down, I looked around the tawdry room. A tunic hung over the back of the only chair and a skirt lay neatly folded on the seat. These garments I handed to her and, after a moment's hesitation, she put them on. As for underclothes, that was up to her. "I want to help you. How are they going to punish you?"

She did not cry very much. As she sobbed out her story, I dragged the unconscious guard in and tied him up with strips of the bedclothes. She reacted to this. But, rather cruelly, I suppose, I considered the fact of the guard being dealt with in so summary a fashion made her see she was committed. She had not cried out for help, that was for sure.

As I listened I realized with sinking feelings of mingled horror and despair that I'd made a right leem's nest of this.

Oh, yes, by Vox! How I'd completely made a stupendous mistake! All the same, this Renata was now my responsibility. Despite what she was, I had to get her out of the temple.

"And they're going to send my darling Sando up to Winlan." Her voice choked up with despair. "And they want to send me to Tolindrin. Oh, what can I do? They'll beat me, beat me terribly."

What a confounded idiot this Dray Prescot was! Here he was, out of his own bravado committed to rescuing a young woman who at the command of His Highness through the Prism of Power, would turn into a raging monstrosity of an ibmanzy!

Then, at a stroke—as they say in Clishdrin—she solved the problem for me. Well, to be honest, not solved it entirely but, as it were, shuffled it off for the time being. Put it in cold storage until, later on but as soon as possible, I could solve the whole issue for good and all.

"If you really want to help me," said Renata in her soft, breathy, frightened voice. "Then take me to my darling Sando."

To my relief, Sando, she said, was not in the temple at the moment but had gone to visit his parents in the city. He didn't know as yet, so Renata thought, that he was to be separated from her. The priests hadn't yet physically punished her for her refusal to go to Tolindrin. They had browbeaten her and exhausted her with their constant orders and mental manipulations and threats.

Now she had materially recovered. She clearly hadn't thought through the way the course of this imbroglio might go. All she could think of was her darling Sando. Once in his protective arms everything would be alright.

The recumbent guard began to stir. It was time, then, to make a move.

"Put this on." The cloak was parti-patterned in a dark red, a dark blue and a light green. I did not care for the effect and it seemed to me that this particular cloak would be easily recognized. Renata, however, had no other cloak. She did have a brown cape. This was the garment I told her to don.

Like many women who have been through an ordeal, and who find themselves continuing in the aftermath of betrayal, ruin or loss, Renata talked. She chattered. Once started, the floodgates were opened and the words poured forth in torrents of abuse and reproach. On and on she went all the time we went down the stairs, she with a bag containing essentials, out the door, across the yard, through a wooden gate in the wall into another smaller yard. Opposite stood an archway of cut stone within the brick wall.

She interjected into her monologue a few words to tell me this was a tradesmen's gate. A bored looking Fristle in an ill-fitting guard's uniform, carrying a spear, lolled against the wall picking his teeth with a black fingernail.

Not aware of the internal social structure of this infernal temple, I felt it wise to assume that it was not usual for a priest to be seen leaving this back gateway with a serving wench. The decision to act the part of an overbearing and domineering nasty kind of fellow with the guard was automatic. This would be the way they carried on in this deplorable place.

Renata's brown cape had no hood. The rain had eased to a light drizzle so that there was an excuse for her to pull her scarf up and let it drape down half concealing her face.

The guard made an attempt to straighten up as we approached.

Giving him a hard stare of habitual authority I rapped out: "Well?"

Renata turned her head away and down. The Fristle jumped to open the small wicket in the main gate. I went through first and Renata trailed on after. A mytzer-hauled cart was just then hauling up and the Relt driver climbed back up to his seat when he saw the guard. He waved and the guard, shrugging, started to open the gates. Renata and I faded into the drifting lines of drizzle.

She said nothing and we splashed along trying to avoid the puddles. Letting her be the guide we walked as fast as I thought circumspect towards her darling Sando's parents' house. Poor Renata! I might thus shuffle her off from the immediate problems besetting me. She would remain a part of the greater problem—the almighty greater evil—of these damned ibmanzies. As I say, poor Renata!

A thought dreadful in its implications occurred to me.

My Val! Because of the horrific seriousness of the threat of these demons from hell I ought to strike Renata down dead right now. Better yet—I should wait until we met her Sando and then kill them both. Just butcher them as soon as possible before they had a chance to turn into insane monsters.

I felt the simple face I was wearing harden into an executioner's mask. Of course, I couldn't do it. Could I?

The closeness of this encounter with a potential ibmanzy made me realize afresh and with greater impact the vital necessity of finding and disposing of this Opaz-forsaken Prism of Power. Doing that would remove the threat from Renata and her Sando. That was the only proper course of action.

Mind you, if it came to another and more frightful course, then my duty would constrain me to it. No doubts of that, no doubts whatsoever, by Krun.

The Maiden with the Many Smiles beamed down all streaming pink radiance and rosy shadows as we walked along the rain-shining streets. An interestingly evil idea occurred to me. A tempting idea, a fascinating prospect of hoisting these Dokerty cultists with their own varter. By the Black Chunkrah! What a beauty!

Once we had the Prism of Power in our possession, why, then, why not use it to turn all the infected victims in Prebaya, in Caneldrin, into ibmanzies?

The idea was evilly fascinating. And right out of the question. That would heap more fuel onto the smoldering beginnings of the fires of destruction due to break out in the sub-continent.

Veda hadn't known how many people had been infected with the ibmanzy potential. A goodly number, she felt sure. She also did not know what date had been set for their use. That didn't surprise me, by Krun. The chief priest of Dokerty, the thin nosed and thin lipped cramph they called His Highness, probably didn't know either. Only one person would know that. The one who would decide the date herself. Oh, yes, the high and mighty regent, C'Chermina, would know and decide the time for her schemes to ripen.

The regent wished to conquer both Tolindrin in the south and Winlan in the north west. The distances to be covered were considerable. No doubt some of the potential ibmanzies would be transported by lifters, the airboats able to make the journeys in good time. But I was willing to wager that the majority of them would travel overland. Some might go by sea. The result was the same; some time had to elapse before C'Chermina's plans would be in place.

In that breathing space we had to act.

Just before we reached our destination I decided that to call the poor people who had gone through the painful initiation 'ibmanzies' was technically incorrect. They would become ibmanzies when the demons took over. They'd been infected by devils. A good name for them would be infectos. When we were admitted to the house and Renata clasped Sando with a thankful sob, I reflected that this couple of infectos, like all the rest, were doomed. Doomed, that was, unless somehow I could lay my hands on the Prism of Power.

Sando's parents were out. He was surprised that a priest should so blatantly go against the dictates of the temple, and looked decidedly frightened. Renata showed that whilst she might not be another Veda she still retained her spirit. "I do not think he is a priest, Sando. But he has helped us. We do not know to whom we are indebted."

I told them my name was Larghos Nath H'Harmen followed by a truly comet-like tail of syllables, ending with sturboin. I said I habitually used the Double and that, yes, I was a priest of Dokerty who had lost all faith in His Highness.

Sando, too, had no memory of the agony of his initiation. Like Renata, he recalled the experience as a divine revelation. They had no conception of the destruction His Highness and C'Chermina planned for them both.

I could only wish them well, say the remberees and depart.

Back at The Harland Lifter I shifted back into my own clothes retrieved from the bottom of the chair and then I dug out poor old Hyslop from his crockery cupboard. He was fast asleep. All the same, I pressed under his ear sufficiently to keep him out for the time it took to strip off his bonds and dress him in his own clothes. The tablecloth and curtain cords went back from whence they came. Then I splashed some raw wine over his face, draped him across the table, assumed a similar drunken pose myself, and waited.

I heard him move and exclaim: "Wha—? Where—?"

So I sat up, swaying somewhat, and said: "You're a good fellow, Hyslop. But when you went out—"

"Went out? Me!"

"Oh, aye. You came back and didn't say what had happened. There was a girl in it, I believe. Then you went to sleep. I've been here all alone, as it were."

His amazement was a joy to see. Damned Dokerty drunk!

In the end he convinced himself. Mind you, by Krun, I wasn't particularly concerned over what he believed or didn't believe. He went off, swearing he'd had a marvelous time, although not altogether remembering the whole. We called the remberees and walked off in different directions as She of the Veils threw down her rosily golden radiance across the still rain-drenched streets of Prebaya.

So what had I accomplished? Nothing! A great round fat zero. Very depressed I trailed off to the embassy. There had to be a way for a bold gallant adventurer to break into the temple and steal the Prism of Power. There had to be. I would just have to start all over again. As to the bold gallant adventurer bit, I, Dray Prescot, felt nothing like that at all, nothing whatsoever like it, by Krun!

Five

Just as I expected, Veda's nose went up in the air as she said: "Huh! It would all have gone very differently if I'd been with you."

We were at the first breakfast. The ambassador ate his clus-fruit and cereal in silence. He did give me a sly little look which meant, or so I imagined, "I wonder!" Of course, the look could have meant, "I don't doubt it." I ate my palines studiously.

Of course, by Vox, that dry little look could mean: "Yes. And if I'd been there, it would all have gone swimmingly."

"Well?" demanded Veda.

"You can't win 'em all the time."

Now whilst this is undeniably true, I had a flash of memory of what my kregoinya comrade Mevancy would have said to that. "Oh, you!" she'd have burst out.

As for my kregoinye comrade, the Kildoi Fweygo, he would have— I halted these rambling thoughts. Truth to tell, Fweygo would have been very handy to have had along last night.

"This serving shishi, Renata." Veda selected a paline with care. "I don't know her name, of course, and probably don't know her to look at. I always felt a trifle sorry for the servant girls. They are not treated properly." She bit hard down on the fruit. "Men!" As she finished this outburst she winced, and then a look of pain flashed across her face.

"Veda?"

"I'm perfectly all right—thank you!"

In the next instant she contradicted that by putting a quick hand to her side. Her white face drained still further of blood so that, for a frightening moment, she looked like a corpse.

After that events moved in ways over which Veda had no control. Well, by Vox, neither had I nor the ambassador. Suzy the Surcease tut-tutted crossly, shook her head, told Veda to go back to bed and said she'd return as soon as possible.

When Suzy did return she had with her a woman of commanding presence. The woman was not apim, although having only two arms and no tail. Her frame was corpulent. Her face possessed heavy ridges over the forehead and around the eyes, which were of that piercing kind which seem to drill right through you. She wore a long gown, simple, of pale yellow girdled with silver. Her hands were large and elegant, supple and unadorned. She was a venahim, of a race of diffs renowned for their mysterious healing powers. She was introduced as Mistress E'Eolana.

When she went to work I felt it a privilege to be allowed to watch. Veda crawled out of bed, looking decidedly shaky, and stood up as straight as she could with her pale blue nightgown falling to her thighs. Mistress E'Eolana stood at the far end of the room. She closed her eyes and quite clearly went into a deep meditation. Throughout the whole treatment the venahim lady did not touch Veda.

Her hands moved gracefully in the air before her, tracing the ghostly outline of Veda's superb body. She seemed, as it were, to caress Veda from the distance separating them.

"This is a technique called schonibium," Naghan whispered. "It is very ancient. Very." He did not pull his goatee. He went on to explain that E'Eolana was calling Veda's ibma—as distinct from her ib—to exert its proper function. Veda had been badly hurt, far worse than I'd realized, and our chasing through the city had exacerbated her condition, as, of course, I had feared. Now her ibma, through remote control as it were, was being drawn forth to put her body and ib back into harmony.

By Krun! Of course! I saw at once how this benign use of these mysterious forces of the spirit world was decadently paralleled in the ibmanzy project. Arcane forces, of the mind and the spirit, fuelled by devout faith, not sorcerous, were being conjured up for two quite opposite purposes.

Could there be, I wondered, some connection, some way we could use this information to combat the ibmanzy scourge?

There were definite stages in this art of healing. Mistress E'Eolana opened those drilling eyes. She had established Veda's body form and now as her supple hands wove patterns in the air she massaged Veda's spiritual shape. The aftershock of Veda's experiences had hit her and I did not doubt that the realization of what the ibmanzy project would have done to her had been the worst shock by a long way. A very long way, by Krun.

The process wended its way, at every stage remaining fascinating. In due time Veda lost the shakes, her features whilst not flushing with blood at least ceased to resemble a corpse's. When at last the two women between them pronounced they were satisfied with her, they put Veda back to bed, stuck a sleep-by needle in her and shooed us out of the bedroom. Meekly, we went.

The more I learned about this subcontinent of Balintol the more, not less, mysterious the place became, and you could say that again, by Vox!

A servant brought in glasses of strawberry colored sazz as Naghan and I sat down in his snug. He shook his head, no doubt about to utter some banal and diplomatic remark about my lack of success. I told him, briskly, that I had another plan.

He already knew most, although not all, of my dealings with the lady Quensella. The fight between her guards and those of the regent C'Chermina outside the prefecture had naturally attracted enormous interest, gossip and scandalous rumor throughout Prebaya. The Vallian ambassador had said, with a little sigh, that it was a pity that our new customs prevented our hiring on mercenaries, except in the most desperate circumstances. "That juruk you created," he sipped his sazz regretfully, "was a most splendid body of men, a really first class guard." As to where they were now, he could not say, apart from one.

I guessed at once. "You took on Erwin the Waggler!"

"Aye."

Well, by Vox, Erwin was a fine lad. I was pleased that he'd found employment so quickly. I was even more pleased that he was here, in the embassy, and on hand to help further my schemes. As a Valkan, he knew I was the strom of Valka and the ex-emperor of Vallia.

The cunning way—that of sneaking in to steal the Prism of Power—had failed. Now it would have to be the blunt instrument.

I told Naghan that despite the new customs of Vallia, which I had introduced and enforced, my scheme would require the use of mercenaries. The paktuns must not be traced back to the Vallian embassy. C'Chermina was maniacal enough to send off her growing army of ibmanzies to Vallia. My Val! The destruction they would wreak before they were put down or blew up beggared the imagination.

Naghan quickly agreed to have Erwin make efforts to trace the members of the guard I had created for the lady Quensella. Everything must be handled with the utmost discretion. A convenient meeting place must be chosen which would afford total security. As these arrangements were concluded I began to feel a fresh and completely unexpected sense of unease.

So I had failed in my sneaky attempt to penetrate the temple. Yes, that was true. But what had caused the failure? I knew well enough that if a similar situation arose, with a poor naked girl like Renata being dragged off, I'd act again in exactly the same way.

I remained the same simple sailorman called Dray Prescot who had first been pitched down onto Kregen. Sure, I was emperor of this and that, and king of somewhere else, but I remained me. But—and this thought stung, believe you me!—I was a Krozair of Zy. Just because this first attempt had failed did not mean that I could not try again. Oh, no, by Djan! Not by a long shot.

Very briefly, curtly almost, I said: "Naghan. I'm going to have another bite at the cherry." And I took myself off.

The advantage of night time when fewer people might be expected to be about was negated by my past experience of temples where the very numbers of people busy about their business made a new face inconspicuous among the throngs. Now. Right now, I'd go back to that damned Temple of Dokerty.

Off I sallied wearing my ordinary clothes—the russet, I thought, very brave in the streaming mingled lights of the Suns of Scorpio. If it became necessary to knock someone over the head—a guard, say—and take his uniform, then that is what I would have to do.

If I bumped into sub-priest Hyslop Nath ti Vernaloin, I'd greet him as an old drinking companion. I'd be comradeship itself. If, regretfully, I could not shake him off in a civilized way, then he'd have to be thumped and dumped.

The best way in would be via the tradesmen's entrance from which Renata and I had fled. There was no difficulty. I walked in abaft a trundling old Quoffa cart with creaking, wobbling wheels, and so melted into the shadows through the courtyards and into the main structure of the temple.

Here the stifling closeness of the atmosphere and the varied smells as I traversed the corridors provided a vivid reminder of my previous unhappy experiences here. I was fully aware that I was pitching myself headlong into a sinister underworld of religious magic, agonizing pain and murder.

The new face on which I'd decided changed my features at the last moment before entering. I now looked harsh and contemptuous. That some people might say this look was quite normal for Dray Prescot was, I devoutly believed, a foul calumny. All the same, by Vox, I must admit it did not sting as much as some other faces I've adopted in my time. Boldly, I pressed on.

As expected, the passages were crowded with various folk about their daily tasks. Priests stalked, mumbling to themselves. There were guards posted at doors and stairways; but these were of the flamboyant, ornamental kind, all lace and feathers and fancy polearms, with monumental helmets polished to a blinding brilliance. None was a Kataki. They'd be guarding the inner sanctums, I guessed, even if the priests of Dokerty would not trust them to guard the most sacred shrines.

This time, for which I thanked Opaz, I did not encounter a naked girl, abused and struggling.

From the directions of Veda's map carried in my head the way remained relatively clear until I reached that portion which the Unruly had marked merely with a blank square. The corridor down which I marched with an assured swing ended in a chamber furnished with benches around the walls. Men and women waited in various degrees of patience, obviously to be called past the balass door at the far end.

A single glance around convinced me this was of no use to me.

Reversing my course I headed off down a side passage towards the next section of blankness on Veda's map.

So far I had seen not a single solitary sign of a secret entrance to the passageways that, I presumed, must run between the walls. Mind you, from my experiences in the palace here in Prebaya, there was every chance that these secret runnels were heavily guarded.

Beginning to feel the mounting frustration as a weight dragging my shoulders down, I came into a sizeable space crammed with all manner of folk. This side of the blank square I sought to enter faced the front doors of the temple. These people looked like ordinary townsfolk. There was a deal of chaffering going on, and over the hubbub the tinkle of coins changing hands indicated that here sacrifices were bought, bribes given and bribes taken, in short, all the usual underhand practices of this kind of religious establishment, debased, avaricious and contemptuous of human values, were carried on.

This, then, was the Autmoil Hall. Moving quietly along, I pushed my way through the crowds, avoiding offers of dangling chickens, strings of beads, mirrors, painted clay images of people with unfortunate diseases or disfigurations. If the priests of Dokerty promised to cure some of the afflictions, they were either miracle workers or charlatans of the most despicable kind.

Leaving the Hall of Strangers by one of the arcades leading around the angle of walls, I followed the line of Veda's blank square.

All the hubbub and commercial confusion fell away abaft and I walked with a measured tread into a long, impressive chamber with tiles brilliantly adorning both walls. Light fell from many lamps. Ornamental guards stood, half asleep, at their posts at the ornate doors piercing the wall. That was the wall that did not abut the blank square. Frustration had to be contained. By Krun! Who said this was going to be easy?

At the end, before a tall double-doors of balass wood, stood a guard of an altogether different stripe. He was a Rapa, and his kit was workmanlike. His fist rested on his sword hilt.

"What is your business here?" he demanded brusquely.

Ready for this question, I had the answer ready. I told him I was a friend of priest Hyslop Nath ti Vernaloin and sought him on a private matter. The harsh contours of my face softened as I spoke.

"I know him. You should know that sub-priests are not allowed through here." The Rapa raised his voice. "Guards!"

Oh, well, this was another attempt that had been thwarted. I kept my face impassive as a detail of guards like the Rapa doubled out of the side door and surrounded me. Their Deldar looked me over, rapped out typical Deldar bellowing orders, and we all marched back down that imposing tiled corridor.

Too frustrated and annoyed, I couldn't even bring myself to hurl a few mental Makki Grodno insults into the indifferent void.

There remained the fourth side of the inscrutable square.

This time, by Djan, would have to be the time!

The Deldar rapped his audo to a stamping halt at the end of the corridor and told me to be about my business. Meekly, I nodded, and walked slowly off towards the commercial hubbub of the Autmoil Hall.

Further towards the front of the rambling structure must be a way around. No doubt there would be guards. Poor old Hyslop had proved worthless in the end. So—!

Indeed, there was an arched opening onto the right direction. Boldly, I marched through. This corridor appeared to be plated in gold. That the surface would almost certainly be gold leaf did not detract from the effect. Some folk would describe the dazzlement as sumptuous. There was more than a hint of Vulgar Ostentation about it for my taste. I walked on towards the flight of marble stairs going up. Elaborate statues of nymphs and satyrs alternately simpered and leered up the walls. The air tasted of rose petals.

The roof came down low enough to conceal the top of the flight of stairs. An odd sensation hit me, as though my insides had been taken out, inspected, and thrust back. A floating sensation in my head came and went like a summer zephyr. Up I climbed. The roof lofted away into a blinding shimmer of gold. The stairs went on up.

Doggedly, on I went. All this flummery of gold had to mean something or someone of great importance resided at the top, surely?

At last, the top came into view—a damned great golden door.

This must be very high up in the temple. I pushed the door open and a blast of scented air racketed past. I blinked.

Everything ahead was a sheer dazzlement of gold.

A keen, penetrating voice said: "Come in, Dray Prescot, Emperor of All Paz. There are matters to discuss."

So I knew.

Six

A sea of gold encompassed me.

A hand up to shield my eyes made little difference. Spits and sparks of gold flew about in the air, the scent of roses grew stronger. I spoke with some heat.

"Look, Star Lords! I'm rather busy right now. There is—"

"We are aware."

Well, by the runny nose and dribbling eyeballs of Makki Grodno! Of course they'd be aware! After all, they were flaming super humans, weren't they?

And, anyway, why were they using these flamboyant methods of summoning me instead of the good old Giant Scorpion and his blue radiance?

"The task you set of uniting Balintol is difficult. There are maniacs who want to set a bunch of monsters loose—"

"The so-called ibmanzies, yes." The Everoinye went on to tell me that they were in advance of that situation. When I'd kidnapped young prince Ortyg of Tolindrin to stop him helping the regent C'Chermina, that had, the Star Lords said, materially set back her programme of conquest. The ibmanzy project was some way to fruition yet. There were other fish to fry in the wider world of Kregen. The breathing space I had counted on did, indeed, exist.

Now this conversation with superhuman beings of incalculable powers induced in me feelings of annoyance when, I suppose, any normal person would feel only blind panic. I'd had traffic with the Star Lords for long enough now to know a little of their ways. I could handle them—given a tithe of luck and a ton of boldness.

Mind you, always, over and above everything else, the threat they posed of sending me back to Earth, four hundred light years away, dictated all my actions. Another twenty-one years back on the planet of my birth, parted from Delia, was something I could not contemplate.

They told me that I must go to Kildrin. A friend was in gaol there and I must have him set free. "No violence, Dray Prescot!" Apparently there were chariot races. I was to bet heavily on a rank outsider, Vando's Lilies. The favorite was Lart's Chavonths.

"Once you have won the money you will pay the fines."

I felt affronted, not to say outraged.

"What is all this nonsense to do with dealing with the regent C'Chermina and her army of crazed ibmanzies!" I fairly bellowed.

"All in due course, Dray Prescot."

They gave me a few directions, cautioned me again in their aloof Everoinye way, and reminded me of my obligations. The golden haze all about began to fade. I felt a chill breath strike my face. Blueness welled up, swirling me about, tumbling me head over heels, a faint after scent of roses died. My feet hit hard earth.

The streaming mingled rays of Zim and Genodras fell athwart the land. I breathed in good clean Kregan air. I stared about.

About an ulm away the red walls of a city rose against the sky. Fields extended beside the dusty road. From a small wood a caravan trundled on towards the city. Quoffa and mytzer carts, a selection of the many wonderful riding animals of Kregen, and trudging people of many races of diffs, made a colorful spectacle. There was no difficulty in walking quietly along with them. This time the Everoinye had left me with my clothes and weapons. That was mighty generous of them, by Krun!

The sole topic among the people of the caravan appeared to be the forthcoming chariot races.

This, then, was the city of Emgidu.

The land looked ripe and prosperous, and this conjecture was reinforced by the surprisingly large amounts of cash these folk said they intended to bet on the races. The colorful names given to the chariots emphasized the importance Emgidu attached to their famous race meetings which extended over four sennights—at least.

Lart's Chavonths were most often mentioned as the favorite rig to win the Autarch's Stakes, the most prestigious event. The rig I was supposed to back, Vando's Lilies, was mentioned only once—and that with a raucous laugh of contempt. Two other chariots might be in with a chance: Naghan's Droombs, and Rolico's Strigicaws.

All the same, mind you, with all this excited talk of betting and the odds and the way the charioteers handled their rigs creating a hubbub all about, I was still seething over what I saw as the high handed effrontery of the Star Lords. By Krun! They'd tasked me with the job in Balintol, and now they casually tossed me down here to get on with something entirely different.

What really cut as I remembered what had passed between the Everoinye and me was their callous comment on my efforts so far.

I'd said: "I have to destroy the Prism of Power."

And that ghostly voice with its echoes of the last bubble in a glass of champagne had replied: "You've not had much success so far, have you, Dray Prescot!"

If I'd had a hat on at the time I'd have torn it off, thrown it down, and jumped on it.

The caravan passed peaceably under the arch of the Hindrod Gate which led onto the wayfarer's drinnik just outside the walls. Here everyone shouted the remberees and in small groups went off about their various businesses. The guards, who looked calmly competent, let me into the city without comment. Everyone from all around, it seemed, was flocking to Emgidu for the races.

The main avenues thronged with folk. Here I saw more Kildois at one time than I'd ever seen in all my experiences upon Kregen. Even so, they were vastly outnumbered by members of other races of diffs. There are not a lot of Kildois upon Kregen.

As you know the various splendid races of diffs have their own ideas on architecture and these very often cut across mere national boundaries. Sometimes the results of this mixing of styles is charming, sometimes dysfunctional, sometimes distinctly weird. Here in Emgidu the results of the jumble of building fashions gave an impression of orderliness found out of chaos. Even the aracloins, which in the normal way are a messy ramshackle collection of tumbledown structures penned between narrow twisting alleyways, here managed to retain some semblance of order, even of dignity. The prime autarch, who ruled as the first peer among equals, kept a tight rein, that was all too obvious. As to the political forces at work here, well, at the moment I knew very little. What I did know was that in following the Star Lords' demands to unite Balintol, I'd soon have to learn all I could and then, having this intolerable burden of being the Emperor of All Paz thrust upon me, to interfere.

Walking along quietly and minding my own business I passed the open door of a tavern—an odd building of many tiny pyramidal roofs—from which the mingled odors of wine wafted. A polsim talking to a group of attentive listeners put a finger alongside his shrewd polsim nose, saying: "Lart's Chavonths—ha! No, doms, my cash all goes on Nath's Hammerers."

"Nath's Hammerers!" scoffed a burly Rapa, green and yellow feathers all abristle. "Nah. No chance, dom. They're all spavined."

Passing on I reflected that the passion for chariot racing infecting this city of Emgidu emphasized the charming inconsequence of the nature of human beings. Too, this reminded me somewhat of the passionate partisanship of LionardDen, Jikaida City, a place in almost the center of the continent of Havilfar where Death ruled many of the games. A simple race of chariots, I thought in my ignorance, would scarce merit much concerns over Death.

With a clattering staccato of hooves and grinding of bronze-rimmed wheels a two-zorca chariot hurtled past perilously close to the group at the tavern door. They yelped with surprise and angry protestations. The charioteer, a youngster in a gaudy tunic, all flashing teeth and glittering eyes and flaring hair, laughed and roared on. Your humble servant hopped smartly out of the way, believe you me, by Krun!

There were many chariots passing up and down the wider avenues, mostly hauled by two zorcas, although there were sleeths and other draught animals. The occasional troika was larger and mostly possessed a driver, with the owner lolling in the back. All the rigs were elaborately decorated and brightly painted. They did make a charming picture under the brilliance of the Suns of Scorpio.

The first thing to do was get the wager down on Vando's Lilies. The Autarch's Stakes would be run tomorrow, so I staked everything I had saving enough to pay for a night's lodgings and meals. As every schoolchild knows, gambling is a mug's game. If you wish to throw your hard-earned money away, that is your problem. Those who have money and can afford to waste it may gamble to their heart's content. It does say a great deal about my relations with the Star Lords that I was thus meekly betting all my cash on what sounded like an unlikely chance.

Keeping back enough money to buy meals was prudent. Holding back cash to pay for the night's lodgings was a waste of time. In Emgidu the nights of the races, bags of gold would not secure you lodgings if you had not booked well in advance. If you had friends living in the city, wonderful—I had not.

There remained nothing else to do but join other unfortunates huddled up in alleyways and corners of arcades. Naturally, it rained. The night passed. Wet and uncomfortable I blinked bleary eyes on the morning suns as they cast down mingled streams of apple green and rose. The earth steamed. I stretched and went off for the first breakfast of this momentous day.

There had been only three attempts to rob me during the night. Sleeping with half an eye slitted open and ears cocked is not only perfectly natural to an adventurer upon Kregen, it is more often than not vitally essential. A few fights had broken out under the arches, struggling bodies toppling out into the rain. Five, I believe, people had been discovered with their throats cut in that particular area, or it could have been six.

The breakfast was good, and I sauntered off with the crowds to view the track with a handful of luscious palines to munch.

The track proved to be totally unlike a terrestrial horse racing circuit. Imagine a wild, unkempt area of rutted surfaces, straggly, thorny bushes, culverts, ditches, humps and bumps here and there. Among this wilderness tall stone pillars had been erected in pairs. Each pair bore a number. So presumably the charioteers started at the first number and chased around following the succession.

Judging that each pair of pillars was just wide enough apart to allow two chariots to pass through made me whistle. Quite clearly, if a rig passed outside a pillar the driver would be either disqualified or penalized.

The whole wide area was situated in a natural depression in the ground and already the crowds were forming on the low hills. White buildings at one end obviously contained the starting apparatus and no doubt special viewing arrangements for the lords and ladies. A wide paved road led into the rear of the buildings from the city.

As was to be expected on a day of high festivity the sellers and entertainers were already hard at work parting the spectators from their cash. Aromas of food rose. Ale flowed. Oh, yes, by Krun, it was all very fine and jolly!

The sightseers who had come thus early to the course to gain advantageous viewing positions had mostly brought provisions. I had not. Discussing with myself the relative importance of actually seeing the races and the emptiness of my inward parts, I reached the firm conclusion that the next meal was of prime importance.

Off I pushed through the throngs back to the city and to spend what I had left from sleeping out in the open in the rain on food.

Spot on the hour of mid the noise from the hills surrounding the course burst up, telling those unfortunates who were not there that the first race had begun. The Autarch's Stakes would be run as the last race of the day. Thinking of that devilish race track I wondered how many chariots would be in one piece by then.

The trouble with me was that I had no interest in these chariot extravaganzas. I hungered to return to Prebaya and get after that damned Prism of Power. The Everoinye must know what they were doing, surely? Hah! They'd made mistakes before, as I well knew, and sure as a Herrelldrin Hell would singe your breeches, they'd err again.

A mangy-looking Rapa with draggly feathers and Krasny-work armor bumped into me. He lurched sideways and the whiff of dopa choked right up my hooter.

"Get outta my way, blintz!" His hand reached down to his sword hilt.

For a single blinding moment I reacted as I might have done seasons and seasons ago. My own fist gripped my sword hilt. Then the memory of the Star Lords' command shafted into my brain. "No violence, Dray Prescot!"

So I stepped aside, turned away, and walked smartly on.

Mind you, by Djan, there went one very lucky Rapa! Even as I thought that, another and altogether more hateful memory stirred. That dopa-fuddled Rapa might easily have been a far better swordsman than was I. Always, my encounter with Mefto the Kazzur stayed with me as a reminder that I was not—as I have never ever claimed to be—the 'Best Swordsman Of Two Worlds.'

A spark glinting from the sky drew my instant attention. Wide wings cutting the air, cruel beak thrust arrogantly forward, the rays of the suns reflecting from brilliant feathers as though they were lacquered, up there a majestic raptor sailed the wind.

He didn't squawk down at me: "Dray Prescot! Onker of onkers!"

He turned, circling me, watching me. That was his job, this Gdoinye, the spy and messenger for the Star Lords. I watched him.

The world turned blue.

The representation of the gigantic Blue Scorpion hovered over me. Coldness bit. I lifted into the air, head over heels, gasping, whirled away through aching emptiness.

Now what did the confounded Everoinye want? Couldn't they let me get on and finish with one task before thumping me down into another fine mess? My feet hit straw-covered dirt and I staggered forward, my sight clearing as the blueness faded and vanished.

The scene before me, ugly and sickening, demanded instant action.

A man lay on the straw with blood masking his face. Just beyond him a man was hitting a third man with a cosh. The barn echoed to this unfortunate's screams. Even as I leaped forward I wondered if this was an open and shut case, or was this another example of picking the wrong side to assist?

There was no uncertainty in the blow which sent the cosh-wielding fellow down to sprawl face-first in the straw.

"Help! Help!" Blood oozed from a scalp cut over his ear and he'd have a prize bruise there; apart from that he looked unharmed. I reached down to support his shoulder, saying: "It's all right now."

Well, he took a little time to recover with the aid of a bottle he took from an inside pocket of his leather coat. His face held a weather-beaten look, with good features and startlingly blue eyes, and a stubborn chin. He was apim, like me.

"You have my thanks, dom. I thought I was done for." He took a drink and offered me the bottle, so I took a swig to keep him company. He asked my name and I said Drajak and he said his name was Nath Seegfreed-han. At my quick, surprised look, he sniffed up his nose and hunched his shoulders, took a drink, and said: "I know, I know. But a fellow's not responsible for his own name now, is he?"

"You could always change it."

He glared, affronted. "You insult the memory of my grandfather! He was a very great man, a warrior, a kampeon—"

He grumbled on a bit, mostly to himself, for he was still woozy from the blow to his head. Then he said somewhat grudgingly: "Well, Drajak, to tell the truth, in business I use the name Vando."

I felt my heart sink.

"Vando's Lilies?"

"Aye." He gestured at the two bodies, one dead the other unconscious. "And there are my first and second charioteers. The second, Narga, knocked down the first, Strido, when I chanced in. He immediately attacked me, swearing Vando's Lilies would not race today. Then you—where you came from I've no idea."

"A lot of money rides on the races? That's the reason?"

"Oh, aye." A great deal of money was wagered, besides items of treasure and property. Apparently the Nine Autarchs who ruled Kildrin incorporated the result of the Autarch's Stakes in their pecking order. Each autarch entered his chariot and the winner was more likely than not to become the Prime Autarch for the following year.

As he spoke I used his kerchief to bind his head up and suggested we find a needleman for him and his second charioteer. He said that his inclinations were to let the blintz rot; but that his grandfather had taught him differently. Then—and the realization hit him like a gut-blow, suddenly, for his dizziness had precluded logical thought—he burst out: "The race! My chariot! My charioteers! The blintzes have done for me, devil take 'em!"

He staggered up wildly, waving his arms about, yelling. His people came running in at last and he did not berate them for their tardiness—well, not much—and quickly order was restored, the bodies dragged off, and, with five young grooms, he went over to the stalls at the end of the barn. Intrigued, I followed.

They brought out Vando's Lilies, the zorcas I had backed with just about all my cash. With a name like that, well, you'd expect grays, wouldn't you? You'd expect gleaming coats of pure white, splendid under the radiance of the suns. Well, my friend, you'd be wrong, sadly wrong.

The five zorcas looked a mangy bunch, dull gray and brown.

I couldn't help it. I burst out: "Sink me! I've bet all my cash on this sorry lot!"

Nath Seegfreedhan—Nath Vando—hopped about quickly like a sparrow to face me when I blurted that unkindness out.

"You bet everything on my chariot?"

"Aye."

"What do you know of zorcas? Look at them."

So I looked. Often in the past I'd ridden saddle animals that looked nothing much but which were superb mounts. Vando's Lilies raced under false colors, that was for sure. Four of them were splendid under their scraggly coats. The fifth was larger and more powerful. Now for a quadriga you need four balanced animals, so how did this fifth beautiful specimen fit in? Vando told me.

"Five? To haul a chariot through those pillars? You really are a crazy lot in Emgidu!"

He laughed at that, and winced and put a hand to his head. He then spat out that he'd nothing to laugh at. He had no drivers. The grooms were too young and nowhere near strong enough. No other drivers were available. He looked at me. My heart sank again.

"You can drive?"

I had to agree, for, as you know, my father had taught me well.

"Then, Drajak, I think it best that you should be the charioteer for Vando's Lilies in the Autarch's Stakes."

Seven

At that, even dear old Makki Grodno failed me.

I opened my mouth to protest and he lifted an imperious hand.

"I see your shoulders. I see your legs, your calves. You can drive as well as you hit people."

"Five—?"

He went through the drill. The five zorcas were named after the mythical Larghos Kraneyzendo's draught animals who hauled his chariot through the thunder clouds and amidst the lightning shafts. The mythology of Kregen is vast in scope and extensive in preposterous stories. Still, Larghos only harnessed four to his aerial chariot. From larboard to starboard they were: Pride, Power, Passion and Perseverance.

"That's Larghos's four," I said. "What about the fifth?"

Vando put his hand on the fifth zorca's neck, rubbing affectionately. "He pulls in the center. His name is Baldur."

I jumped.

He didn't exactly snarl it out when he snapped: "My father's name. A proud name, Drajak, even if you've never heard it before!"

Now the Star Lords had instructed me to bet on this rig, so they must have known something about its chances—this I had thought. Now an altogether different reason entered my old vosk skull of a head.

Vando went on through the driving drill and I listened and learned. Every now and then I was able to interject with a casual question. I learned his grandfather—this Seegfreed—had created a vast fortune and had then met, fallen in love with and married the only daughter of one of the Nine Autarchs. There had been some considerable jiggery-pokery including winning the Autarch's Stakes, that installed Seegfreed as one of the Nine.

"He was a consummate story-teller and made us laugh."

"He is well, I trust? I should be honored to meet him."

The autarch's face clouded. "Alas, my friend. He passed through the mists and the Ice Floes of Sicce some time ago."

"I trust he has climbed the Sunny Uplands beyond."

"Aye. He was often called away on business, and the tragedy happened in a far country—Chobishaw."

I nodded. The king and queen of Chobishaw were good friends.

He brisked himself up. "You'll wear my colors and you'll have to leave your weapons. They will be safe. Here."

One of the young grooms handed me a vicious-looking sickle-shaped knife. I could guess what that was for. If the chariot went smash you'd have to slash yourself free from the reins before the galloping zorcas scraped you bloodily along the ground.

As a simple matter of common sense the five splendid zorcas were harnessed up. Baldur in the center and slightly in the lead, the double doors flung open, and I drove the rig out into the practice circuit penned within high walls. Vando instructed me. His team started slowly and were responsive to touches from the whip.

I looked askance. "I've never whipped a zorca in my life!"

"Quite so." He told me that when I touched Baldur with the tip of the whip he would open up into the full racing stride. I was to leave that until the eighth of the nine circuits.

The team had been acquired not long ago and their quality was unknown to the populace. They had been seen and condemned on sight.

Then we went in to eat a hearty meal. I refused to consider this as the last meal of the condemned man. With care I got Vando into talking again about his grandfather, and this was easy, for he had loved the old man. I said: "Did he ever talk about ridiculous—ah—well—sort of different worlds from Kregen?"

"Did he not! One world of which he told us many stories was so comical we always laughed. Can you imagine? Only one little yellow sun, one tiny silver moon and—wait for it!—no diffs at all. Only apims like us! Hah, we laughed 'til we cried."

So that settled that. No wonder the Everoinye were tender about Nath Seegfreedhan, a.k.a. Vando.

Of course, the next thought hit me like a thirty-two pound roundshot 'twixt wind and water. Suppose, just suppose this Vando was a Kregoinye like his grandfather?

The time approached for the last race and all preparations were finalized. I was togged out in a gaudy red, blue and yellow outfit with a great flaring clump of yellow feathers atop the round leather helmet.

The procession to the racecourse turned out to be quite a pomp and circumstance affair. A band thumped and tootled away. The grooms gentled the zorcas, one by one, and the chariot was put on a cart and hauled by a couple of Quoffas. There were dancing girls prancing about in silver gauze throwing flowers. The whole scene was one of pleasure and brightness and approaching excitement. There was wine in abundance. Everything laughed and glittered under the streaming mingled radiance of the Suns of Scorpio.

I thought of that devilish racecourse—and then did not think of it again.

The nine whitewashed stalls in the starting building each held a chariot and team and the many grooms and handlers. The noise from them and the crowds blew up prodigiously. That noise would blow the sky right off when the race began. The team was harnessed up and you may be very sure I'd gone round to each zorca to whisper in his ear and gentle him. They knew me by now. I climbed up into the narrow railed platform, wound the reins around my waist, made sure the sickle-bladed knife was to hand, and resolutely faced the bright blue doors leading onto the course.

The race did not begin right away. Outside in an area connecting the buildings and the first pair of pillars leading onto the course proper, the nine chariots waited. I studied them as a religious ceremony honoring Midopsort, the deity presiding over the fortunes of the contestants today, chanted and sang to its conclusion.

No other gods were honored, and this was obviously politically motivated, besides being a great relief.

The racing crowd used a slang term for a chariot. A chariot was a mutrowfer. In the typical Kregish way this word contains a number of elliptical meanings. On the surface it means dirt cruncher. Also it infers that the chariot will hit the dirt and be crunched. As a charioteer I was therefore a mutrowferim. This particular mutrowferim admitted to a concern over which meaning of the word would apply to him; too right, by Krun!

Naturally in the Kregish way the word was abbreviated to mutfer. And, again, this word had other and much more unpleasant connotations to do with scrabbling around in the muck.

Trumpets blared. The nine flags ran up their poles and cracked out bravely in the breeze. A violent and distinct smell of dust choked up my nostrils. I wiped a paw over my face. At the signal the nine chariots moved slowly towards the line.

There would be nine drum beats. On the ninth the race began.

The Lilies were drawn three in from the right. Over on the left five brilliantly white zorcas strained at a magnificently decorated chariot—this rig was Lart's Chavonths, the favorite.

Just why this Lart fellow might have the favorite showed on the eighth drum beat. The chariot moved slightly so that on the ninth it was rolling a trifle and shot off to a splendid start. The rest of us followed smartly. Whips were already rising and falling.

There ensued a mad scramble to reach the opening pair of pillars first.

There was no doubt about it, these drivers were a bunch of maniacs!

In a wild turmoil of pounding hooves and flashing wheels, of flailing whips and gouting spurts of dust, the whole mass roared on.

Mindful of Vando's instructions I held onto the reins, allowing my rig to ease towards the center without struggling to be up among the leaders. The first through the pillars could round the first turn on the inside and gain an advantage. As it was one chariot's outer zorca clipped the stone and he winced inward. The rig span. The driver thrashed his whip and a following chariot, unable to swerve, crashed headlong onto him. Both chariots flew to flinders. The zorcas belted on dragging the drivers who frantically tried to slash themselves free with their knives. The first succeeded, the second turned into a bloody pulp as maddened zorca hooves pounded over him.

And this was right at the start!

I swallowed down hard and let the Lilies find their own way past the wreckage. We bounded out onto the course proper and turned sweetly, spewing dust. Ahead, all the field save one roared on.

Seven chariots thundered out along the first straight and the Lilies paced sixth. I wondered if I'd made a mistake from which there would be no recovery. The distance to make up was formidable. The uneasy foreboding plagued my mind.

Then, of course and naturally, it began to rain.

On and on splashed the wheels and soon they scattered sheets of water to either side. Holding onto the reins and being savagely bucketed up and down, I became aware of a pool of blood at my feet.

There was no pain I could feel. Yes, my backbone felt as though some giant was banging it up and down and my skull jolted like a fiddler's elbow. But I didn't hurt anywhere enough to account for blood. The pool widened as I glanced down in between trying to guide the chariot between pillars that flashed past with fearsome speed. Blood?

Red drops dripped and flicked from the bright racing colors. What kind of cheap frumpery had Vando been conned into buying? In Vallia we grow a berry which when crushed and mixed with the proper chemicals makes a red dye that is fast. Most countries had fast dyes. This red dye was not—and had given me a fright. So, bathed in lurid crimson, on I thundered around the track through the silvery lances of the rain.

The headlong chase screamed on. A nasty thought rode with me. It is well known on Earth that horses do not like treading on objects in their path unless they absolutely cannot avoid them. Those zorcas back there had simply trampled all over the unfortunate charioteer. These zorcas then, bred to haul chariots, were unlike the friendly creatures—unless highly incensed—I had known heretofore upon Kregen.

The manifestation of Whetti Orbium passed over the land and the rain stopped. Unpleasant-looking gray clouds masked the faces of the Suns of Scorpio. As the chariots raced on around that dire course gradually the clouds blew over and the radiance poured down, ruby and emerald, and the land steamed.

The rig lurched and bucked horribly under me. More than once my feet were lifted clean off the floor and I clung onto the reins and the low rail expecting to be flung out. Still my position remained the same. The fellow in my rear made a half-hearted attempt to pass, and gave that up, and settled down to the chase. The noise from the crowd howled prodigiously to the sky. Mud-spattered, dyed red, shaken like peas in a colander, I hurtled on.

My knees felt like mashed bananas. All feeling in my ankles which had appeared to be dipped in molten lead now vanished and I wondered how my feet remained attached to my legs. The chariot struck viciously upwards at each ridge and bump. The jarring blow of the descent was just as savage. Springs? Hah! The designers of the rigs no doubt considered such effeminate contraptions to be far too decadent for mud-spattered mutferim.

The ruts gouged by previous races tended to keep the chariots on line so that it became decidedly difficult to lunge out and across in order to pass. The ruts leading through each pair of pillars did have the effect of guiding you through—but not necessarily on the line you wished to take. This whole chariot business was just crazy.

On the fourth circuit the positions remained the same. A rig up ahead made an attempt to pass the chariot in front, and failed as it swerved deliberately, and only just managed to nip back in time to scrape between the pillars.

Overtaking on a devilish course like this was proving to be an almighty monstrous task.

All the same—I had to get past. The Star Lords had commanded.

Coming up to the straight where start and finish were marked by the fluttering flags I seized a slim chance. Giving the reins a twitch and hauling out I yelled at Baldur. I didn't touch him with the whip. Over the surf roar of the crowds he heard and responded.

The chariot bounded and for a moment or two it seemed to me I was flying through the air like Larghos Kraneyzendo himself.

We swerved out with the zorcas pounding along, manes flying, spiral horns glittering, racing up alongside the chariot ahead. We thundered on and the other chariot slid back and back and finally I was able to nudge the team inwards in time to hurtle through the gap.

Only then was I able to take a whooping breath. My Val! That had been close! And as I worked my way up the field I was somberly aware that the quality of the rigs would be better each time.

On the fifth circuit at the same place with Baldur hauling splendidly from the front we passed the next chariot.

Now we lay fourth in the race.

As we swerved back on line sparks spat from the iron bound wheels and stones flew lethally through the air. My arms ached, my body ached, what there was left of my legs ached and my head ached.

No time to worry over minor discomforts like that when there was a race to win, by Krun!

This, indeed, was a race I had to win. I could not afford to lose. So to a Herrelldrin Hell with all the battering my body was taking!

The pairs of pillars were cunningly arranged, not to say sadistically arranged. There were only a limited number of straights where overtaking was practical. Up ahead the startlingly white five of Lart's Chavonths led the field. Closely pursuing galloped on Nath's Hammerers, so that crafty polsim with his finger to his nose had not been as foolish as his auditors imagined. Ahead of me Rolico's Strigicaws held third place. The chariot-eer was making no real attempt to overtake and shortly my splendid five hurtled along on his heels. Naghan's Droombs had flown to flinders in that first maniacal charge at the starting pillars.

The same positions held as we rounded the curve to begin the sixth lap. On the eighth, Vando had said. On the eighth touch Baldur—and cling on with a grip of death!

The mutrowfer I'd passed, Miriam's Zhantils, streamed along in my wake. The mud had not yet dried sufficiently in the heat of the suns to blow and billow about, so the lady autarch's driver did not spit my dust. By the time the race finished—assuming any chariots were left intact then—I judged the dust would be creaming in thick sheets from the wheels. Well, rain, mud, red dye—a trifle of dust would coat all that in a patina like a shroud.

The spectators kept up their yelling. The Suns of Scorpio threw down their mingled streaming lights. The air smelled of drying mud. The chariots raced on.

A serious worry nagged at me. Lart's Chavonths were drawing away in the lead. Just how far could Baldur and his magnificent team afford to let them get away? Could the ground be made up?

On the seventh lap I felt a definite easement in the rapid gait of Vando's zorcas. I could not use the whip on them and it was too early, according to Vando's instructions, to start them on the final run in to the winning flag. All I could do was go along with Baldur's faithful zorca brain and trust he knew what he was doing.

Then, of course, in a swirl and a crashing racket and a glimpse of straining zorcas and gold and silver ornamentation, Miriam's Zhantils roared up alongside and passed and hurtled on ahead.

By the dangling infested eyeballs and congested hairy nostrils of Makki Grodno! Now what the hell was Baldur playing at? We hit a series of ruts angling for the next pair of posts and I jangled about like a puppet on strings. The next curve and we'd be on lap eight. All right, then! Baldur—do your stuff!

Miriam's Zhantils galloped splendidly up to Nath's Hammerers. Twice the mutferim attempted to pass and twice was blocked. On the third try he scraped through and started headlong after Lart's Chavonths.

The curve was coming up fast. A few specks of dust flew. The pair of pillars ahead looked confoundedly close together—the damned things seemed to be closer with every lap of the course.

Miriam's Zhantils kept on a true line. Nath's Hammerers clung on and then swung out and the whip rose and fell. The team leaped forward. The pillars grew larger and larger. Nath's Hammerers kept doggedly on. I watched, fascinated. Now dust peaked up from the iron bound wheels. Miriam's rig swept on. Nath's chariot held on fractionally too long. Frantically the driver tried to haul the team back into line, and failed, and five zorcas, the chariot and the charioteer smashed sickeningly into the stone.

The uproar flowered prodigiously to the skies. Only by a last minute swerve and an immediate bumping crashing across the ruts was Baldur able to avoid the tangle of wreckage. We hurtled through with the stone pillars a savage blur in the corner of my eye.

By Krun! This was warm work!

Ahead now Miriam's Zhantils and Lart's Chavonths were the chariots to beat.

Now we were on the penultimate lap.

Gently, I touched the tip of the whip to Baldur's hindquarters.

The only true description is to say that we took off like a rocket. We flew. The wheels whirred. Dust streamed back in a smothering cloud. Baldur and his team simply took off.

All I could do was cling on and trust.

With Pride and Power to larboard and Passion and Perseverance to starboard, with Baldur magnificent in the bows, we passed Miriam's Zhantils as though they were standing still. Around the course we thundered. When Lart's Chavonths entered the last lap we were closing. Baldur stretched out and his team responded with consummate power and skill. Dust flew to coat Lart's charioteer when we passed. The crowds were going mad. The final flag flew. Vando's Lilies romped home, magnificent, beautiful, sublime.

After that everything became a blur. There was some kind of victory ceremony. Wreaths were placed about the zorca's necks and I still had sense enough left to want to get blankets put over them. Vando's grooms turned up. A tall, gaunt-faced individual in rich clothes with a great golden sash around him and feathers in his hat met us as we re-entered our stall. I climbed down and my legs felt shaky, decidedly shaky, as though I'd been at sea for a year.

"Here, mutferim," he said, and handed me a leather bag. It clinked. "There is some gold with the silver."

"Thank you. Where is Vando? Who are you?"

"I am Nath L'Llonge. The autarch Vando has been called away." He favored me with a mean look under his eyebrows. "And you address me as notor, tikshim. Dokerty take your impudence!"

I didn't hit him; I was still not really back in the world.

"Notor—where are my clothes—my weapons?"

He pointed offhandedly to a pile of clothes on the table. They were bright green.

"There are new clothes for you. Where yours are I don't know."

I sucked in a breath.

My limbs still felt as though they'd been through a butcher's mincer. The Everoinye had commanded that there be no violence. This was a moment for reasonable debate, not fisticuffs.

"Thank you for the clothes, notor. But—my weapons?"

"I've no idea where your weapons are, blintz. Now take your money and clear off!"

Eight

Clad in my new clothes, bright green, hideous, uncomfortable, I took myself off to collect my winnings. At least I'd had a bath and cleaned off the muck, mud, red dye and dust. The disappearance of my armory was serious, yet I did not wish to spend any cash on new swords until I'd found out how much the magistrates wanted for the fine. Anyway, in all probability I'd only be able to buy the Krasny work blades they sold down here in Balintol. Mind you, Fweygo had said that Kildrin did produce fine steel—at a price.

The prison turned out to be a lumpy stone building. The warders had the grim, no-nonsense faces of prison guards. The pervading smells of dirt and burned green vegetables and disinfectant brought back unhappy memories, by Krun!

Waiting at the desk where a Relt wrote rapidly on sheets of yellow paper I looked out into the yard. A circle of prisoners walked around and around, heads hanging, dispirited. A Kildoi walked with them, defiant, upright. He supported another Kildoi who was bent and clearly injured and in pain.

Involuntarily, I spat out: "Fweygo!"

The Relt looked up, his gentle beaked face absent with the work still in his head and to be committed to paper.

"You have brought the fine, dom?"

"Aye."

He said that the prisoner Fweygo had tried to break in and release his father, who was sick. "That kind of behavior is frowned on in Emgidu. Still, I see that, like me, you are a man of peace."

"Oh, aye."

The formalities were gone through with speed. The Relt had a lot of work to catch up on. Fweygo and his father were brought in. When my kregoinye comrade saw me, he opened his mouth, shut it, said nothing as the cash was counted out. The fine took just about all the money I had, including what I'd been paid as a mutferim.

When we were outside in the clean Kregan air, he said: "You have my thanks, Drajak. This is my honored father, Fando."

"Lahal, master Fando. You need a needleman."

"Aye." He held his side and wheezed. Fweygo supported him.

"We can't stay in the city." Fweygo spoke decisively. "We must go to my grandfather's place. Mistress Tilly is there."

Fweygo had given my weaponless belts a startled look. But he did not comment. His own weapons had been returned to him. We had just about enough money to hire a calsany on which Fando perched. Fweygo and I walked. His grandfather had a small farm a few ulms from Emgidu so we trailed along the dusty road. I admit to a feeling of desolate emptiness in my inward parts, not altogether occasioned by the lack of food.

The few ulms turned out to be better than a dwabur and the suns were declining as we reached the farm. On the way Fweygo, no doubt eaten up by curiosity over my lack of a proper Kregan armory, filled the picture in for me. His father had tried his hand at this and that to make a living, usually failing after a season or so. He owned a small shop in an alley where he'd sold brass ornaments. Developments were afoot and the site of the shop was required by the big investors. The refusal had been met by trumped up charges.

At this critical moment, Fando had fallen ill. Debts were called in, and unable to go on, the charges stuck. Fweygo in his immediate way had tried to release his father, and been incarcerated in his turn, with the imposition of a hefty fine.

Just how hefty that was I knew—the calsany had taken all I had, with the deposit, leaving me with just nine coppers.

By the time we reached the farm long ruby and emerald shadows lay athwart the countryside. Despite riding the calsany, Pando was exhausted. Anyway, a calsany is more properly a beast of burden, not a saddle animal. We couldn't afford a preysany, which would have been more comfortable.

The rural smells accentuated the freshness of the air, for the farm was impeccably managed. The muck heaps were all downwind and removed from the farmhouse. As a mutrowferim, I fancied I knew all about falling in muckheaps.

Fweygo's grandfather turned out to be a surprise. He sat in a small four-wheeled chair with a shaft hauled by a young Kildoi lad. He greeted us with some concern. There is this condition, rare on Kregen, of peoples' hair turning snow white. He was introduced as Fweygo Senior. His hair stuck up in peaks either side of a bald pate. His beard was white. His moustache was worthy of the most ferocious Krozair Brother.

Fweygo Junior explained that if he had a son he'd be called Fando, after his father, and the son's son would be Fweygo.

I noticed Fweygo did not say when he had a son, but if. As I say, there are not many Kildois upon Kregen.

A competent Puncture Lady bustled up, and this Mistress Tilly, a Kildoi, took immediate charge of Fando. All the workfolk on the farm were Kildois, about six of them, and none was slave.

The meal we ate was gargantuan, and when we'd finished the last paline from its decorated pottery bowl, we were replete.

Fweygo said his father would be safe now and he had things to do. He'd told me neither his father nor grandfather was kregoinye. I said that I needed to get back to Prebaya as soon as possible, that I had no money to hire a lifter, that riding would take far too long, and that I was forced to wait for the Everoinye to send their Giant Blue Scorpion to transport me back to Caneldrin.

He nodded. "Very well. I shall leave in the morning." He'd take the calsany back and claim the deposit.

We talked into the evening and Fweygo Senior proved sharp-witted. When he asked me what I knew of Kildois, I replied that I'd known several, and that two in particular stuck in my mind.

"One is a good comrade called Korero." They shook their heads. Even in a small race of diffs everyone was not known by everyone else.

"The other was a certain Mefto, who made himself Prince of Shanodrin, Prince Mefto A'Shanofero. Known as Mefto the Kazzur."

The silence around the table echoed.

Fweygo Senior leaned forward from his wheeled chair.

"He was your good comrade?"

I couldn't stop the harsh laugh, almost a cackle. I made a negative motion with my hand. "No! He bested me in a couple of fights—"

"I am not surprised. Yet you still live."

"On the first occasion we were interrupted by bandits. On the second I was fortunate enough to cut off his tail hand."

They sucked in their breaths at that.

I added: "It was a left hand, as I remember."

Old Fweygo Senior rubbed a veined hand over his bald head between the white tufts.

I didn't even consider the chance that I had made a bad mistake and these folk were friends of Mefto the Kazzur. Anyway, there's nothing like the truth to brace a meeting up; even if, as you know, I so often bend the truth around to suit the situation.

Fweygo Senior's wife, Fweygo's grandmother, had long since died. Fando's wife, Fweygo's mother, had run off with a travelling puppet-show master. No doubt this contributed to Fando's failure in life. That tragic circumstance might well have been the reason why the Star Lords recruited Fweygo to be a kregoinye. What little he had told me in the past about himself and his family might very well be not altogether the whole truth.

The fact remains, I liked Fweygo's family.

"Mefto the Kazzur!" Fweygo Senior breathed the words harshly. "Sometimes there comes a time when it would be appropriate for we Kildoi to swear by gods and spirits as other races of diffs do."

"You know Mefto the Kazzur then." It was not a question; I made it a statement.

"Oh, aye. Aye. In his young days I marked him. He had everything." Old Fweygo used his right upper to wipe his pate and his right lower to lift a glass of wine to his lips. "He was like quicksilver. He learned almost faster than—" He stopped abruptly.

I think I'd already guessed. But I said: "Than what, master?"

Old Fweygo shook that remarkable head. "I know with my mind I should not blame myself. But my ib lies a heavy burden of guilt on me. Faster than I could teach him."

I sat back in my chair and sipped the rich red wine.

"So you are a swordmaster. I should call you San Fweygo."

"No more. No more!"

The old man's distress was obvious. I felt deucedly uncomfortable, I can tell you, by Vox!

Mistress Tilly soothed him and fetched a cup of a herbal potion that he eagerly sipped. She sighed. "I think he upsets himself just so he can have a drink of my Herbal Tea." She sat down again. "He is allowed but six glasses of wine a day."

That was two short of the preferred eight meals a day most Kregans believe in. And, judging by Tilly's countenance, there was alcohol of some sort in her famous Herbal Tea.

When Fweygo Senior had recovered himself he said: "I took you, Drajak, for a man of peace, not a man of war. Yet you say you fought Mefto the Kazzur. Anyone he fights ends up dead. Yet you say you cut off his tail hand. This is all a conundrum."

Fweygo cleared his throat. "Oh, Drajak handles a sword—um—clumsily. I have tried to assist him. But he will prance about—ah—like a dopa-maddened Ivarchuck in a scrap." He shook his head sadly. I hid a smile. My antics during a fight were deliberately designed to conceal from good old Fweygo that I did, indeed, have a little skill with a blade.

Why I did this must all be wrapped up with my scorpion nature, a hangover from my adventuring days with my kregoinye comrade, Pompino.

Fweygo Senior's story, once told, was clear enough. He had been a master swordsman, a hyrscreetzim, and was famous as a teacher. He had taught Mefto. In thanks, Mefto had crippled him in a practice bout. When Fweygo Senior learned of Mefto's subsequent devilish activities, he retired from teaching. He would not touch a sword hilt again.

Now Mistress Tilly was far more than just a Puncture Lady, no matter how valuable they are under the Suns of Scorpio. She was chatelaine, farm manager, accountant, adviser—and, as Fweygo said very seriously indeed—a remarkably expert swordswoman.

"She served for a number of seasons with the Jikai Vuvushis. When she met my grandfather her life changed. She devoted herself to him." Fweygo used his tail hand to pick a crumb from the table. "She abandoned the life of a Warrior Woman. Anyway, she did not like being called a Combat Cutie."

"Oh, aye," I said. My glorious Delia had had a few run-ins over being called a Combat Cutie, laughing it off as silly.

By this time my comrade Fweygo and I sat alone at the table. The others had retired. Strangely enough, despite my exertions of the day I did not feel particularly tired. There were items of information yet to be learned.

Fweygo said his grandfather had spoken the truth about no longer teaching, with one exception. "He trained me up."

As I made no comment to this surprising statement, he went on to say that Mefto the Kazzur was a blight upon the race of Kildois. I could see he, like the others, still doubted my claims.

So I deliberately changed the subject. I asked about Nath Seegfreedhan, known as Vando. He'd just vanished—and with him my arsenal. All Fweygo knew was that Vando was in line to become Prime Autarch. He was absolutely astonished when I told him about the chariot race. "Then, as Vando won the Autarch's Stakes, his succession is assured. So he has been abducted."

"No business of ours, dom."

"Well—" He sat back, and fiddled his left upper and right lower in a finger-nest. "I must be off early in the morning." He stood up. "I'll be gone by the time you rise. Moonbright."

"Moonbright," I replied, using the goodnight they had here.

By the morning Fweygo was as good as his word and was gone. After the first breakfast Fweygo Senior had his chair wheeled out onto a scrap of green lawn, surrounded by brilliant flowers, where birds and butterflies flew and cavorted. He made himself comfortable with a glass of parclear on the armtray. Then he demanded to know all my history concerning Mefto the Kazzur.

So, truthfully as far as events not to do with the Everoinye were concerned, I told him.*

When I had finished he nodded somberly.

"I think perhaps you handle a blade somewhat better than my grandson would have us believe."

I had to admit, not necessarily with any shame, but certainly without any pride, that I had done a deal of sword fighting in my time.

"Mefto the Kazzur may be more expert than you, Drajak. I know he is not the better man."

Of course, I said nothing. I report this only to indicate the way Old Fweygo's mind was working.

He went on: "Do you think you will ever meet him again?"

This question, as you who have followed my narrative will know, had plagued me from that fraught day when I'd fought in the deadly game of Kazz-Jikaida in LionardDen, Jikaida City, against Mefto.

"All things are possible upon Kregen."

He nodded decisively. He'd made up his mind, as I thought, that I spoke the truth.

"Between the second breakfast and foremid lunch Mistress Tilly will come for you. Be ready." With that the lad wheeled his chair away back into the house.

Having to wait for the Star Lords to transport me back to Prebaya so that I could continue with the task of tackling the evil ibmanzies fretted away at my feelings. The work was there, to my hand, needing to be got on with, and I was stuck here. The farm did not possess a lifter, and I regretted I had no airboat or flyer and, at the moment at any rate, no access to one.

What I should be doing right now was trudging back to Emgidu to

---

* See *A Sword for Kregen*, Book 2 of the Jikaida Cycle, being Volume 20 of the Saga of Dray Prescot. *ABA*

reclaim my weapons. Vando or his people would have them, surely? I just hoped Nath Seegfreedhan was still alive and safe. You can never be sure of those happy circumstances upon Kregen.

So—instead of returning to Emgidu I waited here. The fascination of talking to the man who had trained up Mefto the Kazzur was far too strong for me to resist.

Promptly on time Mistress Tilly arrived to lead me out to a small walled yard paved in sand. She wore a long gray cloak. Fweygo Senior upright in his wheeled chair watched us. He waved a hand and his attendant lad passed a rudis across to me. The wooden sword was well-made, fashioned to resemble a braxter. I took it and held it down by my side. I did not swish it about in the air.

Tilly threw off the gray cloak. I looked at her, blinked, and looked again. Her legs were bare. She wore a short skirt, a very short skirt, her midriff was bare, and a pair of tiny black triangles clothed her upper body. Her brown hair was scraped up tightly and held firmly in place by a bright red scarf. She looked splendid.

Holding the rudis between my knees I rapidly—and thankfully—ripped off the hideous green tunic-blouse. Tilly picked up her wooden sword and she did make a few whistling passes in empty air.

Old Fweygo cleared his throat and said: "Just fence. I need to evaluate first. Begin!"

Tilly and I saluted each other gravely, as is proper in the practice fence, and we set to. There was no doubt in my mind that crippled though he was, the man in the chair would pierce through any attempts on my part to disguise my skill. So I fought correctly. I did not use the tricks and the unpleasant stratagems, the downright dirty fighting of your swordsman adventurer. Tilly was extremely good, as I expected. She was using only one sword, when she could have wielded five. I fancied I'd have some trouble against her when we got around to that.

On Kregen there are many Disciplines of the Sword, as distinct from techniques of fighting. Some may be blended with others, some with greater difficulty, and some not at all. Formality in what is and what is not allowed as a legitimate target, of course, introduces artificiality which is completely inappropriate on the battlefield when you are fighting for your life.

Marvelous as she was, using only one sword Mistress Tilly could be bested. Old Fweygo watched, his head stuck forward, his bright eyes missing nothing as we foined. Presently he called a halt. Now I do not wish to recount in meticulous detail the events of the succeeding days. Conscious as I was of the pressing need to return to Prebaya, or to hotfoot it to Emgidu to rescue my own weapons, the sheer expertise and brilliance of what Fweygo showed me held me in thrall. I sweated out those days of swording, I can tell you, realizing just why Mefto had the bettering of me back there in Jikaida City.

Fweygo Senior kept many different weapons in his armory and I practiced with them all. Mistress Tilly followed his instructions with supple skill and I responded—and learned.

The white-tufted head nodded at me one bright suns shining morning. "Now I see why you survived against Mefto. You have the edge in sheer speed. That, I judge, alone saved you."

"Aye."

"Lucilli the Radiant sent you to me to comfort me in my old age with the knowledge that justice is not dead in the world."

The Radiant Lucilli, one of the most brilliant goddesses upon Kregen, must have smiled on me, too!

Fweygo said he could teach me no more. Also, he was aware that my own Disciplines of the Krozairs of Zy contained much that was new to him—greatly to his surprise, I may add.

Still without any weapons of my own, I was grateful when he presented me with a first-class braxter as a parting gift. All I could return was a most heartfelt thankyou. I vowed to come back here one day. Here, despite our swording, resided peace.

Eventually, as I knew it must, the Giant Blue Scorpion of the Star Lords hovered and descended over me in a whirl of coldness and rushing empty winds. Up I went, head over heels into the next adventure.

Nine

I, Dray Prescot, Vovedeer, Lord of Strombor and Krozair of Zy, glared at the gathering of warriors here in a small room in the Pronto and Risslaca in Prebaya. They looked a ragamuffin collection of scoundrels and cutthroats wearing dingy ragged clothing. Underneath they wore armor. They looked nothing like the smart guard I had created for the lady Quensella.

Nothing like, by Krun!

Erwin the Waggler had contacted most of the old juruk. The familiar faces, dirt-streaked, stared back at me, ready to go. Their weapons were sharp and to hand under their rags.

"You all know exactly what we're after." My voice sounded harsh and intolerant, even in my ears. "I emphasize again the enormous importance of what we are going to do. I know you will not fail." Then I added a few words very fitting in Balintol. "May your gods go with you."

With that, the briefing was over. They all knew exactly what was required of them. They were doing this for money—naturally, as they were paktuns—but they were in this adventure for the reasons I had spelled out, and, as I truly believed, out of loyalty to me.

Inevitably, Veda started to insist that she should accompany us. She was actually wearing enough clothes so as to be decent. I caught a disapproving shake of the head from Suzy the Surcease. She pursed up her determined Hytak lips and said, very firmly, that the nasty cut over Veda's left breast was not healing properly. There was infection. At this Veda tossed her head and began to rant a trifle, pointing out that she was used to discomfort and pain.

Suzy sighed. "That rascal Naghan the Leaves has faithfully promised me that today a lifter will fly in bringing herbs and jungle plants. I intend to be the first into his shop." She gave a brief description of the herbs and plants she wanted and their purpose in healing. The Kregan doctors are well aware of the healing properties of many of the exotic plants growing within the rain forest canopy. So it was decided. A decidedly sulky Veda the Unruly had to accept the needle, as they say on Kregen.

Just before dawn my little band took up their positions around the damned Dokerty temple.

With me I kept Erwin the Waggler, the hytak Nalan ti Perning and the khibil Perempto the Shorn. With low voiced wishes for success the others went off. We four walked sedately around to the side entrance by which I had first penetrated the temple.

This stout door was obviously locked. This way in led to the passageways on the face of the blank square on the map on the opposite side to those I'd tried before. Here were the chamber where infectos were tortured into being and the observation gallery for the artists who recorded the hideous scenes.

I did not intend to wait for someone to exit the building and so open the door for us. Pulling the two-handed axe out from under my raggedy cloak I hefted it high and brought it down with a rending smash.

Wood chips flew. The door shuddered. Two more blows shattered the lock and Erwin pushed the door wide.

We wore raggedy clothes just in case of capture. I had debated long with myself about the wisdom of bringing Erwin. He was a Vallian employed in the Vallian Embassy. Yet I hadn't the heart to deny him after his efforts on my behalf. Anyway, we were just a bunch of tazll paktuns after the fight with the regent C'Chermina's guards and out for loot. Erwin would come through.

We all carried bundles over our shoulders which were heavy enough and would be lighter by the time we'd finished, splendidly lighter, by Vox!

Tsleetha tsleethi, softly softly—well, that approach had been tried and

I'd abjectly failed. Cunning and sneakiness had not availed me. Now was the time for the blunt instrument.

The corridor stretched ahead, empty, lit by a few lamps along the walls. Moving quickly and quietly we filed along.

Past the tiled and whitewashed corridor we entered the rooms which were carpeted and more brightly lit. I pressed on, alert for footsteps or voices, until we reached the spot where I'd encountered the two lovebirds. From here the way to the observation gallery lay stuck in my memory. The oppressiveness of this damned place, the close stink of incense, the very breathlessness of the air, all combined to give me a most nauseous sensation. The quicker we did our business the better.

Peering through the fretted peepholes into that diabolical chamber where they made infectos, where I'd had to fight with a brass candlestick to assist Veda the Mazarnil to escape the horrendous creatures who intended to torture her until the demon could enter her body, I deemed this a fitting place to begin.

As far as we could ascertain the torture chamber lay empty. Servants would be busily at work in most of the areas of the temple; this chamber was reserved for the priests. Beyond it—somewhere—I was sure would be found the inner sanctum. My blunt instrument of a plan did not envisage pressing on. Oh, no, by Krun!

Our bundles contained all that was necessary. There was no need for orders. Silently we opened the sacks and took out the squat rotund pots. These were not amphorae for wine, their particular shape indicated to all that they contained oil.

If I assure you it was with some satisfaction that I watched the oil gush out and spread, shimmering in rainbow colors, across the floor of that horrendous chamber, I believe you will fully understand.

We did not stint in our endeavors.

By Vox! We laid a gleaming carpet of oil from the fretted screen clear across to the platform. The smell of the oil—cheap mineral oil, not samphron oil—did not offend. On the contrary, it smelled far sweeter in my nostrils than the stinking incense they burned to their Opaz-forsaken god, Dokerty.

Checking Erwin as he went to tip his last oil pot out, I said in a low voice: "Save it. We'll use it on the way out."

"Quidang!" he said—in a whisper.

In his superior Khibil way, Perempto said: "Cadade—I never liked these Dokerty blintzes. I will light the oil."

My amusement at this was short lived. The business was serious—deadly serious. I nodded. "Very well."

Perempto took only four strikes to get his box to light the tump. He breathed the glow into flame. A scrap of cloth blazed up. Perempto tossed it expertly through one of the frets.

With great satisfaction I watched the pool of oil light. Little blue flames danced. The fire front advanced radially. Smoke began to plume. The gilded legs of a chair smoldered and the gilding ran in shining globules. The fire began to speak.

Very shortly the whole demonic place would be engulfed.

The platform where they'd tortured folk to turn them into infectos, the pompous overblown furnishings, the disgusting tapestries, all would succumb to the purifying breath of the flames.

Time to go!

We backtracked to a carpeted corridor where Erwin deposited more oil. When that lit it would prevent fire-fighters from going down to the chamber immediately, for they would have to quench this blaze first.

Perempto made sure the oil was well ablaze before we walked smartly off towards the whitewashed corridor and the way out.

This early in the morning there were few people about in this section; we shrank back into an alcove to allow a hairy Brokelsh to trudge past carrying a yoke over his shoulders from which depended wooden tubs. He looked neither right nor left. He wore the gray slave breechclout.

Perempto put a hand to his sword hilt. I checked him.

When the Brokelsh had gone I whispered: "Probably milk. Even if it was water—what good will two tubs be?"

"Hah!" said Perempto. "Bad cess to the lot of 'em!"

The great blunt instrument that was my so wonderful plan did not include getting into a fight. Fights were to be avoided.

Just how long it would take for the temple to wake up to the unpleasant fact that a part of the place was on fire remained conjectural. One thing was sure—after the initial panic they'd buckle down to serious firefighting. My estimate had been that the torture chamber once well alight would spread the flames from its position into all parts of the building. And so, as usual, I, Dray Prescot, began to worry my old vosk skull of a head over the chances of my plan. Had I done enough? Would the flames spread quickly so as to engulf the entire rotten fabric of the temple?

By the maggoty entrails and diseased left eyeball of Makki Grodno! The fire must spread. It had to!

So, in a fraught frame of mind, I padded along these sinister corridors, not looking for trouble but looking for the way out.

The ominous tramp of iron-studded boots echoed from ahead.

We halted. Perempto pushed open a small wooden door on the left side of the corridor and we bundled in. Standing still and perfectly quietly we waited as the crash, crash, crash, of the boots thudded past.

"They don't seem in a hurry," whispered Perempto.

They didn't—and I was not pleased by that. They should be running hell for leather for the fire by now.

Erwin tried the door. "It's locked!"

"Charming!" I peered into the blackness. Now where the hell would this unwanted detour take us? I lifted the axe to smash the door down and the sound of more tramping feet pounded past.

The axe lowered slowly in my grasp. Djan take it! There was nothing else to do but grope forward quietly and find a turning to the right to take us out of this mess.

Perempto flicked his scrap of burning cloth about. The erratic light showed us a passageway painted a dark green. Cautiously we edged along. Erwin breathed in my ear. "I have read the books. I never dreamed—this is wonderful!"

I tried not to feel sick.

A fine brave young lad like Erwin—and just because he was caught up in a potentially deadly scenario with Dray Prescot of whom he had read fantastic swashbuckling stories of adventure, he was thoroughly enjoying himself. If he only knew the truth!

Padding along quietly in the flickering illumination we came to a door at the end of the corridor. Here we halted. Erwin eagerly tried the door. It was not locked and opened easily.

The carpeted corridor into which we stepped stretched emptily left and right. A fanciful halberd with red and green tassels lay on the floor. A faint smell of smoke hung in the air. Evidently, the guard at the door had dropped his polearm and gone haring off towards the fire.

Erwin went on through and then halted, swinging to face me.

"Which way?"

My bump of direction said we should go right. Perempto started off that way and we had reached halfway to the door at the end when a gout of flame burst through as the door collapsed.

This astonished me.

"Tolaar take it!" exclaimed Perempto, halting abruptly.

Quite obviously we had achieved a more than resounding success with our fire! Nothing else remained but for us to scurry back and run up towards the left end door. The flames leaped at our backs. We could feel the heat funneling down in the confines of the corridor.

Erwin reached for the door handle. It did not budge.

"Locked!"

Almost before Erwin finished speaking my axe whistled around. The door shattered inwards at the first blow and we all tumbled through.

The corridor stretched left and right. It curved away to the right so that we could not see what stood at the end. The left branch ended in a flight of stairs going up.

"Akhchutz rot it!" Perempto glared about. "This warren is a damned maze!"

"Up or along?" Erwin had a hand on his sword hilt, the other arm cradled the rotund oil jar.

"To the right," I said. "If we go up the flames will follow us."

So we ran around the curve of the corridor. There was no doubt the place was well afire now. Smoke sifted after us and the ominous crackle of the flames roared louder at our backs.

We sprinted out into a sizeable room, furnished with chairs and benches, where blue smoke drifted. The heat increased. There was no one about, so they'd all run off, either to fight the fire or to escape. If we knew which way they'd gone, we'd follow, sharpish, very smartish, by Krun!

A number of doors studded the tapestried walls. Now the dull surf roar of the fire beat steadily on our ears and the heat mounted. The flames following us crackled nearer.

Talk about being hoist by your own varter!

The first door Perempto opened led onto a flight of steps. They went up. He span back angrily, leaving the door open, and ripped at its neighbor. The door smashed in on a billow of smoke and dark energetic figures bundled through. Four of them, they halted when they saw us. They were guards, black with smoke and with singed holes in their clothes where their armor did not cover.

The oil jar cradled in Erwin's arms signaled instantly to them that they'd stumbled across the incendiaries. Perempto's scrap of burning cloth merely confirmed their suspicions.

There was no time to think, only time to act.

I leaped for them, the braxter ripping free from the scabbard and snouting forward.

The first had no time to draw. He went down. Perempto engaged the second and chopped him with his sword half-drawn. The third's sword lifted and the braxter slid between chin and mail, tearing out his throat. Perempto sliced the fourth and we stepped back, not even winded.

On the instant the smoke from the door through which these four poor doomed guards had erupted bellowed into flame. There was no way past there.

"Up!"

We bundled through the open door and up the stairs.

Erwin went first, then Perempto, and I followed.

Near the top I halted and swiveled as a hoarse voice yelled from below: "Stop, you Dokerty-forsaken blintzes!"

More guards crowded the foot of the stairs. One lifted a crossbow and loosed immediately. The bolt whistled past my side. I heard a thwunk followed by a crash. Swiftly glancing up I saw Erwin's oil jar had been knocked from his arm. It bounced down the stairs, two, three, four—on the fifth it shattered. Oil splattered down.

Perempto let out a triumphant yell. He hurled his burning rag down.

Evil blue flames spread across the stairs, between the guards and us. "That'll hold 'em!"

Scrambling like apes up we went, kicked open the door and tumbled out onto a smoke-free landing. Our eyes were streaming, our nostrils choked up and our throats raw.

At our backs the flames licked up from the stairhead.

We headed off towards the right. We had to find a way out of this maze before the whole place—and us with it—burned to a cinder.

The fire now pranced and danced and hissed behind us. We had to go on. The next door opened onto a corridor and for a moment we hesitated at the blue tendrils drifting up through the floor. The storey below was well alight and in a very short time this whole corridor would be engulfed. Perempto started off boldly.

The noise of the inferno beat a cacophony in our heads. The heat scorched and flayed like the Furnace Fires of Inshurfraz. The floor as Perempto leaped along began to burn through. Flames ran across the wooden floorboards. They gyrated upwards, orange, red, yellow. In only moments the floor would collapse.

Perempto halted at the far end. He shouted. Erwin started across the corridor floor. Rapidly his youthful figure became enshrouded in smoke. I saw him running on. I saw the floor open at his feet like an evil scarlet lily, devouring.

Erwin flung up his arms. Downwards he plummeted, his shriek lost in the noise of fire and flame.

He vanished. He was gone. All that was left was an unholy pit of engulfing fire like an entrance to a Herrelldrin Hell.

Ten

Erwin the Waggler was gone. He was dead. He was a mere blackened husk falling through the shrieking inferno below.

I, Dray Prescot, could only stand there uselessly. All I could do was consign my young comrade, Erwin the Waggler, a good Valkan, to the mercies of Opaz. I wished him a safe passage through the encircling mists, through the Ice Floes of Sicce, to the Sunny Uplands beyond.

As for me, there was no way back. The flames leaped higher and higher from the pit ahead. I stepped back half a dozen paces. The figure of Perempto wavered and distorted. He threw up his arms. I could just make out his shout.

"You'll never jump it!"

"By the Black Chunkrah!" I snarled to myself. "There's nothing else to do! I will jump it!"

Gathering myself, I ran and leaped.

Sheer heat engulfed me. My eyes were dazzled. I was sure my skin was all singed away. That my clothes did not catch alight was a miracle. Hurtling headlong through the geysers of flame I soared up and over that infernal pit.

Almost, almost, I did not make it. My scrabbling fingers clawed at smoking floorboards. I shoved the pain away and with a savage burst of energy hoisted myself up, tumbled head over heels into Perempto's booted feet.

He hauled me up.

"Well, cadade—if I hadn't seen it I wouldn't believe it!"

The absence of spittle in my mouth prevented me from spitting. I coughed—I coughed my guts up. My eyes were red sore.

Perempto went on: "Erwin! I saw—he was a good lad."

Somehow or other I managed to husk out: "Aye."

The sensation of being bathed in fire persisted. We moved away from the pit, along the corridor to the far end. Fire pursued us remorselessly. Was there no way out of this inferno?

Of one thing I was certain sure. Erwin would want us to get out and save ourselves, before we gave further thought to him. His memory would be honored in the proper ways and rituals later.

After that we scurried along corridors and through rooms trying to avoid gouts of flame and billows of smoke. At one point all sense of direction was lost. Which way should we take in this furnace of a temple?

Eventually, in Opaz's good time, we smashed down a door, coughing in smoke wreaths that coiled about us, and stumbled out onto a flat roof. The glory of the mingled rays of the Suns of Scorpio fell about us, emerald and ruby. We were standing on an extension to the main building. At our backs the streamers of fire burned to the heavens. As we looked a dome crumpled inwards and amidst fountains of sparks collapsed. The whole sky glowed with the glare.

The light breeze pushed the smoke away from us, which was a blessing. The roof looked ugly. Spirals of smoke lifted across its entire surface, and little flames danced here and there, hungrily, striving to take hold and burn the lot to ashes.

"Come on, Perempto! We can't lollygag about here."

With that I started off running for the far edge. The rafters swayed and creaked under my flying feet like the timbers of a ship in a gale. Perempto pattered on after. Breathing became easier once we'd reached the far parapet. We peered over the edge.

The sheer wall fronted a narrow street bordered by a single storey building. Blazing timbers, fallen from the windows below us, choked up the street with fire. No one was about. I pointed.

Even as I shouted above the roar of the inferno the roof lurched. Chunks of brickwork fell from the wall below us. "Jump!"

Perempto's haughty Khibil face blanched—just a trifle, just enough to show he did not relish this at all—then he brushed up those fierce Khibil whiskers. "Ay, cadade. We must jump!"

We stepped back over that swaying, smoke and flame bellowing roof, gathered ourselves, ran—and leaped.

Out we soared, out and down. We came down with two almighty great crashes on the lower roof opposite. Bruised, winded, singed, we stood up, panting. We looked like a couple of chimney sweeps who'd fallen into the fire.

This building would not burn; but the breeze would almost certainly brush the fire onto the buildings on the other side. I just hoped that when the dormitory area went up into fiery destruction all the little servant girls would be safely out of it.

Once we found the way down we took little time in gaining the street and running along to the kyro at the end. Here the square was packed with people, mostly gawping, but some were standing in a hopeless bucket line, throwing handfuls of water uselessly. There was not a single sign of a red-robed priest anywhere.

A hand fastened on my shoulder and I whirled.

It was Sijilo the Oivon, one of the Hytaks in the guard. He was clearly excited by all this. "We have seen nothing, Jik! Not one of the lads I've checked saw the priests leaving."

Sijilo had been promoted to Deldar. I believed him. I snarled out: "The blintzes aren't still in there, that's for sure!"

Perempto demanded: "Did they fly out?"

Sijilo shook his stubborn Hytak head. "No one saw a lifter."

Despite all the burns, the smoke, the bruises, despite even the cat-astrophic death of Erwin, I was still capable of feeling a fresh sense of despair. All the planning had failed, the blunt instrument had failed, I had failed. The fact was that we were not so much no nearer the Prism of Power as actually further away.

My guards had been posted on all sides of the building and by the time we were gathered together all hope that someone might have seen the escape of the Dokerty priests vanished. Veda had not claimed her map showed everything. Clearly, there was another way out. All the same, by Vox, if the priests had run out into any of the surrounding streets one or t'other of my lads should have spotted the blaspheming cramphs.

This dismal meeting was held in a private room of the middling tavern, The Pronto and Risslaca, which I had been assured was safe from prying eyes and ears. We drank down our ale glumly.

"A secret tunnel!" I burst out loudly, wiping froth. "That has to be it." I looked hard at my men. "Make enquiries all about. Someone must have seen them."

"Quidang!" We washed and cleaned ourselves up.

A plan was rapidly devised and they went off determined to find the answer. A few runners were left to carry word to the others when success had been achieved.

This wholehearted support offered me by these men, this immediate and ready acceptance of my orders, had to be put down to the yrium with which I was both cursed and blessed. For good or ill, I possessed this power so much greater than mere charisma. This was the reason, I believed, that the Star Lords had chosen me. I could have done without it, could wish it far and far away, by Vox. Yet—I was stuck with it and the monstrous problems it brought.

In the event the polsim Naghan the Flea brought the news. Polsims with their ferrety faces and quick wits are generally dubbed crafty or cunning by other races of diffs. They prefer to think of themselves as canny or shrewd. He walked into the tavern with that typical unobtrusive, almost slinking gait polsims have. His narrow whiskery face smiled as an ale jug was passed across.

"A tunnel it was, Jik. Out nearby the Temple of Tolaar on the Avenue of Chained Veesons." A veeson is a wild animal of Balintol not unlike a leem. "They headed northwards in the direction of Santoro. A damned great crowd of Katakis guarded the convoy." He slugged back a drink. "They were all well mounted and travelling fast. Devilish fast, my informant said."

"They'll be well gone before we can mount up and follow," exclaimed Harpion the Sallow. "Damned Katakis."

"I want five volunteers," I said.

Naturally, they all volunteered. A hot debate ensued.

Decisively, I selected Molar Na-Fre and Nalan ti Perning. I knew their mettle. Perempto glared at me, so he was included in the party. Because he'd brought the news, and because he was a shrewd or cunning devil, take your pick, Naghan the Flea joined us.

He'd performed well in action when we'd fought C'Chermina's guards. He'd saved Nath the Chanter's hide for him, and they'd struck up an unlikely friendship. So I took Nath the Chanter along too. With these five chosen jurukkers the job would have to be done. I gave instructions to the others, ignoring their downcast faces. They'd join us as soon as they could.

Elten Naghan Vindo, the Vallian ambassador in Caneldrin, had been tapped for cash when the Star Lords released me from Kildrin. All the money I took from our various embassies and consulates around Kregen would be carefully accounted for by my personal stylor, Enevon Ob-Eye, back in our fortress palace of Esser Rarioch in Valka.

So it was that I could pay the extortionate fee demanded by the attendant at the parking lot. My own lifter was a six-place job.

On the way there we passed an ugly mob of Dokerty people ready to smash up any followers of Tolaar they came across. Tolaar's devotees were being blamed for the fire at the Dokerty Temple. This did not please me, you may be sure; but that was the way of things where the two rival religions were always in conflict.

The lifter soared sweetly into the fresh Kregan air. Ah! To feel the scented Kregan breeze sweeping through the hair, the feeling of steady onward progress high above the land fleeting past below, the sheer joy of flying—that is an experience of Kregen never to be forgotten!

The lads were strangely quiet as I drove the airboat on.

No doubt they were contemplating what lay at the end of this exhilarating flight and the damned Katakis waiting for them with naked steel.

I should have known better, by Krun!

They were concentrating on their game back there, a matter of placing numbered squares down in such a way as to complete the winning sequence and deny the opposition that favor. The game was known as San Vester's Challenge, after the sage who'd invented it some thousand or so seasons ago.

These men were hardened paktuns, mercenaries who took their hire and did their duty for the gold. When we reached where we were going they'd consider the Katakis. Until then, a little gambling would pass the time.

The game of Vester's was barely interrupted when we opened the hamper that Indros the Stout, a paunchy little Och who was the landlord of The Pronto and Risslaca, had made up for us. We wolfed down the food and drank off the ale, as the lifter soared onwards.

So we lived from moment to moment. I kept seeing flashing horrific glimpses in my mind's eye of Erwin the Waggler plunging down into that hell hole of fire. The pit of flame coruscated about his young body, burning, incinerating, destroying. Oh, no. I would not forget Erwin the Waggler.

The death of a fine young lad from Valka must be absorbed into the whole life fabric. Life itself went on remorselessly. Now the vital necessity was to look to the future. That future held the Kataki guard. The jibrfarils would be a problem, sure enough, but I knew the damned Dokerty cramphs kept the Katakis out of their inmost secret chambers. There they employed guards of their own dark persuasion. That was a fact of the utmost importance.

The land we were flying over gradually changed from rich agriculture with ordered fields and farmsteads and villages to a forest belt. Beyond that the land turned sour. You couldn't call it a true desert for straggly vegetation managed to find deep-sunken water for tap roots; all the same, it looked highly unpleasant.

Soon after we flitted over the barren land a hump grew out of the desert ahead and grew and enlarged and turned into a fantastic outcrop of naked rock.

I'd had the good fortune to study plate tectonics on one of my recent returns to Earth and that along with continental drift was known to the Savanti of far Aphrasöe. The Star Lords, of course, as far as I could make out, knew just about everything, by Krun! Millennia past the earth had convulsed and these tremendous layers of rock had been thrust upwards and tilted over forty five degrees. Weather and time had eroded them into stark pinnacles and fissures, striations capacious enough to swallow whole villages in their clefts.

Those ancient titanic upheavals had liberated underground water, for greenery clustered in fissures, and on one side a waterfall tumbled over and out onto the plain where it dried and vanished into the dry and hungry sands. There were buildings down there.

This then was Santoro.

In his impetuous Khibil way Perempto ripped out: "We have seen no caravan. By the Imps of Khabriana! Where are the blintzes?"

The most sensible suggestion anyone could come up with was that the damned Dokerty caravan had stopped off along the way for refreshment. They could be anywhere in any of the villages.

At that moment Molar Na-Fre let out a cry. True to his Pachak mercenary way of life he had kept watch faithfully. He flung up a pointing arm. "Lifter!"

The sky was cloudless. Out of the blue an airboat scudded low down across the barren land. Quite obviously the craft avoided us, sheering away, shooting up in a long slant to disappear into a cleft. The speed of the lifter and her direction left us high and dry.

"That's it!" There was no doubt in my mind. "Put us down!"

When I told them what I proposed there was instant argument. I'd have none of it. Overriding their protestations I ran into the deep twin shadows thrown by the massif of Santoro. I looked up at the frowning cliffs above. Their overwhelming bulk toppled against the sky. I swallowed. I was in for it now, I was committed.

Taking the first hand and foothold I began to climb.

Eleven

Dust and fragments tumbled away below. Pausing, I did look down. By this time I was half way up. The ledges slanted from top left to lower right, and the ground looked a good long way off. Dust was already clogging up my hooter, and I sneezed, and took a firm hold, and so swiped away at my nose. Damn dust!

The climb in itself was not particularly arduous. Certainly, it held none of the difficulties I'd experienced before in climbing into danger. I just hoped there were no eyes up there spying on me.

Square cut blocks, mortared together, came into view and I had to skirt around them carefully. My judgment was that this was an outbuilding, possibly a defensive work. Where I needed to go was higher, much higher.

The twin suns of Scorpio moved across the cloudless sky. Some of the strata of the outcrop were sandstone, and this glowed in the light. Beyond that first building the way tended diagonally upward. Craning my head back I stared up. The next building jutted boldly from the cliff face. H'm. There looked to be a wide detour in the climbing itinerary. At once I began inching across the strata upwards and along to the left. This took me back into the shadows for which I was duly thankful. The drop in temperature was marked.

Reaching up past that building protruding out over thin air, I decided it was most definitely a fort, an outwork. The parapet was crenellated, and further back on platforms varters were arrayed, their snouts looking most sinister. Any attack on this place would face severe difficulties. An assault would be a most bloody affair.

Because of the loose stuff everywhere, shale and dust and bits and pieces weathered away, the ascent was slow. The suns moved across the sky, and up and up I went, cautiously.

The top rim of this crag looked for all of two worlds like the teeth of a giant, decayed and broken in. There would be a way into the citadel before I reached as high as that—at least, so I hoped, by Djan!

There is a certain time during a climb when the mind detaches itself from the body. An exhilaration takes over that does not interfere with the technical aspects of climbing. During that ascent I first began to consider what would be looked upon, I suppose, as a ridiculous concept by almost anyone involved. I, Dray Prescot, fully intended to destroy the Dokerty Prism of Power. That was the task set to my hands.

Yes, but—what right had I to destroy a religious symbol? The Prism was regarded as holy. It was sacred to Dokerty. I intended to commit sacrilege. Then my foot skidded and I grabbed on. The phantoms of philosophy whisked away. Yet there is more to this logic chopping you shall hear in due time.

A series of hand and footholds, precarious enough, by Krun, gave way to what could laughingly be called a track, slanting upwards steeply. The side was reinforced with stone dressed to fit. A black shadow looming overhead turned out to be a two storey watchtower.

The dark shape of a man in armor leaned over the parapet.

"Weng da!" His voice challenging me with 'Who goes there!' sounded hoarse. Also, he was surprised. No wonder!

"Hai, dom!" I called up in as friendly a voice as I could muster. "I am mighty pleased to see you, Dokerty save me. Give me a hand up for pity's sake for I'm slipping."

Clever, cunning Dray Blabbermouth Prescot!

He aimed his bow down and loosed.

The arrow struck the stone by my head and caromed off into space. It made a damned uncomfortable sound, I can tell you.

Here was I, pinned to the face of the cliff like a display mounted insect, and here was this fellow shooting down at me.

Most uncomfortable, by Vox!

Now many folk deride the good old Kregan habit of carrying around a veritable miniature armory of weapons. In this situation that derision appeared stupid. I had no sheath of terchicks behind my shoulder so I could not hurl a throwing knife at him. The bow appeared again over the parapet. The arrow head looked black and damned pointed and sharp. The thing would be viciously barbed, too.

He let fly. This time the shaft was on target. My braxter flicked up in time and deflected the arrow and it shot off somewhere.

Below this infernal sentry and his arrows stood a door in the masonry of the watchtower. Taking a breath I made a convulsive leap forward and upward. Before he had time to nock a fresh shaft I plunged up and under his line of sight. If he loosed or not I neither knew nor cared.

Above the door a wooden crane and pulley indicated how they could haul supplies up. The axe unlocked the door and I tumbled inside.

A torch guttered smokily on the rough hewn wall. The passage led straight on to a far door. Putting the axe away and drawing the sword I padded on. The far door opened—and there he was, blocky, uncompromising, with his bow lifted, drawn and aimed straight at me.

The shaft sped true. The Disciplines of the Krozairs of Zy flowed through my being. The sword flicked up and the arrow was duly deflected.

He swore, some mumbo-jumbo to do with Dokerty, and nocked a fresh shaft. I moved on swiftly. Twice more he was able to loose and twice the braxter chingled the deadly bird aside.

Then I was almost on him. He reacted with a swiftness that even in that fraught situation I could admire. The bow hit the floor. He drew a dagger and in the same motion thrust savagely upward aiming for my guts. My forearm flashed across before me. It checked the fellow's arm and forced it inwards. His own vicious drive carried on reinforced by my arm. The dagger struck upwards with tremendous force. It went in under his chin to the quillons. Like a pair of statues we just stood there for three heartbeats.

Stepping back, I watched him. Blood poured from his mouth. His eyes glared madly. He folded up, bending double, sinking to his knees. His head dropped until only the dagger supported it.

I had no intention of killing him. I wanted to ask him a few pertinent questions. But he had, in effect, killed himself.

So, there was just the one thing to do.

He was apim, like me. His uniform and armor, workmanlike but with enough fancy touches to suggest the guard to which he belonged enjoyed advantages, fitted me tolerably well. As usual it was tight across my shoulders; no doubt it would split at the first exertions I might be forced to undertake in this hell hole.

His braxter was merely a cheap munitions weapon, not Krasny work, to be sure; but no doubt it would snap at the first real blow. Drawing the dagger free was unpleasant but was done. The uniform was preponderantly madder red, and the armor was scale. Each scale was larger than high quality construction, and made of bronze. When I examined the arrows I discovered, as I had thought, that the heads were fashioned from obsidian. In a land where iron and steel were of dubious quality, flint or obsidian for arrow heads made a great deal of good commonsense.

The bow was not a Great Lohvian Longbow, not even an ordinary bow, but a composite reflex. It shot flat and well, as I could testify, whatever my comrade Seg Segutorio might say.

There was no thought in my head that I would stand guard in this sentry's stead. Poor chap, he was dead, and would be found in due time. I had to be off about my business here.

The amusing notion occurred to me that my own discarded clothes, blackened, singed, with burn holes, would prove quite a conundrum to the damned Dokerty lovers. Bad cess to 'em!

Very little blood had fallen onto the armor and I was able to clean up using my own raggedy clothes. Now for it!

In a rocky mountain like this I had the gravest doubts that there would be many secret passageways. Oh, yes, of course there would be some. After all, this was Kregen. Building secret doors and passages is considerably easier when you are constructing an edifice from scratch. Tunneling through this rock was a tough business so it was likely there would be few secret runnels between the walls.

All the same, by Krun, I'd keep a weather eye open for 'em, just in case.

Tugging the uniform straight and hitching up my sword, I started along the passage. The door at the end was closed but unlocked.

Yes, I have walked on numerous occasions into hostile fortresses. Yet, as I have said, every time is different. Who knew what lay ahead? All I could do was pad on quietly, keep my eyes and ears open, and be ready for the perils in wait.

The door opened and I felt surprise. The declining suns threw long double shadows across a valley choked with vegetation. The opposite cliffs were terraced and cultivated. A dirt road led down from the stone platform under my feet, winding away until lost in the trees. I turned to look back.

Above the door reared the back of the watchtower. That explained why supplies were brought through the door below. I swung back to look down the track and a sudden and puzzling flash of light seared down my left eye.

At once I looked at the masonry. The stones were gray and—well—just stones. No light glowed there. Odd!

This time I turned back the other way and the same flash of turquoise light struck down past the corner of my right eye.

A thought of so horrific a nature occurred to me that my fist gripped whitely upon my sword hilt.

Turquoise!

Standing perfectly still I put a hand up over my eyes as though peering down into the tree-filled valley below. Slowly, cautiously, I slid my eyeballs in their sockets sideways. Peripheral vision very often picks up and distinguishes objects lost to direct sight.

A turquoise glow could just be made out, tantalizingly there, flickering; but there, solid and real.

Oh, no. It was not real, it was not really in this dimension at all. The details came clearer. Yes, by Vox! It was the Eye, the same damned Eye that had spied on me before.

As large as an orange, with a purple lid and a white tendril curling and uncurling below, it hung unsupported in mid air.

We believed this to be the spying mechanism of the illusionist who ruled Winlan, San W'Watchun. A miserable-sounding nation, Winlan, up in the north west, with their military masters and their ground-down slaves, a people who fenced themselves off from the rest of Balintol. What in a Herrelldrin Hell was the rast doing, spying on me here and now?

On those unpalatable thoughts, the eye blinked its purple lid—and vanished.

Taking a breath I composed myself. Whatever the damned Eye wanted, it was gone, and I had a job to do. Standing on the lip of the paved platform I looked out over the track and the forest.

My foot lifted to take the first step onto the dirt trail.

A rough and exceedingly coarse voice bellowed in my ear. "Idiot! What d'you think you're up to? You drunk? Or have you gone crazy?"

My foot swung forward in that first step even as that hectoring voice shouted. My foot, my leg, my body, my nose, crunched forcefully into a solid and very hard barrier—an invisible barrier.

Twelve

Somebody laughed. The laugh was crude, mocking, and probably that of a Brokelsh.

My nose felt as though it had spread across from ear to ear. The impact brought tears to my eyes. I shook my head impatiently.

"Anybody'd think you wouldn't know how to skin a banana." The hectoring voice continued. "Brassud! Snap up and get yourself together. By Jakar! Walking slap bang into the wall! What a fambly!"

The crude laugh spluttered again and its owner spat out: "Probably on the bottle all day, Deldar."

"Aye. Now get about your duty! Bratch!"

"Quidang!" I got out like a marble block splitting.

Through rainbow distortions I began to see again. There was no damn wall there at the edge of the platform, only the vista over the track and forest. The Deldar was a typical Deldar, and that was enough to know. Sweaty, bulky, straining the bronze scales of his armor, vividly scarlet of bulging cheeks, he glared at me and then swung about and marched off, very military.

The Brokelsh, still laughing to himself at my stupidity, was dressed as a guard in the same style of kit I wore. He gave me a hard look, stopped laughing. "Never seen you before. You new?"

"Aye."

"Didn't they tell you in the guardhouse?" He laughed again then. "In course they didn't! They like their little jokes, they do." He tapped thin air. A sound rang just as though he rapped a pane of glass. "See, fambly?"

"Aye."

He gave it as his considered opinion that I didn't say much.

We were clearly standing in a corridor within the cliff. The Deldar had marched off and when I looked he'd vanished. No doubt there was more illusion at work there at the end of the passage. We were not in the ambient glow of the suns, there was no forest-filled valley below and if this damned hairy Brokelsh didn't shut his black-fanged winespout sharpish it was likely to be shut for him. I forced myself to simmer down. There was much to be learned here, by Krun, and the quicker I learned the better.

This Brokelsh's body hair was very black. "What's your name?"

"Ortyg."

He screwed up his eyes. "Ortyg the Wall Walker! That's what you'll be called." He laughed immoderately. He considered this not only very funny but also extraordinarily clever of him.

I kept my old black-fanged winespout firmly closed.

"I'm Bancur, known as the Bansun. Well, we'll need more guards now."

All this, you see, without a seemly Lahal greeting between us.

More guards... Was that because the Prism of Power had been brought into this clifftop fortress temple of Santoro? That had to be the explanation.

Now the Brokelsh as a race of diffs are, as you know, a pretty uncouth lot. Many races on Kregen enjoy themselves by knocking seven kinds of brickdust out of one another at parties. Brokelsh carry this diverting pastime to an extreme. They'll thwack each other about with mighty blows, and then collapse in a heap with their arms around each other's shoulders, the best of comrades. Such apparently irrational behavior is known on this Earth, of course. I'd been friendly with a number of Brokelsh in my time and adventured with comrades. So I was not surprised when this Bancur the Bansun asked if I was off duty, and at my nod suggested we toddle along to the canteen for a wet. It was, after all, evening.

When we'd walked as far as I'd seen the Deldar go I felt a tiny tingle all over my skin. The next step took me into a masonry corridor that up to then had been invisible. Turning to glance back I saw the vista of forest had vanished to be replaced by a continuation of the wall.

So they had an Illusionist working for them in Santoro. This meant I could not trust anything I saw. I had to learn about this place fast!

The way opened into a chamber where guards, both men and women, were coming and going. The place held a busy air of activity. In the far corner a black square opening just above man-height began to fill with feet and legs descending. As I watched a party of men dropped into view supported by a wooden platform depending on cables from above. Bancur brisked his pace up and as the newcomers moved out into the chamber he stepped onto the lift.

"Come on!"

Three or four others joined us, a plaited red rope was tugged as the signal, and the platform began to rise.

Expecting the elevator to be a jerky ride I was surprised at the smoothness of the ascent. Lantern light streaked the walls as we went up.

The top was reached after a few minutes and we all stepped off into a well-lit hall. Fresh people were waiting to descend. Bancur led off with a swing, obviously eagerly anticipating the first swig. After various passages with doors opening off, we came to the door leading to the canteen. The air tasted of stale ale.

Here off-duty soldiers were relaxing. Grass strewed the floor, the tables were solid wood, the benches wooden and not too comfortable, and servants ran about carrying pots and jugs.

Brokelsh conversation is not extensive except in exceptional circumstances, so Bancur's remark on my taciturnity held greater weight than it would have done coming from a member of another race of diffs. He asked the usual questions, of my place of origin, how long I'd been a paktun, how many campaigns I'd been in, all of which I was able to answer with facile lies. I told him I'd been having a look around when I bumped into the wall of illusion.

A couple of steins of vast proportions were placed before us and we quaffed amicably. "They do a good frazzer here. Try it."

I wiped foam and nodded.

The frazzer turned out to be a bed of imported rice loaded with meats of indeterminate origin, a variety of vegetables, peppers, all mixed into a violently red sauce. "It's hot, Ortyg."

Sharp set as I was I tucked in. My Val! It was HOT!

Sweat formed. Valiantly, I spooned on. This would set up a fighting man, no doubt of that, by Djan!

Bancur could eat and talk at the same time quite easily. Most Brokelsh can and do, minimal conversationalists or not.

He commented on my name I'd given him and went on to say his father was a blacksmith. His father and his father before him had been black-smiths. "My old man always wanted to be an armorer but of course there was no training. He had to follow tradition."

In addition, although Bancur didn't mention it, armorers in many parts of Kregen keep the arcane arts of their craft strictly secret. Sons follow fathers, families cluster; getting in is so difficult that I gave Bancur senior's chances of achieving his ambition as about even with a cotton doll in a Herrelldrin Hell. Still, blacksmiths did progress; he might have done it.

This opened the talk to complaints about the quality of weapons on general issue.

This hairy specimen of his race had saved diligently in order to send away to Kildrin for a weapon of superior manufacture. He touched the hilt. "This does not snap when I hit someone."

We did not have to pay for the food and drink; they came up part of the rations. Another colossal stein was required to assuage the furnace in my mouth. Bancur laughed his coarse laugh.

"I told you so!"

He commented that I'd also acquired a braxter from Kildrin and then said he had a date later in the evening with a shishi of exceptional charm. In a typical Brokelsh way he stood up and took himself off abruptly. I sat for a moment finishing the drink.

My lads out there in the unpleasant countryside would contrive some comfort for themselves during the night. They'd just have to wait out my return. I didn't even bother to contemplate the chance that I might not return. I was about business for the Everoinye and therefore could not afford to fail.

That brought the fretful feeling nagging away at the back of my mind into sharp focus. I knew I'd made a bad mistake. After I'd dressed that poor devil of a guard in my blackened rags I should have tumbled him over the edge of the cliff. But desecration of his dead body in that fashion had been beyond me as I now was. He would have friends. He'd be recognized. There would be no puzzle as I had so stupidly imagined. The evidence was plain.

On that I began to feel eyes in the canteen all watching me. The sensation became intolerable, even though a product of my imagination. So I stood up casually, wiped my lips, and went out.

Two items presented themselves. Of one I was absolutely certain. The second was more probable than not. The first, happily, dovetailed into the second. One: I had to get rid of this uniform, pronto! Two: there would most likely be a different guard of better quality and finer uniform posted within the inner courts. The Katakis, I judged, were out of it for now. So that was what I'd have to do.

No one took any notice of me as I strode along like any off duty paktun along the corridors. There was considerable activity. We'd seen only the one flier planing in for a landing here so I felt sure enough that my drinking pal, Hyslop, hadn't been aboard. He wasn't important enough. I strode on.

When I came to a broad staircase leading up, up I went.

A long corridor stretched ahead with the last rays of the suns striking in through a series of slit windows. This was a defensive gallery with a commanding view of an assaulting force. At the end another staircase up led onto a gallery lined with varters, their snouts projecting out over the cliffside. Soldiers were lounging about. Their uniforms were similar to the one I wore.

Again no one took any notice of me.

How long this would last I didn't know. At last, as I knew must happen, after more passages and chambers, I came out into a wide space where guards wearing different uniforms moved about at the far end. I stepped quietly into the shadow of a column.

This, then, was the area where occurred the interface between the territory of the inner and outer guards. And—by Krun! Not only territory but jurisdiction, authority. If I'd been watching my step up to now, I'd have to watch a damn sight harder from now on.

The outer wall was pierced by windows wider than the arrow slits below. No doubt the architects of this place considered that by the time an attacking force could reach this high, they'd all be dead. The main assault on this fortress, of course, would come from the air. There would be formidable defenses up there. Up there was where I was headed.

On the other side of the chamber, openings and doors led onto a labyrinth of passages and rooms: storage space, offices, rest rooms, ablutions and the like. Here I passed along briskly, edging up towards the far end. I'd had a busy day, and a fine lad had met a fiery death—and would be formally mourned at the proper time—and in all this there just was no time to feel tired. The Star Lords had told me there was time to go to Kildrin; but now? Was that female maniac C'Chermina and her equally maniac male priests ready to let the ibmanzies loose? I tell you, I sweated on that, by Vox!

The fellow I wanted walked into the place where I expected to find him. The ablutions were empty and he gave me a hard, contemptuous stare. "You're not allowed here, blintz. This is reserved for the palace guard. Schtump! Get out!"

He had no time to shout any more abuse for I stepped smartly up to him and sent him to sleep standing up. I did catch him as he fell. I didn't want to mark his uniform.

He wasn't the first palace guard for whom I'd waited. This one wore a uniform I could squeeze over my shoulders. I did that. I dumped him in a stall, bolted the door and climbed out over the top. He'd remain unconscious for some time. When he woke up he'd try to free the gag and the bonds. If he did that before anyone became suspicious about the occupied stall I'd be surprised. The bonds were secured by knots notoriously difficult to untie.

His braxter was a quality sword, so I assumed custody of that and dumped the other one into the trash bin along with the discarded uniform. Stepping out smartly I reasoned that I had a little more time at my disposal before the vosks got into the chicken coop, as they say in Clishdrin.

The owner of this kit was a mortpaktun, and I made sure the pakmort showed its silver sheen at my throat. His pakai was not impressively long; but there were three gold rings among the silver.

Beyond the next series of corridors reared a triangular cleft. The darkness spattered with torchlight. People were standing waiting. I halted. Accompanied by a loud creaking and rumbling of wheels a wooden carriage descended the cleft. The architects of Santoro had boxed clever here; instead of sinking a shaft vertically for the lift, they'd made use of the forty five degree angle. The lift came to rest, people climbed in and out, and I climbed in. With an immense lurching groan we began the ascent.

Then, of course, a most fascinating thought occurred to me. Maybe there weren't two separate sets of guards. Perhaps the units whose rig I wore were not the inner guards. Maybe there were three lots of them. I'd joined the middle guard; the highest juruk up there would probably throw me out if they didn't arrest me.

The carriage squeaked and rumbled up the slope and I threw off those miserable defeatist glooms.

At the top everybody alighted and I gathered they were off for a pleasant evening's entertainment before turning in. They trooped off to the right, chattering and laughing. After a moment I went left.

After the hubbub of the off duty personnel the way lay quietly before me. No one was about. A broad flight of stairs led up to a landing, turned and went on up. The stairs debouched onto a broad well-lit hall. At the far end imposing double-doors with the motifs of crimson animals emblazoned were guarded by a sentry wearing a quite different uniform from the one I had put on.

Steadily, I walked down towards him. He was apim, with a strong body and the look of a seasoned free-lance.

"Hey up, dom! You must be lost. You're not allowed in here. These are the priests' quarters."

I said: "Oh, thank you—" and reached out and put him to sleep. I was gentle with him, for he had not been offensive and was clearly a paktun of honor.

Easing him to the tiled floor I straightened up, already loosening the now useless uniform. One leaf of the doors opened.

A red robed priest emerged. He saw the tableau—one guard unconscious on the floor, another—an unauthorized blintz!—bending over him—and he reacted at once.

"What is going on here?" he demanded in that hectoring tone so habituated to instant obedience. He started to turn away to run back. "Guards!"

Thirteen

In two bounds I was on him. A hard hand wrapped around that bawling mouth and the other jerked his head back savagely. The folds of his hood prevented my fingers finding his neck. His head snapped back. A sharp and distinct crack echoed.

This is the curse laid on us. Without any intention of harming him except rendering him unconscious, here I'd done it again.

He slumped. Quickly I peered around the door. The space beyond was illuminated by lamps, there was fragrance on the air, and, thanks to Opaz! it was empty of life.

Working very rapidly I dragged him back. He was not as big as I was, but there was a tuck in his cloak secured by stitching, and this I snicked apart with the tip of my sword. Then the cloak fitted very well. The uniform of the middle guard went on him with room to spare. I kept my weapons under the red cloak.

Now came the bit I abhorred, shrank from, but knew I must do. These Dokerty lovers intended to inflict the monstrous ibmanzies upon Balintol, and that had to be prevented.

The stairs were hard. I heaved him up and walked down to the landing. Picking him up by the heels, I whirled him in the air and brought him down, head first. His face smashed into the stone.

Very, very quickly I jumped back up the stairs without looking down. Let the poor devil wander where Dokerty would take him!

The Krozairs call that cunning pressure upon the nerve endings Kaonik, where the jolt into the brain knocks one unconscious instantaneously. The guard slumbered. The reverse procedure is called compib, loosely translated as the life spirit. I pressed the right spot and the guard stirred and snorted. Pulling the red hood closely around my face I waited for him to recover sufficiently to comprehend his surroundings, and then bawled out brutally.

"What is going on here!"

He rolled over and stood up groggily. He shook his head where I knew the famous old Bells of Beng Kishi were hammering away.

"Notor! I—I—don't—"

"A guard not allowed up here ran away when I came out the door. Take up your post, sentry. I shall report this!"

"Quidang, notor!"

With an aggressive shrug of my shoulders I swung away, went back through the half open door and slammed it shut.

The front fastenings of the red robe were black braided silk attached to silver acorns. I just hoped if I got into a fight I could get my weaponry out and into action fast enough. The hood threw deep shadows over my face. I marched solemnly on towards the far end of the chamber where another double door barred my progress.

The luck of Five-handed Eos-Bakchi had descended on me so far. As I pushed open the door I trusted to Opaz that the luck would still ride with me.

The space beyond made me blink. The floor and ceiling were more or less horizontal. The side walls sloped at forty-five degrees. This induced a most odd sensation, as though one wanted to lean over to compensate. Guards in their brilliant uniforms, priests in red robes, slaves scuttling in their gray breech clouts, formed a busy scene.

As I passed along guards stood to attention. I carried on as I had before, ignoring the swods and gravely acknowledging those of higher ranks. The way stretched ahead and on I went along that senses-confusing hall. By now I must have penetrated well into the mountain. Just how far did this Dokerty-dedicated labyrinth extend?

Eventually I fetched up before half a dozen square black openings. This time I was not surprised, so I boarded a lift and was whisked upwards. I shared the platform with a most imposing figure. He did not speak. When we reached the top I was in for another surprise.

We stepped out into starlight, with the Maiden with the Many Smiles sailing serenely overhead, casting down her fuzzy pink light.

Trees and bushes showed ghostly branches in that glow. Tall columns here and there supported arches. Buildings dotted the space. Colored lanterns swung lazily in a night zephyr. This was a pleasure garden, no doubt of that.

The imposing figure, hands crossed in sleeves, moved on.

A thick growth of bushes covered in tiny berries gave the place and the chance. His astonishment when I dragged him in was so great he didn't even cry out. A hand over his mouth ensured his silence. I glared down into his face, a countenance engraved with lines of power. I spelled out his options. He chose the one that started him talking. He talked, by Krun, oh, yes, he talked!

Santoro turned out to be quite a place. Originally just a simple shrine in the barren lands used for meditation it had over the seasons become a retreat, a palace, a pleasure park, all protected by the fortress. There were ballistae and catapults in towers and the iron chain netting for aerial defense could be put in place in no time at all—so he claimed.

Once he'd begun talking he gabbled on. I got the layout in my head. Very little inducement prompted him to reveal the proper words and greetings formulae. Yet—yet in the pink light his graven face held a sly look.

When I asked about the ibmanzies his manner changed. The first time I mentioned the Prism of Power he clammed right up.

I reminded him of his options.

"Why should I tell you if you intend to kill me anyway?"

"I do not intend to kill you, although you and your lot truly deserve to be expunged from Kregen." I went on to expound on further options open to his choice. Even as I spoke I couldn't stop myself from that niggling doubt: what right had I thus to interfere or condemn a whole religion on the basis of the evil practices of a part of that community?

He told me in the end, without physical force.

Still that damned sly look twisted up those thin lips.

There was, without doubt, something very nasty awaiting me up there at the end of my quest.

So, thinking to be clever, I said: "You should thank Tolaar for your life."

He reacted to that. His face twisted up and he started to snarl out: "You blintz of—"

The gag went in then, when his black-fanged wine-spout was nicely open. He was trussed up like a chicken for the oven. Into the heart of the bush he went and I crawled out backwards and with a careful scrutiny of the surroundings I stood up.

His name, he'd told me, was Fortro N'Norgoil. Around his neck hung a golden chain with an ostentatious medallion, all gold and ronils in the form of the upflung wings. His expression of sly cunning intensified when I took it. Well, I trusted I was canny enough to know not to wear it. Now it rested in a pocket under the red robe.

The open area around me had seen a great deal of money spent on it. Water management must have cost a fortune. Aqueducts and pipes led water to many fountains and pools. Where the softer strata had weathered away, time and the hand of man had created pleasure gardens filled with an abundance of flowers and greenery. The harder strata, sculpted into fantastic statues, loomed over the little valleys. Moving along was at times like following a nature trail.

The buildings scattered among the glades were given over to all manner of pleasurable pursuits, some agreeable, some intriguing and some best not mentioned. Priests strolled among all this array of hedonistic comfort to partake of their relaxation. Here a Dokerty rewarded his own.

Across crisply shaved lawns, shimmering in weird ripples of color under the light of the moon, and along pale graveled paths, I followed the directions given me by Fortro N'Norgoil.

The temple in which, he'd assured me, I would find the shrine of the Prism, appeared at the end of an avenue flanked by monstrous statues of mythical beasts. The structure looked small for so important a function. This area stood some distance from the main pleasure centers, and in the fuzzy pink light of the Maiden with the Many Smiles I could see no other movement. I walked steadily on.

The doors were solid beaten gold. The pillars lustrous marble. I pushed the door, it gave, and I went in.

Again I was struck by the smallness of the place. It was lavishly adorned with treasure, glittering blindingly in the lights of many lanterns.

The shrine in the form of a three meter high octagonal box was just a mass of gold, studded with ronils. A crystal window in the front glowed with light from within. So I looked in.

The damned winged symbol stood there, plainly. The upflung wings, joined at the tips, were meticulously detailed. Where they thickened at the base juncture the round shimmering device contained the Prism of Power. This was the devilish ancient curse that turned young men and women into doomed raving monsters.

The crystal window swung open on silent hinges.

I reached inside.

I reached for the Prism of Power.

My fingers opened and closed, grasping.

My fist closed on air, on nothing. My fingers went clean through the winged symbol.

At once I saw the truth.

Illusion! Damned illusion!

At that precise moment a hoarse and eerie laugh echoed at my back, reverberating through the temple.

Fourteen

My fingers undid the black silk fastenings of the robe. Slowly, I turned about.

The figure advanced from the door. The lights illuminated a robe of red and black diagonal slashes, heavily adorned with golden ciphers. The hood was pulled forward over blackness. One hand grasped a large staff, wrapped in symbols but without skulls or bells. A distinct smell of rotting vegetation wafted from this apparition.

The hoarse, mocking laugh echoed again.

"You think to defile the sacred objects. Blasphemer! Pervert! Doomed of Dokerty!"

I said nothing. He advanced further, menacingly.

"Give yourself up—or prepare to die!"

Abruptly, from absolutely nowhere, a Chulik fighting man jumped into view before me. His yellow tusks shone with gold. His shaven skull gleamed. His swords snouted for me.

I ignored him.

"You are a dead man!" The hoarse voice shook with passion.

I marched straight up to the Chulik, forged on, marched clear through him.

"Unbeliever! Die! Die!"

Another Chulik appeared from nowhere, swinging his swords at my head. I did not dodge, parry or deviate from my course.

Like smoke wisps he vanished as I passed through him.

The hoarse voice rang and vibrated in the temple.

"Guards! Guards!"

The neck around which I fastened one gripping fist felt thin and scrawny. I choked him a bit. With the other hand I seized his staff, wrenched it away, hurled it along the floor. It rang and bounced on the marble.

The hood of the robe ripped off. He was apim, sallow of face, with drooping black mustachios, dark piggy eyes, a wet mouth.

I shook him. "You should know the Chuliks have gone back to their islands to defend against the Shanks. Your illusions have no power."

He gobbled and spittle ran. Easing the choking pressure gave him a chance to speak. What he was going to say meant nothing. I gave him that old hard look folk call the Dray Prescot Devil Glare. He flinched back. In my old gravel-shifting voice I said: "Your illusions have no meaning now. Either remove it from the Flutubium here in this shrine—or tell me where the real Flutubium is!"

The stinking smell of him was getting right up my hooter. I shook him, not gently. "Hurry up!"

His wet mouth spluttered. He was trembling as though with ague. At the time his distress meant nothing beside the evil he wished to inflict upon Balintol. Later I felt sorry for the bastard.

"Spare my life!"

"Remove the illusion!"

"My staff—"

Caution prompted me then. I walked him across and then stood at his back as he bent down and retrieved his staff. My fingers tightened on his neck, digging into his windpipe. "That is a warning, Illusionist! Now get on with it." I released the constricting pressure and felt his Adam's Apple jump up and down like a fleeing paly.

He lifted the staff and it shook. It vibrated with the terror of his trembling. He mouthed words, archaic mumbo-jumbo. As far as I could see nothing happened. So—we would see, by Krun!

Marching him up to the shrine I kept one hand around his throat, took the staff away with the other, threw it down, and then reached for the winged symbol. The Flutubium felt hard and solid in my fist. Ha!

The thing came out handily enough. There was little weight in it; no doubt it was wood gilded over. The silver pole could be broken off and discarded. I'd seen this diabolical symbol of evil in the company of that gentleman rogue, Dagert of Paylen, and his servant, Palfrey, when Dagert had vowed that, by Hanitcha the Harrower, he wanted nothing of it. A very great deal had happened since then and there was a very great more to happen, that I knew, by Vox!

The Illusionist's staff lay on the marble. I eyed it malevolently. Well, and why not? It might accomplish nothing; it ought to slow the old devil up, surely?

The staff snapped across with a loud crack. Twice more I broke it. I hurled the pieces away.

He made no attempt to run off when I released him. He looked dazed. He shook his head—and a tear ran down his cheek.

Could that moment of emotion affect me? Of course it did. Yet I had to harden my heart and get on with the Star Lords' command to save Balintol and so secure the future of all Paz.

Just before we reached the door the guards for whom he had shouted appeared. There were four of them, clad oddly enough in short red robes over their scale. They were all apim. They saw the situation and leaped forward, swords glittering in the lights of the many lamps.

I gave the poor old devil of an Illusionist a thwack alongside his head and he pitched down. My two swords came out sweetly.

These guards stood in a privileged position as their short crimson robes showed. They fought well and I had to skip and hop. Cannily enough I kept myself between them and the Flutubium on the floor at my back. The blades clashed and scraped. One went down, and then another. The remaining two fought well, and I caught a gleam of gold at their throats. They panted. Now they were backtracking, seeking the right moment in the quick flurry of blades to run off. I couldn't have that.

With a regret that was probably misplaced, seeing just who and what they were, I finished the thing. No doubt at one time they'd been honest paktuns earning their hire. But Dokerty had corrupted them, and they had achieved their present status only to end up puddled in their own blood in their damned shrine.

So, because of that, I did not take their golden rings and their pakais. They were tainted.

Prudence dictated I put as much distance between myself and this benighted temple as possible. A quick survey of the avenue of statues showed red movement at the far end. Reinforcements? So I ducked around the side and dived between bushes, coming out into a scented glade. This was refreshing after the stench of the Illusionist.

The prospect of retracing my steps all the way down through this Opaz-forsaken mountain did not appeal. Oh, no, by Krun! There was another much better way.

In the cover of a clump of bushes I examined the paired wings. They could be broken off leaving the symbol at the base wherein, so I believed, reposed the Prism of Power. This I stuffed down under the robe. Then I started out in earnest to find the way off the blasphemous mountain fortress where evil and pleasure ruled in equal measure.

Even though I'd closed the door of the temple after me and the place wasn't exactly busy, I couldn't believe there would not soon be a hubbub and outcry. If that movement at the end of the avenue of statues had been merely normal and not reinforcements, someone, surely, must visit the temple from time to time. So, as I prowled on alertly, I started to fret over the absence of pursuit.

The Prism of Power had been obtained remarkably easily. Did that mean I was still being fooled? I remembered that damned sly look on Fortro N'Norgoil's cunning twisted face. That made me duck into bushes and check the Flutubium.

The thing was, indeed, a case. It came apart readily under the tip of a blade. A glare as of red sunsets burst up and I flung an arm over my eyes. Tears streaming down my cheeks, with fingers that shook I shoved the case closed. Well, now!

That, indeed, would seem to prove the thing was genuine.

Also, it was dangerous.

Pushing it back under the red robe, I set off once more.

I threw my mind back to the time when my lifter had circled here. The airboat that had darted in so swiftly had landed along this way. I was going in the right direction.

I judged that any illusions in place would now have vanished. That must, I considered, alert the guards at the invisible wall.

When, at last, the place I sought came into view there were, as I expected, a good few guards standing sentry. My weapons had been cleaned on the clothes of the paktuns back in the temple. Some of the black silk braidings were fastened up; enough were unlatched to allow me to grasp the hilts of the swords instantly.

The flierdrome was not a hive of activity. I approached along an overgrown path with the steady priestly step expected here. A few wooden sheds to the left looked incongruous alongside the ornate marble columns and tiled roofs of flanking buildings. Five airboats rested on the landing platforms. They were all middling craft, somewhere between ten and thirty seaters. Most looked to be new, a mark of the wealth of the Dokerty cultists.

Boldly marching up I halted for no one. A guard wearing the short red robe over his armor looked up. He was a Jiktar. I nodded to him with that arrogant superior way the priests had and strode on. He didn't hesitate but stood to attention and saluted.

The nearest flier would not do. There was a fine-looking voller over to the right and as I neared her I was relieved to see she was not chained down. Out of sight of the Jiktar I vaulted over the rail and settled at the controls. Now for it!

At the precise moment I put my hand on the control lever shouting began. Unable to see what was going on, I had to press on regardless. With a smooth practiced swing up we went, the lifter sailing up and out into the rosily-golden radiance of She of the Veils rising after the Maiden with the Many Smiles. I looked down.

Red robes were running for the parked lifters. So be it, then. I shoved the speed lever fully home and we lanced through the air. Very shortly the dark shapes of airboats soared up in pursuit. My lead was slender and I just hoped I had chosen well. This voller had lines of speed. She'd need all the speed of which she was capable if I was to come out of this imbroglio with a whole skin.

A sensible course of action occurred to me if I was to be caught. The voller climbed in a straight line urged on by relentless pressure on the speed lever. The pursuing airboats followed on.

The speed lever was jammed full forward by my knee. I was able to use two hands to take out the case containing the Prism of Power. Carefully—very, very carefully, by Vox!—I put the tip of a blade into the junction line. I held the case over the side of the craft. I shut my eyes. I twisted the blade and opened the case over empty air.

Even with eyes closed the red glare smote through, turning everything to the semblance of blood.

The crimson fire diminished. Opening my eyes I looked back.

The pursuing craft were swirling up in the air, trying to reverse their courses. Redness bathed everything in a lurid glow.

The whole scene swam in crimson radiance.

The world exploded.

Enormous concussions battered the lifter, smashed her end over end, drenched in spurting redness. I was falling into a whirling pit of crimson as the world went mad.

Fifteen

Avalanches, earthquakes, volcanoes, typhoons of crimson fire burned the world into red roaring madness. Coruscating gales encompassed sanity. End over end, upside down—I didn't know which way was up—I somersaulted as the world of Kregen span about the airboat.

How long that red nightmare lasted I do not know. Gradually some kind of order returned. My eyes smarted as though dredged with desert sand. Breathing was a matter of laboriously dragging heated air into my distended mouth. The noise persisted and only half of that cacophony was the Bells of Beng Kishi banging and clamoring inside my skull.

Cracking sticky eyelids open a fraction revealed a monstrous pillar of crimson fire reaching up and up into the heavens. Its base began where the Prism of Power had struck the ground. It reached up in a solid column of fire, lurid, sparking, and the summit turned into a black pall extending across the barrens.

With twentieth century terrestrial science to guide me I knew the Prism of Power was no thermonuclear device. Had it been I'd be a charred cinder now, radiating pollution and corruption.

Of the pursuing lifters there was no sign.

The speed of this lifter with the lever thrust fully on by my knee had whisked me clear of the main devastating effects. The following craft had taken the full impact. Incinerated, blown to smithereens, they no longer existed.

I dragged in a breath of heated air. My Val! Had the whole world turned blue I might well have imagined myself being snatched up by the Giant Scorpion to talk with the Star Lords. That made my lips turn down. They should have given me some warning. Still, that wasn't their inscrutable way. Only since my recent conversations had they appeared to bother themselves over my welfare. Normally if a tool failed them it would be discarded, of that I had no doubt at the time.

The voller gyrated, twisting and turning. Bringing her under control I saw with some amazement that she'd been knocked into a banana shape, her whole fabric dinted in. She still flew, thank Opaz!

The plume of fire roared to the sky and the ebony pall spread a dismal shroud over the land. The stars, the moons, were blotted out. My bump of location told me that Santoro lifted off to the left. Thither I steered the airboat.

The air being drawn hungrily upwards by the red column of fire turned increasingly into a whistling gale. I had to force the lifter down closer to the ground and in the ghastly crimson glow constantly check for the surface. The wind rushed past and the lifter fleeted towards Santoro.

The slanting mass upthrust from the barrens edged with a reflected orange and crimson glow appeared shrunken. The blackness all around burning through with the fiery pillar seemed to me to shrink the very ib in a fellow. That dolorous nightscape was a scene straight from a Herrell-drin Hell.

Skirting around the side of Santoro I was aiming for the black bar of shadow beyond when I spotted a lifter scuttle out into the red madness of the illumination from the fiery pillar. Orange reflections smote all along her side. I recognized her at once.

Swirling up and alongside I saw crossbows aimed at me. I waved. For an instant I thought they'd loose; then someone recognized me in turn and the bows lowered.

"What happened?" The shout attenuated in the wind blast.

I pointed down. Together, the two craft settled to the ground.

The awesome sight of that plume of fire sobered my lads, right enough. I told them sufficient to explain the situation.

Gradually, little by little, the burning violence subsided. The specter of an insane crimson world continued to film our vision with fire. They didn't speak much. Slowly the wind dropped. The flame dwindled, the blackness drifted away, the stars and the moons reappeared. We could breathe more easily.

They'd been in the shadow of Santoro when I dropped the Prism of Power and that had hidden the calamitous effects from them. They'd saddled up and ventured out to see what the hell had gone on.

"The job's done here. It's back to Prebaya for us."

Before leaving I removed the two silver boxes from the banana shaped lifter. They were valuable and always useful. The borrowed flier was torched, with some regret, and we left the smoking wreckage and soared aloft.

The flight back was accompanied mostly by grunts and monosyllables instead of conversation.

We'd all had a hard day and an eventful night. Now it was time for shut-eye. We reached The Pronto and Risslaca without incident and turned in. We slept.

The next morning my lads were still in a very sober mood. They'd gazed upon the face of hell and the experience had been highly uncomfortable, mighty uncomfortable, by Krun!

Still, being good Kregans and paktuns to boot, that matter did not stop them from tucking into a hearty first breakfast.

Difficult though it might be for me to realize the situation, what I had set out to do in Caneldrin had been accomplished. At long last I'd been successful. That, and all thanks to Opaz, came as a great and welcome relief. Now the maniac regent C'Chermina would not have her insane priests turn ordinary folk into ibmanzies and wreak a terrible scourge upon Tolindrin. Now, with diplomacy, the unification of Balintol to resist the Shanks could happen.

For a short euphoric moment I believed this. But I was on Kregen. Upon that wonderful and terrible world nothing can be taken for granted. So, quite quickly, I understood that this business was far from over and perils awaited me in the future—as always, by Krun!

Telling my guardsmen to take it easy for the rest of the day—or until I returned with fresh alarms!—I went off to the Vallian Embassy. Here Elten Naghan Vindo welcomed me with a worried expression, and Veda yelled at me from the bedroom to come in, bratch, and tell her all about it.

This I duly did.

At the tail end of my recital a servant announced a visitor and in strode Fweygo, big and confident, breezy. He carried a long blanket-wrapped bundle which he plunked down on the table with a clang. "Lahal, all!"

Sazz and parclear were brought to assuage his throat, dry from the journey, and miscils and palines to munch.

The day was well on, for the night's activities had eaten up the time. The second breakfast and the meal of mid were past so we soon settled to the middle afternoon repast. Fweygo carried his mysterious bundle in, set it on the floor and began to eat. When the meal was over and the table cleared we sat comfortably quaffing ale. My Kildoi comrade hoicked the bundle onto the table. He looked at me meaningfully.

With something of a flourish, quite ostentatiously, he pulled the binding ropes free and unrolled the blanket.

He said nothing but continued to look at me with that sly, enigmatic stare.

"Well, now," I said.

There, gleaming with oil, lay my armory left with Nath Seegfreedhan, known as Vando, in Emgidu.

I quirked up an eyebrow.

"He was kidnapped. Opponents who did not wish him to become the Prime Autarch." Fweygo went on in an off-hand way to say that he'd tracked Vando, rescued him, and with him my weapons.

"This great bar of steel you laughingly call a sword is, I know, dear to your heart."

Nodding, I said: "True. But as you know a fighting man must be able to use any weapons that come to his hand."

They were all there, the drexer, the sailor knife, the rapier and main gauche, and the great Krozair longsword. This I took up into my fists. It felt good, by Zair!

"I give you my sincere thanks, Fweygo."

"That's what comrades are for." This was handsome. Then, with that little sly smirk, he added: "Anyway, I have to look out for you all the time, don't I?"

To this remark I replied obliquely. "Thank you again."

He sipped his ale. "What have you been up to here?"

Veda, whose stylish clothes were still adhering to her shapely body, piped up: "Drajak destroyed the Prism of Power!"

"Aye," put in the ambassador. "A brave deed well done."

Fweygo just took another sip of ale. He wiped his lips fastidiously.

"That's good news." He displayed no particular emotion, which surprised me a trifle. Kildois do not flaunt their feelings, as you know, except in remarkable circumstances. All the same...!

"So the ibmanzies are finished." Naghan Vindo banged his goblet on the table. "Thank Opaz!"

"Here, yes," said Fweygo. "I managed to get rid of the Prism of Power in Emgidu. Made a hell of a show, all red fire and black clouds. Like some feeble-minded famblys' idea of a primitive hell."

"What!" shouted Naghan Vindo.

"You did what?" cried Veda.

"You mean there's more than one?" I fairly bellowed.

"Well, of course."

"How many?"

"I don't know. Where the main temples of Dokerty are located, I expect. All I can say is that there are more Prisms of Power to be destroyed yet."

My jaw dropped. I could say nothing.

Sixteen

I, Dray Prescot, Vovedeer, Lord of Strombor and Krozair of Zy, took very little time to recover from the shock. Life on Kregen teaches a fellow to expect the unexpected, and the unexpected is usually bad news. So, there were an as yet undetermined number of other Prisms of Power in existence. So all right, then!

We'd just have to find them and turn them into coruscating pillars of fire.

Naghan Vindo did not have an airboat large enough for my purpose, so with a small group of my lads we sallied off to the lifterdrome where Naghan had given me the name of Larghos S'Snaffding.

Now your dealer in second hand airboats on Kregen is not to be compared with second hand car dealers on Earth. There are the obvious comparisons, of course; but when you are dealing with the half-understood, mysterious, properties of the silver boxes, there are vast discrepancies.

As we turned the corner out of Remor Street to cross the Bridge of Relentless Regret—so named for its convenience as a place for suicides—I was leading on at a brisk pace.

"Hai! Ortyg!"

The voice with its coarse Brokelsh accents alerted me at once. I halted and turned, blank-faced, to stare at Bancur the Bansun. He looked as hirsute as ever; but his appearance bore traces of attempts to repair and clean up tattered clothing and dinted armor. He walked up to me with a swing. "Lahal, dom. So you escaped, too."

Speaking in a level voice, I said: "It was a trifle fraught."

He laughed that coarse Brokelsh laugh. "By the Resplendent Bridzilkelsh, it surely was! I was fortunate to get away with only a couple of holes in my hide."

My lads waited at the corner, looking on. With a few careful questions and an easier manner, I soon found out what had befallen Bancur. His description of the column of flame was entirely picturesque, colorful, and so full of profanities it almost matched the cursing he gave over to the Dokerty guards.

"We took the blame, so the upper guards came down and tried to slay all of us, as you know. I was able to get away, like you; but it's not something I want to dwell on, no, by Bakkar!"

He went on to say that the unfortunates I'd dealt with had been found, that it was established that an intruder had been at work, only to tumble down the stairs and smash his face in. "So there must have been two of them." It didn't matter now, but I noted down in my little mental black book that my ruse with the poor devil of a priest had not been discovered. The confusion reigning in Santoro must have been prodigious and splendid to witness. In that confusion many people would be unaccounted for. Anyway, it was done now. What lay ahead should occupy my thoughts.

Bancur pushed his helmet straight. "I'm tazll now, dom, and in dire need of fresh employment."

So, as it had with Dagert of Paylen, the idea of employing this Bancur the Bansun popped into my head.

I said in a voice harsher than I intended: "You took your hire from the Dokerty priests."

"By the Belly of Karibar! I wish I'd never laid eyes on 'em! I soon grew sick of their ways, I can tell you."

"I can offer you honest employment." His hairy face lit up. I went on: "I run a small juruk. Every man is a kampeon. I am known as Drajak the Sudden. Remember that."

He agreed instantly and with mingled gratitude and relief.

"Thank you, Orty— I mean, Drajak the Sudden."

So that was settled. On the pappattu being made between him and the rest of the lads, the introductions formal in the proper paktun protocol, I knew he'd fit in—or else!

Prebaya bustled about its business as usual although this day all the talk was of the tremendous happenings out across the barren lands by Santoro. News travels fast.

Larghos S'Snaffding turned out to be a Lamnia. These diffs are a gentle race in all their social occasions. They are known and respected as honest and shrewd merchants. I'd had dealings with them before and liked them. Now S'Snaffding rubbed a hand across his pale fur and smiled and showed us his stock of lifters.

Without difficulty we struck a bargain. As they say in Clishdrin, a good deal is one where both buyer and seller are satisfied. S'Snaffding took the gold graciously, and we climbed happily into the voller. She was a stout, roomy craft, with a comfortable cabin amidships. Instead of handing over my own airboat in part-exchange, I intended to use her as a tender to the new craft, which was immediately named *Cloudscamper*. Her hull was pale blue with a black-outlined red streak and her upperworks beige. We were well satisfied with her.

Later that day, well-stocked with water and provisions, we prepared for departure.

All my little guard stated their clear intentions of going with me, including Bancur the Bansun.

To my surprise, Veda said in a voice that brooked, as they say, no opposition: "I shall come with you, naturally."

"But—"

"Queyd-arn-tung!" Veda hitched up the shoulder of her dress. "I've a score to settle with those damned of Dokerty!"

Her determination was so fierce that the outcome was exactly that: Queyd-arn-tung, no more to be said. As we all climbed aboard I reflected that, by Vox, she was some girl!

Now, however resilient and tough young Veda was, she remained that 'some girl' in other things besides being an ex-Battle Maiden. She tried to conceal her feelings; but it was obvious she was all a-twitter about flying south. She did say how much she was looking forward to wearing a shamlak. Immediately I had a horrific vision.

There are shamlaks and shamlaks. The garment, as I have said, has a slit or opening all down the front. This vent varies in width dramatically. My vision was obvious to anyone who knew young Veda and her penchant for having bits and pieces of her clothing fall off at frequent intervals. Useless to conjure up Makki Grodno or the Divine Madam of Belschutz. My Val! What a daunting prospect!

Cloudscamper flew on. Ah, what it is to feel the sweet breeze of Kregen flowing through your hair! The glorious mingled radiance of Zim and Genodras streamed in benediction across the land as we soared on. The slanting emerald and ruby rays gave to the face of Kregen that beautiful aspect which conceals so much of the horror lurking beneath.

When the time came around again for a meal we all tucked in. A stir-fry had been cunningly cooked up so that I, for one, was not at all sure of the ingredients. Whatever, it was delicious, if a trifle hot still. Withal, I confess I hankered after a plateful of roast vosk and momolams. After the meal palines could be taken as the benediction the little yellow berries always afford.

The Suns sank in refulgent glories of emerald and ruby fires. The Maiden with the Many Smiles floated among the stars. Ale and wine was broached. Proper lookouts were set, alert, and the rest of the lads congregated in the cabin and started what swods of Kregen will always start given half a chance. They sang.

One mercenary tradition in sessions of this kind is to open with "Paktun's Promenade", which we sang lustily. We followed with "The Maid with the Single Veil". The Torana chavpaktun, Nath the Chanter, now established his right to the sobriquet by warbling out a solo. He chose to give us "Lola the Fair and the Door Handle", which song is ever so, ever so, sad right up to the last line. This is so raucous it reduces listeners every time to helpless laughter.

Recovered from that and wiping our eyes, we bellowed out "The Chariot with One Wheel", and then "The Kovneva Sophie's Wardrobe". You may rely on these hardened paktuns dwelling lovingly on each item in the lovely Kovneva Sophie's wardrobe, packed as it was with exotic clothing of every description.

Presently, amid all this merriment and good comradeship, it was time to speak of our vanished friend. Erwin the Waggler was given a first class send off, a noumjiksirn to remember, a splendid wake.

The proceedings terminated when the watches changed. My years as a first lieutenant in a King's ship, many of which had been spent beating about off Brest, remained clearly fixed in my mind from my days on Earth. So I ran *Cloudscamper* on Naval lines. All the same, even as the captain, I still stood a trick at the controls. This might have been bad for morale back on Earth, here on Kregen with my comrades about me, I fancied it gave my status as cadade something of an extra dimension of authority. Of course, that damned yrium, the mystical power so much higher than mere charisma, that I am cursed or blessed with and for which the Star Lords chose me to further their madcap schemes, gave my command complete authority.

With the stars wheeling above me and the moons shining down refulgently, I found my thoughts straying back to my time on Earth. There was only one small silver moon and, during the day, only one little yellow sun. There was no splendid array of diffs, no marvelous diversification of facial features and physical bodies.

All the same, the Earth has enough wonders of its own. I thought of the battles in which I'd fought, of the thunder of the broadsides and the gushing smoke, the flaming discharges. None of that horror existed on Kregen. I'd firmly set my face against any idea of introducing gunpowder. Kregen would not be the same. So as we soared on towards Oxonium I dreamed of the seas of Earth, and the people I'd known, the ships in which I'd served, the ports and the way of life that, many years ago though it was, remained vividly as an integral part of the person who was Dray Prescot.

A hoarse voice rasped out. "My turn, cadade."

Turning to greet Bancur I caught a fleeting glimpse of color from the corner of my eye. Turquoise!

In the instant that the Eye disappeared I saw the confounded thing, clear and distinct. The pupil shone. I felt a shock of absolute power. Then the Eye vanished.

"You all right?"

"Yes, Bancur, thank you."

"You looked as though you'd seen someone you knew broken from the ib."

That was Kregish for a ghost. The Eye was no ghost. It was someone spying on me, probably the Illusionist of Winlan. I shook my shoulders and Bancur moved up and took over the controls.

"Just old old thoughts," I said. "Moonbright, Bancur."

"Moonbright, cadade."

As I was about to enter the cabin I glanced up to the sky. The Twins, often known as the Dahemin, were rising past clouds tinted rose. I thought of one silver moon, and sighed, and so went in to find a few burs sleep.

I believe there is no need for me to mention the name of the person of whom I thought last, as always, before sleeping.

Anyway, what in a Herrelldrin Hell was she up to now? She was a kregoinya, off about business for the Star Lords. Or, although she'd severed many of her links with the Sisters of the Rose, she could so easily be haring around Kregen on some demanding—and to me, terrifying—scheme for those dedicated ladies.

The next morning some of the reflective mood of the previous night persisted as I partook of the first breakfast. *Cloudscamper* fleeted above morning mists concealing the land, milky mounds tinged with slanting rays of apple green and palest rose. All of my life upon Kregen was not hectic rushing here and there, swinging a sword.

In view of my general unease on the question of just how the animals whipped in races view their treatment for the avarice and pleasure of humankind, I'd made no protest about driving a chariot on that score. The urgency of the moment overcame scruples.

Mind you, Fweygo had done remarkably well, and he'd brought back my armory into the bargain. A fellow of some capacity, my kregoine comrade, Fweygo. And you could say that again, by Vox!

Molar Na-Fre reported, with his Pachak face annoyed, that the water supply was down by reason of a leak. "Molchak the Meddler sends these inflictions upon us."

"If you believe that, Molar."

"These ungodly spirits love to meddle in human affairs. It amuses them and they think it funny in their own interfering way."

"Quite. Also, my friend, it could be bad workmanship."

"Well, yes. But by Papachak the All-Powerful! All these gods they have here in Balintol don't stand comparison with the conniving spirits and their results."

So, this meant we had to touch down somewhere convenient to replenish our water. International frontiers have little meaning when you can fly over them, unless, of course, the border guards fly airboats faster than yours. In our case we saw only a dozen or so ovverers in convoy, their sails reflecting the radiance of the Suns, slanting away with the wind. The mists began to clear and we looked for a likely landing place.

Prudently, we came down out of sight of a small village tucked away in its valley. There were groves of trees, meadows, and a stream beside which we alighted. The sky took on an angry tinge as the leak was caulked and we took on the sparkling water from the brook. That was pure clean Kregan water, untainted by chemicals.

"Storm a' coming," commented the Hytak, Nalan ti Perning. He pushed his longsword back out of the way and shouted at the swods to have a care with the breakers. "That's how the leak started. Clumsy great famblys."

The sky, indeed, looked ominous. The storm through which the Lady Quensella and I had driven master Llanili the Stout's lifter *Sparking Thunder* had been a rough one. The events of that mad flight were not forgotten. I said: "Aye, Nalan. We'll berth here until the gale blows over."

"Quidang!"

Between them my officers cajoled *Cloudscamper* under the cover of trees and set up camp. We were tight as nits in a ponsho fleece as the gale blustered and howled over our heads. The wind flogged the trees unmercifully and the rain fell in bucketloads.

We jolly lads remained snug and dry, eating and drinking.

Useless to allow this delay to fret at my nerves. We'd get where we were going in Opaz's good time, and I trusted that Opaz would smile on our endeavors when, at last, we arrived.

The coat tails of the gale still blew smartly about us as we took to the air once more. The air itself, washed clean, tasted like the best Jholaix, although there was precious little dirt to be washed out of Kregen's superlative atmosphere, by Krun!

Ahead lay Oxonium, a strange city, true enough, built upon its chequerboard of hills. On the summits lived the nobles, the wealthy merchants, the nobs. Festering below in the runnels between the hills the poor folk looked up with useless hatred at the nobs who looked down with supercilious contempt. I'd run with a gang down below, Nagzalla's Nasty Neemus, and I'd done business with the aristocracy above.

Presumably the reluctant King Tom still ruled whilst hankering after a religious life within Cymbaro. I supposed Hyr Kov Brannomar still ran affairs of state. Prince Ortyg had been taken up to prevent his mischievous alliance with the regent of Caneldrin, C'Chermina. So that left Hyr Kov Khonstanton, Khon the Mak, to weave his ambitious schemes. How, I wondered, had he fared in recruiting an army in the Chulik Islands. Not well, I judged, in view of the Chuliks' return home to defend against the Shanks.

In all probability there would be little if any chance of my making a trip to Farinsee to find out how young Tiri was progressing in her religious studies, exercises I'd been given to understand would confer on her strange and mystical religious powers.

Cloudscamper soared on above the clouds. It must be raining down there. The night spread its superb canopy of stars and the moons sailed past, distant, and yet oddly comforting in their rosy presence. Towards dawn we'd reach Oxonium.

A brief twinkle of reflections of The Twins striking back from a lake as we passed over told us the clouds had gone. A dull glow appeared on the horizon directly on our course. The lookout called. That was Oxonium's night lighting, to be extinguished with the coming of dawn. In these moments before the Suns of Scorpio arose over Kregen the whole world breathed quietness and peace.

The glow increased. Now a shaft of fire speared up from the east, precursor of the twin suns. On we flew as the light brightened. There were clouds of dun colored smoke rising within the glow from Oxonium. I frowned and peered closer.

As we approached the city came into plain view, the mingled lights casting radiance upon the eastern-facing domes and towers. The western sides all lay in inky shadows. Many of those shadows were luridly illuminated by tongues of fire.

Oxonium burned.

"By Makki Grodno's—" I started, and then clamped my mouth shut. My jaw muscles ridged. Armored figures clashed in the streets and squares. Dark shapes climbed the sides of the hills. *Cloudscamper* circled above the mayhem and bloodshed below. I saw and understood what was going on. The shrieks and clamor of combat rose into the air like the baying tumult of wild beasts.

Absolute chaos enveloped the city of Oxonium.

"The gangs." I felt the words in my mouth like fiery coals from a furnace. "The gangs have risen!"

Seventeen

The gangs had risen. And Oxonium burned.

Glaring down appalled as flames gouted from wrecked buildings and black smoke drifted like evil fingers clenching around their victims, I saw the pity and the horror of it all. I have seen many fine cities burn, to my sorrow; destruction wrought by greed and hatred and fear. Now the Suns rose higher and their slanting rays illuminated only more calamity and pain.

"Bring her round." My order was curt, brutal.

Cloudscamper swung about, above the flames, above the smoke, high above the hideous clamor below.

Not all the buildings in Oxonium burned. On Grand Central the king's palace, although damaged, remained recognizably intact, as did the palace of Kov Brannomar. These were protected to some degree by the sorcerous arts of Brannomar's sister, Sana Besti. The Vallian embassy was, I saw with great relief, completely untouched. That apparently miraculous invulnerability was the thaumaturgical work of our comrade Wizards of Loh. The

Sorcerers of Balintol might wield unknown powers up in Caneldrin and Winlan, here in Tolindrin the Wizards of Loh had a freer rein. Towards the embassy the quartermaster headed *Cloudscamper*.

"At least," said Bancur, hoarsely, "there is a place to land there."

Slanting lower we caught the stench of burning flesh as we passed over a gutted meat market. The smoke choked streets and avenues crowded with people, running, falling, fighting. There were no lifters or ovverers in view; no doubt every one had taken a full freight of terrified passengers out of the doomed city.

One or two of my guards let rip exclamations of surprise; most of them regarded the catastrophe calmly. After all, they were seasoned mercenaries, paktuns who'd fought in battles and sieges and seen their fill of burning cities. This, anyway, was not their home.

As for poor Veda, had there been a tear in her eye I'd have fully understood. I sympathized with her. How she'd looked forward to shopping in the glamorous souks of Oxonium! How she'd been so excited at the prospect of wearing the sophisticated clothing here! Now all was gone, dust and ashes. Yet, ex Jikai Vuvushi that she was, she said nothing and stood at the rail, stony-faced, staring down at the ruination of her happy dreams of the gracious life.

A humorous thought welled up inside my old vosk skull of a head. By Vox! Oh, yes, Veda was disappointed. But me—plain Dray Prescot charged by superhuman immortals to unite Balintol—me, Dray Prescot, the so-called Emperor of All Paz, what utter disaster had befallen me!

"Do we wait? Or do we go down, cadade?" Bancur's gruff voice jolted the evil thoughts away.

"Down."

The Vallian embassy was laid out in the proper way for an embassy. It had an outer wall enclosing the landing area and gardens, and an inner wall to secure further the apartments within. Acting as helmsman during his trick at the controls, Bancur brought the lifter down smoothly. There was not a soul to be seen on the landing site. In marked contrast to the destruction all around outside, here the gardens with their freight of flowers looked peaceful.

We touched down. Instantly a howling mob broke from the concealment of the bushes fringing the strip and bore down on us, waving weapons, foaming with the mad desire to escape—to escape in our lifter.

Over the hubbub a trumpet pealed. A swift glance back showed a Vallian jurukker on the inner wall. He waved the trumpet at us and pointed back behind him.

"Bratch!" I yelled it out and Bancur jumped. "Up!"

Grimy hands clasped at the gunwales. Ferocious faces lifted into view, whiskery, lined, distraught with passion.

A crossbow bolt thunked into the deck. More scythed in and then, thankfully, Bancur lifted the airboat and we soared up.

Half a dozen of the poor wretches fell away, shrieking, to pulp themselves on the ground. I breathed out. That was close!

We curved round and came down on the inner side of the second wall. Guardsmen, trim in their Vallian kit, surrounded us.

Here came Elten Larghos Invordun, clad in Vallian buff, his wide brimmed hat in his left hand, the red and yellow feathers brave. He was now a diplomat; he'd been a bonny warrior for the Freedom Fighters of Vallia. He knew my identity. He held out his hand, smiling. "Lahal, Drajak the Sudden."

"Lahal, Larghos. Oxonium has fallen on hard times."

"It reminds me of 'The Fall of the Suns.'" This is an ancient poem of a very grim nature. "You might not believe it, but those folk out there who tried to take your airboat are our invited guests. They sought asylum. We could not refuse them. They keep to the outer courts. I feel this is prudent."

"Quite."

He brisked up, then, looking at Veda. Introductions were made and when the pappattu was finished Elten Larghos clapped on his hat and held out his arm for Veda, most gallantly. She rested her hand on his arm like any great lady of the court, and they paced in side by side. Orders were given to attend my lads, and I followed on after Larghos and Veda. Oh, yes, he was a gallant gentleman and she was some lady, by Krun!

Also, I found myself wondering, was our Veda losing some of her contempt and hatred for men? As I walked sedately into the embassy I felt that Veda and Larghos were getting on very well.

Of course, that possibly had something to do with the fact that Veda was entranced by everything Vallian.

She was whisked off by a bevy of serving girls. Larghos held out a glass of parclear, which I took with gratitude. Then I went and cleaned myself up and, before we ate, trotted around to the barracks to check on my juruk. The guardsmen were making themselves at home with the familiar knack hardened campaigners have. I was pleased and not at all surprised to find the Vallian guards getting on with my lads. From the state of affairs cooperation was going to be an essential ingredient of our actions in the immediate future.

During the second breakfast Veda pounded the ambassador with questions about Vallia and, in particular, about Dray Prescot. She flushed up vividly when Larghos admitted that, yes, he had met Dray Prescot, had, in fact, fought with him in many mighty battles. The stain of blood under Veda's pale skin appeared most odd to me. Her eyes were unnaturally bright, and her tongue licked her lips. She wanted to know everything Larghos could tell her.

Callously, I cut across all that. "What's been going on in Oxonium, then, Larghos? The place is a bedlam. Talk about a Herrelldrin Hell!"

"Aye. After the earthquakes we thought things would quieten down. Then, naturally, when the ibmanzies struck, why, the gangs seized their chances and swarmed out of the runnels."

"What?" I bellowed. "Ibmanzies!"

"Oh, yes, by Vox! Scores of 'em, laying waste to everything."

I sank back in my chair. I knew my face must resemble a block of granite carved into harsh furrows over millions of years.

Veda said: "I told you there were more Prisms of Power."

I gave Larghos a hard stare. "Khon the Mak?"

"Aye. He fared ill in the Chulik Islands. He has destroyed his own country's capital city for avarice, for the crown."

"The cramph." The next and obvious thought gave me a jolt of apprehension. "Princess Nandisha and her family—her people?"

Larghos reassured me. Nandisha was safely away in the country and not at one of her own estates. The protection of her numim servants' twins had brought me to Balintol in the first place to meet Fweygo. I guessed that was where the Star Lords had sent him now. The ibmanzies, then, were down to me.

Larghos wanted to know what Prisms of Power were and Veda explained in an animated fashion.

The ambassador nodded. "There is a new chief priest of Dokerty in Oxonium now. An unhanged rogue called Nath G'Goldark. He belongs, body and ib, to Khon the Mak."

Among the few buildings in the city without significant damage we'd observed as we flew in, I'd been pleased to see the Temple to Cymbaro was safe. I'd not been pleased to see the main Temple of Dokerty still stood. The reason was blindingly obvious.

The chief buildings—the king's palace, Brannomar's palace, the Temple to Cymbaro, a number of embassies of which the Vallian was one and, extremely surprisingly, the Temple of Tolaar—remained untaken. In the streets between, the folk who'd swarmed up from the valleys now surged about indulging in looting and drinking and general mayhem. How long would these islands remain intact?

There was no getting off the hills for the gangs and the mobs in the city and below in the runnels, except by flying.

Now if I have given any impression that a state of normalcy existed in the embassy, then that is completely false. Oh, yes, routine went on in the dry way of embassies the world over; but the pulsing sense of impending destruction tarnished everything.

The first thing to do, I suggested to Larghos, was to get these invited but unwanted guests out of it. They could be flown out party by party. My lads would make sure there was no chance of the frenzied creatures seizing *Cloudscamper*. Larghos agreed at once, thankfully.

Taking the other airboat, now used as a tender, I flew out to recce Oxonium—or what was left of that unhappy city.

There was not a single solitary sight of the maniacal form of an ibmanzy. Nary the one.

People looked up and pointed as I passed aloft. How strange a lifter had become to them in these dreadful days! The sight of lifters and ovverers passing and repassing in the skies above the city had—once—been a mere part of everyday life.

Not one cable car route stood undamaged and many of the towers were toppled. No doubt the infamous Kataki Watch had fought; but I suspected that the Whiptails had upped and run as soon as the ibmanzies revealed their true horrific power.

My business lay with the Dokerty cramphs; but first I circled over the Shrine to Cymbaro. The walls were intact. A couple of roofs had fallen in and one colonnade had collapsed like a row of dominoes, otherwise the place looked its usual peaceful self. No one was in sight below and the gardens stretched emptily.

In the process of debating whether or not to land I continued to scan three hundred and sixty degrees of the sky, from below the horizon to azimuth, as any fighter pilot does.

A dot driving straight on for the Vallian embassy resolved into *Cloudscamper* returning for a second load of refugees. As I watched a second dot appeared, fleeting through a straggle of cloud.

"Hullo!" I said to myself. "Now who's he?"

The levers sent the little craft up in a climbing turn to meet *Cloudscamper*. Three airboats riding the sky, cleaving thin air high above the city, we soared together.

The outline and colors of the mysterious visitor became plain.

"By the mucous clotted hair and dribbling diseased nostrils of Makki Grodno! Shanks!"

There was no doubt about it. The hard black hull below the brightly painted upperworks was unmistakable. The Fish Heads' voller looked to be a scouting craft. Their usual vollers were large and carried these smaller craft inboard. The Shanks had need of sizeable ships for they sailed around the curve of the world from their continents and islands to attack the lands of Paz. Hate, detest and fear them though we did, we also had to afford them admiration for their navigational skills and their courage.

Now the Shank voller soared in fast. She was out on a recce mission, clearly, attracted by the smoke. Was she a mere outrider, a loner, seeking information? Or did she portend the presence in the vicinity of a Shank fleet? This could change everything, by Djan!

The lads in *Cloudscamper* had seen her. They curved up and around. They knew about Shanks, by Krun!

One of those co-incidences that so often occur in battles now put the point at which the two airboats would meet over the Temple of Dokerty.

I hammered the controls. Whatever was to happen would happen and I needed to be there!

The two ballistae in the bows of *Cloudscamper* might not be the gros varters of Vallia, but they were useful weapons. She headed straight for the Shank. The streaming radiance of the suns caught and glittered off the weapons in the fists of my juruk on deck.

The Fish Heads' voller was a scouter. She was fast and nimble. I did not think they would wish to hang about for a fight; but with Shanks you never could tell what they would do. The lights of the suns splintered evilly from their weapons, too.

Also, as I saw with a sudden apprehension, scouter she might be, she was still larger than *Cloudscamper*, and stuffed with Fish Heads. The snouts of varters protruded from ports and from a narrow fighting gallery just above the keel. Calmly, I set the controls to carry me straight on and turned to seek out a few firepots.

Setting fire to the wick in its little brass container took a moment or two, and the tump blew up splendidly at the second try. I set the brass box down in its retaining beckets. The port-feu I kept in my hand, ready.

Now firepots are essentially evil devices, given the results of their handiwork on the fabric of fine vessels. Sometimes I have wished that a firepot could fall upon every Shank vessel in existence, and sometimes I have felt shame at the thought. Now, as ballistae bolts began to flash from the black-hulled flier to split the air about *Cloudscamper*, I drove my craft up into the slanting radiance of the Suns.

The red glow of the port-feu in my fist suddenly seemed to me to resemble the evil crimson eye of some pagan devil.

The vollers turned and twisted seeking the advantage.

My lads concentrated on trying to get their varters to bear on the enemy. This meant a series of quick headlong rushes followed by sharp turnaways as the Shank swung broadside on to get in a smashing reply. Some of the bolts were striking home. Neither vessel appeared able to climb above the other. Around and around they went in a locked circle of imminent death.

Laboriously my lifter climbed. Keeping her away from the other two necessitated sudden emergency turns; but we went up—slowly but surely up we went above *Cloudscamper* and the Shank.

Pretty soon crossbow bolts spat up at me as the Fish Heads saw and appreciated my maneuver. This was going to be tricky work.

Had I been the skipper of that Shank scouter I'd have cut and run by now. You could never judge a Shank by what appeared to us in Paz to be normal human behavior. They were alien. What they thought remained locked in their fishy skulls.

Cloudscamper shuddered and abruptly dropped bows first.

"Moxog Makib!" I shouted, the words jolted from me by sheer apprehension—sheer fear!—for my lads aboard.

She righted, her bows came up, she hung on an even keel. Likely a varter bolt must have struck her control linkages. She looked to be back under command now, thank Opaz. The Shank dropped down to bring his fighting galleries along his keel into action.

I shook my head in disbelief.

When chances are given in a fight you must be very careful. The riposte can be deadly. This time the damned Shank had bared his throat. My lifter crossed over the Shank. Half a dozen bolts flicked up. Fish Heads clustered at the rail, most looking down.

The evil demon eye of the port-feu spluttered the fuse of the firepot into red life. I blew. Then I dropped the blazing engine of destruction over the side.

Working as fast as I could I sent a succession of firepots down as my voller paced the Shank below.

"Burn, you bastards," I said to myself without any vestige of chivalry. "For all the misery you've brought to Paz—Burn!"

The black-hulled flier burned.

She swung about and headed down streaming smoke. Flames wreathed her. Shanks swarmed into her foreparts. They hung on and braced themselves for the impact of landing. I saw—with remorseless regret—that their vessel would touch down before the fire could burn its way forward and so engulf them all entire.

The fiery mass, hissing and sparking, pluming a black smear of smoke, came down in the square before the Temple of Dokerty.

Quick, agile figures jumped clear of the wreck. Orange reflections glittered from their armor and weapons. They spread out across the square.

"Makki Grodno take it!" I burst out. "There are enough of the cramphs left alive!"

Of any other human life in the square there was no sign.

No wonder, by Krun!

Cloudscamper wheeled in alongside me. Gently we dropped down.

Everyone watched the Shanks below.

Right up in the bows of *Cloudscamper* Nalan ti Perning pointed.

"Look!"

A red robed figure appeared from the doors of the temple and stood at the top of the flight of steps. He just stood there, studying the approaching Fish Heads.

A lone priest of Dokerty, all in red, a blob of crimson against the doors of the temple, bathed in the fire glow from the wrecked scouter, there he stood, arrogant, contemptuous, almost, it seemed, taunting the ravenous crew of Shanks. He stepped aside.

Four people emerged onto the steps. Four young folk clad all in white, two boys and two girls. They began to walk quietly down towards the square and the waiting Shanks.

Nalan shouted across to me. "Cadade! We have to help them!"

Cloudscamper began to dip down.

Frantically, I bellowed in my old foretop hailing voice.

"Hold! Do not go down! As you value your lives, do not go down!"

Eighteen

"Do not go down! As you value your lives, do not go down!"

My stentorian bellow cut across the gap between the lifters. Nalan jerked upright. A row of faces under helmets appeared at the rail of *Cloudscamper*.

"What—?"

"Just watch!"

On that I switched my attention to the two white-clad girls and two white-clad boys below. They looked fresh and innocent. They looked victims. Well, by Krun, they were, weren't they, the poor duped devils.

The Shanks roared on across the kyro towards the steps leading up to the temple. They intended to take the place over and make a fortress of it against whatever the soldiery of Oxonium might hurl at them. Each individual scaled Fish Head must know he was doomed. They would, in their barbaric fashion, fight until the end, until every single last one of them was dead.

The whole scene bathed in the streaming mingled lights of the Suns of Scorpio steamed with heat. The impression of a cauldron bubbling with imminent violence was compressed by the vision of a vast upturned bowl covering all below.

Now I am well aware that my next thoughts were highly reprehensible if not downright repulsive. Yet they were entirely in keeping with the enormous situation flowering unpleasantly in the sub-continent of Balintol. Oh, yes, by Krun, it is always pleasant to see two sets of your enemies knocking seven kinds of brickdust out of each other. By Djan! Let 'em destroy the whole boiling, and despite the darkness of the proceedings let the ordinary simple folk of the land rejoice!

The savagery of the Shanks as they stormed forward could curdle the soul in a man. The four white-robed figures waited calmly. The deadly transformations, when at last they came, erupted with violence to meet and overmatch the barbarity of the Fish Heads.

The young lads, the young lasses, grew and swelled. Their bodies writhed with the demonic forces pent within and now being released. Claws sprouted from their fingers. Talons ripped their shoes to shreds. The white robes split and dark hairy bodies roped with muscle stretched into raging devils.

Give the Shanks their due. For one horrified moment they halted. Then, screeching their hissing warcries 'Ishtish! Ishtish!' they smashed forward once more.

Blood. Blood everywhere. Bits and pieces of scaly bodies hurled into the air. Chunks of torn hairy flesh hacked away by weapons held in the fists of fishmen already dead. Horror engulfed the kyro beneath our two circling lifters.

The raw stink of spilled blood mingled with the stench of dead fish choked our mouths and stifled our nostrils. There was no loud metallic clamor of sword against sword or spear against shield. The harsh grunting gasps of the ibmanzies as they ripped bodies to pieces formed a hideous counterpoint to the shrilling shrieks of the Shanks.

These were the twin evils afflicting Balintol, the demons and the Shanks that could spill over into the rest of Paz.

My lads aboard *Cloudscamper* looked down in silence. They did not turn their heads away. Each jurukker was a kampeon, a hardened paktun. Oh, yes, they watched the slaughter and did not flinch. If they shared my sentiments, and I fancied they did, then by Krun they were eternally grateful they were not down there!

One of the ibmanzies fell. He—or she, for the grotesque bodies had chests smothered with coarse black hair—fell by reason of having no legs to stand on. As the thing fell it grasped a Shank in each hand, squeezing, so that ichor spouted.

Shank bodies, or parts of bodies, strewed the stones of the kyro. Another ibmanzy toppled. The Shanks had quickly deduced the way to deal with the monsters. Their trouble was that they were likely to run out of men to finish the job.

The third monster with hair matted red staggered, refusing to fall. Its single remaining arm smashed remorselessly at the weaving darting Fishmen. Their axes sliced in return, just as remorselessly chopping the monster to fragments.

It fell.

That left just the one.

The ibmanzy, like the Shanks, had no thought of retiring, of running away. One instinct alone possessed what of brain it had.

Ibmanzies were created to kill until they destroyed themselves.

Ibmanzies and Shanks—they proved opponents worthy of one another. You had to grant them that.

The last demonic monster still had two arms, although one was half sheared through and dangled uselessly. With its other arm it seized up a Fishman and dashed him headfirst to the stones. He just telescoped into a splintering of bone and puddlement of flesh and ichor. Instantly the ibmanzy snatched up another Fishman. The ibmanzy's head bent in a darting motion like a vulture. Yellow fangs ripped out the Shank's throat. The demon threw him at his comrades, and charged.

From *Cloudscamper* Nalan yelled: "He's done for!"

Still Shanks were on their feet, not many; but it looked as though Nalan was right.

The awful destructive power of the ibmanzies was hardly ever revealed more chillingly than in what followed.

One after another the Fishmen were annihilated.

Now the monster limped, and then hobbled; but still it kept up its relentless killing.

If these things were let loose upon the face of Balintol, upon all of Paz, the world would cease.

The crowds of people surging about the streets of Oxonium must be a mixture of citizens, guards, gangs from the warrens, thieves and panic-stricken merchants unable to escape. Once the ibmanzies got among them the loss of life would reach astronomical proportions. Those folk were nothing like the Shanks. Those poor damned doomed Fish Heads down there had put up the fight of their lives—and their deaths—for they'd killed three demons and badly crippled the fourth before they'd all succumbed.

"What's he up to now?" Molar bellowed across.

The manic monster shuffled crookedly across the kyro below. It made no attempt to avoid the scattered bodies. It just trampled over them, heading for the nearest avenue.

The thing must be nearing the end of its existence within the shredded body of its victim. Despite all my years upon Kregen the image that rose to my mind of the ibmanzy's end was that it would blow up. Until the Opaz-forsaken demon did blow up it would maim and destroy anything that stumbled into its path.

"Molar!" My old foretop-hailing voice brisked 'em up over there on *Cloudscamper*. "Crossbows! Shaft the damned blintz!"

"Quidang!"

Cloudscamper executed a perfect one hundred and eighty degree turn and Nalan at the helm positioned her above and to the side of the demon. The thing looked up. Its face distorted into a mask of insane anger. Red lust to destroy animated every single part of it. Its one arm flailed the air, its jaws gnashed and white foam gushed between the yellow fangs. Its eyes were mere mindless pits of fury. The ibmanzy exuded a wave of nausea.

Then the lads shafted the damn thing.

It took many quarrels in its hairy hide. I do not believe the shafts had done their work before the demon within that poor contorted body wreaked its inevitable destruction.

Swelling grotesquely, yellow ribs splintering through ripped skin, eyes bursting, guts tumbling, the ibmanzy collapsed at last, and shrank, and there lay the shattered body of a young girl.

In the kyro among the Shank corpses sprawled the horrendously mutilated bodies of two young men and a young girl. Oh, yes, I had no love for the priests of Dokerty and their power-mad mentor, Kov Khon the Mak.

Shaking my head on these somber reflections I was also aware that these four particular demons had not retained possession of their host bodies for very long. If that had significance I had then no way of telling. The length of time an ibmanzy remained in being was clearly of great importance.

The Suns still shone, a few light clouds drifted by and, incredibly enough, a flock of birds caroled and cavorted around a broken and burned tower. With all the horrors that had shattered this city, the birds could still sing. Amazing!

Cloudscamper turned easily and headed off for the embassy to pick up more refugees. I thought of Erwin the Waggler. He was just as much a victim of the maniacal desires of the Dokerty lovers as those four young folk down there. That—and the black thought rode me evilly—that and my own maniacal desire to halt the ibmanzies.

Erwin made up my mind for me. I could drop the remaining firepot on the damned Dokerty temple right now. But, no. Oh, no! Oh, no, by Krun! I swung the lifter towards the embassy. I'd pick up a whole great mass of firepots, and I'd return here and drop the lot on the stinking place and burn the demon-breeding hell-hole to the ground.

There was the vital necessity of pushing aside the unpalatable fact that in my own arrogance and pursuit of my designs I was adding to the destruction suffered by the city of Oxonium. I had to think of this act as that of cutting out a cancer—a glib excuse, and often used for acts of destruction. All the same, by Vox, in this case it was as true as Zim and Genodras rose each morning over Kregen.

A surprise awaited me at the embassy. No sooner had I touched down than a Blazing Fury leaped at me. Veda actually pummeled my chest with her fists. She was panting. She cried out that I was an ingrate, without pity or mercy, and deserved to have been torn to pieces by the demons.

My fears regarding the way she would dress down here in Oxonium were now realized, for she'd changed into a pale blue shamlak with golden cords. The opening was wide—very wide. As she banged her clenched fists against my chest the shamlak parted company with her.

"What the blue blazing—!" I started, and then grabbed her fists. "Calm down, you little she-leem!"

"You didn't take me! You left me!" She flailed about wildly, breathing open-mouthed, hair whirling. "You could have—"

"But I wasn't." I spotted the ambassador bustling up. That I felt the most onkerish of idiots goes without saying. Elten Larghos Invordun, the Vallian ambassador in Oxonium, as I have indicated, was a perfect Vallian koter. He relieved me of Veda in a supple, suave way that I admired. She backed off with his arm about her.

"If you think those Dokerty blintzes—" she shouted.

Larghos spoke up smoothly. "We shall deal with them, lady Veda, never fear. Now how about a glass of wine?"

Veda's clothes were in casual contact with her here and there. Her usually pale face blazed. "I hate you, Drajak the Sudden!" She was sobbing now. "Yes! I really do!"

"Yes," I said. "I can understand that. After what you have been through. But—"

Her bare legs were kicking the air. Larghos had hold of a she-leem right enough. "You can talk! If Dray Prescot was here he'd act as a great emperor would! He wouldn't go off and leave me—"

So—and I admit with a sense of the humor of the situation—a trifle stung by this beautiful passionate girl's words, I was enough of an onker to burst out: "By the Black Chunkrah, young lady! All right! All well and good! I'm going off to burn the damned Dokerty Temple." I drew a breath. "If you want to throw down fire pots on 'em, then you're welcome to join me."

She had half the shamlak up over one shoulder now and at my words her head jerked up. She glared, her lips opened, then closed and she tugged more of the garment into place. Headstrong young Veda was as sketchily dressed as usual. She lifted one hand to smooth back her hair and the other made a quick grab to stop the blue and gold-cord shamlak from billowing once again to the winds.

"Very well, Drajak! I shall most certainly throw down fire pots." Having smoothed her hair she tossed that pretty little head disdainfully. "But if you think that makes you like Dray Prescot—forget it, fambly."

Only too thankful to have got out of that imbroglio without a punctured hide I made no reply but started off for the embassy's arsenal. Larghos paced at my side. He said, and he meant it and would not be deflected, that he was going to fly with us and hurl down fire pots on the heads of the ungodly Dokerty blintzes.

"The rasts," he said, "shall be burned out of their pestilential nests, yes, by Vox!"

So, shortly afterwards, there we were, the three of us, flying out towards the temple where they manufactured infectos.

Amazingly enough, Veda was managing to keep a vast flying fur around herself—for how long though was a gamble I wouldn't bet on.

Activity still frothed and bubbled in the streets. Oxonium was a rich city and would take some time before the gangs looted it dry. Among the figures down there I spotted Katakis, doing more than their fair share of pillaging. Those jibrfarils would be taking up poor bewildered citizens and chaining them up for the slave bagnios. However much I would like to put a stop to that inhuman behavior, the first and overriding task to my hands remained the ibmanzies. Of course, should a demon and a Whiptail happen to tangle, that would be instructive. Still, that was highly unlikely. So we flew on. The kyro before the Dokerty temple still showed no sign of life. Shank corpses lay scattered. The four dead youngsters sprawled grotesquely. The stinking cramphs of red-robed priests hadn't even bothered to venture out to collect their dead for decent burial.

The citizenry quite clearly were giving the temple area a wide berth. That was the place where they bred devils. A certain very obvious fact had been bothering me for some time and now we were going to try to burn up this temple that fact might topple all our plans into as much ruin as the city itself. Still, you have to try.

During the short flight Veda's face had resumed its normal pallor. As she looked at the handiwork of devils and Fishheads below her face did not become paler; a ridge jumped alongside her jaw. She said nothing. Well, by Djan, what was there to say? She bent lithely and took up a firepot and weighed it in her hand.

Larghos very quietly said: "I will take the controls, if you wish. Then you may throw—"

"It's all right." I looked back and Larghos nodded and in turn picked up a firepot.

Down in that infested place below I'd done some running about. The extent of the buildings would demand all our supply of combustibles. Taking the voller around in a gentle curve I positioned her above the nearest corner.

We'd work our way across, methodically shedding fire upon the damned temple and joy to see the stinking place burn.

A flicker of red appearing and disappearing on a terrace meant that the priests had seen us. Well, bad cess to 'em! They could run or they could fry.

A horrific thought jumped into my old vosk skull of a head.

Even as Veda blew her firepot's fuse into life and hurled the destructive engine down, I thought that, suppose, just suppose, when the temple burned the priests turned any infectos they had left out into the city to become ibmanzies!

If that happened then my lads in *Cloudscamper* would have to join in and deal with the demons. That damned temple had to burn.

As the airboat sailed smoothly across the temple my two companions threw down their fires. Very soon wisps of smoke grew into clouds that rolled upwards. Flames began to shoot up, crimson and orange. Methodically on we went, wielding a flame of destruction.

In a voice I made steady despite the apprehension and anger within me, I said: "Look out for ibmanzies. If you see any I'll fly over them and you must try to hit them with a firepot."

Not, I said to myself, that there was much chance of a bulls eye under these conditions.

The ambassador called out: "They're opening a roof."

Up ahead where so far the flames had not reached a cylindrical roof split down the middle and the two halves began to roll back. We had not reached over the spot when a lifter appeared rising up through the opening. She was a sizeable craft with a double-decked superstructure. Red flags flew from her masts.

"The blintzes are getting away!" screamed Veda.

The control levers shoved savagely forward under my fists. We began to pick up speed; but it was clear the airboat would be well up in the air before we could reach her. There was no need to guess who or what was aboard that voller that sported the colors of Dokerty. We surged up and ahead and then, surprisingly, the Dokerty lifter swung about, turned broadside on.

In the next instant she'd let fly with her broadside varters. Unlike the sailing frigates and line of battleships of Terrestrial seas of my youth, we were not glued in place. All I had to do was deftly swing the little voller up or down and the hurtling rocks would miss.

There was no need to repeat the devout prayer of seamen under fire: "For what we are about to receive may the Lord make us truly thankful." I decided to go up and at the precise instant the varters let fly an evil flicker of turquoise light blinked in the corner of my eye.

My head twitched around. The turquoise light shone out more brightly. The Eye shot into distinct vision. For a long instant the thing glared on me, purple and turquoise and knowing. Then it vanished and a damned great chunk of stone thunked smashingly into our hull.

Two more rending crashes shook the little craft as a leem shakes a ponsho in his jaws. They must have spread their broadside into a barrage to try to hit us no matter which way we went. The tactic was not without merit; it usually failed if the target was nimble enough. In this case that Makki-Grodno diseased turquoise eye had delayed my response.

We were hit and as the voller sagged I sensed we were badly hit.

"We're going down!" yelled Veda. As she shouted she still hurled a fire-pot. She looked splendid, wild, with her hair blowing.

"Hold on, lady!" shouted Larghos, grabbing her.

We were hurtling down, out of control, the temple wreathed in flames lurching up at us like the mouth of a volcano.

Desperately I juggled with the controls. My heart gave a jump as I felt a tiny response. Hauling at the levers I managed to drag the nose up a fraction. Now we were slanting down across the fires, feeling the heat beating up at us. Smoke engulfed the airboat. Noses and throats and eyes choked and streamed as we plunged down over the blazing temple towards the kyro beyond.

We'd been knocked out of the air and the stones of the plaza would be extremely hard. Larghos and Veda huddled down among a pile of furs. Veda called to me to protect myself; but I clung to the controls frantically trying to coax the voller into more level flight to make the impact more of a glancing blow.

We shot out of the smoke, eyes streaming, lanced down towards the ground.

Blurrily I looked down and saw— Oh, yes, they'd not forgotten anything, the Dokerty-loving cramphs.

Standing just beyond the edge of the flight of steps leading up the temple facade two figures stood. Two youths, waiting for us, two youngsters dressed all in white.

They stared up at us and lifted their arms, waiting.

Nineteen

Speed. Speed was our only salvation. I felt reasonably confident that with a little luck I could deal with one demon. But two—!

I had to get to those poor kids down there and mercilessly chop them before their hideous transformations were complete.

The streaming mingled radiance of the Suns of Scorpio threw twin shadows from the scattered Shank corpses and the grotesque remnants of the four young people. The two waiting down there for us appeared not in the slightest concerned about the sight of four of their companions so gruesomely torn to shreds. Duped, believing, they wished only to serve their great god Dokerty. Poor devils!

And, of course, devils they were in all sober truth.

Up there in that bedecked lifter the chief priest, this Nath G'Goldark, would be lifting the Flutubium and intoning the word of power —"Dokomek!"

As our voller hurtled headlong for the ground I had no idea of the time left. All I knew was that I, plain Dray Prescot, had to act with the swiftness and violence of a rashoon of the inner sea.

We hit in a rending smashing as of the end of the world. The little voller flew to flinders on the instant. Bits and pieces of wreckage skidded helter-skelter. At the moment of impact I hurled myself off, relaxing, rolling over and over like a kicked ball, using all my skill learned from the implacable Disciplines of the Krozairs of Zy as the instructors train you on their mat-less marble.

It hurt. By Krun, it hurt. The ground mashed and pounded at me as a fat cook mashes potatoes in a pan.

Somehow or other I was on my feet, swaying a little, partially dazed. The kyro swam about me. No time—there was no time for anything other than leaping up, drawing the Krozair longsword, and hurling myself at the nearest white robed youth.

Already he was changing. Talons and claws sprouted. The robe split over his chest and black hairs sprouted through above plated muscle. He roared, fangs beginning to sprout.

In a single heart-stopping attack I rushed straight at him, brought the Krozair brand down in a monstrous cleaving motion. He was cut through to the breastbone. His blood—poor little devil!—spouted in a gory fountain.

In the next instant I leaped aside, instantly and without thought. Talons whistled through the air where my head had been.

Tumbling away I whirled to face the demon. I saw—! I saw the lithe frantic form of Veda rushing up with sword raised. I saw Larghos haul-ing himself up, a smear of blood about his head, drawing his sword and charging. These two companions of mine were throwing themselves at the ibmanzy, reckless of the consequences!

This vision of courageous action flashed upon me in a heartbeat. I was appalled. But, horrified though I was, recognizing that Larghos had been a kampeon of the Freedom Fighters and would expect to fight for his emperor, the true horror and admiration was for young Veda. She was no screaming fainting fragile maiden. She'd been a Jikai Vuvushi. She wanted to, as they say, get stuck in.

"No, no!" I yelled and swirled the Longsword so that—and damned luckily, too, by Djan!—it chunked a gobbet out of the demon's lifted arm. The ibmanzy let out a roar of insane anger. I shouted, and I verily believe by all the gods and devils in Steurbdin, that I shouted louder than the ibmanzy. "Get away! Stand clear!"

Veda's flying furs were long forgotten. As she bounded up the sham-lak flew back like a pair of wings. She looked ferocious and beautiful and brave all at the same time. What a girl!

Both she and Larghos were shouting but their words remained unrecognizable. Their faces were inflamed, their mouths distorted. They'd fight splendidly; but they were doomed if they did so.

There was only one way I could think of to save them and as the Krozair brand swirled dazzlingly before the ibmanzy and I slid sideways out of the clutch of his talons, I bellowed again.

"Stand clear, both of you! Larghos, drag Veda off out of it! Elten Larghos Invordun—that is an order!"

He'd caught up with her by this time and my vicious words brought him up short. That famous, blessed and cursed yrium, the power so much greater than mere charisma must have burst from me like an exploding supernova. He caught Veda clampingly around the waist, hauled her back, kicking and raving as she was.

"Quidang, majister!" he shouted.

There was no time for anything then but the ibmanzy.

Like any of the many wild and ferocious beasts I have been forced to fight in my time, he could be subdued by the application of fighting methods. As I have said before, and no doubt will say again, I take no joy in this. It was a messy business.

He foamed and dribbled. He exuded a disgusting stench. His eyes showed the redness of utter madness. A devil, wanting only to destroy, he must for the sake of Paz receive what he sought to serve.

Around the corpse-strewn kyro we circled, bathed in the refulgent rays of the twin suns. He didn't care if he trod on a dead body or part of a dead body or not. His talons shone yellow and his fangs shone yellow and presently a couple of his ribs shone yellow, streaked with blood red.

He tried to kick, slashing with his claws—and they shone yellow, too.

I had to cripple him. Unpleasant but necessary, the tactic was the best in this kind of combat. We'd seen the horrific capacity of these demons to stay on their feet and battle on despite horrendous wounds. By this time I was sweating a trifle. I leaped and cavorted away from his brutal thrusts, bore in to strike, jumped back to avoid the return slash. In one passage the Krozair brand lopped a claw-filled hand away so that it dangled from sinews, spraying blood. He didn't mind. He just roared in again, insensate with killing fury.

Like any novice I slipped on a patch of drying blood. Over I went, sliding down, desperately holding the sword up so that his blow hammered into the blade. It bit deeply. But such was the force and power of the demon that the sword was forced back. With an agile squirm I tried to slide away and a damned great claw ripped all down my side. I let out a yell.

In the next instant I'd scrambled wildly to my feet and run off a space. I turned to face him again as his bandy hairy legs bounded that massive body on. I went one way, swayed back, took an almighty swipe at his thigh as he went past.

The blood felt both warm and cold, running down my side.

Oh, yes. I've said that I fought the ibmanzy with a method I'd use against any wild and savage beast. But this unholy thing was not just any old wild animal. This monster was a demon, charging with a devil's spite, insensate, intent on one sole object—to destroy anything in its path. Insane, makib, it would struggle on and on until it was cut down or exploded with the dark fires of the demon spirit animating the body.

The cut on his thigh did not discommode him in the slightest. Even as I slashed again and skipped away out of the reach of his talons, I wondered if his blood would ever run dry.

Another slicing blow almost hit the same spot on his thigh. So I'd hew away as one chops at a tree trunk. Make a vee cut and work inwards and outwards, cutting deeper and deeper with each blow. Once more his talons ripped down and scored my chest, tearing the cloth away. This fellow was even more stubborn than earlier ones. Again and again I got through and hacked him down. But he would not go down. He stayed swaying on his bloodied legs, reaching out with hatred and the blind lust to kill.

There is a somber saying among my comrade Krozairs of Zy. "It is futile to argue against a Krozair longsword."

All I can say is that these Zair-forsaken ibmanzies put up one of the best arguments I ever came across.

The thing had to be finished now. This disgusting combat had to be brought to an end. His hair-matted chest heaved with the violence of his panting. He was smothered in gore. He lurched forward to get at me again, never stopping. He lifted his arm high, talons gleaming ready to slice down and rip off my head.

This then was the final moment.

Without pity or remorse I lunged forward and drove the Krozair brand full into his chest.

The blade struck in deeply. I twisted.

I twisted again. Savagely I worked the blade within him. My head went down and forward and his talons scythed past, missing.

When at last the bestial work was finished I withdrew the superb sword with a last grunt of effort. I stepped back. I drew in a deep lungful of the stink-laden air. He stood. He stood for a long moment. His arms dangled. He shone with blood. He stood—and then, slowly—oh, so slowly!—he fell.

He sprawled upon the stones of the square and soon the transformation took him and the demon vanished back to his own hell and the pathetic twisted corpse of the young lad lay there. I turned away. I admit it, I felt sick.

Oh, no, not for the gore, the blood and guts. There have been plenty of those in my time on Kregen, for my sins, as you know. Two more youngsters lay among the dead. My sickness was for these poor kiddies, duped, tortured, betrayed. I leaned on the sword for a moment, breathing hard, trying to clear my mind.

Finally I looked around. There was no sign of Larghos or Veda. Only the dead companioned me in the kyro of blood.

I had to brisk up. Brassud! as they say on Kregen.

Was I or was I not the brave, famous, wonderful, exotic Dray Prescot, Emperor of All Paz? There could be no shillyshallying about now. There was work to be done. The emperor bit you could take and shove it. All the wonderfulness you could take and throw into a leem pit. I was saddled with my destiny. And, as they say on Kregen, Queyd-arn-tung!

The voller that had flown up out of this demon's nest and shot us down had quite obviously been carrying Khon the Mak and the chief priest of Dokerty, Nath G'Goldark. Also, she'd been taking the symbols sacred to this pestiferous Dokerty. The Flutubium with all its dark and secret powers was being carried off to safety.

With somewhat of an effort, and a grunt that startled me, I straightened up. Pain rivuleted down my back as though boiling lead poured from shoulders to hips. The damned ibmanzy had clawed me then, in that lethal grapple, and in the fury of the contest it had passed me by.

Now you, Dray Prescot, I said to myself, have to be sensible about this. You must walk back to the embassy and seek a needleman. He'd soon have me sorted out and patched up. Larghos would be well able to take care of Veda and my order would have sent him off to the embassy. He carried a Vallian drexer which should deal more than adequately with the inferior local braxters.

The streaming tangled radiance of Zim and Genodras tinged with blue. I halted. I looked up. The world of Kregen turned blue.

"Not now!" I shouted. I kept my temper. "I've a damned great lot of work to do. Not now, confound you!"

The blueness deepened and the colossal form of the Giant Scorpion hovered overhead. In a weltering of coldness and storm up I went, head over heels, thrown this way and that, thumped down into a shiny chair that hissed along a columned passageway.

Oh, well, when the Star Lords call it's up you go, my friend. Sometimes I'd managed to avoid that; not often. Now I sat in their marvelous chair, not leaning back, I assure you, and went hissing along to hear what they wanted now.

The chamber into which the chair carried me contained a table with a single leg carrying a flagon and a glass. I poured and drank gratefully and did not wipe my lips. I did say: "By Mother Zinzu the Blessed. I needed that!"

The voices whispered out of thin air. "Dray Prescot! We are disappointed. You have failed—"

"You think I don't know that?"

"The devices you call Flutubiums should never have been allowed upon the face of Kregen. All must be rendered harmless."

"I had," I said with some acerbity, "worked that out for myself."

Agony lacerated every corner of my back and chest and thigh. A torment so intense I contorted with a violent bellow as pain washed all over me. It vanished as quickly as it arrived. I drew in a huge lungful of air, and blew out, and flopped back in the chair.

The Everoinye had never done that to me before. In all our dealings despite their cavalier treatment they'd not—and, mind you, as far as I knew—sought to torture me.

"What the Makki Grodno—?" I began, and then stopped, abruptly abashed. I felt refreshed and fighting fit. All the aches and pains inflicted by the ibmanzy were gone.

"You, Dray Prescot, despite your yrium, are of little use to us if you are not in proper condition for your work for us."

So, by Vox, that put me in my place!

"Anyway," I said in what was almost a snarl. "I give you my thanks for patching me up."

They ignored that in the way of a grand seigneur. Not for the first time I wondered if in their millions of years of life they'd forgotten what simple gratitude was. They'd been human once, though.

A single whispering voice sharpened. "The Flutubium is being taken to Winlan. There is a Dokerty temple there in Winbium."

"The capital." I nodded. "But there's a wall all around—"

"A trifle. We are sending you to Winbium. You will arrive before the flier carrying the Dokerty symbols. You know what to do."

"Oh, aye." I reached for the wine glass. It evaporated in my fingers. Blueness drenched me. I was falling. I was cold.

Blueness receded and the emerald and ruby fires of the Suns of Scorpio lanced into my eyes. My feet hit flagstones. The hum of many people filled the air. My vision cleared.

I blinked. Before me stretched a busy crossroads, with traffic and citizenry and slaves about their different activities. The architecture was remarkable. Buildings were supported on clusters of thick pillars. The upper storeys projected over the lower giving an odd effect, almost as of upside down structures. Rising and descending from the flat roof landing areas many lifters and ovverers flitted against the evening suns shine.

From what I knew of Winlan there were warriors and slaves with merchants tolerated for business purposes. These class distinctions were readily apparent in the crowds before me. That made me glance down at myself. The Star Lords had done me proud, quite unlike those old times of adventures when I'd first landed upon Kregen.

The russet tunic was brand new. I carried all my weapons. They'd even given me a golden pakzhan to wear on silken cords, and an almighty long pakai, glittering with many gold and silver rings. So I was supposed to be a mercenary hired by a merchant. That made good sense. The warriors stalking about were indeed a mighty haughty lot, always ready to kick a slave out of the way. The Star Lords had decided not to attempt to integrate me with them, and they'd felt that being a slave would cramp my activities.

The scent of blossoms giving forth their perfumes for the evening, and the tinkle of fountains could not conceal the essential unpleasantness of the social arrangements of Winbium in Winlan.

At the center of the crossroads rose a slender tower which served the purpose, as I supposed, of guiding the traffic. I looked at it again. I sucked a breath. At the top and facing the four points of the compass were placed Eyes—Eyes remarkably like the one that had spied on me.

The sense of oppression weighed me down as the Eye facing me stared unblinkingly. I could feel the damn thing prying. I stepped back into the shadows of a thick column.

No one took the slightest notice of me. Like in any great city, these inhabitants were gearing themselves up for the night to come. Slaves scuttled. A grand lady wheeled past in her zorca drawn chariot with mounted guards, paktuns for a certainty, fore and aft.

A crowd of warriors strolled along, very high and mighty, swishing their scabbards and flirting their extravagant neckerchiefs. All that was peer pressure and response to the pecking order. One of them, an apim youngster with a too-florid face gave me a casual glance. Not quite sure of the proper response, I gave my head a little incline, a kind of bow. Drat the fellow! I just hoped I'd done the right thing.

When I straightened up and looked he'd already turned away. Phew! Mores and customs vary wildly; some remain almost the same.

Just as I was relaxing a giant voice bellowed. It thundered over the crossroads and shook the windows over my head.

"Arrest that man! That is Dray Prescot, the blasphemer! Seize him!"

Twenty

"Arrest that man! That Is Dray Prescot, the blasphemer! Seize him!"

The casual party of warriors abruptly became casual no longer. They looked over at me. Their hands went to their sword hilts.

Again the gargantuan voice bellowed.

"Yes! That is Dray Prescot, the Great Blasphemer and Defiler of Dokerty! Take him!"

My Val! What a mess! I turned smartly about and started off at a dead run between the thick pillars. The street into which I burst was wide; but because the buildings overhung so much the tops were close together and admitted little of the suns' light. I ran along in a gloom I fiercely hoped would soon be total darkness.

That damned Opaz-forsaken Eye! The diabolical thing had been spying on me. Now it—or the Illusionist who peered through its lenses—had recognized me without delay. Once more I was a hunted fugitive.

So much for the Star Lords' impressive plans for my welfare here in Winbium! If I didn't get out of this with a whole skin the Everoinye could whistle—their grandiose schemes would be blown with the breeze.

Sprinting along the street I looked for somewhere—anywhere!—that might afford refuge. This city was an astonishing jumble of top-heavy buildings, kyros, narrow alleys and hopeless dead ends.

This street led on to another at right angles. Some of the warriors among the passersby halted to stare at me. I stared at the crossroads.

By the pestiferous dangling eyeballs and pustular infected nostrils of Makki Grodno! In the center of the crossroads a tower lifted with the Opaz-forsaken Eyes situated at the top.

Before the gargantuan voice had time to start braying like an onker kicked up the rump I was off, fleeing down a side alley.

Now those warriors in this street joined in the chase.

Sprinting between massive columns under a building I catapulted across the next street and so roared on between a fresh set of columns. Directly ahead loomed a wall stretching from ground to third storey level. Clearly, then, all the buildings were not of the top heavy variety. I shot off to the left.

The need to think this situation through was imperative. The mob baying at my heels probably knew the city well enough to try to head me off. Perhaps—I hoped devoutly—the suburbs would contain smaller buildings of more traditional structure where alleyways would lead on to sanctuary.

The noise of pursuit bayed on, more faintly now, so that I slowed my headlong rush as a couple of warriors hove into sight ahead. Like the others of their unpleasant kind they wore shiny armor, some plate but mostly scale, and they carried a plethora of weapons. Their neckerchiefs were marvels of color and crimps and folds.

Walking up briskly I prepared to pass them with a polite nod.

They weren't having that, no, by Krun. One of them gave my shoulder a push of some authority whilst the other tried to kick me.

Now this was, in the view of a civilized person, conduct quite out of order. In addition to that consideration, I'd had a somewhat fraught day. Recovering from the push I caught the foot of the fellow who wanted to kick me, twisted hard so that bones snapped, and swung him at his comrade. I followed that up smartly with a couple of good hefty thunks under ears. As I walked off I didn't kick their recumbent forms, much though the cramphs deserved that.

A crossbow bolt went sizzling past my head. A flashing glance back showed me the pursuit foaming up from under the columns. The high and mighty swording warriors had bowmen with them now, then.

Running on fleetly I saw a man step into the street. He was apim, very scrawny with a frizzle of white hair on his naked chest. He carried a pole across his shoulders from which depended two baskets. They were heavy, for they bent the pole into a bow. His lined and grimy face looked the picture of abject misery.

A crossbow quarrel flew over my shoulder and thunked solidly into the slave's chest. For a moment as I neared him he stood looking down stupidly. Then a transfiguring expression of joy transformed his features. He dropped the basket-laden pole. He lifted his skinny arms high. "Thank you, Oelefer! Thank you, thank you!" Then he fell to slump into a pathetic huddle.

Without stopping I raced past. I said, aloud: "May your Oelefer have you in his keeping." Then I skidded around the corner.

The death of a slave clearly meant nothing to these brave fighting men of Winlan. The pathos of the slave's end affected me.

Rust and verdigris shadows stretched long across the road. The suns were declining. Perhaps, in the night, I'd avoid these confounded Eyes? The wall continued on at the side and the next sets of buildings indeed were smaller and less imposing than the others. By pure chance I'd fled into an area less frequented than the center. I considered this chance; I doubted the Everoinye had a hand in it.

There was no doubt I was running faster than the pursuit and once again the blood-thirsty baying faded to the rear. The slaves I passed merely gawped at me. I saw no brave bold warriors to kick.

Dimness stole more and more upon Winbium. The verdigris and rust light stole higher and higher up the walls. Maintaining my breathing at a steady rate, keeping the old leg muscles going, I sprinted on.

Here the buildings were of more normal construction, with walls that stood vertically and with alleyways between. Lights shone from few windows, indicating this to be a business area and those the lights of watchmen. Just the place, then, for a hunted man to hide.

The next alley looked promising. I started along it and a faint fuzz of blue light abruptly shone into being twenty or so paces ahead. I stopped sharply. I sucked in a breath. Could this be one of my comrade Wizards of Loh? Could they have succeeded in circumventing the Sorcerers of Balintol's interference? I watched.

The blueness deepened. The color ran to the edges and a form gradually became clearer. I looked—and I looked and my heart gave so resounding a thump I swear it could have been heard on the other side of Kregen.

I couldn't get hold of my emotions. Joy. Passion. Bitter anger. Gut-wrenching fear. Complete panic. I lifted my head and shouted like a madman. "Star Lords! No! No! You will destroy— no! Send her back!"

But my Delia stepped from the blue radiance and lifted her arms in that old heart-rending gesture of welcome.

Delia! The Star Lords must have sent her to help me. But—!

Frantically I ran towards her dear form. I now felt cold, as cold as the Ice Winds of Gundarlo. If these fine warriors of Winlan trapped my Delia! Absolute terror gripped me.

She was dressed in her russet hunting leathers. Her rapier and main gauche were scabbarded to her slender waist. The embroidered bag containing her Claw was hitched under her shoulder. She smiled and stretched out her arms and I ran like a lunatic to clasp her.

Her lips shone darkly red in that light, her hair a marvel. My arms went about her and through her and she was not there and a massive iron-meshed net descended about me and dragged me down in its chilly folds.

I felt nothing more. The cloak of Notor Zan engulfed me.

My next impression was smell. The stink of charring flesh conflicted nauseatingly with heavy musky perfumes. I was lying on a hard floor, marble by the damned feel of it. People were talking and as my senses quickened the hum of conversation bore in like a heavy surf pounding rocks. The rocks were all in my head.

If that disgusting stench of burning flesh meant what I suspected it meant, then no doubt the conversation was of more interesting ways of inflicting the hot irons.

I could feel cold iron about my wrists and ankles. Not rope. So I was manacled and fettered. I was not going very far, then.

Carefully I slitted half an eye open. Light struck in like a poniard. By the time I had both eyes fully open and working I'd come to the conclusion that no one was taking any interest in me. For the moment, at any rate, by Krun!

In these fascinating situations one always has to take stock of the surroundings. I was naked save for the brave old scarlet breechclout and all my weapons were gone. Rolling my eyeballs I saw.

The chamber was not overlarge and was draped in tapestries of various myths and legends of Kregen. People stood about in groups. One lot of splendidly attired warriors stood by the brazier with its irons heating nicely. They were practicing on a haunch of vosk, making their disgusting stench.

Another group wore the red robes of Dokerty and looked decidedly unhealthy.

A third group looked to be merchants, decently clad, worried.

Rolling my eyeballs I made out a fourth party wearing black robes with tall black hats on their heads. Near them stood another small group of men and women wearing mustard yellow robes. Somehow they struck me as being cowed by their surroundings.

So, at last, that brought me round to stare at the figure seated in his curule chair.

At his back a line of paktuns with impassive faces stood guard. They were all zhanpaktuns with immensely long pakais.

The figure in the curule chair looked shriveled. He was very short and his little legs rested on a velvet cushion. He wore all black, with a brimless hat far loftier than even those ridiculously tall top hats gentlemen wore in the middle of the nineteenth century.

His face puzzled me. Very white, only slightly lined, with a sharp nose and decided chin, with thin but red lips, the face would have been interesting in its own right. But his eyes like glass gave the whole countenance a feeling of pent up power. He rested a gloved hand on his belt and the other hand supported his chin.

This, then, was the renowned Illusionist of Winlan, San W'Watchun.

He brooded on me. I could feel his stare as a physical force. At last he spoke and the conversations in the chamber died instantly.

"I have waited a long time to meet you, Dray Prescot."

That struck me as banal. I started to reply and found my mouth would not work properly. It felt as though it was filled with cinders. I tried to swallow and my mouth was as dry as the Ochre Limits. I shook my head—and that was a nasty mistake. All the famous Bells of Beng Kishi started up a cacophony in my old vosk skull of a head so that I blinked wetly.

At last I managed to get out: "What in a Herrelldrin Hell d'you want with me, W'Watchun?"

Some muted gasps from the congregation made me feel I'd hit the right note.

A magnificently-attired warrior, burly bold, aggressive, stepped forward. "Let me have him, San. I will—"

"Not so." The voice I'd expected to be thin and reedy from this scrawny little Illusionist boomed out full and rich like a best red from Jholaix. "Your torture would fail."

The whole air of unease in the chamber, the sense of impending events of vast proportions, the closeness and pressure, gave me a most queasy feeling, I can tell you. I was in for it, there was no doubt about that, by Vox!

San W'Watchun made a small gesture. At once a couple of hefty paktuns strode down and hoisted me up like a side of ordel. I was thrust down kneeling before the Illusionist. A broad hand in my hair hauled my head up facing W'Watchun.

His thin white face bore down on me. His eyes like glass caught the light and flamed.

He looked into my eyes.

Challenge of Antares

Dray Prescot

Dray Prescot is a man above middle height with straight brown hair and level dominating brown eyes. His shoulders are enormously broad, to the despair of his mother as he grew so rapidly out of his clothes, and now he has a superbly muscled physique. He moves like a savage hunting cat, silent and lethal. There is about him an abrasive honesty—which has not served him well—and an indomitable courage that has sustained him during his darkest hours.

Born in 1775, he joined the Royal Navy as a boy when his father died from the sting of a scorpion, and his mother followed soon after. The life in Nelson's Navy, harsh, intolerant, formed and molded him.

Dray Prescot has been consistently passed over for promotion, even though he has fought his way from the lower deck through the hawsehole to the quarterdeck. Now, together with the rest of the world, he considers himself a failure.

Just recently he has been experiencing unsettling dreams, of weird places and animals, strange beyond the comprehension of a plain sailorman. Through these eerie nightmares he occasionally glimpses the vague face and form of a woman who touches him profoundly and for whom, not really understanding why, he knows he would lay down his life.

As we join his story he is serving as the first lieutenant in His Britannic Majesty's seventy-four gun ship *Roscommon*.

At this juncture in his life, Dray Prescot sees no future at all for him on Earth.

Alan Burt Akers

One

I, Dray Prescot, First Lieutenant of His Britannic Majesty's seventy-four gun ship *Roscommon*, leaped for the struggling form of Mr Midshipman Simpkins entangled in rigging as the main topmast collapsed upon him.

The ship writhed in the gale and the deck went up and down like the swinging hips of those beautiful girl dancers of Tahiti. Simpkins screamed on and on, a thin kitten mewling snatched away in the maelstrom of noises. The physical force of the wind battered our senses, ripped the breath from our mouths, clenched with the pressure of a torturer's tongs upon our brains.

There was no time for all that. Skidding on the water-running deck I nearly missed him. He was a fresh pimply-faced youngster scared out of his wits. Savagely I wrenched myself about, grabbed for him. His arm felt sparrow-leg thin in my grip.

"Come here, lad!"

A monstrous sea washed inboard spinning us about helplessly. With that water-buffeting momentum and my desperate wrench he slid free as the main topmast hammered down.

The gong note of mast against deck rang clear through the boiling confusion of the gale.

The mast slewed viciously, dragged by the trailing rigging, and gyrated across the deck. The main top-gallant smashed down and across the lee bulwark, snapped and in a smother of parting lines vanished over the side. There was no hope in my mind that the top-gallant had really gone, oh, no! The damn thing would be held up and penduluming and in the moment the thought occurred the first jarring thump shocked through the hull.

"Get that raffle cleared away!" I used the old foretop hailing voice to pierce through the racket. Another vibration through our feet made the men jump—perhaps not as much as the savage quality of command in my intemperate bellow, I dare say—and they moved in warily on the wreckage. The top-gallant would puncture our hull if we were not sharp about it.

Everything was going up and down and around and around.

The hands were right to be cautious. Lines snaked everywhere across the deck ready to snatch up an incautious man like those damned great pythons of the jungles. Axes lifted and descended and keen edges bit.

The light was going, a ghastly blood-red glow through the turmoil, and a man's life was cheap, far cheaper than the value of one of His Britannic Majesty's ships of the line. First Lieutenant or not, was I not Dray Prescot? Was I an officer to send my fellow human beings into peril and hang back? Well, of course, in the right circumstances certainly I was. But not now. Seizing an axe as Simpkins collapsed, I jumped at the raffle of wreckage.

The whole mass shifted threateningly and it was a business of nip and tuck. One by one the tangling lines parted. The manic banging of the top-gallant overside acted like some imperative drum, driving us on.

We'd been badly hit in the fight with the French eighty and some blood had still not been washed from the decks. There'd be shot-holes below the waterline, into the bargain, although the Froggy had played the usual French trick of shooting at our spars. Well, the monsieur had done that well enough. The main top-gallant, injured in the fight, had now fallen; we'd already lost the mizen top-gallant. Rain slashed at us, streaming water and sweat down the men's faces. They looked like a bunch of imps crazed from hell. But we hacked and cut, jumped and dodged, and all the time the ship pirouetted and the damned timber overside smashed at our hull.

Captain Parsons appeared at my elbow as I leaped back, just avoiding a cut line whose end would have guillotined me nicely.

"Get to it, if you please, Mr Prescot! That mast will hole us if you delay."

Parsons was incompetent to the point of imbecility. There was nothing else I could say but: "Aye aye, sir!" and leap at the rigging again, axe flailing.

And—danger brooded malevolently in Captain Parsons. He was one of the famous Mad Captains of the Royal Navy. A captain was God Almighty aboard his own ship. This affected certain men, the corruption of power infecting them insidiously over a period of time so that in the end they turned out to be as mad as March hares in their addled brains. No doubt the dreadful conditions of those under their command and the well-nigh intolerable burdens of command serving an Admiralty that demanded perfection accelerated the process of mental decay.

All that meant was that I, plain Dray Prescot, had to give the captain a wide berth and bear his tantrums with what equanimity I could muster.

Thankfully with the onset of night the gale began to abate. The dark seas laced with creamy marbling rushing past eased. Urging the hands on to fresh efforts, taking chances to get at the inner coils of lines inextricably entwined, hacking the raffle free, at last I was rewarded with the sight of the topmast swiveling, swaying, stabbing its splintered butt dangerously at us as we leaped back, and finally toppling overboard. I dragged in a lungful of air, storm-washed, refreshing, scented with the smells of the sea. All the time the manic captain pattered on in a monologue, a harangue of threats and descriptions of what he would do in the way of discipline aboard his ship.

A portly, florid man, he had a whining nasal voice. Now he gave me a hostile look and said: "Jury masts, if you please, Mr Prescot. And as quick as you like."

"Aye aye, sir."

God rot the confounded fellow!

Mr Harcourt, the carpenter, running sweat from his exertions, turned his head away; but not before I'd seen the look of contempt upon that mahogany countenance. I took no notice. Mr Brace, the bosun, shouted at the nearest hands, panting, sweaty, pawing their faces where sweat and rainwater mingled. If a king's ship had no top hamper by reason of it being shot away by the French, why, then, Bigod, sir! it must be restored with a jury-rig immediately.

There was no such thing as rest aboard a vessel of the Royal Navy until all that had to be done was done. And done all shipshape and Bristol-fashion into the bargain.

Giving the Second and Third of the ship their instructions and knowing that the carpenter would manage things with the bosun, I became aware that the gale had gone right down. The night breathed gently with the merest puff of a breeze. Someone, then, must be keeping a friendly eye on us sorry mariners.

Now the sky blazed with stars. Drawing a breath, I looked up. As ever my gaze was drawn with hypnotic power to the constellation of Scorpio with its arrogantly upflung tail. There blazed the red star of Alpha Scorpii, Antares, as though a lighthouse seen from afar off in some strange and unfathomable way was beckoning to me. Since my father had been killed by a scorpion when I was a little lad, always that red speck of fire in the heavens appeared to me to contain some hidden meaning.

A voice at my elbow said: "You are wounded, Mr Prescot. Pray allow me attend you."

For the moment a trifle bemused, I glanced around. The surgeon, a snuffy, strange little creature, reached out for my arm.

To my surprise I saw blood on my shirt sleeve. My coat had long since been discarded. "Come below, sir. I must dress—"

"It is nothing, I thank you, doctor. A mere scratch. And I've the jury masts to rig."

This surgeon, Doctor Milius, shook his narrow head. His thin face screwed up in annoyance. I tried not to look at his face, for he had the most amazing eyes. Pale, like glass, they seemed to drill through me.

"You will vastly oblige me, sir, if you will step below."

There was no pain from my arm, and where the confounded wound had been collected I had no idea. *Roscommon* hummed with activity under the lamps. This crew had been hand-reared by me and knew what to expect if they failed me in the exactitude of their duty. The manic captain towered like a leering monster over us all, of course.

The work going on now was so familiar to me from many many years at sea that I knew the jury masts would be up and canvas set in good time despite the fatigue of the hands. All the same, I couldn't leave now.

"Come, sir, I pray you." Milius held out a hand.

He spoke with the normal florid courtesy demanded so that I could find no fault in that. When the captain said he would be vastly obliged—he'd probably say obleeged—if a person would do what he wanted done the effect was much the same as the bosun's starter thwacking down viciously on a waister's rump. I started to speak and Milius turned away abruptly. He trotted in his odd pigeon-like walk over to the captain. What was said I could not hear.

Captain Parsons looked across at me. "Mr Prescot! Would you kindly take yourself below, sir, and have your wound bandaged."

"Aye aye, sir."

All the ordered confusion of the deck could be left. I could go below to the wardroom. Amazing! What the blazes had the surgeon said to our raving captain?

The wardroom looked exactly the same as I remembered it when I'd gone up on deck at the beginning of the action. Not a single shot had penetrated here. The action itself was already history, the French eighty gun ship, mangled and near-derelict, flown with that quick gale into the night. I felt the supreme annoyance of a fellow deprived of honest Prize Money.

The odd thing was, I reflected as I led the way into my cubicle of a cabin off the wardroom, I'd been absolutely convinced we'd taken the Frenchy. Monsieur Jean Crapaud's blue white and red had still flown from what mastheads he had left to him; but I was already anticipating the feeling of the gold in my pocket when he struck.

"The damn Froggy," I said, my thoughts spilling out resentfully into a grumbling growl. "He's laughing up his sleeve at us now, I'll warrant."

The surgeon pulled my blood-soaked sleeve back. "You do not like the Frogs."

"Like 'em? What's that got to do with it? We're at war with 'em. And that's an end to it."

He gave a non-committal grunt and went off to fetch his medical chest. In the few minutes he was away I tipped some water from the pitcher into the bowl. There was a quantity of blood on my arm; I could feel no wound.

When he returned I pulled the little hinged table down. Something odd, something that was not quite right, was niggling away at my mind. He put his box on the table and opened the lid. Then he pointed a scrawny forefinger at my sea chest whose lid was thrown back.

"A handsome pair, Mr Prescot."

A highly-varnished mahogany box lay open on the top of my meager possessions. Certainly, the brace of dueling pistols did look mighty handsome. The red velvet was thick and plush, the gunmetal gleamed with the dark blue of superb craftsmanship, the furniture superb with a deep polish and the locks marvels of the locksmith's art.

I looked and shook my head.

I didn't own but I recognized the dueling pistols; but before I could speak Milius took one out in his thin hand and turned it over. "I must see to your arm first, Mr Prescot; but then I would be vastly in your debt if you would tell me about this weapon."

He weighed it a moment, holding it extraordinarily awkwardly, then returned it to the box.

"Now," he said, more to himself than me. "Bandages, yes. Scissors, yes." He rummaged about in his own medical chest. "Where are the needles?"

"Needles!" I burst out. "Sink me, Doctor Milius, the wound can't be so bad as to need sewing up!"

"Not those kind of needles—"

He looked up swiftly at me, his thin ferrety face somehow altering its planes so as to produce the semblance of a demon.

I looked around. Now I knew what had been niggling away at my brain. The wardroom couldn't look just as it had been before the action. Impossible! Everything would have been struck down as we cleared *Roscommon* for action!

He saw me looking at him, he saw my face.

"What the blue blazes is going on?" I brayed out.

The surgeon straightened up.

"Dokerty take it!"

He turned towards me and his strange eyes like glass bored piercingly into my eyes.

Two

I, Dray Prescot, First Lieutenant of his Britannic Majesty's seventy-four gun ship *Rockingham* glared with malignant helpless fury upon the destruction of my ship. *Rockingham* was doomed. Immense seas, darkly green bearded with foam, crashed upon her, all her masts were gone by the board, her hull was breaking up and the scraps of humanity aboard were being tossed about, with the cruel inhumanity of an indifferent fate.

Down off our lee the coast of West Africa waited menacingly.

Sheets of water cascaded inboard, hurling the detritus of battle into the scuppers. The sheer prodigious volume of noise numbed a man's senses.

Up and down we went and around and around, the darkness of hell's gates gathered above us and the end could not be far off.

The action we had just fought—and won, Demme! won!—had brought ruin on us. The gale was in truth one of the worst I'd experienced in my many wearisome years at sea. Crippled by the Froggy's shot, blasted by the gale, we were buffeted helplessly.

In these last moments before we struck there was time for me to contemplate my life. Not that there was much of life in it to contemplate and certainly none with relish. Wearisome, yes, that had been my lot. This was the year of Trafalgar and once again I had been disappointed of my step. Captain Anstruther had been washed overboard some time back. I found it very difficult to feel any sorrow for the fellow, for he had led me a miserable dog's life.

The stern of *Rockingham* went up and down like a pendulum, the waves towered, immense, awe-inspiring. If we weren't pooped we'd broach to and then we'd never strike the shore.

The flying wrack prevented me from seeing the stars. I could not even take that strange not-understood comfort from looking at the red spark of fire that was Alpha Scorpii, Antares. Weird how that star had come to dominate my inner thoughts.

Some of the hands were trying to lash themselves to baulks of timber. Others just waited for the inevitable end in a passive, almost stupid state. The master stood grasping the wheel and his face, streaming water, turned upwards with a serene countenance that took the final strength from his unshakeable beliefs.

The surgeon, Doctor Brighton, stood grasping the rail near me. A small snuffy man he surprised me by his complete absence of emotion. He stood with one foot on his medical chest, anchoring it against the maniacal movements of the sea.

"Not long now, Mr Prescot!" His reedy voice reached me through the shriek of the gale.

"Aye."

"We are all in—" He paused, checked himself, and went on: "We are all in God's hands now."

When a surgeon talked of God was the time, in my experience, to worry.

The end came with the startling suddenness of a pistol shot.

We struck the sand shoals at the mouth of one of those vast rivers that empty out of the heart of Africa into the Atlantic and shivered to pieces instantly. I surfaced in that raging sea and caught a baulk of timber and was swept resistlessly on and flung half-drowned upon a shore of coarse yellow-grey sand. I just lay there sodden, abandoned, water dribbling from my mouth.

Why I had been spared from the wreck was past my comprehension.

Life held little of joy for me; my promotion, my dreams, had all faded away and were gone with the days that had passed. I was weary of going on and on in a meaningless ritual. I felt my life had been wasted. The struggle to stay alive in that wicked sea had been merely reflex, my habitual answer to opposition and injustice, with no thought to why I should thus bother to save so worthless a life.

The sand scratched wetly at my cheek. I rolled over listlessly and stared up.

Yes, the arrogantly upflung tail of the Scorpion shone down on me. Inevitably my eyes were drawn to the dot of red fire that was Antares. That Scorpion star fascinated and compelled me. I did not know why save for the manner of my father's death and that my birthday was the fifth of November. I felt awe, and could not explain myself to myself.

What I did know was that I was shipwrecked on the west coast of Africa and for all my emotions like to perish here if I did not start thinking and planning to continue my meaningless life.

The slapping sounds of footsteps on the wet sand snapped me to attention.

"I am overjoyed to see that you have survived, Mr Prescot."

"Aye, doctor," I said, and stood up stiffly, dribbling seawater.

He walked up with his odd mincing gait, twisting his head birdlike to peer up at me. "It will be dawn very soon." He still carried—and I saw this with some surprise—his box under his arm.

"Aye."

His clothes were wet; but not as wet as mine. He did not appear in the least discomposed. He put the box down and sat on it, very awkwardly, first with his knees up past his chin and then with his skinny shanks outstretched. "I have seen no other survivors."

I couldn't say I was surprised but I made some formal noise of sympathy and relapsed into silence. This little fellow and his strange glassy eyes gave me a queasy sensation in the midriff.

"Do you think, Mr Prescot, that there are head-hunters in these parts? Cannibals?" He did not sound disturbed.

"Depends where we are. There will be slave trader stations along the coast, I dare say."

As the light strengthened and we could see the river streaming out to sea I realized with some concern that there was not a single sign of human habitation. In between the slave factories there might well be the headhunters the surgeon mentioned. I had never touched the disgusting Triangular Trade; and whilst I was well aware that would not stop an incensed native African fellow sticking his spear in me, I had no real belief that he'd pop me in his pot for lunch.

He cocked his narrow head up at me. Then he stood up, picked the box up and tucked it under his arm, and said: "Then, Mr Prescot, it would seem advisable for us to find some shelter."

That was fair enough, so I nodded and side by side we plodded up the beach towards the tree line. Birds were already out and about flaunting their gaudy colorings. The special and particular aroma of Africa wafted all about us, spicy, rich, exotic.

Just inside the trees Doctor Brighton stopped, put his box down and once more sat upon it.

Despite my feelings of the worthlessness of my life I still had to think of what to do and plan our next steps. We'd have to make our way along the coast until we ran across a factory. If there were people living here who had escaped the slavers chains—or who were the rump of families who had not—they would not look upon us with kindly eyes. No, sir!

The more immediate annoyance—to pitch the discomfort no higher—came from the myriads of creepy-crawlies and flying stinging insects. I was flapping away more or less continuously although I noticed with considerable resentment that the pests attacked Doctor Brighton far less than me. Maybe there was some vinegary substance in his blood that repelled them.

Eventually I found a suitable length of wood which felt hefty enough in my fist. This was not a weapon for the stinging pests. If we did meet up with hostile Africans I'd have to fight until they overcame or killed me. That is, if I couldn't parley with them first.

There was no question, absolutely no question at all, of a parley. A shining black fellow simply leaped out of a tree full on me.

His spear whistled past my ribs as I swerved, a most ugly sensation. He had a yellow bone through his nose and his hair stuck up ferociously. He was vengefully acting out years of resentment against people who looked like me. I couldn't blame him. But, being Dray Prescot, I had to stop him from degutting me.

He was active and quick and his spear looked to be damned sharp. We circled and he darted in and I deflected the spear along its haft with my left arm and clouted him over the head with the timber.

He fell flat with a whoofling whoosh of expelled air.

Standing back I saw the surgeon pointing a pistol at the recumbent form. His ferret-like face bore an expression of absolute fury.

So his precious box had not been his medical equipment at all. He shook the pistol and then glared at me. I avoided the gaze of those strange mirror-like eyes with difficulty.

"The powder's wet," I said. "No wonder."

A shout from the direction of the beach swung our instant attention there. A line of warriors, brave with feathers and spears, moved into view, angling along the sand towards the trees.

"We're in for it now." I put my foot on the chap I'd downed and rolled him over. He slumbered. It was not in my heart to kill him. "We'd best make ourselves scarce, doctor. If you would kindly lead on I'll follow."

"But—" he began. Then: "Yes, very well."

If we ventured too far into the forest, we'd become lost.

We had to keep in contact with the sea and make tracks as fast as possible. We were, there was no doubt about it, in an extremely parlous position.

A few moment's thought convinced me I could do more damage with my length of lumber than with the spear, which, although sharp, looked relatively fragile. As we set off I saw with a bemused amusement that the good doctor clutched his box with its brace of pistols as a drowning man clutches at a floating piece of wood.

I had to say: "You might as well leave that, doctor. The pistols are completely useless without powder."

His reply astounded me.

Speaking very earnestly, he said in a controlled voice: "Then, my dear Mr Prescot, you will have to manufacture some powder."

There was no rational answer I could give to that right off. So I contented myself with pointing along the fringe of the trees. His face contorted with an anger he could not suppress.

If he thought I could make gunpowder on a deserted African beach he'd have to think again. The idea was ludicrous. Mind you, I suppose if you found some saltpeter and some sulphur you could always make the charcoal from the forest. The inanity of the concept amused me, for I've always been a fellow who took amusement from situations perhaps not as salubrious as they might be.

One odd little thing made me grip the length of wood. When I'd grasped it in the first place to hit the chap who'd jumped from the tree I'd had a strange and powerful urge to take it into two fists instead of one. The need to deflect the spear with my arm also came oddly—but later, after it had happened. I felt obscurely that I could have slipped the spear aside with the wood held in my hands and then struck. Odd, as I say, odd.

The warriors moved away out of our sight to the rear. I fancied we'd not seen the last of them.

Doctor Brighton was clearly working himself up to say something. Taking the lead I ignored him and plodded along at the edge of the treeline. The sea roared away beyond the beach and the birds swooped and called and the smells of Africa wafted all about. By this time I was feeling decidedly peckish and began to wonder what the forest might offer in the way of edibles to a desperate and starving man.

There was no wreckage from poor old *Rockingham* scattered along the beach as one would expect. I found that strange—but, then, there were a lot of odd things going on that I couldn't figure out.

Midday when the sun took on its African ferocity we could do with our cocked hats. They'd gone with the ruination. Our naval uniforms were not exactly suitable for the climate, either.

The surgeon pattered up alongside. I had to admit that he did not appear at all apprehensive about the presence of hostile men wielding spears.

"Why, Mr Prescot, do you not make some gunpowder?" He sniffed. "We are, after all, are we not, in dire need of some?"

Exasperated with this little pettifogging fellow I said in a rather curt tone: "It's not that simple."

He'd had the presence of mind as *Rockingham* struck to bring pistols along. But then, surely, he knew only too well that they'd never fire once they'd been in the sea until after they'd been thoroughly dried and drawn and reloaded. And where were the charges to come from? Make 'em ourselves!

"What is the problem?" Now his voice took on a sharpness.

I told him that if he knew anything about the arcane art of manufacturing and milling gunpowder he'd know we did not have the wherewithals to hand.

"What do you need?"

This was becoming ridiculous. I sighed. "We could probably make some passable charcoal—"

"Charcoal?"

"But as for the rest of it, Doctor Brighton, I think it highly unlikely. In fact, my dear sir," I went on, trying to keep the annoyance down, "I think it as likely as seeing the cow jump over the moon."

The sharpness in his face changed in a subtle way to an expression of mulish obstinacy. The anger suffusing him, although controlled for the moment, put a tiny tic at the corner of his mouth. He mumbled to himself, shaking his head, not looking at me.

Satiated with his nonsense I set off at a smart clip. The way was probably the most difficult part for fallen branches and tangles of creepers. I certainly had no desire to venture further into the forest nor did I wish to reveal ourselves on the beach to the warriors.

Now this fatuous Doctor Brighton wasn't, I supposed, too imbecilic a fellow. Clearly he knew practically nothing about guns. He'd been trying to help. Relenting a trifle I slowed my pace. He was quite ignorant of my powers of hearing for he muttered on to himself in the way folk do who are wrought up by frustrated fury. I took the distinct impression that his anger was not directed at me; rather he was profoundly annoyed with himself.

His disjointed mumblings contained a recognizable sentence:

"I suppose I'll have to start again at the beginning." And another: "Extremely tiring business."

That was true, trying to walk through the tangle of the forest floor.

My mind caught a fascinating and not altogether impossible idea. The gale might have driven other ships towards the coast. On the thought I scanned out to sea, seeing the horizon rim as a silver bar against the blues above and below. Not a speck of sail could be seen.

The surgeon was continuing to complain away as I searched that empty ocean. Abruptly he let out a sharp cry, which was followed by a heavy crash. I swung about.

He'd caught his foot in a creeper and fallen toe over tip. Now he was struggling away and further entangling himself in the vines. He was cussing a blue streak, too, good round Naval oaths interspersed with odd, barbaric-sounding names I'd never heard of.

Reaching him and concealing my unkind amusement at his plight, I ripped vines away and took him under the armpits and stood him up. As I did so I swiveled around to face the sea.

Holding the surgeon I gaped out across the water like a loon. Less than a league off from the beach a long line of hills rose from the sea, green hills, with clumps of trees and streams running down in pretty waterfalls.

The familiar distant bar of the horizon so familiar to me from years at sea was gone. Hills!

Hills! Growing out of the Atlantic Ocean!

The sun must have addled my brains. I shook my head, blinked, looked again. The range of hills remained solid and firm rising from the sea—and! And now the rich golden sunlight changed. Distinctly before me on the sand shadows stretched foreshortened, twin shadows, two shadows of me, one tinged a ruddy red the other suffused with green. The hills under that ruby and emerald light curved around north and south to enclose the Atlantic Ocean into the compass of a lake.

Stresses and strains had taken their toll. Perhaps the trick of light was my brain trying to escape from reality, perhaps the sun had done for me, perhaps I was truly going insane.

Doctor Brighton twisted in my grasp and looked out to sea.

"Oh, Dokerty take it!" The sheer fury in him shook his slight frame. He turned his face up to glare on me.

Those strange glassy eyes looked into mine.

Three

I, Dray Prescot, First Lieutenant of His Britannic Majesty's seventy-four gun ship *Roscommon* stared in utter amazement at the file of Royal Marines as they answered the summons of 'Clear for Action!' 'Beat to Quarters!'

The drums roared and throbbed through the ship. Men were fitting chain slings to the yards and preventer stays, rigging nets. The powder monkeys were sloshing water over the decks and strewing sand. The guns were being readied, loaded and run out, twelve pounders on the upper deck, twenty-fours on the gundeck, for *Roscommon* was a leaky old tub of a vessel and well past her prime. All the ordered confusion of a line of battle ship sailing into action pulsed around me; but I gawped at the red coated Marines.

Barefoot! All the Marines were barefoot just like ordinary seamen! Even as I stared, incredulous at such a display, a sudden sheet as of lightning flashed down across the deck and was gone. I blinked. All the Royal Marines wore decent shoes.

Useless to shake my head. I had undergone a vision of some kind and now normalcy had resumed. I swallowed down—hard. Bigod, was I going insane after all my arduous years at sea? Still I had not been posted, and not likely to now, and so would remain a lieutenant until my hair went grey and I was tossed onto the beach to rot.

The sun shone, there was no glitter of stars above so that I might seek out that enigmatic spark of red that was Alphii Scorpio, Antares. How incongruous that a grown man living in despondent depths all his life should fancy he received some surcease from a mere star! Maybe I was going insane. There were very many famous mad captains in the Royal Navy, and we had one aboard *Roscommon* with us now.

The slight form of Doctor Hastings came into view as I turned away from gawping at the Marines. He favored me with a small grimace, and looked away. That pleased me. I didn't like his damned glassy eyes, believe me!

Ostentatiously I hauled out my watch and consulted it. Now this was an action completely abnormal for me. Oh, yes, I'd check the times of setting and handing sail, of loading and firing the guns. That watch dominated the lives of the hands. But now we were really going down into action was not the time for flamboyant gestures of that sort. On the thought the watch whisked away. I took a turn up and down, hands tucked into the small of my back, cocked an eye aloft, performed all the rituals of a sea officer on duty.

The Frenchman bearing down on us was a damned eighty.

We'd fight. We had to. All the hallowed traditions of the Royal Navy enshrined in this ship and her company dictated no other course. And, naturally, no other course would enter the mad block head of our captain. So I shrugged off the weird hallucination of Royal Marines improperly dressed and took a long look at the Frenchman.

She looked a beautiful sight, there was no gainsaying that. She appeared to gleam out there across the water, her sails puffed to the breeze, the canvas drawing sweetly as she bore down. She was an eighty and her captain must fancy his chances against an old seventy-four. The difference was not merely that of six guns. Oh no! She was brand new. She was sizeably larger than us, longer and broader. She carried long forty-two pounders and twenty-four pounders against our inferior armament. She was built massively yet so balanced as to form one of the best fighting machines afloat. Her complement would be far greater than ours, perennially short of men as the Royal Navy was. I felt my fists clench at the prospect before us.

"You do not like the Frogs, then, Mr Prescot."

Doctor Hastings, like a sparrow, sidled up. He stared at me in his disconcerting way. Oddly enough I detected a calculating quality in that look.

"What's that got to do with it?" I turned back and looked once more at the Frenchman. "They're a fishy lot, to be sure, but—"

I halted my babbling tongue. I wasn't going to tell him that the French were a brave and determined race of people who'd given us enough bloody noses in our time. That kind of honest appraisal of the enemy, Monsieur Crapaud, was not in tune with the thinking of the period. It was all: "One Englishman's worth three Froggies"—that kind of nonsensical rubbish. My habit had always been to keep my lips buttoned, and, certainly with this odd little surgeon, there were the best of reasons not to change now.

The fact that he was on deck at all at this time as we prepared for action meant he had completed his below decks arrangements. The surgeon's loblolly boys and the purser would have placed ready the canvas to carry the wounded below, the blankets spread on sea chests, the buckets to carry away portions of anatomies sawn from living bodies.

With everything prepared, it was now time for the captain to give his speech. Captain Parsons gripped the quarterdeck rail and lifted his ranting voice. Insane he might be, intolerant, lacking patience; he remained a serving captain in the Royal Navy and he knew what was required in this situation.

He told the hands that the miserable snail-eaters were lacking those great traditions of the Royal Navy, he bombasted how the English always won, he roused the hands out of his own simple beliefs in the service he had known all his life. He finished: "God save the King!" The hands cheered. This did not surprise me in the least. Now those jolly seamen could let go of all restraint and where in every day hardship they were disciplined and bullied and kept down with a rod of iron, now they could lash out and vent all their frustrated spleen.

This was not the first time I had been in action. I knew what horrors to expect. All I could do was carry out my duty with the same intolerant eye as ever. As, for instance—"You, Jock! Get that tackle straightened, you blagskite!"

The twelve pounder captain of the gun, this red-haired Jock, jumped and snarled his gun crew into putting the truck tackle ship shape. These men no longer were surprised I knew their names, an unusual accomplishment for a gold-laced officer. At the next gun along the gun captain, a magnificent fellow, Hans, who'd once been a Pomeranian Grenadier, laughed with his crew at Jock's discomfiture.

In normal times he'd have been triced up to receive a red-checked shirt at the gratings for insolence. Now, times were different.

The surgeon was peering at the gun with an intent scrutiny.

"Should you not be below, now, Doctor Hastings?"

He was quite calm. "I shall go below, Mr Prescot, when my presence is required."

There was no point in taking this any further. He was, after all, not a junior officer to be ordered about without consideration. But, the little snuffy fellow did stick to me like a burr.

The two ships neared. Silence fell, pierced by the rattle of blocks, the slatting of canvas, the rush and gurgle of the sea.

Captain Parsons, mad or not, knew how to handle his ship.

Both vessels maneuvered for position, one trying to bring all the massive destructive power of her broadside to bear, the other seeking to veer away and sneak up in the attempt to rake. Parsons was good; but it became instantly apparent that the French captain had other ideas. He did not wish to play at long bowls. Under topsails and topgallants he surged in with the clear intention of laying alongside and boarding.

The first shots fired out, flame and smoke gushed. The sound struck me as odd, muted, the full-throated bellow of big guns replaced by far lighter concussions. A seaman fell to sprawl motionlessly across the sanded deck. I could see no blood on him, and all his limbs were intact.

The Frog neared. The two vessels were wreathed in brownish smoke. The sounds reached me as though from underwater. In all my years at sea and the many actions in which I had been engaged I'd never experienced a battle quite like this. There was something deucedly odd about these proceedings.

The dead man was unceremoniously tipped over the side. Well, that was something usual and expected. Our mizen topgallant lurched, bent, smashed down in a shower of blocks and tackle. The chains held the yard at an angle; but detritus showered down through the nets. Smoke blew to obscure my vision.

I saw Hans, the ex-Pomeranian Grenadier, point his gun and then pull the lanyard. At that moment a block fell to smash into the deck less than a yard from me. I jumped, I admit it. Doctor Hastings let out a squeal. In the instant that I automatically turned towards him I caught sight of Hans stepping back, of a gush of smoke from his twelve pounder. The gun did not recoil. Then I'd swiveled to face Doctor Hastings.

He put up a hand and snapped out: "It is perfectly all right!"

Ignoring him I swung back to Hans. He was busy trying to reload the gun in its run out state. That he couldn't do this seemed to puzzle him. He must have failed to load the shot on top of the powder, although I couldn't believe that a Pomeranian Grenadier would fail in any item of duty.

"Haul in, you lollygagging blagskite!" I fairly yelled at him.

Smoke now settled about us like a shroud. Hans had his crew haul the twelve pounder in so that it could be reloaded.

The incoming shots must be hitting us, for I could hear screams and the rend of timber; here we seemed to be isolated in a tiny segment of the surrounding madness.

A billow of smoke wafted down about us. I sniffed. That didn't smell like gunsmoke. It smelled for all the world of woodsmoke with damp leaves thrown onto the blaze. Odd. Deucedly odd, by thunder!

A drilling pain as though a shipwright was driving his auger through my brains made me wince my eyes up instinctively. I'd suffered from these damned headaches on and off now for what—a couple of months or so—and I'd no idea why. I was having bad dreams, too, and as that eerie smoke writhed about the deck I had a flashing, lightning-stroke moment of dream recall. My nightmares were filled with vaguely seen bodies of men and women whose heads were half-concealed by clinging vapors but which appeared monstrous, uncanny, demonic.

Men and women with grotesque heads cavorted about me, mocking me, waving swords and spears at me, malefic.

But—but really only sensed and not seen in the way of dreams, there was a presence in the background, a form surrounded and infused by a roseate glow, a face, a face I knew I yearned for and could not reach. If only I could see that face all my problems would vanish and wisp away as the smoke wreathed me now.

The fact that Doctor Hastings had not gone below to tend to the wounded didn't bother me as it should have done. I did not know why this was. But it was so. He stood close by me, jumping in reaction to the crashes as shot struck us. He looked calm. I felt a little twinge of appreciation of him. His snuffy little figure had courage, there was no doubt of that.

A little powder monkey scuttled across to Hans's gun carrying his wood and leather bucket of cartridges. He looked like an imp from the nether regions, blackened with smoke, sweating, bare feet leaving a trail of blood across the sanded deck. He showed the signs of a lad who'd been in action a long long time. I frowned at that.

As usual, it seemed now, Doctor Hastings was looking at me. I checked a snarly little growl in my throat. The fellow spent most of his time staring at me, and although I found it in me to concede his courage, this perpetual observation was irritating, highly irritating.

Considering it high time I took a turn about the deck to check that the hands were sticking to their duty and their guns, I said: "We seem to bear a charmed life here, doctor. I'll—"

At that self-same moment the powder monkey let out a shrill yelp of pain. His thin boyish voice struck a pang into me. How well I remembered my days as a ship's boy, the hell of it, the fetching of powder in the midst of blood and death!

He sprawled all a-tumble. The shot had struck into his powder bucket and the charges, broken, scattered their contents over the deck. I stepped forward instinctively, quite unable to stop myself. I was the ship's First Lieutenant, far above helping little powder monkeys to their feet. But something in my blood would not be denied.

Hoicking him up and seeing he was not wounded, I felt my foot crunch the spilled powder. The first almost panic reaction vanished. The decks were sanded and well-watered so there was little chance of an explosion from the nails in my cheap shoes. I looked down.

Strange! I bent and lifted a pinch of the powder spilling from the broken cartridge. Sand! The gunpowder was sand!

Bewildered, I straightened up. What the blue blazes was going on!

As though on cue to wrench my mind from this baffling puzzle I saw a towering hull shoulder bluntly through the smoke overside. The French eighty was on us! She lifted high above our freeboard, two decker or not. Her gun-ports were open and the muzzles of her guns belched all along our quarterdeck. She rammed in with her fo'c'sle nuzzling our waist, swinging in, so that the bulwarks were within jumping distance. With the degree of tumblehome in ships necessitated by the need to mount the great guns as far inboard as possible, no real way of boarding could be found if the vessels merely lined up beam to beam. I had never been particularly fond of grasping a rope and swinging across the gap, as some foolhardy fellows did, for the waiting opposition. Now we were going to be boarded.

There was no time now to fret over sand instead of gun powder in a cartridge. That must be the evil handiwork of criminals in an arsenal conspiring with the gunpowder millers. God rot 'em!

In the old foretop hailing voice I bellowed.

"Prepare to repel boarders!"

And, again, louder still:

"Stand by to repel boarders!"

Noise wrenched the hearing from my ears. Smoke choked in baffling swathes and folds. The Frenchman's hull closed and when she touched the shock shuddered through old *Roscommon* like an earthquake.

A sea service pistol was gripped in my left fist, I only vaguely recalled drawing it from the sash around my waist. Three more sea service pistols snugged there, so that four Froggies would never live to reach our deck.

I drew my sword and faced that lofting hull.

Figures clustered along the bulwarks and up the ratlines. Quick, active fellows, Frenchmen, bold and brave. Their trouble as sailors in their navy was that they seldom put to sea, so their gunnery was nowhere as effective as ours. But they could fight!

Dark energetic shapes readied themselves to leap down on us.

At that climactic moment I felt the surgeon bump into my side. Instinctively my gaze switched from the menacing forms of the Frogs to his pallid face.

"Not now!" I fairly snarled at him.

Men were leaping down, their boarding pikes and cutlasses looking as deadly as our own. I saw those men. I saw them fair and square. I could not believe what my eyes were showing me.

They wore seamen's dress, yes. But their heads! Their faces!

They did not have human faces. Snarling with the ferocity of their attack they leaped down, frog-faced, fish-faced, snake-faced!

Men with the heads of fish crashed down onto our decks, hissing, shrieking, utterly impossible!

Doctor Hastings lifted himself up. He looked into my face. Even as his weird glassy eyes fastened upon mine, from somewhere so deep within my psyche I could have no coherent understanding, a word burst up into my brain. A single word screamed out into the madness.

"Shanks!"

Four

I, Dray Prescot, Second Lieutenant of his Britannic Majesty's thirty-two gun frigate *Aventure*, put a quick hand to my head as the blinding pains lanced through my brain. The world went black. These damn pains had been drilling into my head for some time now and I had absolutely no idea why.

Taking a measured breath I held very still, waiting for the agony to cease. Slowly the world brightened, the pain dribbled away, I could see again and my brain—my whole body—felt like a wrung-out dishcloth.

Aventure was in the process of picking up her buoy in the roadstead and in short order I'd be instructed to take the longboat and proceed to the arsenal. Across the calm water the busy activity of the port went on, the usual forest of masts and yards serrating the skyline. Smells of tar and seaweed, of cooking smoke, permeated the air. Up on the quarterdeck the captain, a useless, idle sort of fellow called Captain Stancher, was talking to the First Lieutenant, Mr Lawrence. He ran the ship with my assistance, and between us we kept everything taut, tight, and all ship-shape and Bristol fashion.

A slight form moved at my side and Doctor Worthing said in his reedy voice: "I would accord it a great favor, Mr Prescot, if I might be allowed to accompany you ashore."

"To the arsenal?"

My surprise was obvious.

He mumbled something about needing supplies and that a trip around the arsenal would be mighty interesting to a surgeon.

Seagulls cavorted overhead, flashing shapes of glinting white in the light, and they squawked no more shrilly than this little snuffy fellow with his weird and unsettling glassy eyes.

The surgeon went on: "You promised to instruct me in the arts of—ah—gunnery, and the manufacture of powder."

"I did?"

He nodded.

Sink me, I said to myself, I had no recollection of making any such promise. Still, if he said so, I suppose I had, probably when he was badgering me and the pains had been plaguing my addled brains. Anyway, there was no harm in it. Although why a respectable surgeon should wish to know about guns and gunpowder was beyond me. Probably he liked going shooting for sport. Not that shooting wild animals was my idea of sport, not at all, no sir!

Doctor Worthing favored me with a shrewd look.

"You did not sleep well last night, Mr Prescot?"

"No, Doctor, I did not."

In a few words I told him I'd been suffering the most odd, unsettling and damnable nightmares. All demonic creatures, vague monstrous-headed shapes, insubstantial threats from half-glimpsed forms. I wondered if he had something to give me a decent night's sleep.

As I watched him his reaction puzzled me. He did not exhibit the sort of professional concern that a doctor would show in dealing with his patient. Rather, he looked worried. He looked decidedly rattled. Something I'd said had touched a raw nerve, made his pale narrow face grimace in an expression I could only interpret as one of apprehension. Why should whatever was wrong with me make him frightened?

Deliberately changing the conversation, he swallowed, and said: "This—ah—art of gunpowder, Mr Prescot. It is dangerous?"

"Decidedly so if you're not as scrupulously careful as a nun."

He digested that as the last twinges of pain dissipated from my skull. He looked out over the bulwarks. I followed his gaze. The sight that greeted me made me frown. Odd. The familiar skyline, the frieze-like silhouette of the buildings of the dockyard, looked shrunken, somehow. Smoke rose from chimneys, busy activity took place in what I fancied was a circumscribed compass, and that, of course, was a nonsense. We were in the heart of a mighty machine of naval might, throbbing with the sinews of war, wholly devoted to the fight against those rapscallion revolutionaries, a nation of Jean Crapauds led by the Corsican bandit.

The surgeon coughed, a light, delicate sound. "I greatly appreciate your kind consideration of me, my dear Mr Prescot. How exactly is the danger to be apprehended?"

Sink me! I said to myself in something like despair over his callowness. Surely, in his naval service, in these sporting hunts at home, he must know? Surely? Country parsons, if that was where he hailed from, were notorious in their shooting proclivities.

A twinge of pain hit me, only a slight one, rather like a twelve pound shot caroming around inside my skull instead of a thirty-two. Why I hadn't mentioned to this weird little surgeon the face I tried to see in my dreams I felt was because that belonged to me, too deep down. Ah, that face and form! Tantalizing, shrouded in roseate mists, hidden, I knew that I would give all the world to reach out and seek the surcease for which I craved, not understanding, yet knowing that nothing, nothing whatsoever, was more important to me—even my life.

Who was this tantalizing woman, this unreachable lady for whom I knew without any question whatsoever I would lay down my life and joy in the giving of it?

Everything around me in these latter days somehow appeared at an angle to reality, a remarkably idiotic observation but one I felt obscurely to hold more truth than I realized. Doctor Worthing, for his part, clearly harbored some inner apprehension. For all the turmoil simmering away within him you had to grant he possessed impeccable manners. He remained exquisite in his profusions of interest in all there was to know of gunpowder and guns. Damned odd.

I gave him a quick glance. I was still uneasy about those damned staring eyes of his. His face, always pale and drawn, looked now positively haggard. With a little shock I realized the man was tired out, holding complete fatigue at bay only by an effort of will.

Just why I should feel sorry for him I couldn't say. The fact remains, I did.

A fellow like myself who'd clawed his way up onto the quarter deck through the hawsehole seldom if ever had time for pitying anyone. My life had been one of hard knocks and struggling just to stay afloat and of having hopes of promotion denied time after time.

All the same the agitation and exhaustion in the little surgeon affected me. About him there clung now a distinct impression of a man haunted by a doom he struggled futilely to escape.

All the routine tasks required of a ship's company tying up in port rattled on about us. These things were so much a familiar part of my life they passed remark only when anything that should not occur took place. Then, like any ship's officer, I became hell on wheels.

Turning to flick my gaze along the larboard quarterdeck carronades, I swung back to stare hard at the first twenty-four pounder. A raffle of ropes lay untidily half over the carriage and slide. I knew my face contorted instantly into a black mask of fury, a reaction I could not halt—nor would I wish to do so.

Hands were just standing by, doing nothing. At least they had the sense not to be jabbering away.

I shouted.

"Get that raffle stowed, you idle layabout blagskites!"

I glared at a bosun's mate. "Use your starter on 'em!"

He jumped, a brawny raggedy sort of fellow called Joachim, and rapped out a quick: "Aye aye, sir!" before swishing his rope's end down smartly. It cracked against tight white trousers.

The hands seized on the mess, heaving. A line was caught underneath the carronade. What happened then made me blink, shut my eyes, open them again in total disbelief.

A couple of the seamen simply lifted the whole carronade up, others hauled the lines free, and the weapon was plunked down again.

That couldn't happen; but it had.

I put a hand to my head. No pain had returned; but I felt completely disorientated. Was I going insane?

About to ask Doctor Worthing what he had seen, I was halted by his quick words. "A boat is putting off towards us, Mr Prescot. I wonder what their news is."

Despite my own confusion I could not fail to notice his obvious alarm. He was fairly hopping from one foot to another. He stared over the rail and his narrow face drew down into lines more haggard than ever. He looked sick.

The port officials would naturally come out to an incoming ship—the Port Admiral would have something to say if they didn't—so I couldn't understand what the surgeon was worried about. That he was deeply disturbed was obvious.

Still, that was all a part of his enigma. I tried to get my fuddle brains around what had happened with the twenty-four pounder carronade. The men hadn't even used handspikes! A hail from the approaching boat brought me back to what was happening, so I would have to push the conundrum aside till later. Odd, though, mighty odd!

The boat hooked on and the first aboard was a hefty-looking lieutenant. He just stepped straight inboard and marched towards us without as much as a word or a salute. Ready to give him the rough edge of my tongue for so flagrant a breach of naval etiquette, I was further astonished by the altogether unacceptable state of his uniform.

The fellow was big, all right, with bright blonde hair and bright bronze face. The brightness did not extend to his buttons which were filthy, as were his shoe buckles. And—he wore no hat. I opened my mouth to let rip, and closed it with a snap, and just stared, appalled.

Doctor Worthing let out a kind of whimpering moan and scuttled to crouch at my back.

The bulky lieutenant's strange uniform split along his arms and legs. Those dirty buttons flew off like bullets. He was swelling. He grew. His shoes cracked open and he stepped forward on splayed and hairy feet. Hair sprouted over his face and body as the uniform disintegrated. He grew monstrously. Arms raked up and hairy claws extended in a gesture of malevolent fury. The fellow turned into a monster, a demon from hell! He roared in insensate fury and rushed down upon us in the grip of uncontrollable rage. He foamed, the white flecks flying from that wide, cruel, fang filled maw.

Seized in a killing frenzy the demon charged!

Doctor Worthing clung to my coat and screamed.

He shrieked over and over.

"Ibmanzy! Ibmanzy!"

Five

I, Dray Prescot, Vovedeer, Lord of Strombor and Krozair of Zy, remembered. I remembered!

In all the crashing avalanche of memories that smashed into my brain, one and one only was of any true significance. Not who I was. Not the Dray Prescot who was emperor of this and king of that. Not my friends, not my family. Certainly not this crazy ibmanzy lusting only to rip my head off my shoulders.

No, oh no! One person—Delia! Delia of the Blue Mountains, Delia of Delphond!

The racket the ibmanzy was making got on my nerves. The damn thing was interfering with my thoughts, my luxurious thoughts, of Delia. Ah—and I'd still half-remembered and still hungered for her through those roseate mists that had clouded my mind. Still, by the Black Chunkrah! I'd have to do something with this pesky demon before he ripped me into little pieces.

Even as Doctor Worthing shrieked and the ibmanzy roared, I experienced a jolt of guilt that I had so cavalierly disregarded the love I bore for my family—no, I could not forget them or my blade comrades.

With a single all-embracing sweep I discovered what really was the frigate I'd thought was *Aventure*. A mock-up, a sham, a thing of thin wood and canvas, the carronades mere lumps of wood painted grey and black. No wonder the fellows had hoisted one up so easily.

On that realization I checked the pistol. A stupid lump of wood and metal fashioned ludicrously into the likeness of a sea service pistol, the thing was completely useless. I hurled it straight at the charging demon, grabbed Doctor Worthing around the waist and jumped overboard.

But no! This was not Doctor Worthing, ship's surgeon, nor was he Doctors Milius, Brighton or Hastings.

Sink me! I said to myself as we hit the water in a fountain. I know who you are, you cramph!

Oh, yes, this was the Illusionist of Winlan, the famous Sorcerer of Balintol, San W'Watchun. As he tried to struggle in my grip and I took him in hard and started swimming to the shore, I recalled his Opaz-forsaken glassy eyes. He'd had me in a mind spell from the moment his gaze locked with mine in his confounded palace in his capital city of Winbium. He was the Illusionist who'd erected a damn great wall around his country. The place was infested with mighty warriors with their own harsh codes. And me, Dray Prescot? The Star Lords had dispatched me here to destroy the damned Dokerty lovers' Prism of Power, the very agency that created the monstrous ibmanzy. The thing was prancing up and down on the laughable imitation of a thirty-two gun frigate of the Royal Navy of Earth, foaming and screaming and—would you believe it—beating its Opaz-forsaken and hairy chest.

The monstrous thing did not show any willingness to follow us into the water. It simply followed what it was created to do, and programmed as a devilish killing instrument it started across the deck tearing off the heads and limbs of those unfortunates not quick enough to escape.

This W'Watchun of the various terrestrial names culled from my memories, spluttered and tried to struggle. He was clearly not used to the water and presumably knew little of swimming. He tried to say something, clumsy words after the fashion of 'help me', and water sloshed into his mouth so that he choked and spat.

"Keep quiet, san," I said in a voice understandably harsh and uncompromising. "I ought to wring your scrawny neck for all the trouble you've put me through."

"You don't understand—" he managed to get out before he took another mouthful of water.

I understood what my eyes told me. The dock buildings were mere facades, like a film set of Earth. The whole arrangement was set in a lake, and the green hills I'd seen growing out of the Atlantic Ocean were really and truly there, rounded hills with trees and grass and silvery waterfalls.

The obvious conclusion about the slovenly lieutenant who'd turned into a demon was that he'd been sent by person or persons unknown to kill San W'Watchun and probably also me. If the ibmanzy had been created by my old adversary Kov Khon the Mak then I was certainly the target. I had the niggling feeling that what W'Watchun had been up to tinkering with my memories had to do with his welfare. He must have enemies, too.

Just how great were his powers, anyway? They must be prodigious for him to have created all the illusions that appeared real to me. Making me see the small yellow sun of Earth instead of Zim and Genodras streaming their mingled beams of ruby and emerald across the land had to be sorcery of a very very high order indeed.

Everything else he'd made me see had been extremely well done. In those moments of stress or surprise his concentration had faltered, so that I'd glimpsed a small part of the truth through the torn curtain of deception. Then he'd simply hoicked me out of that situation and started me on another section of my memories. When he made a mistake—as in the case of the bare-footed Marines—he'd corrected it instantly and no doubt considering I was sufficiently under his control had simply gone on instead of starting afresh. This made me guess that each scenario took time to prepare.

The shock hit me. How long had all this been going on?

The Star Lords had sent me here to Winlan to destroy the devilish Prism of Power concealed in the Flutubium that Khon the Mak and his crony priests of Dokerty had flown out of burning Oxonium. If they were allowed to make more ibmanzies and let them loose upon Balintol, I would have failed the Star Lords. Then I could look forward to being flung ignominiously back to Earth, four hundred light years away. That, I could not tolerate.

Yet, despite all this, despite the fact I was probably surrounded by enemies, that I might be subjected to the designs of this Illusionist again, that a monstrous great demon thirsted for my blood, the wonderful fact remained. I was not really on Earth. I was on Kregen! That, alone, was recompense enough—for now, by Krun, for now!

The Illusionist lollopped along in my grip, spouting water every now and then, towed along like a waterlogged hulk. Over his head I could see the make-believe frigate. The ibmanzy was dancing up and down like a crazed dervish and the pantomime crew were jumping off like fleas leaping from a smoked ponsho fleece. I didn't smile.

The fraught question remained. Just how long had all this been going on?

That was going to be the first question I asked W'Watchun when we reached shore. A quick glance in that direction showed me considerable confusion among the folk gathered there. Some wore the black robes and tall black hats that were the clothes of Illusionists. There were guards, too, bulky mercenaries in brass and leather. There were women in the groups, no doubt many of them slaves.

Oh, yes, I might have found in my flinty heart some jot of sympathy for the little surgeon aboard one of His Britannic Majesty's ships; for the Illusionist of Winlan of whom I had heard nothing but evil since my arrival in Balintol I could harbor only vengeful resentment. What he wanted or what his plans were—apart from his pathetic desire to learn the secret of gunpowder—I could have no idea.

Whatever he was up to, he most certainly had not gone the right way about gaining the friendship of the fellow who was supposed to be the Emperor of Emperors, the Emperor of All Paz. And then, as I sloshed along towing the sorcerer, you may well imagine the comical disgust with which I realized how my thoughts were going. All this emperor nonsense meant nothing. It was dreamed up by the Everoinye in furtherance of their plans for Kregen. I had to go along with it or risk being banished to Earth.

So, with memories restored and thoughts all jumbled up betwixt ironic sympathy and malevolent resentment, for W'Watchun had me unsure of my own feelings, I reached the shore.

Naked arms reached down for us. We were dragged out by brawny slaves wearing the dismal grey slave breechclouts. Water sprayed as we shook ourselves. W'Watchun sneezed. Slave girls wearing grey loincloths wrapped fluffy yellow towels about him. A general fuss was made as I stood there, dripping water, watching the mercenary guards. They were of a variety of races of diffs and looked useful. Clearly, they were waiting for orders regarding my fate.

Whilst it looked as though this was a ticklish moment, I had no real apprehension that the Illusionist would have me killed. Had he wanted to do that, the thing could have been done when he'd taken me up with his diabolical illusion of Delia. No, he wanted to know about gunpowder. I wanted to know why he wanted to know.

Very carefully I refrained from looking at his face.

Eventually he cracked out in his reedy voice: "Dry him down, you onkers. Bratch!"

Immediately the half-naked slave girls started on me with their towels. The unreality of all this—this apparently normal way of drying off the master and the man who had saved him from drowning—could not be allowed to affect me. The situation was not normal. The damned ibmanzy was still prancing about on the tatty deck of the imitation frigate. The guards by me on the bank wanted to use their swords on me. The confounded Illusionist could stare into my eyes and then—Vox knew what might happen or where I'd imagine myself to be.

Mind you, the little fellow looked done in, exhausted, the pallor of his face turning green at the edges.

The other Illusionists in their tall black hats crowded around him, half a dozen of them, all very grave and drawn-faced. What they said I could not overhear. They kept pointing out to the ibmanzy. How much, I found myself wondering, could poor old ruthless W'Watchun trust them?

Presently a litter carried by eight Brukaj arrived with a grim-faced Chulik in charge. His attire was slightly unusual in that he wore a grey tunic of simple cut without adornment but his belt carried two swords and two daggers. His tusks were clean and without any gold or silver banding. He cleared the guards out of the way with a balass wand, gold knobbed. He was most brisk.

Following the litter came two sylvies almost clad in flowing draperies. You know my feelings about sylvies, that they are too voluptuous, too much of pulchritude, yet often good-hearted. These two clearly served the Illusionist along with the Chulik. W'Watchun was picked up in powerful Yellow-Tusker arms, deposited in the litter. The sylvies hung over the sides, oohing and aahing, and off they went.

A bulky Rapa, his feathers violet and green, strutted over to me. He was clad in the glittery way some cadades like to dress and as the captain of the guard had clearly received instructions about me. Expecting rough treatment, I was surprised.

"You come along with me, dom. We'll soon fix you up with dry clothes." He swiped a fist along his beak. "Proper clothes, not those fantastic things you're wearing. Haw! You look a right sight."

So much for the blue and white uniform of the Royal Navy!

A chorus of startled cries burst out like echoes of his words. "Look! The Monster!"

Before I turned to look out towards the frigate I knew what was happening. The demon was smashing the poor human body to pieces. The thing bloated, flailing its arms about in manic gestures of supreme anger. It began to melt and then dropped down so that the final deliquescence vanished beyond the fake gunwales. On the shore a kind of shiver passed over the people clustered there.

A Royal Marine climbed up out of the water, blowing after his swim. His coat pooled drops of red dye and I was irresistibly reminded of the way my red coat had dropped imitation blood about my feet in the famous chariot race down south in Kildrin. "By Uri!" he exclaimed, and spat more water. "That monster nearly took my head off!"

"Well, he didn't!" The cadade glared at the dripping marine. "And get those stupid clothes off and get yourself back into uniform, you great fambly!"

"Quidang, Jik!"

The guard captain made a disgusted noise in his throat and turned back to attend to me.

That little incident perked me up. The situation was completely familiar to me. These were people of a kind I'd dealt with all my life. They stood guard over the shrunken form of the Illusionist. If only, I said to myself in a distinctly disgruntled frame of mind, if only I could make up my mind about the blasted fellow!

The hectic incidents of the past moments appeared in retrospect to be marvelously alarming to these folk—and no wonder! As the various parties moved off a distinct cooling of the emotions could be felt like a visible miasma. I shook my head. Was I still suffering hallucinations? Was that scheming cramph W'Watchun up to his diabolical tricks again?

The violet and green feathers of the Rapa captain of the guard ruffled in a slight breeze as he took stock of me. "I am Jiktar Ronun ti Bjorfling. I know who you are. You call me Jik. What do I call you?"

This strict attention to protocol did not surprise me. After all, ranks are ranks, even if I generally despise them, and the military mind has to have affairs organized down to the last jot and tittle. This goes for two worlds, at least.

I considered.

The correct way to address me was Majister. You know my feelings on that score. This Jiktar Ronun seemed a decent sort of fellow, and I did not add in these latter days of mine upon Kregen, 'for a Rapa.' So I said in a firm voice: "You call me Majis, Jik."

"Quidang!"

With that settled Ronun bellowed to his men and we all marched off very smartly, heading away from the lake and towards the cluster of white buildings set against the side of a green hill.

The Suns of Scorpio were moving across towards the late afternoon, shedding their streaming mingled radiances of emerald and ruby. Ah! What it is to breathe the air of Kregen! I opened my lungs and stuck out my chest and strode along and almost—almost—broke out into a rollicking song of Vallia.

As I had so often thought during my adventures upon this gorgeous and terrifying planet, so now I hungered to get the task for the Star Lords over and race back home to Vallia and Valka. Would Delia be there? I lengthened my stride and the guards moved more briskly to keep up. Even in these latter days of mine upon Kregen the power of the Everoinye still dominated all my actions.

The Prism of Power must be destroyed before maniacal ibmanzies swept all of Balintol into ruin.

The cadade was most punctilious. As the guard captain for the chief person of this country he stood in a high and privileged position. He called me majis without demur. I was ushered into a building of white walls and green roofs, with little of the odd architecture that characterized the capital. Plants grew and fountains tinkled. All very nice. I stayed alert.

Conducting me into an anteroom furnished in some luxury, Ronun excused himself and said he would order food and that he would be back shortly. Perhaps he saw through all this emperor nonsense and discerned in me a kindred mercenary spirit, a brother paktun.

A guard was posted outside the door as was perfectly proper.

Presently food was brought in by a charming little girl who wore only the grey slave breechclout. She put the tray on a side table and glanced up shyly. In all the grandiose plans I had been following for the Star Lords, the issue of the abomination of slavery had rather taken a back seat of late. In no way—no, by Krun, in no way!—would I ever accept slavery if I could put the infamous practice down. At the moment the evil had to be accepted for what it was. Perhaps, if what I considered the impossible dreams of the Everoinye to make me the Emperor of All Paz came to pass, why, then slavery would be declared illegal by the stroke of a pen.

The food's aroma awoke my taste buds and I realized that perhaps my little erstwhile shipmates Doctors so-and-so etcetera had not been feeding me properly. I tucked in. By the time I reached the silver dish of palines I was in a more sanguine frame of mind over my immediate future. A muted thump from the corridor outside the door made me frown. I wiped my lips with the yellow serviette and stood up. By the time I'd reached the door and opened it and looked out the corridor was empty of life.

This intriguing world being Kregen, I at once suspected the unfortunate sentry had been thumped on the head and carted off.

Naturally, there were many other more rational explanations—but! Oh, no, by Vox, I said to myself. Something fishy is going on.

Just about to close the door I saw a couple of people come trotting along the corridor. They wore decent servant's clothes, so they were not slaves. They were both apims, the man and woman, and they both wore expressions of great anxiety.

"Majister!" said the man, almost stammering. "Please pardon our dereliction of duty!"

"Your clothes, majister!" The woman made an encompassing gesture. "Please, come with us. We have fresh dry clothes ready."

The Suns of Scorpio had dried my rig and it was not uncomfortable to me. Besides, who was more used to working in wet clothing than your barnacled old sailorman?

Still, these two were insistent. The thought of shifting into some proper Kregan clothes was tempting. I nodded brusquely and we set off along the corridor.

They conducted me to the end of the corridor where we entered a narrow passage with a crystal roof. The Suns were almost gone and the slanting rays of red and green lay sharded and patterned on the walls. At the far end a short corridor led to what was clearly an anteroom. The two servants had not spoken and the silence seemed to me to lie a trifle oppressively.

They showed me into a luxuriously furnished chamber. Through an open door I caught a glimpse of a bed in the adjoining room.

The thought did occur to me that all this was more illusion. Maybe W'Watchun was at his tricks again. I didn't think he would give up his quest for the secret of gunpowder easily. Still, the sight of a wardrobe packed with Kregan clothes of the many varieties worn here in Balintol cheered me up. The most important, as you who have followed my narrative will know very well, was to secure a red breechclout about me. The two servants remained mute in a corner. I rejected a shamlak and chose a nice but sober tunic of yellow linen with silver around the hems. At once I felt at home.

The sounds of light laughter and happy chattering heralded the entrance of a troupe of young women. There were six of them and they were all sylvies. The two servants bowed and left. I stared at these voluptuous maidens in their diaphanous gauze. They stared boldly at me and in the next instant, I knew, they would leap passionately on me.

My flinty old sailorman's heart sank. "Oh, my Val," I said to myself. "Now what?!"

Six

An avalanche of flesh swept me off my feet.

Multi-colored veils and scarves, chiffons, silks, swirled about me. Rosy limbs flashed before my eyes. Rippling hair, blonde, auburn, black, poured like a cataract over me. Red lips, moist and pouting, greedily sought to plant wet kisses anywhere they could.

I tell you in all sober truth, that feminine onslaught of pulchritude made me blench like any outright coward far more, far, far more, by the Lady Fayreen the Abandoned, than any vove cavalry charge of the wild Clansmen of Segesthes!

Over I went and clutching hands grasped my feebly protesting form. In a riotous rout of shrill laughter I was carried off into the adjoining bedroom, thumped down on the bed, and smothered with eager ladies who in that time had contrived to discard all their draperies.

By Krun! I felt like that fabled idiot who felled a tree upon himself and was entrapped all night in the leaves and branches.

Something, quite clearly, had to be done, and done with the utmost promptitude. Something drastic, too, into the bargain, by Vox!

My first attempt at levering myself up merely afforded these wanton damsels the opportunity to tear off my nice new tunic.

Only when these highly-excited ladies began to get extremely familiar with my person was my courage restored. As gently as possible I disengaged an arm about my neck only to have another wrap itself lovingly about me. I heaved to no avail. All the time the Sylvies kept up high excited cries. They were enjoying themselves in their own particular fashion. If I didn't escape soon then I was done for.

With a gigantic heave I rolled up into a cowering ball. All tucked up I managed to roll myself off the bed and in a screaming tangle of naked arms and legs we all fell on the floor.

Lusting after me as they were and mighty rapid with their advances, these easy ladies could not quite match the speed of a warrior, a paktun, a fellow whose sheer speed has got his neck out of many an ugly scrape in his hectic life. I reared up like a stag with the hounds clinging to him.

"Enough!" I bellowed in the old foretop-hailing voice. "Ladies! Have done!"

"But we haven't!" squeaked a lass whose fingers were hooked into my red breechclout.

Reaching down I removed her dainty digits very firmly. I sprang away from the tumultuous heap of rosy forms. I own I panted a trifle, too, after this slight exertion. What a pickle W'Watchun had got me into now! No doubt he thought I would readily succumb to this amorous assault. No doubt he imagined one or t'other of these over-endowed maidens would whisper in my ear among the sweet nothings, the question: "And, my love, just how do you make gunpowder?"

Standing back from them by the door I watched suspiciously as they picked themselves up and sorted themselves out. Truth to tell, they were really lovely examples of girlhood, although sylvies. What, I couldn't stop myself from wondering, might have happened had W'Watchun sent beautiful young apim girls?

One thing was absolutely certain. These damsels of pleasure were not about to give up the struggle. They gathered themselves. They prepared to renew the combat.

There was no point in me staring appalled at them. They had to be shuffled off, sharpish. Very sharpish, by Krun!

They moved forward like a phalanx. Slowly, step by step, one shapely limb after another, they stalked me.

Reckoning my best avenue of escape was to slam the bedroom door and lock it, I seized the handle. They'd be locked in the one room of which they had most experience.

A deafening gong-note crashed through the room, jarring my ears, vibrating the furniture. The girls did not jump in startlement.

Their high laughter changed to shrill cries of lament. They looked shattered. Their heads drooped. Bent of back and resentful of feet, they trooped past me out the door, across the lounge and into the corridor. The last one did not slam the door after her, and that would have been perfectly in keeping with their dejection and disappointment.

So, I said to myself, rescuing the yellow tunic and donning it, the next Act is to follow.

The cloying scents of the women hung on the air, clinging, slow to clear and overpowering.

In keeping with many of the great nobles of Kregen, the fellow who entered was preceded and flanked by guards. These guards were not mercenaries. A single all-embracing glance told me they were young aspirants to warriorhood. They were not Kregan equivalents to terrestrial squires, although, I suppose, many of their rituals would harmonize with the concept of being a squire to a lord.

These youngsters were magnificently attired, girded with swords, and devoted to their lord to death.

As for the lord in question, at first glance I found some difficulty in placing him among the group of warriors I'd seen in San W'Watchun's private chamber before the Illusionist's damned glassy eyes had packed me off into a dreamland of Earth's Royal Navy. He'd been there, though, of that I was sure, lurking somewhat in the background of the forceful warrior group. He wore evening lounging robes of sober blue, massively gold-trimmed. All the same, despite his evening wear he had two swords strapped to his waist, and a couple of daggers on the other side to match them.

His face was unremarkable. He did have a reddish scar extending from just outside his right eye to the corner of his mouth. This, I judged, had been administered by a left-handed fighter or a fellow dealing out a backhanded blow; either way the stroke had caught this lord by surprise. His lips were thin and firm. His expression was haughty—but, then, of course, that was the normal facial grimace of these puffed-up great ones of the world.

The little whipper-snapper of a fellow at his side looked to be his son or nephew, aping his betters, callow, weasel-faced, and an unpleasant way about him of which one should be extremely wary.

On the lord's other side stood one of the illusionists with his tall brimless black hat a hand's-breadth shorter than the one worn by W'Watchun. This man's face, although he was apim, reminded me of a frog. His eyes bulged and his mouth pouted. What, I wondered, were his powers and how did they compare to crafty old W'Watchun's?

For a moment complete silence enveloped the room.

The lord lifted a be-ringed hand. A yellow lace kerchief dangled elegantly from his fingers. "You refused my hospitality. You, perhaps, do not care for sylvies." He made a graceful gesture. "They are overpowering to one of taste, I agree."

I nodded. I said nothing.

The little whipper-snapper made a snorting noise through his nose. "Perhaps he cares for—ah—others." He giggled wetly.

With a deliberate half-turn of my head which made it perfectly clear I was ignoring both the offensive remark and its perpetrator, I spoke to the lord. "There are no lahals between us. We have not made the pappattu."

A flush seeped along his cheekbones. If my deductions from the conversation with the cadade were right, protocol formed a very high priority in these stuck-up onkers' lives. He licked his lips.

"I am Kov Barca L'Lambton na Freydin. Llahal."*

"Llahal, Kov. You, I believe, know my name."

The son or nephew sucked in a sharp breath. His tight face went even tighter—and mean with it.

Now if my estimate of the power of formality and protocol among these people was right, if they were bound in a culture of manners, then I ought to chance my arm. I decided to play the great one right along with them—and bad cess to 'em all, the cramphs!

"Yes, indeed—" He seemed at a loss for words.

"Then you will do me the courtesy of addressing me properly."

He swallowed. For a fleeting moment I wondered if I'd overdone it. But what the hell! I had a job to do here and a pack of larded-up warriors must not be allowed to stand in my way.

The young warrior I'd considered as unpleasant shifted on his feet, from side to side. That weasel face screwed up even more. Mind you, as in previous cases, an unfortunate face and manner do not necessarily signify an unpleasant character. I could be misjudging him out of prejudice, and that, by Vox, would never do for an emperor.

He opened that moist mouth but before he could speak Kov L'Lambton cut in: "May I have the honor of presenting my nephew, Strom Marlo M'Maringo na Schull."

---

* Here Prescot gives the Kov's full name. He then adds that these ridiculously long names of multiple syllables are both tiresome and unnecessary to his narrative. Apparently the more wonderful deeds a warrior performed the more syllables he tacked on to the end of his name. *A.B.A.*

I just stared at him. I looked at him down my nose. I do not believe I wore that famous look men call the Dray Prescot Devil Look; but it must have been close, by Krun, pretty close!

He swallowed again, licked his lips. He stammered just a trifle. "Ma— Majister."

I nodded my head perfunctorily. "Lahal, Strom."

Of course, all this was petty, pettiness carried to an extreme that gave some malicious enjoyment. In addition I felt a stab of guilt at my own pettiness. Still, they deserved lessons like this. The real facts here were now becoming clearer. This pretty bunch had not been sent by San W'Watchun. The sentry outside my door no doubt really had been thumped on the head so that I could be spirited away here—wherever here was. The illusionist could easily have set up the whole thing. The walk through the corridor with the transparent roof could quite easily have brought me a considerable distance from the white building to which I'd been escorted. This place could be miles away and well out of W'Watchun's reach.

I decided I would wait to see what happened next.

"May I offer you some refreshment—ah—majister?"

Graciously inclining my head I indicated that would be in order and agreeable.

Scurrying servants brought in wine and glasses. They all looked half-scared out of their wits. Fortunately for what might have followed not one of them made a mistake and received a punishment that I might have been unable to tolerate.

We drank and the young warrior guards looked on impassively. They could not be left out of this equation, no, by Krun!

Gradually as we spoke of this and that the tension eased. My questions about this place, very natural given the circumstances, were evaded politely. I did learn that this Kov Barca L'Lambton possessed overweening ambition. This came out more in what he didn't say, and his bitter comments on a certain Kov Grogan G'Gulandor. The hatred between these two kovs could be sensed as Barca spoke like a fetid miasma in the air.

What also was interesting was that whereas I had assumed from the way the groups stood about in W'Watchun's chamber that they lined up by class, it now became apparent that alliances were formed across classes. This illusionist, whose name was Furney, worked for Kov Barca. Furney's name had no double initial; he lacked the Double, and his rank was obvious from the way the nobles treated him.

Truth to tell, I began to fret at this conversation. I was not tired. The jabbering went on and I wanted to say to Barca: "Get on with it, man! Tell me what you want."

He got around to that in a circuitous fashion. He mentioned W'Watchun a few times in the most general terms, only once allowing his passion to override his politeness. With great acrimony he spoke of the Illusionist's famous Wall. I gathered readily enough that he thoroughly detested the Wall.

Going on from that and recovering his poise, he came out with The Question. For a moment, I was disappointed. I'd quite thought he was going to ask me how to make gunpowder. Instead:

"Tell me, majister, what did San W'Watchun desire of you?"

By the dangling eyeballs and pustulated nostrils of Makki Grodno! So that was it! This fellow had no idea what W'Watchun was up to. Well, by Krun, no more had I. The secret of gunpowder was required quite apart from the obvious reasons for some other and much more pressing reason. W'Watchun's desperation was witness to that.

"The san? Oh, he was interested in my plans for Balintol."

I rather enjoyed that! Let 'em stew over the thought that I intended certain things for Balintol. Maybe, very probably, they'd be things that these high and mighty muck-a-mucks would not relish.

Mind you, this whole situation was highly farcical.

Here was I, supposed to be the Emperor of All Paz, kept as a virtual prisoner. I did not suppose if I asked to leave they'd let me go so tamely. Yet they were held in a kind of stasis of their own creation. Just because I'd been the Emperor of Vallia, and was known pretty well as Dray Prescot over the face of Paz, my reputation preceded me. This was not my doing. Well, not entirely. It was a combination here of that blessed or cursed yrium and the protocol of this warrior culture.

"I understand, majister, that some of the southern nations have accepted you as emperor." He sounded uneasy. Whipper-snapper sitting at his side kept fiddling with the hilts of his swords.

I nodded. "That is so, Kov. It is highly necessary for the welfare of Balintol that the nations co-operate against the Shanks."

"Once the Wall comes down we will—" He checked himself.

I didn't follow that. One thing you could say about this famous Wall was that it might keep the Shanks out of Winlan.

No knock on the door heralded the agitated entrance of a young warrior with blood upon his fancy neckerchief. He spotted Barca, rushed straight to him, bent down and whispered rapidly in the Kov's ear.

Kov Barca's face tightened into a meaner frown than even his nephew's weasely features could manage. He stood up abruptly.

Strom Marlo jumped up alongside his uncle. "What—?"

"Come along, Marlo. Don't chatter!" With that the kov strode for the door. He drew one of his swords. The young warriors were all attention at once and trooped out after him. Furney the illusionist slipped along with them. I nipped very smartly over to the door and caught the arm of the last young aspirant.

"What's going on, lad?"

He twisted his beardless face up to me. His expression was all sick worry. "Please—ma— majister—" He stuttered in alarm and confusion. "My lord—I must follow my lord—"

"Tell me what's amiss."

"Majister! I do not know. Please, let me go!"

I cast him off as one might cast away the hard rind of a heel of cheese. They schooled these youngsters well in obedience!

He fairly flew out after the others, his swords flapping up and down wildly. He, like his fellow aspirants, wore only a small neckerchief. Presumably these ridiculous folded, crimped, laced, flamboyant neckerchiefs were the insigne of warriorhood, like a terrestrial knight's spurs.

Oh, well, I said to myself. Let's just toddle along and see what there is to see.

Outside the room I looked around at once perceiving this palace did not resemble the corridor through which I had been conducted.

So the transparent-roofed corridor had been illusion at work, as I had suspected. This must be the palace of Kov Barca. Off I went in the direction of a hubbub of noise, shouts and screams and the evil sliding scrape of steel on steel.

This cacophony of noises were sounds very familiar to me during my headlong career upon Kregen, by Krun, yes!

Yes, this building was a palace with columns of marble, floors of marble, walls of marble. Much golden fancy-work adorned every cornice and ledge. Candelabra—no doubt imported ware—shed a mellow light. The scents were a trifle off, though, with a hint of drains seeping through the hanging flower baskets.

One of the young warriors stumbled past me, holding his head. Blood shone greasily and I saw he was trying to keep his ear from falling right off. The blow that had done that had been savagely delivered. Mind you, whatever fracas lay ahead, neither side might claim my allegiance, oh no, by Krun!

The lad staggered off and I moved on cautiously.

Standing just inside a tall doorway with golden zhantils prancing on the doors, I looked into the chamber beyond.

Well, they were at it in there, hammering away at one another. Every combatant appeared to be a warrior. I judged there were no paktuns present. This, then, must be a fight between the nobles. Of one thing I was absolutely sure. I wanted no part of it.

So I just stood there for a moment or two, at my ease.

These warriors had been trained up from childhood in the mores and customs of their warrior class. That included being unpleasant to slaves and anyone not their equal or superior. Also, it included long and intensive training in the arts of combat. My gaze sized them up with the cool professionalism of your experienced old fighting man.

Yes, and, well, they were good. No doubt of that. There did not appear to be any one single fighter far superior to any other.

They were all much of a muchness. They fought with academically-learned skills, very correct and very stiff. All the same, when a blow connected it did its work with dire results, as witness the poor lad whose ear had been nearly cut off.

There was some shouting, cries of encouragement and rallying shouts to a name. There were very very few calls of warning, from one warrior to another.

I felt in a most luxurious frame of mind, easy, casual, very comfortable. This was just like a spectator sport. This was, as you will readily perceive, highly unusual for me, Dray Prescot, who was far more accustomed to getting stuck into the combat and dealing and taking blows. But these people meant little to me, even as the Emperor of All Paz. I didn't like their customs. If they wanted to kill one another then that was fine by me.

There was one regret. I'd far sooner they got themselves killed fighting the damned Shanks.

Kov Barca was not in there fighting, as far as I could make out. By the richness of their armor and the ludicrous extent of their neckerchiefs, some of these combatants were nobles of various ranks.

That I couldn't see the nephew, this Strom Marlo, didn't surprise me at all. Still, to be fair to the pair of them they'd not been wearing armor. Maybe they were donning their metal as fast as they could buckle it up right now.

At a rough guess there must have been thirty or forty men on each side. On Barca's side there were about half aspirants and half fully-fledged warriors. Their opponents were all grown men. The combat roared on and more and more of Barca's followers joined in, running from various places within the palace. Just how this little lot would finish escaped me.

The obvious thought occurred to me that this Kov Barca L'Lambton had shown me courtesy after a fashion and hospitality that, naturally, he wouldn't know was not welcome. So, then, did that mean I had to rush in on his side? By the distended belly and massive thighs of the Divine Madam of Belschutz, no!

A veritable giant of a Fristle, swinging his scimitar in practiced sweeps, leaped from a shadowed alcove a few paces off from me and plunged towards the fray. He was a mercenary as his flying pakai testified together with the absence of a silly neckerchief.

One of the invading warriors with a curved moustache down to the lacy neckerchief under his chin and flailing two swords about, jumped for the Fristle. The blades whirled. The Fristle's scimitar became a blur and the overconfident warrior ducked smartly, thrusting up one of his swords to parry the blow. At the same time, with a nice precision a follower of Kurin could appreciate, he thrust his other blade straight forward into the cat-man's armpit crevice.

I blinked.

Somehow or other the Fristle was still standing and the surprised warrior surged forward off-balance. A young man of Barca's force stepped forward and chopped his opponent, sending him down spouting blood. The Fristle spun away into the conflict and I lost him among the battling bodies.

All the same, by the Black Chunkrah! That blade had gone right through him. And the weapon uplifted to deflect the scimitar had not done that; the scimitar had gone on to slice right through the warrior in the instant he had thrust.

So that meant that the illusionist, San Furney, was lurking somewhere in the shadows of a tapestry or column. He was sending phantom fighting men into the combat. They proved effective, no doubt of that, by Krun! The young lad had struck with the confused warrior at his mercy.

Oh, well. This farce had gone on long enough. There was no excuse for me to stay lollygagging about here enjoying the free spectacle of various self-important onkers knocking seven kinds of brickdust out of one another. I had to make a move. Now in all the turmoil was my chance to clear off and find out where I was and decide on my next actions.

The uproar really was a turmoil. The arched decorated ceiling bounced back the echoes multifold. The tinker hammering of weapons, the sharp pings as the defective steel of braxters snapped across, the screams of the wounded and the groans of the dying blended together with the ferocious roarings of the combatants. The whole scene was taken straight out of bedlam. To my shame, I was all too familiar with such scenes, Zair forgive me.

The noise was prodigious but it did not prevent me from hearing metallic footfalls approaching along the corridor from the opposite direction I'd come. I turned cautiously.

The group of warriors approaching were not members of Barca's household. The cut of their neckerchiefs resembled those of the invaders battling away in the arched chamber. It appeared reasonable to assume that each great family delighted in their own particular fancy neckerchief design. The group, harsh, grim-faced, weapons out, marched towards me conveying a deep sense of deadly purpose.

Clad only in a yellow tunic over the brave old scarlet breechclout and without a single weapon apart from those nature and the Krozairs of Zy afforded me, I felt it inappropriate to challenge these new arrivals. This decision was based on the circumstances, not on my weaponless state. Had my people been fighting in there and this lot about to attack my comrades, then you wouldn't see me for smoke as I got in amongst 'em. No, by the Blade of Kurin!

From nowhere a sudden gust of air brought the raw red taste of blood into my mouth and nostrils.

The man leading on the group was not, I judged, the leader. He was just as big, just as ugly, just as ferocious as the rest of them, with that extra little edge that marked him as the captain of the guard quite apart from his fancy finery. He brandished a sword and the blood suffusing his face gave him a demonic appearance.

The real leader, the noble, of these people who marched along a pace to the rear, I recognized from that meeting in W'Watchun's chamber. There he'd wanted to torture me to get the information he required. Now, with all that had happened since, I wondered if it could be possible that he wanted the secret of gunpowder. Somehow, I doubted that.

These gallant bully boys could see how I was dressed and that I carried no weapons. I was not a part of the fight. With a little gesture of my arm I stood aside so that they might enter the chamber and join the combat.

The cadade's flushed face appeared to bloat up as he reached the door, looked in and saw what was afoot. He raised his sword. The hilt was studded with gems. His mouth opened to reveal gappy brown teeth.

Right out of the blue, like a thunderbolt on a calm sunny day, he shouted: "Out of my way, lackey!"

In a single vicious arc he brought the sword down blurring towards my defenseless head.

Seven

Oh, no, by Zair! Oho no! This detestable rast wasn't going to catch a Krozair of Zy with a despicable trick like that. His engorged face, his fancy armor, the jewels all subsumed themselves into that bar of steel slashing down towards me.

The leap aside was conducted as a pure reflex. The blade hissed past and the tip clanged into the marble floor and the damned thing snapped across with a brittle crack.

I, Dray Prescot, laughed.

"You blintz!" He appeared to be having difficulty in drawing breath. "I'll—I'll—stand still—"

He ran out of breath then. He hurled the jeweled hilt to the floor and dragged out his second blade. Long before the steel had cleared sheath I'd made up my mind there was no profit hanging around any longer. As a parting present I gave him my toes betwixt wind and water.

Not even bothering to watch him turn green and double up, retching, I span about and hared off along the corridor.

A passionate voice lifted at my back. "Don't kill him! I want him alive!"

All the sounds melded: the ferocious roar of combat, the shouts and the demented commands of the lord, and the hard clatter of running feet swiftly following me. Well, if I couldn't outrun a measly pack of these cramphs, loaded down with armor and weapons as they were, I didn't deserve the medal, did I, by Krun!

Feel no surprise that I thus meekly ran off. I wanted nothing to do with these unpleasant folk. I needed to get on with my job for the Star Lords.

Like most of the palaces and temples of Kregen, this ornate edifice contained many passages and chambers, many secret runnels between the walls. My first imperative was to get outside, finding secret doors at this juncture was only a second option.

Even though that choleric lord back there had shouted to his sycophantic warriors not to kill me but to take me alive, I was not about to trust to that pious hope in as savage a world as Kregen.

The noise of pursuit continued as I galloped along.

At the second corner I came across I swung sharp right. The pack following me appeared to consist of warriors; the chance that there were crossbowmen among them was an unacceptable risk. I'd have to keep ducking and diving about along corridors and turnings so as not to afford a clear shot to any bowmen there might be.

The people who stood out of my way as I sprinted along were slaves or servants. The fighting men had rushed off to the defense of their lord. Passing a turning where the doors were patterned rather prettily with leaping styloxes, all graceful slender legs and curly horns, I swung the other way smartly. The smell of drains there blew up in a most pungent fashion. My nose crinkled up in distaste—me, a tarpaulin old sailorman who'd smelled the bilges of rotting ships from a tender age!

The obvious thought occurred to me. Why had these warriors chased off after me instead of hurling themselves into the fray? The lord had bellowed loudly enough that he wanted to take me alive. Why?

Was it presumptuous of me, was it paranoia, to imagine the reason for this raid was not to do damage to Barca; could it be that I, Dray Prescot, was the object of all the bloodstained combat?

As I pounded on, steadily outdistancing the pursuit, I remembered what Kov Barca had so bitterly said about Kov Grogan G'Gulandor. My bet was that he and the vicious lord after me now were one and the same.

Although I knew I was steadily drawing ahead of the warriors whooping and hollering after me, I found to my annoyance that I could not shake them off completely. After a series of quick corners and doubling back and following a most erratic course, here they were again, yelling after me like—well, I suppose they were like a pack of damned werstings.

In my flight I'd taken enough notice of the surroundings to steer the course I wanted and to avoid falling into the trap of doubling back without enough care to ensure I didn't run slap bang into the pursuit. Now, I decided, it was time to take a closer look. Already I had the direst suspicion of what I would discover. And, by Krun, I was right! By the mucus-fouled nostrils and slime-filled eyes of Makki Grodno! There the damned things were, neatly camouflaged against the casual glance, obvious to a close scrutiny.

Eyes! Damned eyes of the Illusionists, snugly fitted into the cornices and turnings and doorways.

Taking time to pause and examine one over the lintel of a door with fantastic sea monsters picked out in pearl and jade, I saw the Eye from an angle. The thing was perhaps twice the size of a human eye, with carved lids which fitted unobtrusively into a scrollwork. Peering deep within the pupil revealed what appeared to be a dull turquoise glow. The dim radiance seemed to emanate from a point far beyond the confines of the eye or the lintel. Just looking at it made my own eyes water.

How the blue blazes was I supposed to get out of this moil without being spotted everywhere I turned?

By Krun! If I'd been wearing a hat I'd have torn it off and thrown it to the floor and jumped up and down on it!

By this time the Suns of Scorpio must be gone from the night sky of Kregen. She of the Veils was due tonight—then I laughed at my own stupidity. I'd no idea of the elapsed time since I'd been hypnotized. Still, unless it was a night of Notor Zan, there'd be some of the Moons of Kregen floating past up there.

The corridors were lit by lamps, mostly using samphron oil in the better parts, mineral oil in the lesser.

Suppose I went along smashing all the lamps?

They'd still see me as I entered a new lighted area; but the darkness might make following more difficult. The scheme remained an option.

Quite obviously I had no idea of the layout of Barca's palace. Yes, I'd had considerable experience of the design of palaces on Kregen and could venture an educated guess about the best way for me to go. Because I'd been making all these random twists and turns the watchers had not been able to predict my course and so hurl a posse of warriors in my way.

The spy eyes fixed in points of observation were Kov Barca's, arranged for him by his tame illusionist Furney. Furney evidently did not have the ability of San W'Watchun to send a floating Eye to spy for him at a distance. Spying at a distance was one of the arts of Wizards of Loh and as I ran on seeking an exit I wished heartily that one of my comrade Wizards of Loh would put in a phantom appearance and show me the way out. Too true, by Vox!

So far I'd kept on the same level. When next I came across a stairway leading up off the main passage I reached up and smashed the lamp there. Then I sprinted on along the passage. If by that they thought I'd gone up the stairs, so good, and bad cess to 'em!

Mind you, this amorphous they I needed to outwit—well, just who in a Herrelldrin Hell were they, this they?

Furney had been busy sending insubstantial fighting men into the combat. Could he now be at his post, scanning what information his eyes showed him? Or could it be that Kov Grogan had dispatched his own illusionist to that observation room? Maybe he'd taken over.

Well, to the Ice Floes of Sicce with 'em all! Who was watching me didn't matter. What mattered was for me to outwit the lot of them and make good my escape. My work lay out there, to make sure the damned Dokerty rasts made no more ibmanzies. The Prism of Power brought here by Khon the Mak had to explode with the violence of a hundred suns. Only then would my work for the Star Lords be done.

You may well believe I felt most resentful of these damned eyes. In an odd, almost humorous way, one could feel they were unfair. In a blood-rousing chase like this they gave far too much advantage to the pack baying at my heels. Surprisingly, that feeling had not been experienced over the use of signomants to observe at a distance by Wizards of Loh. How were the thaumaturgical techniques of the Wizards of Loh and the Sorcerers of Balintol to be compared?

To the ice caverns of Gundarlo with the lot of 'em! I was totally disenchanted with this running away. I had no weapons and no armor. But for those damned eyes spying on me I'd have been long gone. To test that theory I struck along in as straight a line as possible and in short order a parcel of guards appeared ahead. They were mercenaries, which probably meant the warriors not chasing me were still tinker-hammering away back there.

Reaching up in a deliberate gesture I smashed the lamp over my head. The paktuns might well take that as a gesture of defiance. Just as easily they could take it as an insult. Either way didn't matter to me, by Krun! I turned around and sprinted off.

After three or four more lamps smashed to ruin I found myself back in an area I'd already travelled through, for it lay in darkness. The darkness was not complete, of course, with the occasional slant of moonlight through a window. With what I was coming to believe was the Star Lords' handiwork, I could see perfectly well in the dimness.

Just how well could these damned signomantic eyes see me?

Now you can hardly say that I came up with a Plan, called the Plan. The scheme, quite apart from its obviousness, might not work and might get my head parted from my shoulders. It might land me in a dank and draughty cell, barred with iron from Zenicce, with the schrafters queuing up with dripping jaws to chew on my bones.

Logic told me the scheme should work. But logic is not always in good supply on the mysterious world of Kregen, no, by Vox!

The decision made I began to trot along back the way I'd come. Inevitably the tramp of iron-soled boots echoed from ahead.

Now the dimness should be my friend!

Finding a niche in which to hunker was not difficult. Shards of yellow lamplight began to extend fingers down the passage. The warriors were no longer running. They must be just as resentful as was I for the diametrically opposite reason.

Their lamplight brightened. Their clumping noise approached. Squirming back into my niche and blinking my eyes I watched them pass.

The warrior cadade led, meaner than ever. The lord, this Kov Grogan G'Gulandor, marched next. Lamplight splintered from the gems spattering his armor. A warrior held the lamp at his shoulder. I looked at the next man and a sensation as of a balloon filling my throat fair choked me up. I looked hard and balefully upon this arrogant fellow as he strutted along, the great lord among inferiors.

I barely took note of the red-robed pair who followed, armored under the red robes of Dokerty, swords in their hands.

This great high and mighty lord's face showed just as pallid in the lamplight as I remembered it. His black hair—as I recalled when first he'd appeared to me I'd thought, as they say in Clishdrin, Black as the Raven's Wing—was longer than before. Maybe he'd been so busy with his nefarious schemes he'd had no time for a haircut. His armor was black, cluttered with jewels. His two swords remained in their scabbards. Their hilts were fussy with gems.

The sharpness of his white chin jutted. His eyes pierced.

So he passed along with the searching warriors and I watched him go. So part of my mission was falling into place. I'd found him.

Oh, yes, and I'd see him again, without a single doubt.

I had a pressing appointment with Hyr Kov Khonstanton—Khon the Mak.

Eight

Khon the Mak! So I'd found the unhealthy kov, despite all. At once I made up my mind. The famous Plan, called The Plan, could now be abandoned. My ploy had been to trot along to the fight and find out who was winning. If Kov Barca's people looked likely to beat the invaders then I'd find a weapon, and armor if I was lucky, and wade in to join them. Barca had been polite. Of course, there was no guarantee he'd stay that way for much longer.

Had the invaders been winning then I'd have had to take off if I didn't wish to be caught and tortured.

Now I could break out of this place, find the residence of Kov Grogan and secrete myself therein until he and Khon the Mak turned up. Splendid, by Zair! That, my friends, was what I called a real Plan!

As for Khon himself, well, there he was, the cramph, and his red-robed followers of Dokerty with him. The priests of Dokerty were the unhanged tapos who created ibmanzies. By using the Prism of Power hidden in the Flutubium, and by ghastly pain inflicted on the victims, they opened up a man or woman's ib to the entry of a demon.

A warm glow, most invigorating, took me. By the hairy armpit of the Dancing Nun of Schweyenza! As it were in a twinkling, the whole world of Kregen brightened. Now I had a Plan I could believe in.

By this time, naturally, the whole palace would be in a turmoil, like a wasps' nest prodded by a pointy stick.

Confirming that, a party of slaves hove into sight carrying torches and looking about them with rolling eyes. I let them go and then crawled out into the passage.

The quick patter of soft footfalls at my back brought me around sharpish. The sight was pathetic, and, at the same time, heartening. Heartening in that even at so fraught a time as this for the slaves and servants, the palace routine had somehow to go on. The courage of the little Fristle fifi servant was indisputable.

She wore a decent lime green tunic and there was a flower in her hair. She was young and barely formed and her tail boasted a pink ribbon. She carried a tray on which was perched a candle and a pot and plates and cups. The candle afforded little light; when she saw me she let out a squeak and stopped dead. She did not drop the tray.

Well, I tried to smile for her. She flinched back. I sighed and said: "Hush, hush. You are perfectly safe."

What I said hush for I really can't say. She wasn't screaming. Rather, she stood there, leaning more on one leg than t'other, and scrutinizing me very keenly.

A little pink tongue wet her lips.

Then: "You are the bandit they're all chasing?"

"I'm no bandit. But, yes, some of 'em are chasing me."

"Well, you'd better hurry up and run for it. There's been a big fight—all blood it was—"

"There's been?" I cut in sharply. "D'you know who won?"

"Why, the lord of course."

"Yes, right. Which lord?"

"You are funny! Why, our notor, Kov Barca."

There was loyalty for you, and a blind belief in one's own!

So they'd sorted out the combat and Grogan and Khon the Mak would be hurrying for the exit. Confound it! So much for my wonderful new Plan to get into Grogan's palace first.

I looked at her tray. She stood still regarding me much as though I was an interesting new addition to the animal larder.

The candle showed cups of dark liquid and plates of cakes. The little Fristle fifi's mistress liked an early night snack. The pot contained a bright orange paste to smear on the bread and butter. I picked it up. At once she became alarmed.

"What—?"

"Tell your mistress a horrible bandit with many swords threatened to cut off your head if you didn't give him the paste pot."

"But—but you wouldn't, would you?"

"No. But, then, suppose I said I'd eat you up?"

"Silly!" And she giggled so that the tea rippled.

"What's your name, young lady?"

"Felice."

She regarded me as one of her own class, she gave me no title, she wasn't frightened of me, and she was undeniably pretty. I just hoped the fellow she married realized what a wonderful match he had.

"Off you go, Felice. Remberee—and thank you."

She gave a toss of her head, bright-eyed. "Remberee—but, why do you thank me?"

"For showing me some honest decent behavior in a crazy world."

She laughed again. "I said you were funny!" And, with that, she was off, her candle sending flittering shadows along the walls.

She hadn't asked my name, which presumably meant she already knew it. But then why call me a bandit? What false information about me had been spread abroad? A drikinger could be slain on the spot out of hand. Maybe, just maybe, Barca had given up on politeness.

Anyway, I'd been under the impression that bandits were thin on the ground here in Winlan on account of the puissant warriors infesting the place. Mind you, their presence might have the opposite effect and create gangs of bandits roaming the back hills.

161

The pot contained sliptinger paste, very tasty. Even as I sucked my finger the sounds of people arguing reached me from ahead.

Light shafted from a corner. The slaves were going round replacing the lamps I'd smashed.

In my shrinking pool of darkness I refused to feel like a hunted animal, trapped at the end, waiting for the kill.

Another finger load of sliptinger paste was sucked off as I walked along. My original requirement of the paste from Felice looked as though it was past history. Anyway, would that scheme have worked? Would I be able to reach up and smear the sticky paste over the eyes?

The infuriating trouble was, of course, that knocking out the lamps or the eyes as I reached them could not stop the watchers from seeing me as I marched on into the next lighted and observed area.

By this time I'd come to the conclusion that this building might be lavishly decorated in what my comrade Sjames would describe as Vulgar Ostentation: it wasn't really large enough to be classed as a palace. The size indicated a luxuriously-appointed villa.

Turning away from the chattering party of slaves replacing the lamps I speeded up and sprinted hard along the next two corridors. At the end lamplight glowed. I did not slow down but charged on in a beeline. Moving very rapidly I kept straight on.

The arrangements of the watchers must be quite efficient over all. Only a villa—yes. But that meant a considerable number of passages and rooms had to be scrutinized. I trusted my speed would carry me past before they had time to organize an ambush party ahead.

Well, that wonderful Plan almost worked.

Coming out into a hall whose marble floor in black and white checks would make a splendid surface for Jikaida I spotted an arched doorway in the opposite wall, with curtained windows in rows each side.

So that was the way out—at last.

The trouble was, standing before the door four warriors saw me, lifted up their swords, and whooping wildly charged.

Sicce take 'em! I snarled to myself. I was in for a fight and I'd been trying to avoid having to fight. Oh, well, if I was in for a calsany I might as well be in for a zorca.

So anxious were they to attack that in their headlong rush two, side by side, pounded out in front of the other two. I could not draw my sword. The semi-mystical power of the Disciplines of the Krozairs of Zy were now about to be put to another test.

These bully boys quite clearly had every intention of spitting me. They hungered to shuffle me off to the Ice Floes of Sicce. So Kov Barca's store of politeness had really dried up. I set myself.

Two blades swirled in at me, one to the midriff, the other to the head.

These warriors, as I had noted, were quite good, if somewhat stiff and rigid. They were certainly slow. Too slow.

A supple sway to the side left the sword going for my head slicing down empty air. A twist left the midriff-aimed sword going straight past—again through empty air. I had to be quick, now. A flailing foot crunched into a throat above the corselet rim. A pair of fingers gouged deeply into a pair of eyes. Both men let out yowls of pain and sagged away.

Without stopping my movement I bounded to the side. Two of these puissant warriors were groveling on the ground, kicking up a screaming din. Their comrades, undaunted, bore in. This time I dived to the side, whirled, hit one right at the nape of his neck below his helmet brim. Before he had time to yell, my forearm was around the other's neck, gripping and lifting. In the yelling I still heard that characteristic snap, thick and soggy, not at all sharp. I dropped him and dealt with his yelling companion. The two on the floor were still yodeling away.

I turned my back on them and sprinted for the door.

Naturally, it was locked.

Hard footfalls bounced echoes from the marble floor as a fresh posse of these pesky warriors broke into the hall and started for me.

Still I refused to feel like an animal in a trap.

I glared about and I daresay my face looked pretty wild.

There was only one thing for it. It was a desperate chance. But it was a chance I had to take.

Moving back towards the oncoming killers I switched about. Mentally hitching up my sword belt I put my head down and ran hard straight for the nearest window.

With a muscle-cracking bound I leaped up and hurled myself headlong at the window.

Nine

The luck of Five-Handed Eos Bakchi lifted me up on one of his outstretched palms as I sailed through the air. Rolling into a ball, arms protecting head, everything tucked in tight; I hit the window with an almighty crash. The cracking of glass and the splintering of wood crackled all about me with one long drawn horrendous roar.

The drape saved me from serious injury. With the curtain wrapped about me I simply went helter-skelter through the window. The curtain trailed along behind like a trawl. Bits of frame clung around my neck. Out I went, out and down.

The ground might well be covered in a nice green lawn; it hit me a shrewd enough blow between the shoulder blades, by Krun!

The shock of that had to be pushed aside. I was in a hurry.

There ensued a farcical interlude as I wrestled with the curtain that had turned from a savior into a dratted mantrap. It wrapped about me like an octopus. Hopping up and down and flailing yards of material away with one hand only to have fresh folds close in about me, I struggled to rid myself of the clinging thing.

When, at long blessed last, I wrenched myself free I quite expected to feel the steel-tipped bite of crossbow bolts.

Swiveling to look back I could see the wall and the gaping hole where the window had been. A couple of heads craned out, black blobs against the light. For a tiny moment yet I was still safe for they couldn't make me out in the shadows. The light from the window struck down very close, perilously close, to where I'd danced my jig.

Looking the other way I felt enormous disappointment.

I was not out of the palace or villa or whatever the damned place might be. This was a courtyard, with the massy outlines of shrubs and small trees. The small space was not even out in the open air, for darkness extended above, without stars or the friendly pink and golden glow of She of the Veils. At once, keeping to the shadows, I set off for the opposite wall. I had to get as far away as possible from those haughty cramphs of warriors. I'd heard these famous warriors referred to as Tchekedos. I preferred to call the lot of 'em blintzes, in the insulting terminology of Balintol.

Mind you, logic indicated that I had been lucky to hurl myself through an interior window. The last bits of wood frame were knocked off. Had I tried that with an outside window I'd have either bounced or waffled myself on the iron gratings.

Somewhere along the way the pot of sliptinger paste had been lost. Now it was gone with Beng Dithermon the Gatherer. Pity. Although not really hungry yet, I could have done with a spot of the sliptinger paste even though I'd no bread and butter on which to spread it. The opposite wall looked promising. Admittedly the garden was on the dim side; still I could not make out any spy eyes.

Lights spattered into life at my back as men carrying torches poured into the courtyard. Time was running out fast.

My feet hit gravel and I looked down. A wooden cover on the ground showed up a few paces off. In the wood was a recessed bronze ring. Mentally rubbing my hands together I moved quickly across, took the ring into my fist and heaved up.

At once a familiar sickly smell assailed my nostrils.

Drains!

In the dimness a flight of wooden steps showed up greasily. On the small landing or platform at their head stood a box like a cupboard. I rather fancied I knew what lay inside that, by Krun!

Instantly I dropped down onto the platform and opened the cupboard. Yes! Torches lay neatly racked with a couple of simple tinderboxes before them. Making a mental note of the layout I reached up and carefully lowered the wooden trapdoor down over the manhole. In total darkness I struck flint and steel, got the tump going, blew gently, transferred the flame to a torch. Tucking a couple of spares under my arm I pitched the rest down the steps and sent the tinderboxes down after them.

At the bottom on the stone ledge that ran alongside the drain, the smell was worse but still tolerable. I kicked the torches into the stream of brownish water. About to follow them with the tinderboxes, I checked. I kicked one in. The other I picked up and held in the hand of the arm under which my spare torches nestled. The flame-giver was not broken, thank Zair. Suppose I tumbled into the water and the torch was extinguished? Mind you, that fall might also wet all my torches. Trusting in whatever Fate might guide me, I set off.

The sewer construction was that of a proper tunnel with arched courses of bricks that now, alas, were grey and slimed. The water flowed at a reasonable pace, indicating sewer engineering that understood the trickeries of gradients. The orange torchlight splashed along the walls and sparked glints up from the water. My footfalls are soft, a useful habit that had not been entirely learned with my Clansmen. Even so, echoes ran like mice ahead of me along the tunnel. The sensation of this confinement, the tinkle of the water, the odd shadows and shards of torchlight, did not strike me as eerie. I suppose in all truth the surroundings would be weird enough for a person with a heightened imagination and who had little or no experience of eerie happenstances.

The stink was the worst part of this trip, believe me!

No other runnels entered the main channel. From this I deduced we'd left the villa and were heading out into the countryside. The sewer still stank—ponged as they say in Clishdrin—but it remained wide with a reasonable ledge at the side on which to walk. Perhaps we'd pick up the effluent from another villa along the way to wherever we were going. That could be the lake where the fake ships had been set up for my benefit, a river or the sea.

Although still not hungry I felt I could do with a wet and a sandwich. That brave young Fristle fifi, Felice, seemed to me now to have tricked me into not taking some of the cakes. Something about that odd encounter with her had been bugging away gently at the back of my mind. Her whole attitude had been enormously surprising given the circumstances. I mean—come on! A young girl suddenly confronted with a great hairy fellow whose intentions might be of the most murky kind—and she didn't scream and drop the tray and run off!

Then I sighed in resignation. I suppose that was the answer to the riddle. As I walked along that greasy ledge among the stinks I had to recognize that Felice, knowing my name, simply had not believed what her lord had told her. Oh, no! She believed the stories she had read in the brightly colored books, the plays she had seen and the puppet shows. Oh, yes, by Zair! Then I had to laugh.

Sometimes the legends surrounding the name of Dray Prescot paid dividends!

All the same, I considered as I reached a point where the ledge had broken away, there was more to that encounter with Felice than I could fathom at the moment. Now this crumbled brickwork posed a problem. The gap was too wide to jump. So that meant there was only one thing for it. Unappetizing, unpleasant and downright unwanted, it had to be done.

Some of the material had toppled sideways into the main stream and a little dam had formed. The water surged around and filled the space between the two broken ends of the path.

So, distastefully, I stepped down. To give the stuff a polite name, I stepped down into the brown liquid. With jaws clamped, I edged along the section of jagged footing until I could climb back onto the ledge. My legs dripped.

Trudging on in a most ungrateful frame of mind I saw in the flare of torchlight a rushing bubble across the surface of the water and shortly thereafter halted at the brink of another sewer entering the main channel. By the dangling eyeballs and dangling intestines of Makki Grodno! Of course the confounded new sewer had to empty on my side, didn't it? Oh, well, the sticky end had been my lot in life, so what the hell—what difference did it make now, anyway? I ponged.

Negotiating that obstacle on I went. More side drains emptied in, coming now from both sides. When, at last, at blessed last, I reached the outlet and stood looking across a river with the stars of Kregen scintillating above, I was in a stinking mood. By Krun, yes!

With a huge running jump I dived into the river upstream.

For a good long time I swam and swam, enjoying the feel of clean water lapping me. When at last all the muck washed away I reached the bank and climbed out onto grass. I lay there, breathing evenly and deeply. Ahead of me lay many things that had to be done immediately. But I just reclined on the grass for a bit. To the Furnace Fires of Inshurfraz with the lot of 'em! Let 'em wait, by Vox!

Ten

Something hard and jagged croaked away at me like a rusty wheel turning on a rusty axle. I opened my eyes and turned and sat up. The sky held that ivory sheen patterned with streaky cloud and vaguely lit in palest apple green and rose that said the twin suns, Zim and Genodras, were about to burst in all their glory over the horizon.

The raucous cawing sawed again at my ears.

"All right, all right, Bird of Ill Omen," I shouted. I stood up and shook myself and whirled my arms about my head. My Val! Here I'd just drifted off to sleep on the grass like the veriest coy, the greenest young idiot afloat!

Up there that tremendous raptor sailed in hunting circles. All gold and scarlet he blazed in the light of the Suns that had not yet reached the surface of the world. I blinked. "You nurdling great onker! What d'you want?"

The Gdoinye carrying messages and spying for the Star Lords hadn't bothered me much of late. Could I believe the Everoinye were tender of my fate and wished to give me this horrendous early morning call to wake me up before some inquisitive guard investigated?

The bird cawed again, croaking a ghostly laughter at my expense; he did not speak to me.

I shook my fist at him and he circled and rose higher until at last a mere black dot he vanished.

As though he had given a signal, at that precise moment the Suns rose one after the other, piercing the slight mist, and the world of Kregen became drenched in light and color.

Quite automatically my thoughts turned to the state of my inward parts. By Beng Trunter the Nosher! I could've sworn my stomach was plastered against my backbone!

Therefore it was time to consider my position. The grassy area was bounded by trees and bushes and I looked to have hove up in a park. Only a few flower beds showed closed petals in muted colors. Was this a public park or a private garden? I was someway away from the sewer outlet and over the trees the strange top-heavy buildings of Winbium toppled against the dawn sky. Private garden, I judged, and beyond the gate would be the villa.

Here I was, stranded without money or weapons. The yellow linen tunic was perfectly proper wear for evening almost anywhere; it would scarcely pass muster during the day in this damned place. The classes were too strictly demarcated for that. I did not look like a warrior, a priest, a merchant or a wizard. I could be a mercenary out of uniform, I supposed. As for being a slave, the brave old scarlet breechclout prevented that in the most emphatic way imaginable, by Krun!

Since W'Watchun had erected his confounded famous Wall around the country most, if not all, of the foreign embassies and consulates had pulled out. Isolation was the idea here. I doubted if Drak, Emperor of Vallia, had either continued or replaced our consulate.

So that meant there was no easy way for me to obtain supplies. My stomach groaned as visions of succulent food floated before my yearning eyes.

Another of my famous Plans occurred to me. Well, by Vox, it might work if I put on a hang-dog expression. There was always the technique taught me by Deb-Lu-Quienyin by which I could alter the look of my face despite the pain of a million bee-stings. If I put on my renowned idiot face the Plan might work.

So—and you who have followed my narrative and understand will know that this was not for the first time—I hitched up my non-existent sword belt, and said: "Very well, then. Let's go for it." And, with that little outburst out of the way, I set off for the gate among the trees.

My clothes had dried. Commenting on the vagaries of well-organized Plans, and mentioning Makki Grodno, I turned and slunk off towards the river. Here I dived in, rolled over and swam back.

Suitably wet I could now march boldly up to the door of the house beyond the gate.

The gate was locked.

To each side extended a wooden fence of stout construction. In, as they say, for a zorca in for a vove. A spring up, two fists gripping the top rail, a lithe sideways pivot and I was over the gate.

Up ahead the house looked more comfortable than ostentatious. Whoever owned it must have a tidy amount of cash for the riparian rights alone would set him back a goodly sum. The building lofted three storeys above a forest of supporting legs. Each higher storey balconied out over the lower. Funny ways, here in Winlan, yet the house was pleasing and looking at it I almost pitched headfirst into a deep trench.

A convulsive heave and contortion of my entire body brought me back to the grass. The damned thing wasn't quite a ha-ha; it reminded me of a fortification the sappers dug. At the bottom an ankle breaker promised injury to anyone trying to cross incautiously.

Now these vee-shaped trenches with ankle-breaker slots at the bottom are the very devil to cross. I looked about.

In a matter of moments a loose branch was in my hand. If you slipped and slid down the trench the chances were your feet would catch in the slot and as you twisted you'd break your ankle, or both. Believe me, I lowered myself down with exquisite care, gripping any purchase that offered, keeping low, and finally—and with a breath of relief—reaching the bottom safely.

Even with the branch to assist me the climb up was more difficult. Twice I slipped and only a frantic brake with the branch and a flailing grip of a white root saved me. At last and all thanks to Opaz I climbed up over the lip.

"Not many folk could do that, dom," said a baritone voice.

"Well, dom," I said as I stood up. "I could find no bridge."

He looked to be a smart lad in his immaculate uniform and rather young to hold the position of captain of the guard. His three swods were all older, a trifle careworn, although their kit was well cared for, and I judged them to be long-time retainers.

"You could have rung the bell."

"Ah!" I said, in the same casual way. "Now that I also did not find."

He was apim. One of his men, a Hytak, cleared his throat and spat out: "Jik! The bell was removed last night for repair."

"Well, dom," the cadade said after a pause, "if your visit is entirely legal then I must apologize for your travails."

I didn't smile; but I quite liked that.

Assuring him I was entirely legal, I was escorted up to the house. He could see I had no visible weapons; all the same he was very correct about the escort, by Krun!

They didn't take me around the back, as I expected. We climbed a set of stairs and went in the front door. "The master will see you at once."

The hallway and room into which I was ushered confirmed my opinion of the house. The atmosphere was one of comfort and quiet elegance. The man who rose at my entrance was a Lamnia, so that told me at once his occupation and explained the wealth discreetly displayed. Not all Lamnias are merchants, of course; but here in Winbium, he could scarcely be anything else.

The cadade explained in his baritone voice why I'd climbed over the gate. The merchant looked surprised at the account of my passing his trench. He stroked his light-colored fur and looked judicious. "So why did you do all that?"

Here was my chance, so I launched into my story.

When I was done, the merchant said: "You were out with friends on the river and your boat capsized? Rather early."

"Ah, yes, well, horter, we made an early start for the fish."

Lamnias are usually gentle folk, and his smile was warm.

"I see you are all wet."

I mentioned that if one fell in the river, one got wet.

"Quite, quite." His voice was ruminative. "I happened to be admiring a particularly fine paline tree in my garden this morning. Oh, yes, quite fine. I like to look at the river, also. If you'd fallen from your boat, why was it necessary to run off from my gate and dive back into the river?"

I didn't say: "Ulp!" But I felt like it.

"I see there is no use trying to deceive you, horter. The simple truth is that I fell in the river last night and only just managed to reach the bank. I was so exhausted I slept. This morning I felt that might not be believed, true though it is, and so I had to become wet again to prove my story."

He reflected on me for a time, then: "Llahal. Your name?"

"Llahal. I am called Drajak the Sudden." This name I'd used so often since meeting my kregoinya comrade Mevancy came out promptly and with the authority of habit.

"I am Dorval ham Hesting. This is my cadade, Jiktar Larghos Frenden." He smiled again. "Known as the Quick. Lahal."

When I returned his greeting, the sound of the L single, and not the Welsh guttural, I felt relief. He might or might not believe me. He was not about to order my head off.

What was a disappointment was that I'd not heard his name first. He was Hamalese. How useful it would have been to use my own real inherited name of Hamun ham Farthytu, Amak of Paline Valley!

This Dorval ham Hesting was no noble. The correct address for him was horter, not notor. As a merchant in this warrior dominated society he was tolerated for the trade he could bring. The location of his house, fine though it was, also revealed his standing in the community. It was situated downstream of the capital, Winbium. They let that foaming brown liquid out of their sewers only a short distance below Hesting's house.

Hesting eyed me. "You are employed at present?"

I shook my head. "No, horter. At the moment I am tazll."

The two men exchanged looks. Jiktar Larghos Frenden said: "Yes, it is quite clear you are a paktun. What ranks have you held?"

In the mercenary trade you take the jobs as they come. There are many less openings for jiktars than for swods.

"I've served in all capacities, Jik."

"All?" Frenden the Quick sounded very sharp, very sharp, by Krun! "You are telling me you've served as Chuktar?"

There was no reason for this. I said, shortly: "As Kapt."

Jiktar Frenden opened his mouth and the Lamnia cut him off with: "And your last employment?"

"As a swod."

If they offered me employment, as I could see was in their minds, I'd have to decline. All I wanted, by Zair, was food!

Hesting obviously made up his mind. He nodded briskly. "I have business to attend to. I shall see you at the hour of mid."

And, with that, and no remberee, he walked out.

The mention of food being delicately raised was rewarded by the information that I would have to wait until the second breakfast. This severe task I managed to survive. When we did sit down in a wide bright kitchen in the guard's quarters my patience was rewarded.

They ate well, these jurukkers in Horter Hesting's employ. Replete, chewing on a handful of palines, I felt a new man.

Naturally, Frenden had asked me questions and I'd contrived a story that, at least for the moment, appeared to appease his curiosity.

On my saying that I'd better cut along, and thank you for breakfast, he dismayed me by saying that, since he needed a stroll, he would accompany me to my lodgings.

"It is not right that a paktun should walk the streets weaponless. No, by the Blade of Kurin. Then we can stop for a draught and be back here well in time for the meeting with the master at the hour of mid."

"I'd hoped you'd forgotten that."

His hand brushed the hilt of one of his swords.

"I earn my hire by taking care of the master, dom."

Now what in a Herrelldrin Hell could I do? I had no lodgings. As to my weapons, they'd been taken off me by W'Watchun and his confounded glassy eyes. By the creased thighs and hairy nostrils of the Divine Madam of Belschutz! I needed another famous Plan—and quick!

A shambles of a plan occurred to me, so I nodded, and all very politely indicated his company would be most welcome.

Because when I'd scrambled up out of that detestable ankle-breaking trench Frenden and the guards had come on me so unexpectedly I'd been wearing my own face. I could give my old physog a few cunning twitches to change it a trifle; I just couldn't alter it all the way.

Ruminating on my problem I set off with the cadade who left the Hytak Hikdar, Quarnus, in charge. Going out of the grounds past a stout stockade towards the rear of the premises brought us to an unpaved road. This led straight to the city. Fretting away about how to avoid those confounded damnable prying Eyes, I still managed to take in what there was to see. Naturally, I had no idea of the layout of Winbium, save of the central area and a slice of the suburbs through which I'd fled with the megaphone voice braying after me. That had taken place almost as soon as the Star Lords had dumped me down here. How long ago was that, then?

My heart sank lower and lower as though a weight dragged me down. My Val! I didn't stand a chance. What hope had I of getting away with it? There were the ever-watching Eyes. I had no lodgings to go to. The cadade kept step with me and his eye was very sharp on me, most sharp, by Vox!

My Plan, to enter some establishment and either pretend to have been there—perhaps all my belongings had been stolen—and get out quick, just wouldn't work. The Eyes would see to that.

My head ached. A dull throb continued somewhere in my old vosk-skull of a cranium. That had been going on since my discovery that I was no longer a lieutenant in the Royal Navy of Earth. Any of my wild Clansmen, any Krozair, knows that pain must be used. As fear must be used to strengthen courage, so pain must enhance resolution.

What was an unpalatable fact had to be faced. Undoubtedly I'd been acting oddly lately. I was not acting in the way Dray Prescot usually went about life and its problems. The damned buzz saw in my head, despite all my efforts, seemed to me to be sapping my will.

Could this lassitude on my part be the malign work of San W'Watchun?

Why didn't I just walk off? Why didn't I just knock Frenden over the head and take his gear and weapons? What held me back?

Well, for a start, tight on security though he was, the cadade had treated me reasonably. He was affable in his own strict way. What sort of fellow would I be if I recompensed him by blattering him?

The city drew nearer as we walked along, the road was graveled, the walls and gates of houses lined our way. Time was running out.

Giving my shoulders a shake I tried to remind myself that I was Dray Prescot, emperor and king of this and that, etc, etc, ad nauseum. My yellow linen tunic had dried out quickly. Although it was not entirely proper for daytime wear, it would pass—one reason I had selected it in the first place. That idea perked me up. Earlier I'd imagined I couldn't walk abroad in the yellow tunic. Maybe if I tried harder I could throw off the yoke W'Watchun had slapped on me.

Something had to be done, by Zair! The Suns of Scorpio beamed down their opaline radiance without a hint of cloud to interfere. The temperature rose with the Suns and the day became warmer than would normally be expected at this latitude. This I took for a good omen.

A tavern hove in sight, a modest place without the supports to raise the structure into the air. There were two storeys, at least, and this lifted my hopes.

"The day grows hot, Jik. I could do with the wet you promised."

He wiped his forehead. "An excellent suggestion."

"You will recall I have no wherewithal?"

"Aye. It all went into the river, you said."

"Just so."

With that we directed our steps to the tavern, The Spotted Gyp. The place was more or less what one would expect to find in Balintol. The tap-room was over half-full; so other folk were feeling the heat. Frenden called a serving girl over as we sat on a bench with the ale-ringed table before us. The room smelled of beer and sawdust on the floor with early cooking preparations wafting their scents from the back quarters. At least, there were no damned prying Eyes, either in here or in the street outside.

The clientele were mostly mercenaries off duty, with a sprinkling of Tchekedos wearing their ridiculous neckerchiefs. Now a singular fact

I had noticed since my arrival in Winbium was the marked absence of women, apart from slaves and servants. There had been a lone lady of quality sitting in her carriage, flanked by armed outriders. I assumed that in a warrior culture women occupied a rather different position in the social structure from most women in Paz on Kregen.

The serving girl brought the ale. It was drinkable.

Very quickly the stares of the drinkers became obtrusive. Apart from the absence of women, there were no merchants there. My yellow tunic looked decidedly out of place. As you may imagine, the taproom was stuffed with weaponry of all kinds draping the armored bodies of paktun and warrior alike.

Quite obviously, Frenden knew this place and had marched in without a moment's thought about my attire. In Winlan the warrior class and their great lords owned everything except the merchants' businesses. The landlord, a Gon with bald buttered head, would be a vassal or slave of the warrior who owned the tavern. He looked decidedly uneasy and kept shooting worried glances in my direction. He was called, in rather overweening jocular terms, Nath the Vosk.

The explosion could not be long in coming now. I gave thanks to whatever gods or spirits—hardly the Everoinye!—for this interesting situation. Poor old Frenden suddenly woke up to what was going on. He didn't bother to finish his drink. He stood up. "Best we should be going, Drajak. They don't like merchants here and you look—"

"Sit down." I spoke normally but firmly. "I shall finish my drink. I shall tell them I am a zhanpaktun, with a pakai longer than their arms—should they ask, that is."

He looked abruptly helpless. "By Cymbaro!" he said, and then looked about with swift sudden apprehension in case he had been overheard. He took a breath. "They will do you a mischief, for they will not believe a paktun walks abroad weaponless."

My mention of my pakai, the string of trophy rings taken from defeated paktun opponents, was quite truthful and had been provided for me, quite uncharacteristically, by the Star Lords. Trouble was, my pakai along with my weapons reposed somewhere in the keeping of San W'Watchun—wherever he was now, Gaynor Turnush the Gatherer of Souls take him, the great hulu!

Do not forget, in all this petty imbroglio, I, Dray Prescot, must plead guilty to hubris, which, as you know, is foreign to my nature. Everything that had happened was like the pus forming under a boil. Frustration brought the boil to a head. Now this idiot warrior swaggering up to our table affectedly playing with his neckerchief, his right hand already clasped around the hilt of his sword, was going to prove the surgeon's needle that would lance the boil.

In my imagination I supposed he would ask me to leave. He wouldn't be particularly polite about it. I didn't expect him to be. But at the least I did expect him to give me the chance to walk out, given that Winlan was a civilized country.

Fat chance of that when this bully boy had a victim!

He marched up to the end of the table. Frenden remained standing. The Tchekedo abruptly reached down, seized the end of the bench on which I was sitting and lifted it straight up. That was no mean feat of strength.

I tumbled onto the sawdust in a tangle of arms and legs with my left fist gripped around my beerpot struggling to keep it vertical. Some beer was spilt, I admit: not a lot.

"Notor!" burst out Frenden in alarm. "He is a paktun—"

"Keep out of it, blintz! You brought him here. I'll deal with you when I've finished with this vagot."

So this person was a lord. Even better. He stood, blocky with his booted feet near my head. The hubbub in the tavern turned into jeers and catcalls and vicious remarks about kicking my head in.

In a spinning motion on my hip, the beer held aloft, I swiveled about, avoided both table and bench, caught his legs in a scissor grip between mine, and so brought the rast crashing to the floor.

He roared. Oh, yes, by Krun, how he roared!

Frenden squawked out something in horror at my suicidal behavior. He was perfectly audible for the taproom had gone suddenly very quiet.

Standing up and continuing to hold the beerpot I said in a calm and controlled voice: "You tumbled me over and I tumbled you over. That makes us even. Let us make the pappattu and so—"

He scrambled up. There were white flecks at the corners of his mouth. He was shaking so that he had to make two grabs to get hold of the hilt of his sword. What he said quite escaped me for he shrieked incoherently as though a leem had him.

His sword came free of the scabbard at last. He swirled it twice and then launched himself at me.

Warrior in this unsavory society he might be; he was not much of a warrior balanced against the places I knew outside Winlan. To have to make two grabs at his sword hilt! To shriek like that! If he wanted to do me mischief he should simply have got down to it.

His ferocious slash went past my left ear as I sidestepped. The use of one of the more elementary techniques taught by the Krozairs of Zy brought his sword into my fist as he surged past. I refrained from helping him on his way with a toe up his rump, as is taught and expected.

This famous Tchekedo hauled himself up and turned to face me. Sheer murder blazed in his engorged face. A sound hissed around the taproom. I squinted sideways to see. The warriors had drawn their weapons. Those blades pointed at me. A ring of steel formed about me.

So I lifted the beerpot in my left fist, saluted them all with a grave inclination of my head. I toasted them. "May Beng Dikkane smile on you all, doms."

With that I downed the beer and so stood there, surrounded by malignant warriors thirsting for my blood.

Eleven

Someone laughed.

The circle of blades about me did not waver. I couldn't see who thought my predicament funny. The mercenaries very sensibly kept out of this warrior affair. Frenden moved to join them and I didn't blame him one little bit—after all, who was I except some stranger who might have been trying to break into his master's house?

The situation as these warriors glared balefully upon me did not appear at all funny. I'd made a leem's nest of this Plan. I'd made a colossal mistake, and not for the first time, by Krun!

Although despising myself for seeking a confrontation in the way it happened, I'd fully expected in a warrior society dominated by codes of conduct to face off against one of the Tchekedos. Oh, no! The whole boiling of these bully boys was about to start on me! Great!

The lord had stopped his shrieking and was breathing in huge draughts, his fancy gilded scale armor going in and out like a fish out of water. I glared at him and rapped out: "I see you have to have your friends to hold your hand. They probably wipe your nose, too."

The light laugh rippled again, filled with amusement.

I shouted: "Whoever you are, you may laugh at me when I can't see you. Come out here and stand before me and laugh in my face—if you dare!"

As you will perceive, I was becoming a trifle warm, somewhat annoyed. In fact, I'll go so far as to say I was becoming belligerent. Now that is totally unlike Dray Prescot. Even in my early days on Kregen when I went charging about like a crazed chunkrah I'd adhered to the sage advice that you don't tell a fellow you're going to hit him. You just blatter him instanter. So was the Illusionist still crawling about in my addled brain?

Not for the first time I brushed away the horrific thought, that all that was happening was mere illusion. By Zair! That couldn't be allowed to sway my actions!

The warriors still stood in their ring of steel staring upon me. I had no stupid conceited conception that they were afraid of me. They awaited a signal. Not, I judged, from this pathetic apology for a lord and warrior; oh, no—probably from the cramph who laughed at me would come the signal to pounce.

The light amused voice said: "I think, Ramley, you will allow he is indeed a paktun?"

Then a surprising thing occurred that filled me with a good feeling. Jiktar Larghos Frenden, known as the Quick, suddenly shouted: "My lord! He is a zhanpaktun. Drajak known as the Sudden. My lord, I apologize for bringing him in improperly dressed, but—" Here good old Frenden related my story of falling in the water.

The unpleasant fellow, Ramley, who'd toppled me off the bench had drawn his other sword. He swished it about. His voice held a sullen note. "That's all very well. But the blintz insulted me." The gilded scale still betrayed the depths of his anger. "He must apologize or I shall cut him up."

The light voice gave its amused laugh again, although, this time, a sardonic note toned it to a deeper shade. The lord sounded highly sardonic indeed, very, by Krun!

Whoever the fellow was, it seemed most likely that he outranked the others and ran the roost here.

I stepped a pace towards Ramley, whereat he flinched back. I held out his sword, hilt first. "Your sword, notor."

He looked undecided. Two drops of sweat rolled down past his temples. Eventually he slapped the blade he was holding back into the scabbard. He reached for the hilt of the sword I held out.

I watched his eyes.

He grasped the hilt. I saw his intentions in his face.

"You blintz!" he screamed, and thrust.

A supple sideways lean allowed the blade to pass harmlessly. Then, I confess, thoroughly impatient with this fellow, I allowed some of my tetchiness to spark my next action.

Allowances: I'd allowed him enough of those, by Vox!

The palm of my hand slapped around. It cracked along his cheek and helped to propel him with his own angry thrust staggering into the ring of warriors.

A swift chingle of steel and his blade was deflected safely. The warrior who did that efficiently grasped Ramley and held him. He growled: "Stand still, Ramley, and stop making a fool of yourself."

Now I was totally unsure of what would happen. To say I was thoroughly disenchanted with these whole proceedings would be a gross understatement. The very nature of this tavern indicated it was of no high quality; rather, the reverse. Paktuns patronized the place and these high and mighty Tchekedos were of the lower ranks.

The situation with the circle of warriors about me inevitably brought resonances of my past vividly before my eyes. There exist these poor sick individuals who light a ring of flame and entrap a scorpion in the middle. They expect the creature to sting itself to death because it dare not brave the flame.

Whether that be so or not—I have heard the story is pure myth—it most certainly did not apply to me, Dray Prescot, despite my life-long involvement with the image and icon of the Scorpion. Oh, no, by dear old Makki Grodno's putrescent eyeballs and slime infested nostrils! Oh, no, by Krun!

To repeat myself—I was tired of the farce of these proceedings. Ramley could bellow like a wounded vove; bad cess to him. The amused lord could laugh his head off: so let him. I had business elsewhere.

This wonderful yrium I possessed, this super charisma that could make folk obey my wishes, existed. I could not deny that. The Star Lords had chosen me to further their grandiose plans for Kregen because I possessed the yrium. As you know, I am reluctant to use the power. It makes me feel embarrassed. Sometimes it flashes out quite involuntarily, and then, believe you me, folk jump!

So, now, I summoned up my Dray Prescot Devil Look, and stared arrogantly around. "That will be sufficient. I shall now leave. Notors and horters, I bid you remberee."

With that I bore straight down on a youngish warrior whose neckerchief was on the modest size. He'd give way. I knew it.

As I turned a sharp spark of turquoise light splintered into the corner of my eye.

I halted at once and cocked my head up. The Eye! The damned spying Eye of San W'Watchun hung there in the corner of my vision.

A voice spoke in the rich, fruity tones he'd used in his own chamber, quite unlike the reedy whisper he'd adopted as a surgeon aboard one of His Britannic Majesty's ships.

"Stand aside! The man Drajak is mine!"

There he stood in the open doorway, clad in his black robes, his tall cylindrical hat, brimless, towering over his head and as black as the Kov of Hell's riding boots.

His face wore the haggard look I remembered, pale and with sweat beads gleaming on his forehead. His strange eyes surveyed the taproom's occupants with a blank glassy stare. I checked the Eye still remained floating, trailing its white tendril. Why did he still need to peer through the Eye when he could see me as plainly as I could see him?

Two other Illusionists stood just to his rear. There would be guards outside, no doubt of that. His hands remained at his side but when he spoke again it was as though he pointed a rigid forefinger at me in absolute command.

"You! Drajak! Come with me!"

The ring of warriors remained perfectly still. As I walked to the door I reflected, as I had when I'd first heard of this famous Sorcerer of Balintol, of the power he must possess to keep a herd of unruly savage warriors in check. Well, by Krun, I'd had personal experience of that awesome power!

No one moved apart from myself. I reached the door and W'Watchun turned and stalked off ahead of me, followed by his associates. Four guards waited for him. Again a flash of turquoise caught my vision. The Eye floated along above the ground. I stared at it and I stared at W'Watchun and his Illusionist comrades and his guards.

Before committing myself, it was vitally necessary to check what those cramphs back in The Spotted Gyp were doing. The doorway remained empty. I swung back to glare at the sorcerer.

I laughed.

Oh, yes, I, Dray Prescot, laughed.

The road held a few people going about their business. There were not many as the hour of mid approached and folk were anxious to reach home or inn where they would wrap themselves around their midday meal. I wondered if they could see W'Watchun and his retinue.

What I had to do now was get about the business of the Star Lords that had brought me here. No more shillyshallying. Briskly, I set off up the road completely ignoring the sorcerer.

What he said surprised me so that I halted and swung back to face him. "Majister! Please! Come with me—"

I surprised myself that my voice was not the harsh old gravel-shifting bellow that would chop him down to size. "It's not on. I have things to do. I do not forget what you have done. You have interfered with my plans and delayed me. Now have done."

"I tried not to harm you, you must know that. But—"

"Forget it, san. I'm off."

So, turning again to leave his phantom image I saw a flier plane down into the road ahead of me and lithe forms leap out.

The first to hit the ground and start running for me was a Chulik wearing a grey tunic. He did not carry a gold-knobbed wand. Now he held a wicked-looking sword in his fist. At his back crossbowmen levelled their weapons at me.

These grim-faced guards were real. They were not illusions.

So the confounded Illusionist had caught me up in his toils once again! I just stood there, fuming futilely. All my famous plans had been ruptured yet again!

Twelve

No manacles secured my wrists. No fetters clamped my feet. No shackles weighed me down. The room was comfortable, even luxurious, with silken upholstery and gilded chairs. Samphron oil lamps filled the room with a warm friendly glow. The windows were closed.

Everyone around me treated me with exquisite politeness. Wines, miscils, palines, dainty delicacies, everything was instantly provided by a bevy of attendants. All the same, I was a prisoner and I knew it.

The Chulik overseer, Chekaran the Balass, told me his master would see me as soon as some tiresome duty was dispatched. Until then, would you please, majister, take your ease.

Perforce, I waited. I did not waste the time. Everything that had happened to me since I'd stared into W'Watchun's eyes went over and over in my head. There had to be a pattern to all this, and the pattern involved the Illusionist's desperate desire to know the secret of gunpowder.

On the way here as the lifter whirled above the top-heavy buildings I'd been able to see precious little of the layout of the city. All the same, the place where I now was, to all intents and purposes, incarcerated, couldn't be any of the villas I'd been in before. This place, too, couldn't be the main residence of W'Watchun, of that I was convinced.

I owed the Illusionist for what he'd done. The pain in my head was now just about gone; but I didn't forget it, I can tell you. All the evidence pointed to this fellow W'Watchun being in deep trouble. If that trouble involved ibmanzies, then my duty was to investigate. Should that investigation land the sorcerer in more trouble—then I did not think I would mourn overmuch.

When at last he came in with the Chulik, Chekaran the Balass, he walked slowly, stooped over, and if a fellow didn't know what skullduggeries he'd been up to he'd attract a deal of sympathy.

"You have everything you require here?" He sat down heavily.

"No."

His head went up. "I see." His voice, although not as full and fruity as when he commanded, had lost the thin reediness of his surgeon impersonation. "You refer to your liberty?"

"As to that, I'll take it when it is necessary. No. I refer to explanations."

"That is why I am here."

We spoke together normally, without all the majisters and the sans. Our conversation was not interrupted, and Chekaran himself saw to pouring wine for us.

"Your country is defended by your sorcerous Wall. Why then is it so important for you to know about gunpowder?"

His smile was weak, almost deprecatory. He told me that I had fallen into the common error. "Oh, no. The Wall is not to keep enemies out. It exists to keep the warriors in."

Digesting that impressive item of information I munched a paline or three. He went on to say that sorcery of great force held the warriors within Winlan. The Wall effectively barred them from the rest of Balintol. Otherwise, he said, they'd go rampaging over the other lands, looting and burning. Rapine and pillage and general destruction would follow.

Taking the character of the Tchekedos into consideration, this hideous forecast rang true. "And the ibmanzies?"

He brushed a thin hand over his face. He took the tall black hat off and the Chulik placed it on a side table. "Those demons from hell—whatever hell it is they come from—have altered my plans."

Of course, it turned out to be Khon the Mak who'd altered the balance of power. The priests of Dokerty here had not yet perfected their creation of the monsters. When Khon the Mak arrived fleeing from Oxonium, he brought not only a lad who was an infecto but the dread secret. That poor lad had been let loose aboard the frigate. "I think," he said, "I think, although I am not sure, he was sent for you."

"Not you?"

"The secret of the Wall is—" he stopped himself. Then: "They will not kill me until they are sure they can destroy the Wall."

The Dokerty-lovers here had been trying to make ibmanzies and that was the reason he wanted to know about gunpowder. He'd seen its effect through my experiences. He was probably quite right. A good solid thirty-two pound roundshot smashing into a demon would most certainly make it sit up and take notice, by Krun!

He was quite unrepentant about trying to fool me with his clever hallucinations. He'd correctly surmised I would not willingly bring gunpowder to Kregen. Now he was at his wit's end, for the red-robed priests would even now be hard at work creating infectos to be turned into ibmanzies.

Quite softly, I said: "I have a personal reason to rid the world of ibmanzies. And, another, is to unite all of Balintol. That includes you, San W'Watchun, and your country of Winlan. Don't forget it."

We talked more around the various subjects. His powers highly impressive though they were, had limits. His fatigue was obvious. He let slip that the Wall was maintained independently of his immediate control. If the warrior lords discovered that secret location they would bring the Wall down with the disastrous consequences he had outlined.

My reply reminded him of the need to unite Balintol against the Shanks, whose invasion plans were at the moment on hold according to my information from the Everoinye. His bloodthirsty warriors would find their satisfaction in fighting gratified to the hilt when they went up against the Fish-heads.

He confirmed that magic had been used to transport me from his bedroom suite via the transparent-roofed passageway. That had been San Furney's doing. Here W'Watchun shook his head and pursed his lips.

"Furney is clever. He is ruthless. Kov Barca may discover that one day when Furney's use for him is done."

"You don't care for him?"

"For neither of them. One way of keeping a little order among the Tchekedos is to encourage them to fight one another." At my lack of surprise, for divide and rule is an ancient method, he nodded, understanding. Kov Grogan G'Gulandor considered himself the naturally ordained leader of all the warriors, and Kov Barca L'Lambton disputed that. There were factions. If the warriors could organize themselves to stand against W'Watchun then life would be a lot harder for the sorcerer.

On my mentioning the absence of women among the principals of Winlan he just said that there were odd customs in other lands of Kregen. In Winlan a woman kept her place, which was in the home caring for husband, menfolk and children. The truth was probably much darker than that.

Naturally he wanted to know about Earth and just as naturally I spun him a few yarns. By careful slanting of the talk I made certain sure he had no knowledge of the Star Lords. The Everoinye know how to cover their tracks, and that's for sure, by Zair!

On that I became uneasy. Here I was gathering vital information for the tasks ahead set by the Star Lords and it might well appear to them I merely sat chatting aimlessly. When intelligence becomes available only a fool ignores the opportunity to learn.

Time was moving along and it was now well into the night.

The Chulik began to make his presence obvious, rattling the plates, lifting glasses and putting them down with sudden bangs. This, I judged, from my own experience of retainers and the loyalty Chekaran clearly displayed for the sorcerer, was not because the Chulik was tired and wanted to go to bed. I said: "If you will excuse me, san, I believe bed calls."

As I spoke I cast a questioning glance at the Chulik. He responded at once, coming forward and masterfully assisting W'Watchun from his chair. We spoke the remberees and off they went, the Illusionist leaning heavily on Chekaran. I closed the door after them, and heard the Chulik half-whisper to me: "My thanks, majister."

Now you may judge of my total interest in what we had discussed that only as I prepared to retire and went through the familiar routine was I struck by a number of notable absences. My Val! The headache was almost gone, so I couldn't blame that. Oh, no, it was the importance to my mission of what we had talked about that had driven other thoughts from my old vosk skull of a cranium. First thing in the morning, then, I'd tackle W'Watchun or Chekaran about my weapons.

Yes, it is difficult to believe that a Krozair of Zy, a wild Clansman, a canny old leem-hunter, a zhanpaktun, should not carry the necessity of an arsenal of weapons to gird about his person in the forefront of his mind.

They served me the first breakfast in the same room. The serving girls were demure, pleasant, deft. The pleasant perfume of lavender wafted about their neat persons. I ate well and the moment Chekaran came in to check that everything was satisfactory I tackled him. He smiled that knowing smile of a paktun when it comes to armaments and beckoned. A couple of slaves entered carrying burdens.

They were all there, thank Opaz.

The Star Lords had done me proud when they'd hurled me into Winbium. The russet tunic was brand new. The link armor was as fine as any that came out of the Dawn Lands of Havilfar. The rapier and main gauche were by now old friends. They'd included a drexer, which delighted me given the inferior quality of most of the steel around here. My old sailor knife went sheathed over the back of my right thigh. The bow they'd supplied was a great Lohvian longbow, although the shafts were not fletched with the feathers of the zim korf. These flights were blue and of high quality.

So, as you may easily imagine, I have left to last in this little inventory the item of greatest import. Oh, yes, by the Blade of Kurin! After all my travails I can tell you it felt—well, is there any other sensation quite like grasping a great Krozair longsword in your fists? Well, yes, just one. And that, of course, is holding a Savanti sword.

Buckling up my equipment and closing the dulled silver buckle of the lesten hide belt with its array of pouches, I felt a new man. By Vox! I felt like two newly-born men!

"Thank you, Chekaran. Now I must be on my way."

"What—but, majister—the master—"

"Quite, quite. Thank you for caring for me. Remberee."

With that I made for the door.

Just how far would the Chulik go in trying to stop me? I felt for his predicament, for although W'Watchun might be a kindly master, he would view with great disfavor his overseer's dereliction of duty. Stopping, I swung about and told Chekaran to inform the Illusionist that I was about the business we had discussed. There was no doubt I could be found if required, none at all, by Krun!

The time for lollygagging about had passed. Now was the time for a spot of action. I now knew a considerable amount about the situation here in Winlan I'd not known before: there was much still to learn.

"If anyone asks," I called back as I went out the door, "I am a zhanpaktun employed by San W'Watchun to assist you." I heard myself speak in a hard no-nonsense way that I'd not consciously intended. So when I finished with a not altogether polite request to know if he understood, the word "Dernun?" rattled out like a thunderclap.

He jumped. He bellowed. "Quidang, majister!"

Deeming it politic not to let him see me change my face I reached the front door and changed my countenance there before stepping out into the morning suns shine. My face stung; but I could sustain that for the time I anticipated I would require.

How glorious to walk out under the streaming tangled radiance of the Suns of Scorpio! All sheening emerald and ruby, the lights set the windows of the top-heavy buildings aflame and cast multi-colored shadows across the pavement.

How wonderful to breath the pure air of Kregen! Ah, magic, magic! On I walked and found I was in a capital mood.

I even hummed half under my breath the little ditty about the fair maid who pined for love of a mercenary, "She kissed the mortilhead." My own pakzhan glinted gold at my throat, and the pakai was wound neatly out of the way. Oh, yes, as I strode along I can tell you, I was your hyrpaktun to the life!

No one took any notice of me and when I spotted groups of Tchekedos taking the morning air I avoided them circumspectly. The Eyes glittered four square from their pillars at crossroads. Was the sorcerer spying on me through them right now? Or some of his minions? Now I still didn't know where I was in the city. Somewhere near the center, I judged, in view of the architecture. The idle thought occurred to wonder how often the forest of pillars beneath the buildings gave way. The idea intrigued me and I pursued it. How much effort on my part would it take to sabotage the pillars? How many would have to be weakened before the building collapsed?

Thus fantasizing I walked on towards where the clump of taller buildings against the sky indicated what must be the center.

Although W'Watchun had not said as much, I felt pretty sure when he spoke of San Furney that the sorcerer employed by Kov Barca was fully capable of preventing the Eye from spying on them. Otherwise my journey would probably not have been necessary.

My guess proved correct. The edifice I sought was not a top-heavy building, as I'd half-expected, but it did lie at the center.

The damned place had its red-robed priests going in and out. Warriors hung about the steps outside and I guessed this was a kind of open-air club where they'd meet and talk and boast before going to the taverns. I saw no merchants patronizing the place, and only a handful of mercenaries. Perhaps it was entirely my imagination; but I sensed an aura about the stones, an exudation of wickedness.

The Tchekedos cast idle glances at me as I walked up the entrance steps and passed under the vulgarly ostentatious portico.

Prudently giving them a humble inclination of the head I advanced into the shadows. Nath G'Goldark, the chief priest of Dokerty, had been brought here by Khon the Mak. How was he rubbing along with his opposite number in Winbium? By Krun! I hoped they were at each other's throats like leems!

The Dokerty religion, W'Watchun had told me, was used by him in his control of the warriors and was why the gargantuan voice had called me a betrayer of Dokerty when I'd arrived. There was no reason for me to delay here. All I wanted to do was gain the intelligence I required and then depart. Then a magnificent Plan would have to be drawn up and acted upon, Opaz willing.

Most temples of the same religion are built along similar lines and my previous fraught experiences in Dokerty institutions, I fervently hoped, gave me a grasp of the general layout here. Moving on swiftly I took a side corridor leading away from the entrance. Red robes passed me without question. I was struck by the complete absence of priestesses. Women must be kept apart from the men even here. They probably had their own entrances and exits.

As I spotted a door that looked promising I wondered if the warriors had never progressed from or if they had regressed to their ancient barbaric beliefs. If the Tchekedos believed women were unclean they were worse idiots even than I'd given them credit for, by Vox!

No one was about as I pushed the door open. It creaked and resisted my initial efforts. It came open with a final rush and dust puffed up about me. The short corridor beyond looked as though no one had disturbed the dust for centuries. The air felt clammy.

The door at the far end proved almost as difficult to open. Glad to get out of the dust I moved down a dimly-lit corridor. So far I'd spotted not a single solitary sign of a secret door in the walls.

A low moaning from ahead grew in volume as I padded silently along. Sweeping curtains hung from brass rails half-concealing an opening came into view as I rounded a corner. Still no secret doors...

Cautiously I put an eyeball around the curtain. Golden tassels offered concealment. The scene within the chamber, lit by tall sconces, struck me as macabre beyond reason. The place was filled with totally naked women. They were flogging one another with thorn ivy and rose branches and stinging nettles. Their moaning rose and fell more like a chant than simple cries of pain. There were women of all manner of races of diffs there, all bare as the day they were born. Their bodies gleamed in spots and streaks of blood against skin and fur and hair. I stood, not moving, utterly revolted.

The woman nearest to me gave a final slash with her rose stem and walked towards the curtain. She was well-built, an Extran girl from the islands, superb, with her black skin gleaming with dark blood. She panted. Her face was mostly concealed by that typical flowing mass of ebony hair the Extrans weave with flowers to make look beautiful.

She approached me directly. She halted just at the edge of the curtain. A single brushing movement swept her hair up away from her face. The face was the thin white face of San W'Watchun!

"Majister! You must leave at once or you are a dead man!"

Thirteen

My face slipped.

W'Watchun's face turned into that of a beautiful black girl and the flopped mass of hair fell to conceal over half.

"Hurry! The women cannot see me. If a sorcerer is spying I trust this disguise will succeed. Now, go!"

Without any more ado I switched about and galloped along the passage to the creaking door.

What had happened was perfectly clear. With the ridiculous state of women in Winlan extending here to religious matters, the idiots even partitioned off their temples. Looking for secret doors I'd stumbled through into the women's section. The dust puffed again as I sprinted for the far end and the other creaking door.

Give the sorcerer credit. I'd had the suspicion he was watching me and waiting on events hoping that my crack-brained scheme would work. Well, by Djan! He'd been quick!

The door opened and I slid through. Once again the passage lay empty of human life; but sounds of people talking floated faintly up from the direction I'd arrived. To brave it out and go boldly back that way? Or avoid confrontation and seek one of the other exits I knew would exist in the temple?

Immediately I turned to retrace my steps. I knew this way out and did not care to risk losing myself in the damned maze this place was sure to be. As I marched along briskly towards the voices I reflected on the interesting fact that W'Watchun apparently didn't know the layout of the Dokerty temple. There was no help to be hoped for in finding the door out of this hell-hole.

The voices turned out to belong to a group of servants carrying water barrels on poles and slings. They stood aside as I strode past, bowing their heads very respectfully.

Quite obviously the relationship between the classes here was far more complicated than I'd at first imagined. If the sorcerer used the Dokerty religion yet was not familiar with this temple, why, then, that must mean he was no Dokerty believer himself. This thought cheered me up.

Around the next corner two paktun guards stood against the walls. I blinked. One was a Hytak, the other a Fristle. They looked familiar. I stared and then with a little shock recognized the russet tunics, the arsenal of weapons exactly similar to mine. Without a word they fell in before me and as a trio we stalked along the passage and so came out into the ante chamber which led to the outside portico.

Now priests in their red robes thickened upon the ground. A clump of warriors barged in through the doorway, their rough voices falling silent as they entered the temple. Now would be the testing time. Still I marched on flanked by the two phantoms in my image created by San W'Watchun.

The truth was, although aware of the cleverness of the Illusionist in thus fouling the scent, as it were, I was not at all sure if his cleverness was not overdone. Inevitably, we attracted attention. The warriors were respectful of the priests. We three moved sideways out of their path, inclining our heads dutifully.

Now if these confounded Tchekedos started a rumpus, then I, for one, would take to my heels. The Wizards of Loh could create illusions of fighting men with swords, which, if believed in, could strike with physical force. Their illusions could kill you. Were the apparitions of the Sorcerers of Balintol able to do the same?

As far as I could see, there was no reason for these oafs in their ridiculous neckerchiefs to stop us, apart from their own bloody-minded natures. Into that calculation I hoped would go the normal reaction of anyone in the church of their religion to act with due respect for the holiness of their surroundings.

Not that, by Krun, I felt any holiness about this Opaz-forsaken den of iniquity!

Among the warriors who were now standing talking in their idle way there stood—of course, of, by Krun, course!—that Lord Ramley who'd been so upsetting in The Spotted Gyp. Then I relaxed a trifle. I must be very tightly wound up, indeed, to imagine he would recognize in the zhan-paktun the yellow-tunicked quasi-merchant.

Anyway, my face was sufficiently different now.

Now we three were up level with the knot of Tchekedos. I found myself thinking that if they wore bones through their noses that would be exactly right. In the right culture a bone through the nose is a proper symbol of high rank; in other cultures it provokes other reactions. These famous warriors had poured out of the northern mountains relatively recently to fashion Winlan in its current state. The original inhabitants had fled, been killed or joined the newcomers.

Now we three were past the clump of warriors. The door to the outside stood open. The slanting rays of green and red flooded in.

"Hey! Tikshims! C'mere—we want to talk to you."

The coarse voice held just that note of casual arrogant authority to get up a fellow's nose. What the speaker demanded was acted upon instanter in his everyday experience. Well, we've met plenty of high-flown cramphs on Kregen. I walked on firmly. If he started to shout and identified me as his target I could always say I was unaware he was talking to me.

He must have been surprised I didn't turn about at once in a respectful manner to find out what he wanted. The two phantoms quickened their pace and I speeded up with them.

"You! Mercenary blintz! Yes, I'm talking to you!"

Now I had grown more than just a little tired of all these overween-ing voices of authority, these arrogant warrior lords imposing their wills uncaring of anyone else. I could feel the eyes of my blade comrades upon me, Seg and Inch, Turko, Balass, Tyfar. Many and many a good comrade seemed to me to be peering down at me, at plain Dray Prescot. What to do?

These warriors would have their bullying fun with a paktun. If he wound up dead at the end that wouldn't disconcert them in the slightest. Probably, the rasts, it would add to their enjoyment.

What to do for the best?

San W'Watchun and his apparitions settled the issue. I acknowledge that this indecision was not untypical of me in these latter days on Kregen. My hesitation came to an abrupt end as the two phantoms simply picked up their heels and ran headlong out of the temple.

Perforce, I ran after them. Even then I couldn't think of this as a flight. I wasn't fleeing from the warriors. Rather, I was running to keep up with a couple of phantom paktuns. By Zair! What a situation for a fellow to be in!

We raced outside and clattered down the steps as people turned their heads to stare in surprise at this unseemly behavior. We were, after all, to the praise of the great Dokerty, respectful of his temple, were we not? That, no doubt, was how their thoughts ran.

Now some credit became apparent in the Illusionist's idea of tripling me for we could hare off in three different directions. This we did and the last I saw of my two phantom comrades was a couple of wisps of russet disap-pearing into the crowds...

Before I rounded the nearest corner of the temple I cast a glance back. The crowds had mostly given up staring at these three maniac paktuns and were going on with their business. A few warriors clustered at the top of the steps and shook their fists. They did not follow. Bad cess to 'em, then!

Once out of their sight I halted. At the center of the kyro fronting the temple lifted a column on which were mounted four Eyes. There had been no sign—at least, none that I detected—of a freely floating Eye and with the departure of his illusions in different directions W'Watchun would no doubt banish them. I started off briskly.

Walking along towards the temple came a double column of people. They were of mixed diff races, young men and women, and they paced along with their hands folded into the sleeves of their robes and their heads down. A priest in red led them. I stared at these young folk and I felt sick.

All were clad in pure white robes.

So Khon the Mak had urged the priests into action already. These doomed ones, already kitted out in the white robes, must be going into the temple to become infectos. They had no idea of the torments they faced. W'Watchun called infectos, people who had gone through the initiation ceremony to prepare them for the invasion of their bodies by demons, the sublimes. Sublime! That was cruelly unfunny.

They walked on, heads bowed, silent, and I could not stop watching the poor devils until they rounded the corner and so paced on out of my sight.

If these deluded folk were really going into the temple to be tortured into sublimes that did not mean the Prism of Power hidden in its Flut-ubium would be there. My guess was they would stay close by Khon the Mak and his tame chief priest. All the same, it might be worth going back. There would be exits and entrances to the temple in a quiet back street. At once I set off towards the rear of the temple.

Around the back in exactly the quiet street I expected stood a lenken door, brass-studded. Two lamps, unlit at this hour of the day, were brack-eted out above. The other side of the street was mere blank walls above short but thick pillars. Through the gaps I could make out only a hazy greenery. This was just another proof of the power of Dokerty hereabouts.

Not even bothering to check if the door was locked I found two deep shadows, tinged red and green, and concealed myself beside a pillar. The wait was not long.

An under priest strutted busily into view, going towards the door. He carried a silver-knobbed cane. With this he kept prodding the grey breech-clout of the slave who tottered along under a chest of vast proportions. The chest was leather-covered and bound in brass strips and corners. It looked heavy. The slave, a Trinkim, with bald swollen head and staring eyes, almost fell. The cane prodded mercilessly and I stepped forward into the light of the Suns.

My intentions were perfectly simple. After a polite request for the under priest to open the door, I'd go into the passage within and tie priest and slave up out of the way. I'd bind the priest with pleasure; the slave with regret.

The falling droop of jaws! The widening of eyes! The panicky hand to trembling mouth!

"Get on with it, rast," I said in no friendly way.

The Trinkim slave dropped the chest. He didn't just let it go. It appeared he tried to hold onto it. I knew the ways of slaves. He gave it a good old-fashioned slam-bang onto the ground. Glass chimed from within.

The key opened the door. There was no point in taking the key; the red-robes would change the locks.

The passage was paved in white and black tiles, the walls and ceiling were painted cream. Mineral oil lamps burned at intervals. Telling the Trinkim to haul the chest inside I looked at their clothes for suitable bonds. The Trinkim brought the chest in and slammed the door. He liked slamming things, evidently, given the chance.

The situation was well under control. The priest was far too frightened to scream and the slave was enjoying himself.

Then, and of course, everything went wrong.

By the pendulous belly and massive thighs of the Lady Dulshini! I fairly snarled to myself as half a dozen warriors hove into view at the far end of the corridor.

A considerable amount of running away had been done by me lately so in theory there should have been no problem in my switching about and sprinting off. Clearly there was no profit to be had in taking on this bunch of Tchekedos. The sensible action was to depart.

The problem was caused by what these oafs were doing.

They had a couple of young girls being manhandled between them. Strips of material hung about the girls' thighs and swirled out as they twisted and squirmed trying to escape. The warriors were laughing in that meaningful way that bastards like this do when they anticipate a little—in their words—fun and games.

Because of their activities they didn't at first appreciate the situation of the priest and his slave. He was, anyway, only an under priest and could never influence their actions. They barged on, shouting and guffawing, coming straight down the corridor intending to exit and go about what they meant to do in some tavern or other.

The passage was a trifle cramped for longsword work. The drexer came out of the scabbard sweetly. Without a sound I leaped.

The first warrior went down without understanding his fate. The next let go a girl's arm. He yelled, and this time in anger and alarm, and hauled on his sword. He went down. The others set up a squalling and a racket and milled about and one of the girls got in my way so that I had to skip side-ways and let her tumble over. I didn't waste time telling her I was sorry. A blade slashed at me. That was taken on my sword and deflected and the drexer swept back and bit.

As so often in a scrap of this nature it was then vitally necessary for me to duck and dodge the savage attack that instantly followed. They were shouting their usual threats, pushing forward, faces contorted, weapons brandished as I skipped out of their reach.

A figure wearing black robes and a tall black hat appeared through the warriors, materializing between them and me.

"Majister! What do you think you're doing? I need help! Please—come at once—"

The figure wavered, blurring, vibrating. It vanished.

For the moment shocked off balance I saw the warriors hurl themselves upon me, shrilling their Dokerty warcries.

Fourteen

"Come at once!" he'd panted in that pleading voice. Come where did he mean? What did I think I was doing? Couldn't he see what I was doing? There were three nasty customers and a wounded one thirsting for my blood. In that tiny fraction of time before they reached me I regained my composure and fronted them.

There was absolutely no question of my abandoning these girls now. For one thing the warriors would butcher them out of hand because they had witnessed Tchekedo humiliation at the grubby hands of a mere mercenary.

The steel crossed and screeched, the blades slashed and thrust, and one warrior was down without a throat and I leaped back and nearly went base over apex across that confounded chest.

Staggering up I knocked a sword away, luckily enough catching the flat with my left forearm. The rast nearly had me then. My sword flicked before the others' eyes. The flicking stopped as it switched sideways and sliced into the nearest ear. The fellow let out an almighty screech, dropped his braxter and clapped a hand to his dangling ear. Before his hand even reached the mangled remains of his ear my drexer slashed the other way. I admit it was a neat cut. The edge bit in over the top of his armor and almost took his head off.

The other one essayed a powerful overarm cut, my drexer chingled against his braxter and his weapon snapped clean in half.

The fourth, the wounded one hanging back, decided this was enough. He yelped out something about going for help and scuttled back up the corridor.

Giving these shints no time to recover I roared in on them and with a quick flurry which bedazzled the eyes but was in reality quite a charming passage of arms, I cut them up sufficiently.

The stink of blood must have upset them. They yelled—but they ran off.

The two girls were clutching each other with white knuckles. No time was allowed me by W'Watchun to lollygag about, I gathered from his desperate plea. I did not wish to leave the ladies here. I glared at them, seeing the tears streaking their faces.

"Keep up with me if you wish to get out of this hellhole."

"Notor—" one of them managed to get past ashen lips.

They were not slaves. That was at once evident by the softness of their bodies and their well-kept hands. The draperies hanging from their waists consisted of silks and satins of a variety of colors. They made shift to haul the dresses up but the straps had been broken when those hairy bullyboys ripped them down so the clothes hung about their thighs. I felt for them, well, by Opaz, of course I did! But San W'Watchun—what in a Herrelldrin Hell was going on with him?

The under priest and his slave cowered away as I stalked past. I gave the chest a kick. The confounded thing had nearly delivered me up to a sword thrust through the guts.

Outside in the air, even city air, the smell of blood could be breathed away. Once more I spoke to the two women, who were clearly two ladies.

"You may keep up with me. Or you may go to your friends."

Both of them wore fancy sandals, fragile affairs of narrow straps and glittery gemstones.

"We cannot—" said one. "We dare not—" said the other.

They were both able to speak better now; but their words were choked with tears. They babbled on then, something about their fate, and how they were doomed. Somewhere in there they said they'd follow me. They did not, either of them, say a thank you.

The apparition of the Illusionist which had been clearly visible to me could not have been seen by these ladies or the warriors. Despite the debt I owed W'Watchun for what he had put me through, I felt more than a twinge of apprehension for his safety. If his life lay between these ghastly Tchekedos and their desires to lay waste to the rest of Balintol, then, without question, my duty lay with him.

On the other hand, as a simple matter of humanity, did I not owe a duty to these two poor creatures? When two instincts clash, why, then, my friend, you're in for a devil of a lot of bother!

In truth, W'Watchun's house was not all that far away from the center of the city. Brusquely, I said: "I am going to Swan Street. If I see you there after—afterwards—I will help you."

On that, and without a remberee, which I felt would be too final for the ladies, I was off.

Oh, yes, I reflected as I sprinted along. After what?

Swan Street, so named for an ancient fountain graced with stone swans, was soon reached. The fountain was obviously a relic of the people who'd lived here before the Tchekedos moved in. The water merely dribbled, indicating that no one bothered to keep the fountain in full working order. The noise became apparent at once.

A gang of warriors congregating about W'Watchun's house set up the racket. What they were trying to do was not immediately apparent. A lot of fist waving and sword brandishing was taking place. The steps had been drawn up into the house and the warriors might well be waiting for ladders. All this I saw in a single flashing glance.

What attracted my instant attention stumbled helplessly along Swan Street. His hands were tied with rope and rope between his ankles allowed him only short steps. Two warriors prodded him along with swords. I pursed my lips. The warriors up at the house had not seen me; these two became aware of my presence as I stepped out into the suns shine. They did not halt. They shouted insults at me to get out of the way, blintz.

I said: "If you untie him now I shall not kill you."

The beaked head of the prisoner snapped up and his violet and green feathers bristled. The Rapa, Jiktar Ronun ti Bjorfling, who was the captain of W'Watchun's guard and who had treated me with kindness and respect, stared as though I was an apparition.

The Tchekedos snarled the expected words of insult, swirled their swords up and came at me headlong to cut me down.

The drexer had been cleaned on a dead warrior's clothes as I spoke to the two ladies. Now it flicked out of the scabbard bright and ready for fresh business.

Quite clearly there was little time left, judging by the sorcerer's frantic appeal and the mob of warriors trying to break into his house. These two were dealt with circumspectly and brusquely.

As you know I am always conscious that one day I shall meet another swordsman of the skill of Mefto the Kazzur. I never boast or even think that I am 'The Best Swordsman in Two Worlds.' That way, apart from being infantile, leads on to megalomania.

A couple of passes, the swift chingle of steel, and the two Tchekedos sprawled on the ground. Only one of their braxters had broken. Finishing the last stroke with a slice at Ronun's bonds I cut his hands free.

"Majis!"

"What's going on, Jik?"

He spoke as he freed himself from his bonds. His words were frequently interrupted by profoundly ferocious curses concerning Tchekedos and all their doings.

San W'Watchun's fears had become reality. A Sorcerer of Balintol, one San Partagus, once apprenticed to W'Watchun, had returned from Loh. What his studies there had revealed no one could know.

"One thing," Ronun spoke passionately. "Treachery!"

Partagus had persuaded Furney to leave Barca and join forces with him and Kov Grogan. They'd suborned some of W'Watchun's allies. The outlook was serious. Ronun, trying to parley, had been taken prisoner by these thugs. The sorcerers were not here; they were trying to break down W'Watchun's resistance. Then the Tchekedos would finish off the Illusionist.

Looking along the street, I wondered how much time we had.

"Round the back, jis!"

At the rear we could distinguish the prancing idiots between the pillars. We couldn't have much time left before the ladders arrived.

How wrong can prior assumptions prove! By Krun, I was all wrong about those dratted ladders! A flier skimmed into view going over us and then the house. Around the corner of the building she was just visible as she touched down by the Swan Fountain.

Instantly, without thought, I started to run.

Despite the general opinion of Paktuns that the famous warriors of Winlan were puffed up windbags of braggadocio, they'd do for us and the Illusionist. Numbers would tell. So I sprinted for the lifter, managing to find breath to bellow to Ronun to keep up.

Between the pillars I could see the Tchekedos as they pranced off towards the voller. They called vollers lifters here in Balintol. As I sprinted flat out I could see she was a roomy craft with a midships cabin and even a rudimentary gallery alongside her keel. No need for the warriors to wait for ladders, by Vox. They'd land on the roof and that would be the end of San W'Watchun. If he was locked in an occult struggle with these other two wizards he'd most likely be able to see and speak; he'd find moving about difficult. He'd be butchered mercilessly.

The lifter had touched down by the fountain as the nearest spot on her line of approach, having to fly over the house. I ran. Oh, yes, by Zair, I ran!

The pilot came out of his cabin and leaned over the bulwark. Acutely aware of the mob of warriors at my back I raced up to the lifter and shouted: "Hai, dom! I'm the new pilot!"

With that I leaped up and grasped his arm. Using him as a boarding net I climbed up over him as he tumbled head over heels out. He let out a yell before he hit the deck. A single glance showed me Ronun almost up to the flier and the warriors hard on his heels.

"Jump, Ronun!"

He leaped; I gripped him somewhere and hauled him inboard. Without stopping the pivoting motion I hurtled into the cabin and thrust the lift lever over all the way. With a surging bound like a zorca clearing a fence, up we shot.

The noise the Tchekedos made below us sounded quite like music, by Krun!

Up and across we flew and so descended on the roof. Jumping out I realized that, for a short time anyway, the urgency had gone. Before those cramphs brought up another flier we'd have to move. We had ourselves a tiny breathing space.

Because this situation told me that dreadful events had occurred, I told Ronun that it was necessary to shift his master. I intended to take him away to a place of safety. W'Watchun could fight his thaumaturgical battles well enough; his physical body was vulnerable. "Jik, you and your juruk need not fight the warriors. The san and I will be gone and—"

"Yes," said the voice of the Chulik, Chekaran. "And I shall be with you." He walked up clad in armor and girded with swords.

"Very well." So it was settled, or so I thought, until Ronun said: "I believe if we stay the Tchekedos will massacre us all."

The lifter was certainly roomy enough. I nodded and said I would go down and see the san. I found him in a quiet and darkened room, the shades drawn, lying on a bed. He looked like a newly-hatched chick fallen from the nest.

He saw me. He croaked out: "They are trying to kill me."

At my nod his head moved restlessly on the pillow.

"You must understand—" he started to say, and stopped and his haggard face drooped even more. What was going on in the arcane realms of magic I didn't know and, frankly, didn't really want to know.

"I understand. This mage Partagus is the key. Kov Grogan wouldn't try to kill you or he'd never knock the Wall down. No, Partagus knows how and where the Wall is sustained."

He tried to wipe his lips, and failed. His hands trembled.

"Yes. And he is on his way there now to destroy it all!"

Fifteen

By the odiferous orifices and exuding excrescences of Makki Grodno! The consequences of this new turn in developments were horrifically apparent. If—I refused to countenance when—if W'Watchun's Wall came down a raging torrent of these uncouth warriors would be let loose on Balintol. Despite their own boasting I fancied they'd be dealt with smartly enough by the other fighting men of the sub-continent.

No, not the warriors only. My concern was the flood of ibmanzies that would be let loose. My Val! Khon the Mak would glee when his monstrous creatures tore the heart out of Caneldrin. By that time he'd reckon to have Tolindrin in the palm of his hand.

There lived people I knew in both those countries—friends and foes. My struggles in Balintol had largely been on their account. If I failed them and thus displeased the Everoinye no need to worry where I'd end up!

Chekaran could be heard shouting from the next room, telling Nath the Swagger, a Brokelsh, one of his underlings, to go round and make absolutely sure everyone was accounted for. The Chulik came in, very businesslike, and took W'Watchun up in his arms. He cradled the sorcerer like a baby. My opinion of Chuliks had, as you know, changed over the seasons of my life on Kregen. All the same, by Vox, this Chekaran was not at all typical of his race of diffs.

We all went up onto the roof. The household was not large for this was a private retreat without formal political functions and I guessed W'Watchun was annoyed it had been discovered.

Of course, I reflected, as the people boarded, the mage could easily have put a geas on the Chulik. With all the magic floating about around here that would hardly be surprising. In addition, the sorcerer could have fixed me up with a geas, which would explain a lot of my actions lately. Well, if he had he might find it necessary to cancel the geas with the occult fight he was waging right now.

The cook clambered aboard dangling pots and pans. She was on the plump side—to be kind—and was a Gon whose beautiful silver hair which normally hung to her waist was now bundled up in a turban of impressive size. She was Glima the Pie—and famous for her pastry.

Last aboard, I observed the fantamyrrh, and then went to the controls. The craft soared up cleanly into the fragrant air. Below us, the warriors looked as though they might rupture themselves, so great were their paroxysms of anger. They clustered by the house, a splodge of raging oafs.

Just beyond the Swan fountain a flash of color caught my eye. It was not turquoise. There were reds and oranges and blues and yellows, and two frightened faces. Instantly, I slanted the flier down, aiming to alight as closely as possible.

"Have your people ready to haul 'em inboard!" I yelled at Ronun. He jumped. He looked back. "The Tchekedos—"

"Aye! We must be quick."

Chekaran shouted: "We cannot go down! It is too dangerous. The master—"

"We'll do it!" I fairly snarled at him.

The whole crazy incident took but a matter of moments. The flier swooped like a striking bird of prey. She eased alongside the two women and brawny arms reached down from the lower gallery and hauled them inboard.

Ronun bellowed up: "Take it away!" for, of course, I couldn't see below the keel. I thrust the levers over and up we went.

The warriors pounded along the street whooping and hollering and missed us by a whisker. They had no bowmen and Ronun must have given the order to his juruk not to shoot. I concurred with that decision, although probably for different reasons.

W'Watchun's Sylvies took the two trembling women away into the rear cabin. Chekaran cast me a questioning look. I shook my head.

"They were about to be nastily handled by these cramphs of warriors in the Dokerty temple. I told them I'd try to help them escape."

"In this country women of quality have no place other than in the home caring for their warriors."

"I suppose we'd better see if the Sylvies can find out what the story is."

"Aye, majister." He took himself off to speak to Glima the Pie.

When he returned saying that enquiries were under way I checked with him that we had a pilot aboard. He nodded. "Naghan the Rash. He flies well; but hold onto your hat."

By this time we were all in need of sustenance. Perforce, we'd have to wait until Glima was finished with the strange girls and could see to the meal.

With Naghan the Rash at the controls, Ronun and I took a tour of the lifter, assessing her fighting ability.

She had a single catapult for'ard, a small battery of varters along her sides in a single tier, and another along the gallery. Ronun ventured the opinion that his men could fight her well enough.

Now as you will appreciate, I'd gone along with Chekaran's direction for the course of the flier. Clearly, W'Watchun had told him where we were headed. Venturing to ask Ronun just where we were flying to, I was not at all surprised when he laughed, shortly, and said he ran the master's juruk. When we got where we were going, then he'd know. Naturally, the Illusionist had kept his secret all this time and revealing it would come hard. That Khon the Mak and the priests of Dokerty now knew had not swayed him, lying on his bed and struggling with phantom forces of evil as he was.

Back on deck after our investigations of the vessel we found Glima the Pie ready to tell us what she, in her turn, had discovered.

Because of the downtrodden state of the female sex in Winlan marriages for girls were arranged. This was quite normal in the circumstances. These two had been betrothed to men for whom they both cherished an active dislike. They preferred the company of each other.

"So they ran away together." Glima wiped her hands on her apron. "I can't say I approve; but then, I'm not a lady to be told just who is going to climb into bed with me."

There was no doubt from what I'd seen of them that the two women kept holding each other all the time, out of fear, as I'd seen, and out of affection as I now learned. Well, good luck to 'em both!

"They were caught and their families tried but could not persuade them to accept the arranged marriages. So they were sent to the temple to mend their ways and keep the warriors happy." Glima frowned. "I feel sorry for them, I suppose. But they deserved it."

The names they'd given—Rena and Tansy—were obviously not genuine. Glima went off to see about the meal and wondered what in a Herrelldrin Hell I was going to do with these two ladies.

Just before Glima beat the gong I took a turn down to the stern. The lookout here, a Hytak who rejoiced in the name of Marsippo the Melancholy, acknowledged me with a salute; but said nothing.

For a time we scanned the sky aft together. The rays of the two Suns streamed down in mingled magnificence, drenching the clouds in emerald and ruby glory. A few birds cavorted here and there, dots to be observed and noted. The land sped past beneath, mostly forest glimpsed between cloud banks below.

Just how long the warrior lords would take to organize the inevitable pursuit I didn't know. What I did know was that there would be a chase and it would not be long in arriving—always with the assumption that the Tchekedos possessed faster lifters than this one. Her speed was upwards of middling, so there was hope. Her name, painted on her bows and stern, was *Galloping Zorca*. If that reflected the truth of her speed, which I doubted, we should be all right. I left Marsippo the Melancholy to his vigil, telling him that food was on the way, and went back to the cabin.

Rena and Tansy stayed in the rear accommodation and food was taken in to them. They were both frightened out of their wits. The enormity of what they had done meant that eventually they must face retribution from their outraged families. Through their fear I could see the courage they must have shown to run away. Maybe it was the courage of despair; but they were both brave girls.

During the course of a meal in most of the countries I'd visited so far in Paz on Kregen polite conversation was general. Of course, what was polite in, say, a camp of the wild Clansmen of Segesthes, would have appeared savagely barbaric in the capital cities of Vallia or Hamal or Hyrklana, for example. Theatre and Art were always fine topics for discussion and would be fiercely debated among everyone from noble lord to kitchen maid. My surprise quickly evaporated when I learned at the table that here in Winlan theatres and puppet shows and similar entertainments were virtually non-existent.

Oh, yes, the proud Tchekedos liked to go to see the dancing girls with ankle bells and waving disposable silks. But of real Art they knew nothing and cared less. As they say, by a nation's Art shall ye know them.

One ray of comfort cheered me up. Any paktun worth his salt will sing the traditional old songs of his profession. I could look forward to that with the mercenaries, at least, thank Benga Eva.

Except—and whilst I would normally say 'of course' in reference to a Chulik, here it might be more appropriate to say 'possibly'—except Chekaran. If he was so different from fellows of his race he might cheerfully join in singing. The meal also afforded an opportunity to find out some of the histories of these folk. What can one say about this Chulik from that? They are trained up as fighters from almost the day they are born. That is their trade. Some, as I had previously discovered, did have some shreds of humanity. Chekaran, polishing up his tusks after the palines, quite broke the mold.

As for Ronun, he said he came from Rinaldrin, and greatly missed the company of his twin brother, Norun, who'd gone for a paktun to Havilfar.

"D'you know where in Havilfar?"

He shook his head ruefully. "Not really, majis. I did hear he'd been in some place called Migladrin."

Memories ghosted up. That seemed a long time ago now.

Ronun stood up. "Time to change the watch."

He went off and shortly thereafter the changed watch came in for their meal. Marsippo the Melancholy just sat down and started to help himself from the central dishes with their freight of various foods. All were delicious for Glima knew her job.

I stood up to go out on deck and everyone at the table stood up sharply. Waving them to be seated I reflected that the ways of protocol here in Winlan could become tedious. I had the suspicion that this kowtowing was not altogether the work of the Tchekedos.

The folk of Winlan were willing to be led and foreigners serving here followed the ways of the country.

The shout soared up just as I stepped out onto the deck.

My legs and body started to turn aft for a fractional moment. Then my brain registered the shout as hailing from for'ard.

Switching about, my legs almost got themselves into a tangle. A few moments brought me to the bows where Garnath the Stout perched up like a prijiker on the stem pointed ahead.

There were four of them, four black dots just breaking through the clouds. As they soared closer and took shape red and green light flashed reflections from their polished sides.

So our pursuers had boxed clever! By occult means they had sent a message ahead. Now four lifters stuffed with warriors flew down to trap and destroy us.

Sixteen

"I suppose," I said to Chekaran, who stood breathing heavily at my elbow, "you headed directly for the san's secret location?"

"Aye, majister."

"Humph," I said, and left it at that.

Ronun came up to join us and I suggested he'd better put a crew on the catapult. "We'll have to duck and dive and dodge them." Turning away I half-swung back to yell up at Garnath the Stout. "Come down here if you don't want to be thrown off during the maneuvers."

"Quidang!" he shouted and jumped down like a monkey.

Back in the control cabin I could see the oncoming lifters clearly through the forward windows. They were windows, not scuttles, and afforded excellent views forward and on the beam. Deciding not to take the controls away from Naghan the Rash I suggested it would be a good idea if he took the flier down to hide among the clouds.

He, too, snapped out: "Quidang." Down we went in a rush.

Now you will notice that I'd not been ordering these folk about. Just who was in command aboard was a tricky question. For the moment and particularly if we had a fight on our hands that problem would sort itself out very rapidly.

Among the juruk served an Undurker from the Undurkor Islands off the south west coast of the sub-continent. Called Ulak the Eye, he'd given my Lohvian longbow a very odd look at our first meeting. He used a compound reflex job and, with his borzoi-like face and powerful build, he'd be an expert shot. Still, if I had my way should there indeed be a scrap, he'd not come within range of the enemy. He'd have to serve the varters, and if necessary with his skill aim each ballista himself as others spanned and loaded.

Fluffy scraps of cloud started to speed past the lifter as we plunged down. An amusing thought occurred to me. Suppose those ugly-looking fliers diving down towards us had not been sent by Khon the Mak or Kov Grogan. Suppose they'd been sent by the two families of Rena and Tansy. An interesting idea; but one I felt unlikely given the way the ambushing lifters knew our course

At that moment, I sincerely believe, Opaz smiled. I stepped out onto the deck to try to get a better view. A piercing shriek—and, believe me, by Krun, it was piercingly piercing!—shrieked up at my back followed instantly by another and even shriller scream.

I swiveled around. Rena and Tansy flew out of the rear cabin. They had their arms about each other's waists, clutching as though they were drowning. Their scraps of brightly colored draperies fluttered like distress flags. They plunged for the gunwale.

In the instant I hurled myself at them a distraught Sylvie appeared at the door from which they'd bolted. "They're going to throw themselves over the side!" Her voice cracked with the horror she felt.

My arms clamped around their waists over their own arms and I hauled back like a driver pulling a team of runaway nikvoves.

They almost went over the side, and me with them, too. Their momentum dragged me along and my feet skidded on the deck. Their hideous screaming racketed up and down like a rusty axle. Haul, I snarled to myself, haul, you great fambly!

With a final wrench which checked their suicidal dive I dragged them back and we collapsed in a tangle. The Sylvie grabbed an arm and others of the crew ran up and grabbed other parts of the ladies who kept up their caterwauling nonstop. Extricating myself, I stood up.

I let out a big breath. That had been damned close!

Glima the Pie carrying a rolling pin turned up. For the moment the hullabaloo resounded aboard *Galloping Zorca*. They'd all, apparently, forgotten the four lifters who intended to shoot us down.

A few harsh words brought them to their senses. The four fliers were one minute hidden by scraps of cloud, the next in plain view racing down towards us. Putting my head in the window of the cabin I yelled at Naghan the Rash.

"How Rash are you, dom? Dodge 'em, dodge 'em!"

"Quidang!"

The lifter began gyrating, flitting like a gnat among the clouds. Now I could turn my attention to Rena and Tansy. They were crouched in each other's arms, sobbing to break the heart.

Quite clearly the Sylvie had told them we were being chased. Instantly they'd realized that no matter who captured them, they would be returned to their families who would then condemn them to the temple devoted to the cult of Dokerty. That was a fate far worse than simply jumping over the side.

Their problems tore at my emotions. Yet the hostile lifters out there pouncing down on us to rend and destroy posed a threat to all of Balintol, and eventually to all of Paz. If they stopped us, if they succeeded in preventing us from saving the maintenance of W'Watchun's Wall, the consequences would be horrific. It wasn't just a matter of these infamous warriors of Winlan riding berserk across the sub-continent. Oh, no. I recalled the white-robed youngsters marching so docilely into the Dokerty Temple. Khon the Mak and his confounded Dokerty priests would be manufacturing infectos, sublimes, waiting for the moment when the Wall came down.

My assumption was that the ibmanzies would not be used in Winlan. They were being husbanded for use to conquer Balintol. Of course, if our adversaries saw the chance of getting rid of us by using an ibmanzy, then they'd do it. By Krun! I detested the lot of 'em!

The tricky little question of just who was in command aboard *Galloping Zorca* appeared to have been tacitly settled. No one else had given orders and although we'd dived down to hide among the clouds, we maintained our original course.

If either Ronun or Chekaran fancied they were in command one might assume they'd have changed course by now. Chekaran had favored me with a questioning look. The escapade with Rena and Tansy had, for the moment, occupied our attention. I decided it would be proper for me to acquaint the crew of my intentions.

"If we keep on our present course in the clouds, we must hope those blintzes up there will calculate we've turned and run away."

Chekaran nodded his head so that his pigtail vibrated. "Neat." Then, after a pause, he added: "If it works."

"Aye."

"They're warriors," put in Ronun. As far as he was concerned that settled the issue. He didn't have to say he thought Tchekedos had lumps of wood for brains.

I hesitated. Slowly, I said: "True. But if my guess is right they have an unhanged rogue with them called Khon the Mak. He's a Hyr Kov out of Tolindrin."

Nothing could be seen of the hostile lifters through the clouds that swept across our deck like white wraiths.

"Naghan the Rash," I called through to the control cabin. "Twitch our course a trifle left. Not much."

Chekaran said: "A wise precaution, majister."

At that precise moment we flew out of the clouds into drenching suns shine. A massive mountain range lifted sharp peaks before us, cloaked in snow, looking like a serrated row of teeth ready to rip us into shreds. The snow glistered in changing patterns of white, toned and tinted in emerald and ruby. The spectacle in normal circumstances would have been very fine, some would say awesome. To me, the challenge was perfectly clear; somewhere in that forbidding massif must lie the hidden location where the famous Wall was maintained.

A hail screeched up from aft.

"Lifters!"

We all craned around to look. This time there were three of them just visible over the roof of the cabin. They were above the clouds now and they saw us and started to dive down.

Marsippo the Melancholy said: "We'll never avoid them."

Not even bothering to reply I searched frantically for a place, any place, where we could hide.

A bank of cloud, detached from the main formation, off to our left, offered a chance.

I pointed. "Go for it, the Rash! Bratch!"

Galloping Zorca whipped her head around just like the noble animal for which she was named. We hurtled for the clouds.

I gave Marsippo a look. He was a tailless Hytak. No one seemed to understand why some Hytaks were born with tails and others without. Many of the diffs who were not fighting men curled their tails around their bodies under their clothes. Fighters, of course, welcomed the opportunity to strap a dagger to their tail. That was an extra weapon with which to blatter their opponents to the greater glory of Hravimond the Perfect Jewel.

Reckoning that the lack of a tail made Marsippo the recipient of his soubriquet, I could sympathize with him. But I most certainly could not have him sowing unease and potential lack of morale among the crew. Luckily enough the two girls had gone back to their cabin. Their fresh outcry at Marsippo's words would have been highly distressing.

"Now, Hytak," I said in a sufficiently firm voice so that he understood I meant business, although not so strong as to make him flinch back. "That's enough nonsense. There are only three now, so that's one we've got rid of."

He said nothing, although he looked down at his feet.

"We don't want to have to fight," I said, speaking to them all. "But if we do we'll do them a lot of serious mischief. Now all of you find something useful to do to ready us for a fight."

"Quidang, majister!" They shouted that with meaning.

I fancied that Jiktar Ronun's little juruk would prove handy, mighty handy, by Krun, in a scrap!

The impressive mountain range lay a goodly way off and the country between looked difficult. Two options stared us in the face. We could make a run for the mountains or we could take cover among the clouds until nightfall. The afternoon wore on, true; but the twin Suns appeared to crawl across the heavens.

The choice to make was up to me. The advantages and disadvantages of each course of action were perfectly plain.

In the same firm voice I said to Chekaran: "Go and see your master. Find out what is happening. I need to know how long we have before it is too late."

He acknowledged the order and marched off brusquely as the vessel turned again under Naghan's helm. Chekaran simply swayed with the movement and forged straight on into the cabin. A useful man indeed.

If we stayed in the clouds until nightfall we would be safe, certainly. We might be too late. If we made a run for it we could easily be shot out of the sky—and that would be the finish, no doubt of that, by Vox!

I didn't bite my fingernails. This situation was the very time and place for fingernail nibbling, right down to the quick.

Then, waiting, I fretted over the decision to send the Chulik. I'd calculated that W'Watchun would speak more freely to his faithful retainer than to me. Perhaps I should have gone myself?

Eventually, after what seemed a half-a-dozen lifetimes, Chekaran reappeared. The Suns didn't appear—to me at least—to have changed their position in that time.

Many folk on Kregen say that Chuliks have little or no facial expressions in any other category than anger and hatred. I plead guilty to that belief during my early days on this horrendous and fascinating world. But I learned differently. Now Chekaran's yellow face bore lines that could only indicate suffering. He looked down when he spoke and fidgeted with his swords' hilts.

"The master is very weak and growing weaker. That slime Partagus is killing him. The coward Furney is helping."

Not replying, I waited until Chekaran got himself more under control. In a strange husky voice he told me that the two hostile sorcerers were slowly but surely beating down W'Watchun's resistance. "The master has been totally deceived by those he trusted. The mages he put in positions of responsibility—" Here he swallowed and licked his lips. "They are split, for and against. I'd like to take 'em and—by Chimula of the Golden Skin! I'd—I'd—"

"Aye, Chekaran."

He recovered a little. "The mages wage a ghostly battle. They are evenly matched. It is these two—the blintzes Partagus and Furney, who are tilting the balance." His yellow fist gripped so hard on his sword hilt, the knuckles looked fair to split their skins. "Sorcery! Give me my sword, and—"

"Aye," I said again. "How long?"

"The master tried to say; but could not. Not long, for sure." Anger began to replace the suffering on his face, which cheered me up. He railed against this blintz Partagus who had been an apprentice and who learned all he knew from W'Watchun. "He went off to Loh where he learned much. Those Wizards of Loh. They are hard people, hard."

This information cheered me up even further. By the Seven Arcades, as my sorcerer comrades would say, perhaps the Illusionists of these magical parts were not as all-powerful as we had dreaded.

Taking stock of the whole situation, modified by Chekaran's news, I felt a sensation that I can only describe as sinking. And, yet—By the pestilential navel and putrescent armpits of Makki Grodno!—there was no need for me to remind myself that I was Dray Prescot.

Yes, I was, for my sins, Dray Prescot of song and story, and the burden weighed heavily upon my shoulders. But, the fact remained incapable of denial, I was that same headstrong, reckless, passionate Dray Prescot who'd bashed and slashed his way about Kregen for many and many a season. I decided I was constitutionally incapable of skulking in a cloud when villains were hallooing away for my blood outside.

Using a very calm and smooth tone of voice but one which I made deliberately hard and flat, like a sword-blade slicing around, I told the crew of *Galloping Zorca* just exactly what we were going to do.

They didn't quite put up a cheer; but they spruced up visibly. They'd do. W'Watchun had chosen wisely when he'd hired on Jiktar Ronun to form his juruk. Some cadades formed guards that were no better than gangs of masichieri, little removed from drikingers.

In addition, Marsippo the Melancholy actually cracked a joke. It wasn't much of a jest and does not bear repetition; the fact alone spoke volumes for the morale of the crew.

Of all the many wonderful Plans I have concocted during my rackety career upon Kregen, so many did not work I sometimes wonder why I bother. All the same, this time my Plan worked a treat—well, as this was Kregen and nothing can be truly unexpected—almost a treat.

Ronun wore the gold pakzhan at his throat, as was proper for a captain of the guard. Chekaran also wore the gold, although he normally kept his pakzhan out of sight, I'd spotted its glitter when he'd been so upset. Also, the Chulik carried a clantzer, the local longsword copy of the longsword of the Clansmen of Segesthes to the north. He, like others, took my Krozair brand to be a clantzer.

"By Likshu the Treacherous!" quoth Chekaran. "Let us do it!"

Condensation set up strings of spectral diamonds along the rails. The effect was very pretty to anyone, even those poor wights about to risk their lives in mortal combat. The decks shone with moisture; it needed only a word to these paktuns to warn them of the dangers of slipping. The clouds, as is the nature of clouds, billowed about us in winnows and streaks, one minute closing in all vision for'ard of the cabin, the next giving us a view through a cleft out into the Suns shine.

When we lunged for the cleft the spectral diamonds all blew away like an opera house of broken necklaces.

Out into the mingled radiance we shot. Every pair of eyes on deck swiveled three hundred and sixty degrees.

Garnath the Stout, who'd clambered up to his prijiker perch high on the stem, spotted the hostile lifter first. He yelled.

"There!" His rigidly pointing arm left him with only one to hold on with. Abruptly he rolled over and hung upside down from the stem, still pointing, still yelling.

"Get yourself inboard, you fambly!" I roared. "Before you fall overboard!"

Naghan the Rash had his orders and needed no further instruction. *Galloping Zorca* surged forward as the levers went over. Naghan swung wildly. I really thought we'd lost him. Then his other hand clapped around the stem and with an agile wriggle despite his bulk, he deposited himself on the deck at my side.

"I was a tumbler in Master Rinkitter's circus between hirings as a paktun. These Tolaar-forsaken Tchekedos stopped all that."

I sniffed. "You spotted him. Now we are going to blatter him."

"Quidang!"

How strange it was, and yet, not strange but truly wonderful, how much at home I felt with these hairy paktuns!

Suns light struck low and level across the world as we raced forward. Over to the left the horizon glowed russet and viridian with sheets of light striking upwards in a blazing fan of opaline radiance. Sunsets are spectacular affairs on Kregen, never more so than when the two suns are close together. Like a stooping raptor we hurtled headlong upon the hostile lifter.

Ulak the Eye lined up the for'ard catapult and let fly.

The chunk of rock barely missed the larboard quarter. Ulak twisted up his long borzoi-like nose in disgust with himself. The crew wound the catapult like demons, *Galloping Zorca* closed the gap, Ulak aimed again and loosed. The rock went somewhere into the airboat's stern. We saw bright yellow chips of wood fly. Naturally, the crew set up a cheer—well, who could blame them?

"Quick and clean!" I yelled and went right forward, elbowing Garnath the Stout out of the way.

Now we were up to the stern, another rock went smash into her and this time a couple of bodies flew up into the air. We inched forward, bulwarks scraped together, and I leaped.

Garnath the Stout was the first after me, and the others tailed on. Men wearing short red capes met us, trying to set up a wall of steel. We gave them no time. Like berserk leems we were into them, chopping and slashing. In the wild melee these decadent adherents of Dokerty were thrust back, back and back, until they fetched up against the opposite bulwark.

They fought. You must give the Dokerty-lovers credit for that. No thought of surrender entered their heads, even when time after time we asked them to throw down their arms. In the end the ghastly business was done, and we could sag back, panting.

The shadows lengthened. For a moment I hesitated, then I shouted for Ronun to send a prize crew aboard our capture. She might prove useful. Careful scanning all around disclosed no sign of the other two airboats. We went back aboard *Galloping Zorca*. The two vessels sailed off in company into the deepening shadows.

As I say, the Plan worked almost a treat. Oh, yes, we'd done what we needed to do and were on course. But I stared down at the body of Garnath the Stout, saw where a spear had penetrated, and mourned.

Seventeen

Foliage before my face parted silently under gentle fingers. I peered out across the open space fronting the cliff. Camouflage mud smeared my features. Around a sputtering fire a dozen or so men lolled, half the guard posted here. The other half stood around, I fancied somewhat helplessly, doing all the fruitless things men do when standing sentry.

This was a side entrance into the mountain lair and, like the main entrance around the front, had a segment of a Wall created by W'Watchun to prevent entry. Khon the Mak's guards could not get in. Equally, no one was coming out without a fight.

The entrance itself gaped like a risslaca's mouth. Chekaran was proven right: there was room for the lifters to fly in.

A couple of varters, one each side, were going to make that course difficult.

The Twins, eternally circling each other as they circled Kregen, cast down their ruddy light turning leaves into a subtle purple color. There'd be illumination enough for these paktuns to shaft us and dart us as we flew in, bad cess to 'em!

Carefully allowing the twigs to fall back to their positions I eased back down the little slope to where Ronun and Chekaran waited. The two fliers were further down still at the spot we'd picked to land when we'd skimmed in low and out of sight of those further up.

In a low voice I sketched the situation before the entrance.

"The master," said Chekaran, "will drop the Wall long enough. We will have to be quick though."

"Aye."

"We will," quoth Ronun, bristling up his feathers, "have to fight these blintzes to get in, by Rhapaporgolam the Reiver of Souls!"

Unfortunately, there was no counter argument I could think of. The two airboats would have to wait until we'd cleared the entrance and then fly in. When I mentioned we'd need a signal to let the two pilots know the coast was clear, Chekaran simply said that the Illusionist would know. So that was a Queyd-arn-tung situation, all right, by Krun!

Quite an armory had been discovered in the lifter we'd taken so crossbows could be handed out. A blizzard of bolts would do wonders for our chances. With everyone ready and knowing what their positions were and what they had to do, we lined up and stared hungrily out onto the clearing and its occupants.

Beyond that portal stretched a warren of natural crevices and cracks, many artificially enlarged into chambers. This whole mountain complex was highly unusual. At some remote period in the past titanic convulsions of the earth had split a huge segment away and subsequent upheavals had left the back of the mountain sheered off straight. The drop went down a long way, a damned long way, by Krun!

When we'd flown past that impressive rockface and I'd craned over the rail to look down, all there was to see were shadows coiling in the depths.

A strange aura of terror breathed up from below, very unsettling, I assure you, very unsettling, by Djan!

We were on the flank of the mountain here. Ulak the Eye looked down his long Borzoi-like nose at the crossbows. I told him to take care of the varter men this side, I would take the other one.

Then, remembering the times with Seg on shooting forays, I said to him: "A small wager, Ulak."

He nodded. "Very well. But I do not think you will win."

So it was quickly settled; a set time, the amount of gold involved, the fine distinction between a wound and a kill. How fighting men find these petty pastimes to lighten the burden of combat!

Looking along the line of Ronun's juruk, seeing the determined faces, fierce, with downdrawn brows, I sighed. How many of these fine fellows would bite the dust in so short a dreadful time? How many would join Garnath the Stout on his journey through the clinging mist, into the Ice Floes of Sicce? How many would find their way to the sunny uplands beyond?

As for Garnath, he would be decently buried in the proscribed form and words spoken over him to comfort him on his journey. Then we would hold a Noumjiksirn and wax merry remembering him as he was in life. The lads of this juruk, I fancied, might drink more than was good for them.

The decision had been taken and the schwerpunkt—rather, two of them as there was a brace of varters—had been selected. The design called for the famous blizzard of bolts to sear the clearing, whilst Ulak and I dealt with the ballistae. Good. I must rouse myself and forget these morbid thoughts. Brassud! as my old dom Seg Segutorio would say, nocking his shafts and letting fly so fast the eye could scarcely follow.

The Twins shed their mellow fuzzy pink light. The fire sparked and sputtered yellow and red. The lads were ready.

I gave the signal.

In the first sleeting discharge of quarrels not a one missed its mark. Bodies toppled. Screams split the night air. Concentrating on working the Lohvian longbow as fast as I could and, as ever, conscious of Seg's intolerant eye on my performance, I had no time to spare a glance to see how Ulak was progressing.

The scene out there, luridly lit by the fire, could have come straight from a Herrelldrin Hell. Men were leaping about trying to find cover. Many sprawled motionless. Two—the glitter of gold and silver at their throats proclaiming their status—began to shoot back. Switching my aim—a dreadful thing to do, Djan knows, I took out the zhanpaktun. A crossbow bolt dealt with the Mortpaktun.

Now, I knew, was the time.

At that precise instant the prow of *Galloping Zorca* nosed up into view at our backs. The captured lifter followed.

"All aboard!" I used the old foretop hailing voice with intent. No one missed the order.

Both varter crews were gone down to the Ice Floes of Sicce. All the same, we had to be slippy about this maneuver.

Ulak leaped up over the bulwarks, the lads tumbled up around him. Arrow nocked and the string drawn back to my ear I looked about on the shambles. No one moved. Satisfied, I relaxed the bow and flung myself aboard *Galloping Zorca*. She went up like a Congreve rocket, the second airboat kept pace, and we hurtled full for the dark opening.

All my doom-laden forebodings had come to nothing. We'd not lost a single man. So much for the pusillanimity of command!

Even then, even with that chastening thought still ringing in my old vosk skull of a head, I still felt a tremor at the fresh thought that W'Watchun had not fashioned an opening in his damned Wall. We'd hit square on and at the speed we were going we'd fly to flinders instantly.

For a handful of moments the darkness clung about us impenetrably. I felt absolutely no change, either in my body or head; but we were through. With dramatic suddenness lights bloomed about a low and narrow cavern. The walls shone with mica from the torchlights' radiance. The air was chilly. The torches did something to illuminate our surroundings—dispel the gloom as they say in Clishdrin—but this place held an aura as of catastrophe waiting to happen.

There was no one in sight. Ahead of us the cavern narrowed to a tunnel entrance, dimly lit. The smells of damp oozed up.

Naghan lowered *Galloping Zorca* to the gravel floor.

"Now we walk." Chekaran went into the cabin and emerged carrying the Illusionist, as before, cradled like a baby.

The Sylvies assisted the two runaway ladies over the side.

"Keep together!" snapped Ronun, and led off.

Leaving the Rapa cadade to the vanguard, I tagged along at the back acting as a rearguard.

We walked along for some distance, rounding corners, and as we went on so the torchlights died at our backs. The effect was eerie. No one spoke much. Echoes rolled against the walls.

Mind you, what I found strange, not to say weird, was the fact that we were walking through a mysterious tunnel under the ground without let or hindrance. There were no traps. There were no monsters. That, to me, was the oddest thing about this place, by Krun!

Apart from the slight noises we made, the tunnel lay wrapped in deathly silence. I kept looking back over my shoulder, fist on sword hilt, just in case.

Up ahead white light blossomed. My companions became mere black silhouettes before me. Around the corner a few more steps took us to the entrance of a vast chamber. The sight was macabre.

Everything could not be taken in at once. As my eyes adjusted to the tricky light and I began to make out details, a young lad wearing a black robe and with a cylindrical black hat on his head approached us. His hat was less than half the height of the other Illusionists' headgear. His face was pinched, the eyes smudged, and his young mouth trembled.

When he saw W'Watchun he cried out in terror.

The sorcerer managed to mumble a few barely intelligible words. The lad shouted in a voice that spurted out shatteringly in that hushed place.

"A chair for the master!"

Four Brukaj appeared, as if from nowhere, carrying a sedan chair into which Chekaran gently seated W'Watchun. I heard the Illusionist breathe the words: "Hurry, Nalgre!"

The Brukaj swept off with the sedan chair with this Nalgre trotting along at the side, one hand gripping the polished wood. They evidently knew what they were doing. This, after all, was why we'd flown here. Now I could look around this mysterious chamber.

The first impression was of an office, with rows of neatly aligned desks filling the central space. Soft and somehow creepy music wafted on the air. The impression of an office was completely shattered by the absolute immobility of the people sitting on the floor before the desks. They were in the lotus position. Their heads were bowed. Many of those heads were crowned with white hair, yet the people were not Gons. They were suffering from chivrel, that dread disease that people did not care to discuss. All the doctors I'd spoken to had no idea from where or how the disease came into existence.

Most of the people looked old, which happens to folk on Kregen only during the last few years of their long lives. Some men were not old. These appeared to be strong and fit, and yet there they sat among the old fogeys, not moving, their eyes closed.

A little Och lady went down the rows spooning some slop into their mouths, which opened automatically at the touch of the spoon. Balconies extended around the walls, some curtained. Many thick pillars rose from floor to roof between the rows of people. The smell lay thick on the tongue, heavy, musky. This, by Vox, appeared to me to be a pestilential place.

The chair pressed on ahead and I followed. Chekaran paced beside his master opposite Nalgre. Ronun gathered up his juruk and went off to escort the ladies to a place which had been assigned to him by Chekaran.

If this was a secret location, what, I wondered, were our chances of ever leaving it?

Better, one had to believe, than the folk here in their lotus positions. They employed a shift system, for an Och led up a fellow who walked like a zombie. He took the place of the man hoicked up by the Och, who led him off into the shadows under a balcony. There were all manner of diffs here, although few Hytaks could be seen and absolutely no Pachaks whatsoever.

Moving after the sedan chair and looking keenly about I did not think that Ulak the Eye had forgotten our wager. What the result was I'd no idea. I rather fancied he'd know, being an Undurker and therefore not only touchy about his bowmanship but arrogant with it after the fashion of his race of diffs.

This wagering on matters of death is, in reality, most distressing. It is a part of the face that is put on by those whose livelihood is fighting for a wage. It is just the same reaction as the apparently callous continuing with business after a fight when ordinary folk would be shaking with the horror of it all. No one who struts about swashbuckling a sword and boasting would really last very long among some of the societies I know on Kregen.

What, I found myself wondering, not without a little frisson of malicious glee, would the famous Tchekedos make of the fighting men of the outside world if they were let loose?

These apparently somber reflections cheered me up a trifle. This place depressed a fellow. It was enough to give anyone the willies, as they say in Clishdrin. Also, it breathed an aura of menace that could not be ignored.

At the far end the little procession passed beneath an arch under the balcony. A few short corridors, carpeted and lit with lamps, brought us to an anteroom. Nalgre and Chekaran took the Illusionist out of his chair and stretched him out on a chaise longue. A woman rose from a seat where, clearly, she had been waiting on our arrival.

These proceedings were performed sedately; yet unmistakably the sense of urgency gripped these people. The woman, a Venahim, with the typical heavy ridges around the eyes and over the forehead, was not as large as Mistress E'Eolana. Her eyes, however, were just as piercing and just as drilling. Her gown, too, was pale yellow, girdled with silver.

Chekaran said softly to me: "The master is not in pain. We do not need a Puncture Lady. Mistress H'Havalini will relax him."

So, without touching W'Watchun, the Venahim healing woman moved her hands in the technique called schonibium. W'Watchun began to respond and in a miraculously short time had regained some color and was clearly far less distressed.

Nalgre brought a golden goblet of wine and W'Watchun drank a little. He sat up, erect, although still black shadows haunted his eyes. He spoke in his resonant voice.

"Take me in, at once!"

"Yes, master," chorused Chekaran and Nalgre.

The Sorcerer needed only slight assistance as they passed out of the anteroom through a door over which fierce, predatory devil faces leered down. I followed, willy-nilly, leaving Mistress H'Havalini lifting a goblet of the wine to her firm lips.

The place we entered was as strange, if not more so, than anything I'd witnessed so far.

The chamber was not over large. Tall green candles burned with a bluish flame, straight and unwavering. Nine golden couches were arranged in a semi-circle. Five of the couches were occupied by men—not a single woman existed in the chamber—who lay rigid, pale-faced, sweating slightly. Each stretched out his arms and clasped the hand of his neighbor, save the one who ended the five just over halfway around the semi-circle. They wore black illusionist clothes. The silence bore down with physical force. The smell of decay and long dead corruption smoked on the air.

Assisted by his retainer and acolyte, W'Watchun lay down on the next golden couch, reached out and grasped the hand of his neighbor.

The five men gasped, a sudden retching, and their supine bodies twitched as though branded with white-hot irons.

"Master!" The five men croaked the word, almost mumbling.

"Concentrate, sans!" The sorcerer spoke with intolerant vibrancy. "Concentrate, or we are doomed!"

The atmosphere choked about me, clinging like strands of spider silk, oppressive, magical.

Nalgre beckoned. Thankfully I followed him and Chekaran out of that weird chamber. I breathed deeply in the antechamber and reached for the flagon.

Then, resentful of the eerie circumstances, totally uneasy with the suffocating sensations of rampant magic, I drank down a draught, wiped the back of my hand over my lips, and said: "By Mother Zinzu the Blessed! I needed that!"

With that simple gesture, those few familiar words, I brought my old vosk skull of a head back from the dread realms of thaumaturgy to the practical problems that faced me.

From the strange activities of this place what was going on here was perfectly plain. The large cavern with the rows of folk all sitting in their lotus positions provided the mental power to maintain W'Watchun's Wall. The sorcerers on their golden couches were fiercely resisting the onslaughts of the mages trying to break in. Nalgre—whose name was Nalgre S'Scholian—elaborated. The people were using their inner resources under the guidance of the sorcerer to maintain the Wall; that was true. The force was not exactly mental power, nor even the ib, but a deep inner source of strength that could only be drawn out and used by a thaumaturge with the knowledge and skill.

They were condemned criminals in the main, offered the chance to escape execution, and not knowing what quasi-life they were accepting. They did not leave here.

As for the Illusionists, well, out of the nine—the magical number on Kregen—four had deserted and betrayed W'Watchun. They'd been led by this San Partagus, who fancied himself as the next chief.

The magical attacks were fairly evenly balanced with W'Watchun and his five versus Partagus and his four. Furney chipping in was a serious handicap; but according to Nalgre San W'Watchun could hold the attacks. The discrepancy in numbers, Nalgre said, was because the four who had defected were more powerful in general than the five who had remained. I said nothing. But I wondered if that was for the very obvious reason that usually explains the betrayal syndrome.

The healing lady no longer graced the antechamber. The flagon was empty. Well, good luck to her, she had to keep up her energy with the power demands put upon her.

I'd had a long day but activity kept me alert and I did not feel tired. Food was a different matter and Nalgre organized a meal. Munching palines he escorted me off to a room dimly lit by a couple of tapers. A young lad wearing illusionist black rose as we entered. He'd been watching a blank white sheet hung upon the wall.

"Nothing is happening, Nalgre."

Nalgre's young, unlined face, grimaced. "Good."

Now magic is a potent tool for those who understand the arcane arts. Yet its manifestations can be grasped by lay folk like myself. So I fancied I could guess what was going on here.

As though sensing my thoughts, Nalgre gave me a lowering look. "I can show you, if you wish."

"Please."

He walked around and put his fingers to my temples. I felt the pressure as a gentle soothing sensation. For a moment nothing happened. Then—well, by Krun, I blinked, I can tell you!

A picture formed on the blank white sheet. The scene showed a typical campsite, with paktuns around fires cooking food, tents of varying importance, guards pacing. I could see no saddle animals. The night sky, spattered with stars and with the Twins rolling along, reminded me of fresh air and I swallowed down the taste of the place around me. I knew what I was seeing.

"The Illusionists are in the tent with the black flag," Nalgre told me. He spoke glumly. "There are a lot of mercenaries."

Before I could answer I saw the rast. Hyr Kov Khon the Mak came strutting from a tent emblazoned with banners, chewing on a chicken bone which he flung over his shoulder. He was clad in armor. With him pranced along Kov Grogan. Those two unhanged rogues demanded attention, and here was I, lollygagging about amongst a pack of sorcerers being stifled by magic!

Some of the fury of my early days on Kregen swamped over me.

By the distended belly and massive thighs of the Divine Madam of Belschutz! Magic played its indispensable part. Now I, plain Dray Prescot, must go and play mine.

The information about locations and tunnels I required I got from Nalgre readily enough. He shook his head doubtfully.

"You brought the master here to fight them. But to go outside—"

"I'm going."

I spoke very calmly. I knew what stood in that fancy tent of Khon the Mak's.

"I doubt, then, that I shall see you again." He sighed. "Rememberee, majister."

As to that, I rather fancy Opaz and Zair, not to mention Djan, will have a say. "Rememberee, Nalgre."

With that I started off for the tunnel that would take me outside the mountain.

Eighteen

No wonder this entrance was secret!

Pressing myself as flat as possible against the rock at my back I edged with exquisite carefulness along a ledge less than two handbreadths in width. The ledge slanted down across the sheer face where the mountain had been sliced off aeons ago. The drop lay shrouded in darkness.

Of course, it was raining. Of course, the wind howled around my ears like a pack of maniacal banshees.

Wetness and bluster encompassed me as I edged along.

Invoking both Makki Grodno and the Divine Madam of Belschutz, I found to my relief that the ledge broadened as it curved around the flank of the mountain. Now the wind, which had been blowing full at my face, screeched against my side. I remained with my back flat against the rock and edged along: had I tried to walk normally the wind would have whisked me off like a feather.

The cave opening from which I'd exited onto the precipice held three tunnels and I'd come out of the center one. They had a Wall, too, which had been dropped for me. The Eye high in the roof monitored my progress. There was the snap of magical discharge in the air when the Wall went up again. The cave twisted three times before reaching the outside. Now I was out, feeling like a flea on a dermiflon's hide as his owner scrubbed him down.

It wasn't absolutely pitch dark. Occasional gleams of pallid light struck down through the racing wrack above. Because, as I believed, the Star Lords had gifted me with the ability to see remarkably well in gloom, I could distinguish enough to take each step along that confounded slippery and dangerous ledge. This scotopic vision served me well during that wild night. Without it I might well have fallen off the precipice and plunged headlong into those shuddery depths below.

A gigantic bolt of lightning streaked from the heavens above and struck furiously into the mountain flank ahead and above. Boulders and chips of stone flew spraying outwards, chips of flashing light in the remaining dazzlement of the lightning bolt. For a moment I could not see a damn thing. My vision cleared; but I just stuck there, not moving, getting my breath back.

The thunder rolled in and I just hadn't bothered to count.

After a space I took a huge breath and forged on. By this time I was wet through and my russet clothes must look black.

The formidable range of white-capped peaks lay well to the north and it was from there that this confounded weather originated.

By the time I'd worked my way around to the south side of the mountain, which was far less of a gradient, the wind dropped, blocked off. You could still hear the howl of it as it attacked the north face, borne in over the hiss and splash of the rain.

A miserable looking fellow stood at the point where the so-called track debouched onto the reasonably level clearing. He was huddled up in a cloak and he neither heard nor saw me. He went to sleep standing up, and easing his body to the ground, I pressed warily on.

The shapes of the tents, mere black splodges among the dimness, looked like beached hulks. Practically no one was about in this foul weather and the second sentry joined the first in peaceful slumber. Calling up the layout of the camp I'd seen through the thaumaturgy of the Eye, I located the tent over which, when I crawled closer, I could identify a sodden black flag hanging down.

Were there golden couches in there, too? Well, by Vox, we'd soon find out!

This stealthy crawling might be necessary, given the concealment of the rain. What it did was to add a thick layer of mud to my already forlorn clothing.

About to steer around a straggly bush, I halted. The leaves were beaten down by the rain. Moving rapidly and with great economy of effort, I unshipped the longbow, laid aside the drexer and rapier and main gauche. Stripping off the russets, which felt slippery between my fingers, I bundled up my armory, arrows as well, and stuffed them under the bush.

I kept—need you ask!—the brave old scarlet breechclout and the Krozair brand.

The temperature was quite bearable to an old sailorman. I've adventured around Kregen wearing the scarlet breechclout and wielding the Krozair longsword. Many and many a play and song, many a puppet and shadow show have celebrated my doings—mostly violently colored and highly exaggerated, to be sure. Still, I felt comfortable in my familiar old kit.

In addition, the sailor knife snugged over my right hip.

The rain fell steadily, occasionally gusted about by flaws of wind curving around the mountain's flank. The canvas of the tent ran with water. A muddy and water-running trench at the base tried to run off the overflow. Because these high and mighty ones of the earth always demanded the most luxurious accommodation, the tents ranked in the grand category. There would be compartments within, and rugs, and proper furniture; not your flimsy campsite rubbish. The effort of slaves and servants in carrying all this impedimenta about would not, of course, trouble the minds of the lords. No, sir!

Usually when I went gallivanting about Kregen kitted as I now was, I was out to rescue someone. That, after all, was why the Star Lords had recruited me in the first place. That was my job.

Only later, when the Everoinye recognized that I possessed the yrium that both cursed and blessed me, had they employed me differently. Now, they wanted me to be the Emperor of All Paz. Pah!

The notion of cutting guy lines and bringing the whole tent down I'd rejected instantly. That ploy had been used with great success to curtail wrestling bouts when I'd hauled Turko the Shield back to Esser Rarioch.*

Now, I judged, even in this foul weather the collapse of the mages' tent would bring guards, Tchekedos—someone—running.

The sailor knife bit cleanly through the sodden canvas. A slit vertically, then a crosscut, allowed me easy ingress. Beyond the tent wall one of the compartments I'd expected showed me stacked sacks, boxes, stores and provisions. The door was flapped with brown canvas.

Through this, and another area revealed a mineral oil lamp smoking unpleasantly with an untrimmed wick. Three Itemos, slaves by their grey breechclouts and whip-marked backs, their shocks of untidy greyish hair confined in fillets of rawhide, their down-drooping dew-lapped faces slack and idiotic, slumped over, breathing stertorously. These three I put to sleep and hoped their deeper slumber would bring better dreams.

---

* See *A Victory for Kregen*. Book four of the Jikaida Cycle, Volume 22 of the Saga of Dray Prescot.

The next compartment contained four acolytes, as the short cylindrical black hats proclaimed. They slept by the light of a samphron oil lamp. Just the same, they went into a deeper sleep.

A short canvas passage, adorned with fanciful embroideries of mythical beasts, led to the place I sought.

And—would you believe!—there were golden couches!

Six of them, arranged in a horseshoe, and containing the forms of the traitorous Illusionists. There they were, stretched out, like chickens with necks waiting to be wrung.

Their faces were contorted with the strains wracking them. They were putting forth all their combined kharrna in the supreme effort to break down the defenses of W'Watchun and his mages and destroy the Wall.

So I, Dray Prescot, stared down on these men who held in their magical arts the means to send me back four hundred light years to the planet of my birth.

That was true in the Light of Opaz. If they succeeded I would have failed. The Everoinye would not tolerate that failure. I would be punished. I would be hurled through the void back to Earth.

Yet—and yet! Oh, by all the Blessed Names! Could I simply kill these men in cold blood?

Was that what all the high adventure on Kregen had come to?

Their eyes were closed, so that they were completely helpless. I gazed about. The canvas was concealed by gaudy silken drapes. Tall green candles burned with blue unwavering flames. Stinking incense smoldered from a bronze vessel in one corner. The closeness of the atmosphere bore down sickeningly upon me. I took out my knife.

I looked at the knife in my fist. My hand did not tremble.

That surprised me.

With a motion at once ferocious and helpless, I flicked the knife up into the air and caught it as it spun. I caught the blade.

Partagus was immediately recognizable by the height of his black hat which stood on a cushion beside his head. He was a fine full-fleshed fellow, with lines of self-satisfaction engraved on his saturnine features. Even if you didn't know he was the leader his whole appearance, even in the throes of exerting all his magical powers, showed unmistakably who was kingpin here. Next to him lay Furney.

I favored them all with a sour glance, of longing, and regret that I was unable to do what ought to be done. Was this not irrefutable proof that I was not fit to be an emperor? Emperors would order their heads off without a second thought. The concept that my lad Drak, the Emperor of Vallia, would do so chilled me. But I, Dray Prescot, of Earth, must therefore be so pusillanimous as to be a coward. I had to be. Why couldn't I just slit their damned throats?

A fluke of wind gusted in strongly and shook the tent. The tall blue candle flames wavered. I felt a prickling all over my skin.

The opposite flapped opening swung up and a Tchekedo stalked in. He was just like all his brethren, big and bulky, girded with weapons, intolerant. He saw me and his eyes bulged. "What—?"

The sailor knife blurred. It buried its blade in the warrior's neck. He looked just as puzzled as though he'd been asked a difficult question. He gurgled a trifle and then fell down.

Time was running out for me. The decision I had to make could not be taken. I retrieved my sailor knife, wiped it clean on the warrior's fancy neckerchief, and set about the business.

Each Illusionist, starting with Partagus, was struck cleanly over the head. When Partagus was hit, the others all gave a little jump, a frisson of expiring energy. They all, the whole damned six of them, sprawled unconscious.

I must admit, grasping the sailor knife by the blade between fingers and thumb, I'd hit the cramphs with the hilt very hard, very hard indeed, by Krun, to the greater glory of Djan!

An exquisite scheme entered my head only to be dismissed at once. As Partagus was dragged off his golden couch by the scruff of his neck, I couldn't see anyone being fooled if he was replaced by the warrior in black illusionist clothes. For all the fun we paktuns had at the Tchekedos' expense, the fact remained they were hard, fierce fighting men, for all their lapses. This fellow's face, arrogant and contemptuous, might match the physiognomy of Partagus, equally arrogant and contemptuous. But the sorcerer was soft with good living, his face flabby; the warrior, at least, had the tough leathery look one expected from his kind.

Long twisted golden ropes reached around each couch, with golden tassels hanging down tastefully. The work of a moment saw a length of rope ripped off and the tassels discarded. I gave Partagus a stare. The fellow would be unconscious for a goodly time yet. Still, better to be on the safe side. So he was trussed up like a turkey and a gag of black cloth ripped from his robe stuffed into his mouth.

After the eerie blue glow of the candles I closed my eyes for a space and then stuck my head out into the canvas passage. All lay clear. Slinging the traitorous Illusionist over my shoulder I padded swiftly along.

The acolytes slumbered. The Itemo slaves slept. I walked past them light-footed. Outside, the rain continued to pour down.

The smells of rain and green vegetation and mud came most gratefully to my nostrils after the decadent stink of the sorcerers' tent. Carefully looking about in the rain-streaked darkness with my scotopic vision enhanced by occasional random gleams of starlight, I reached the bush where my weapons and clothes were stashed.

Here Partagus was dumped down unceremoniously on the other side where he wouldn't be seen but where he was well away from my edged weapons. How resourceful he was in physical matters I didn't know; but I did not care to put temptation in his way.

The whole time taken in dealing with the sorcerers and extracting their chief had not been long. Just when the guards were due to change might, in this weather, be delayed as the reliefs groaned and rolled out of their blankets and stretched and thought about going on guard. Much of that would depend on how strict the Deldars were.

All the same, the sense of urgency pressed hotly upon me.

The tent I wanted, more of a marquee really, was marked by its grandness and the limp flag atop its pole. Thither I went.

I went cautiously, not making a sound. As I had suspected, a guard stood by the closed flap of the entrance.

Giving him a wide berth I crept around to the back. The sailor knife did its work sharply and efficiently. Easing the flap aside I put an eyeball to the opening.

My nostrils carried out the first reconnaissance. The delightful aromas of cooking wafted sensuously from the dim interior. These were not scents from the many and various dishes they ate up here but the spicy, heady aromas of further south. Khon the Mak had brought his own cooks with him. Sensible man, the black bastard.

Inside, a crack of pale light indicated a flapped opening. You could hardly call these openings doors; but that was the office they served, and beyond this one canvas walls led me on to another.

In that room two Tchekedos were playing the Game of Moons. They lost all interest in the game, one after the other. Thinking what Ronun would contemptuously say, that the warriors didn't have the brains for Jikaida, I moved soundlessly on. The floors were covered by rugs, and as I penetrated two more of these canvas rooms, the furnishings grew more elaborate. Two more Tchekedos were put to sleep in a room I fancied led to my goal. Mind you, thanks to Opaz, I'd had fantastic good luck. Oxkalin the Blind Spirit, also, must be guiding me.

The guess proved correct. In this room silks adorned the walls, elegant chairs and a chaise longue occupied half the space with a wash handstand. The other half was almost entirely taken up by a bed of massive size. A flapped door hung half-open opposite.

Khon the Mak reared up from the bed as I entered. His hair, jet black, was rumpled. On his pallid face two spots of color glowed on his cheeks. He looked wrought up, impassioned. He was not quite naked, wearing a bright yellow singlet. He saw me.

Instantly, like a striking risslaca, he leaped from the bed. He leaped away from me, towards the opposite opening.

A white, frightened face appeared above the low bed board. She was young, heartbreakingly young. She sat up and her brown hair fell about her shoulders. She, too, was not quite naked, having two or three strings of colored beads about her neck. Her hands flew to cover her bareness. Her carmine lips, shining, parted to emit a scream that tore at me.

Without stopping my forward movement after Khon the Mak, I raised my left hand, palm outward.

"It's all right. You are quite safe."

She took no notice and went on shrieking. Well, by Vox, who could blame her?

Rounding the bed I sprinted for the opening. Lights blossomed in the next apartment. So the wasps' nest was aroused!

From the entrance I could see in, and see the doom that waited.

Nath G'Goldark, that chief priest of Dokerty raised up by Khon the Mak, stood forward as the kov ran yelling past him. Khon pointed back, shrilling almost incoherently. But his meaning was perfectly and hideously plain.

In G'Goldark's fist was gripped the Flutubium. The two curved wings joined at the top and glinted in the lamplight. In there, in that symbol holy to Dokerty, reposed the Prism of Power.

So I knew and, I admit it, my first thought was of sorrow for the poor little lass in the bedroom.

"Do it, do it!" screamed Kov Khon Khonstanton, cowering at the chief priest's back. "You know who he is!"

The priest still wore his deep red robes. He lifted his arms. He pointed the winged symbol past me, pointed it through the opening, pointed it at the screaming little maid cowering on the bed.

"Dokomek!"

Nineteen

I looked back.

The horror began.

That beautiful young maiden just burgeoning into womanhood began to bloat, to swell. The strings of multicolored beads snapped and cascaded in a rainbow flood to the bed. She stood up, and, just for a moment, appeared glorious in her nakedness. Then the bed collapsed, her legs bowed, hairs sprouted over her body. Her hands turned into talons. Razor-sharp claws sprouted from her feet. She emitted a gargling cry. Could I detect in those moments of horror the desperate lost cry of a bewildered girl?

She stepped off the shattered bed. Her hands lifted. The claws raked forward in instinctive movements of destruction.

Absolute determination to kill and go on killing turned her face into a virago's, a demonic mask, the visage of a devil from hell.

The stench of her pervaded the room nauseatingly.

With a leap as lethal as any leem's I sprang forward at Khon the Mak and his priestly companion.

A single savage blow from my fist struck Mak Khon senseless to the rugs.

I took the Flutubium into my left fist and hit the damned Dokerty priest so hard he flew back against the silks gracing the canvas walls. He collapsed with blood pouring from his ruined face.

Gazing down for a fleeting moment at the prone form of the hyr kov, I regretted I couldn't take him with me. But I was apim, with only two arms. I doubted if the blow had knocked any sense into his head; but it was a start.

The bellowings from the bedroom rose up the scale. The ibmanzy was working itself—hardly herself, by Krun!—into that dread killing fury.

Without wasting any further time I ran towards the other door. The chances were that the demon would follow me. I was the moving target and there was every possibility that the ibmanzy would ignore the two senseless men on the floor.

So, perforce, I ran.

A series of canvas cubicles and passages led into a larger space where the uproar at my back aroused the sleeping occupants. These were not, as I fully expected, mercenaries of Khon the Mak's personal bodyguard. They were not priests of Dokerty, either. They were not Tchekedos.

They'd been calling in surprised alarm, wondering what was going on, and when I appeared in their sight they started a shrieking caterwauling very distressing to the ears.

What they made of me, clad only in a breechclout, mud and blood smeared over my body, Opaz alone knew. I lifted the winged symbol and shook it.

"Ladies!" I bellowed above their panicky screams. "You must leave here at once!"

They were very well used to obeying orders. There were a dozen or so of them, all neatly arranged in two rows of camp beds; and quietening down at once as my words penetrated, they started to gather up their clothes and possessions.

"No time for that!" I bellowed. I made them jump more than the sounds of crashing and bashing drawing nearer. "Leave everything! Run—Run for your lives!"

I did not want their messy deaths on my conscience, no, by Vox!

By the state of noise along the way I'd run I judged the demon was in the process of dealing with some unfortunates who'd gone to investigate. If it got among these girls—well, I couldn't have that. "Hurry!" I yelled again. And, then: "Shoo! Shoo!" That, I confess, was highly ludicrous; but it fitted the chaos around.

Dangling strings of beads, brightly-colored garments flapping along like forlorn flags, the girls ran for the exit.

Shepherding them along into the outside air I followed.

The rain had eased considerably. One or two stars were even visible, high above and remote, coldly twinkling. The wind fluked about unpredictably.

People were running about, scrambling out of tents, shouting. At any other time the rumpus would have been splendid; as it was, it was a confounded nuisance.

The cave entrance into the side of the hill could now be made out by the erratic light of The Maiden with the Many Smiles streaming through broken clouds. The black gap of the hole looked just that, a dark opening; inside it stood W'Watchun's Wall.

There would undoubtedly be an Eye in the entrance cave. I had very little time left to act. If I sprinted into the cave, would the young acolytes see me on their white sheet? Would W'Watchun be able to drop the Wall to let me in in time? A nasty shiver took me as I reckoned the chances and came to the unpalatable conclusion that there would not be time enough.

The screaming women vanished in all directions, clutching what they'd managed to save. Only when they'd all gone had I the nous to grasp just what I might have done.

Onker! I snarled to myself. Get onker! Of course!

Each one of those sweet young ladies could be an infecto, a sublime. Each one could be turned by the Prism of Power into a foaming maniacal ibmanzy. Dolt! I chastised myself. Cretin! And yet... and yet, by Zair, what else could I have done at that precise moment?

Best not to fret over what was done and could not be changed.

Mud-smeared as I was I could easily pass as just another mercenary running about with the rest of the paktuns in bewilderment.

But if I entered the cave and the Wall did come down, a whole pack of Tchekedos would stream in like leems for the kill...

The idea of retracing my steps up that narrow trail winding around the mountain did not appeal. There was the possibility that I wouldn't be able to find where it started and I might go blundering about the slope of the mountain for the rest of the night.

And—by Krun, that reminded me that the night was drawing to a close. Zim and Genodras would be rising in their mingled opaline glory all too soon.

The acrid smell of burned wood and water warned me, so I was able to skirt around the drenched ashes of a campfire. The cooks had been forced to prepare the lords' suppers under cover, with care, as I'd scented entering the first tent. Well, and, by Krun, I was sharp set again!

This moving about was useless. The main entrance was no good. Ergo—I'd have to go painfully back up the mountain trail.

By Makki Grodno's diseased left armpit and dangling right eyeball! What a confounded trek for a fellow who just wanted some grub and a warm bed!

Making sure no one was too near, I went back to my bush.

Partagus was feebly trying to move, and odd little gargling sounds dribbled from the gag. I said: "See what your evil ways have brought you to, sorcerer," and hit him over the head.

He slumbered once more.

His tall black hat was gone with the waters of the oceans. I ripped the black robe up around the bonds holding him. He wore a fancy black vest underneath and this I allowed him to keep. See how great was my munificence!

My arsenal of weapons went back on, strapped and buckled up.

I left the pathetic sodden lump of clothing. I regretted abandoning the russets; but I didn't fancy putting them on, all clinging and wet and unpleasant as they were.

My journey had barely begun with the sorcerer slung over my shoulder when a paktun loomed up, suddenly brightly visible in a random shaft from The Maiden with the Many Smiles.

"You all right, dom?"

"Aye, dom, my thanks. You?"

"What," he said in a hopeless voice, "is going on, by Lasal the Vakka?" By this I knew he was a light cavalryman and hailed from Vallia. "Have they all gone crazy?"

"There's a damned great demon around somewhere, dom. Best get out of it while the going's good."

"Aye." He cast a puzzled glance at the form of Partagus. "What's up with him?"

"Went makib at the sight of the monster. It's for his own safety." I shifted the Illusionist higher on my shoulder. "Well—"

At that instant a colossal bellow burst up, shattering across the clearing. So the ibmanzy had fought his way out and was now intent solely upon destroying anyone in its path.

"That's the demon," I said. "Right, dom, I'm off."

Then I checked, and because he was a Vallian and his first words had been friendly, showing concern, I said: "May Opaz go with you. Remberee."

Just before I swung back I saw his face show a tiny ripple of shock. He started to move forward. I waved the Flutubium in parting salute, and marched off at a very brisk pace, very brisk, by Vox! You never could tell, what with all these stories about Dray Prescot circulating where folk read books and watched plays.

His voice reached me. "And Opaz with you, dom. Remberee."

The Maiden with the Many Smiles vanished behind clouds and darkness fell. I moved on smartly.

Mind you, the friendly paktun was from Vallia. He could easily have served with me in the Time of Troubles, when I was the Emperor of Vallia.

The winged symbol atop its silvered wooden staff was becoming a nuisance. Breaking the staff away I took the case into my free hand. I was not, you may well understand, going to open that! Stuffing the demonic thing into a secure hold in my harness I loped on.

The edge of the clearing, vaguely visible as a massy bank of bushes and small trees in the erratic light, looked remarkably similar all the way along. Well, by Krun, I'd debouched out of there somewhere and if I wanted to keep my head on my shoulders I'd have to find the path and devilish quick, too!

I'd been on my feet for a day and the best part of a night. There had been adequate if not voluminous amounts of food along the way. Well, an old sailorman, a Clansman, a Krozair of Zy, can cope with fatigue and lack of grub quite comfortably. In my body, sinews and muscles, enough energy remained to carry me through this adventure. By Krun! There'd better be!

After all, this going on, this determination, this will to beat down all the perils thrown in the path, well, by Zair, that was part of what Dray Prescot was all about, wasn't it?

The noise of the demon pent up in a young girl's body crashed and smashed about the clearing. Mingled with all that roaring the thin screams of people having their arms, legs and heads torn off reached the ears like the mewling of kittens.

If it was my old beakhead of a nose or my bump of location I neither knew nor cared. Oxkalin the Blind Spirit must have smiled, for I found the overgrown entrance to the trail as I remembered it in only a dozen or so heartbeats. Giving Partagus a hitch on my shoulder, and with a silent 'All thanks to Opaz!' off we started. The trail went well at first and we made good progress. Presently, as we mounted higher the way became steeper and narrower.

Thinking of those last stretches before the cave entrance was reached would be a mistake. The fact was, that part of the climb did not bear thinking about, by Krun!

The clouds were rolling away now as the wind got up again, taking the rain with them. Also, as the Maiden with the Many Smiles began to shine more strongly, they were taking away my cover.

A raucous caw from above jerked my head up.

There he was, perfectly visible in his shining gold and crimson glory, the Gdoinye, circling arrogantly. He was the spy and messenger for the Everoinye and, as both my hands were occupied, I did not shake a fist at him.

He cocked his head to one side to fix me with a black and beady eye. "Dray Prescot! Prince of Onkers!"

Oho! So this time he was condescending to speak to me.

Without replying I continued to plod up the trail. The ledge narrowed all the way and I'd have to do something about the Illusionist soon.

"Dray Prescot! You must destroy the Prism of Power! The Everoinye command—"

"I know, I know!"

"Cast it into the depths, then, oh Emperor of Onkers."

Now I knew exactly what the Prism of Power would do when it hit the ground. The explosion was not nuclear; it was a damned good counterfeit, I can tell you! The shock would shake the mountain. The demonic red glare would blind anyone foolish enough to look on the titanic coruscation as the devilish energy burst all restraints.

"You must do it, Dray Prescot! You must!"

"Aye, aye! When I reach the top."

"And then, onker of onkers, take care of your skin. The Everoinye have use for you and do not wish to see you damaged."

Well, I didn't laugh. All the same, there was no doubt that the Star Lords had changed tack where I was concerned.

I halted and lowered the Illusionist to the ground. Now I could shake my fist at the Gdoinye. This I did, and I bellowed up.

"Fly off, you crazy bird!"

A mocking caw, a harsh rattle like that of a dying man, and the magnificent raptor swung away on wide wings, climbed, and vanished.

Taking Partagus by the scruff of the neck I began to drag him up along the ledge. I was careful with him. After all this effort I didn't want him pitching over into the abyss.

Without dignifying what I intended to do with the title of 'The Plan', I knew exactly how I was going to work this somewhat tricky business. After all, by Zair, I wouldn't want to disappoint the Star Lords, now, would I, and get myself damaged?

The last part of the climb was something I do not care to dwell on. All noise from below dwindled away and probably by this time the ibmanzy had torn that poor little girl's body to shreds.

Going on and up, pace by pace, flat against the rock face, with Partagus inched along painstakingly, gradually I neared the cave opening.

The fluky wind proved a nuisance. One minute it whistled past me, so that I stopped and waited; the next, absolute calmness wrapped me as though the world had halted.

At last, at long and thankfully at last, the end of the ledge came in sight. I admit, I dropped Partagus in the entrance and just slumped back and took a breather. My eyelids closed.

As though struck by lightning I leaped up. My Val! I'd nearly nodded off! A crime, Dray Prescot, a heinous crime, and you are found guilty! I wiped a hand over my forehead and took the case containing the Prism of Power out of my harness.

A low moan past the gag reminded me of the sorcerer's presence. Back went the devilish case. Gripping Partagus I hauled him into the cave. We went around the three corners and I dumped him down where the three tunnel mouths began.

"Just stay there, mage. I'll be back."

At least, I said to myself as I retraced my steps, I hope so.

Kregen lay still in the thrall of night. More stars were visible and the Maiden with the Many Smiles went rolling down the sky.

A gust of wind tore at the bare mountainside and died away.

The chance that the Gdoinye wheeled in his wide hunting circles up there, watching me, checking to see if I did indeed do as the Star Lords commanded, was not a wager I'd care to accept.

Light though the case containing the Prism of Power was, when I took it out of my harness again it weighed like lead in my hand. All nonsense! I snapped at myself, disgusted. The thing was going over the edge, that was for sure. By the time it hit the bottom and the world exploded into redness and fiery destruction I'd be in the cave with Partagus, snugged down in the cover of the corner.

Why, then, did I delay?

The hell with it, I said, and threw the damned thing as far out as I could. For a fraction of a moment I stood watching it flying through the air, a small, dark, inconspicuous little thing.

A furious blast of wind lashed in. The wind seemed to concentrate all its fury and venom into a single hurricane of power.

The case span up, gripped by the wind. It whipped over and over. The wind caught it and played with it and drove it directly back at the cave entrance.

A sudden crack of lurid red light splayed from the case as it began to open.

I stood, appalled.

The unholy thing flew through the air straight at me.

Twenty

For what seemed like half a lifetime I stood there like a loon. The unholy red glare broadened as the case opened and swooped in the teeth of the wind. My eyes squinted shut. Move, man, move! I screamed at myself.

Spinning about, mouth open, with half-closed eyes, I ran madly into the cave. Three times I stumbled and crashed into the walls. Three times I recovered and tore on.

Gasping for air I hurled myself into the angle. Partagus made gargling groans beneath the gag. He saw my face. At once, he understood what terrible deed I had done.

His eyes opened to glare madly upon me. His face twisted into an expression of absolute unutterable horror. The gag vibrated to his panic shrieking, like a wild beast trapped far below ground.

Knowing exactly what was going to happen outside didn't help: rather, the awful knowledge made me scrunch up into the tightest ball I could manage. The only hope we had, the frailest chance, was that the wind in fluking the damned Prism of Power at the cliff face would not hurl it into the cave entrance. It had to—by all the Names, it had to!—drop down below the lip of the precipice.

That I can tell you of these fraught happenings is proof enough the opening case did indeed fall and strike below the opening.

The whole world turned red. Virulent crimson burned through my eyelids. The intolerable glare lasted and lasted until the concussion smote.

Everything shook. We vibrated up and down like dancers on a trampoline. Enormous pressures funneled down from the entrance and buffeted us with the force of the worst rashoon of the Eye of the World. The redness faded and an eyelid could be cracked open.

Sliding cracks appeared like diseased veins across the walls. Chunks fell from the roof and dust smothered and choked us.

Gradually the hurricane wind subsided. I knew what was happening outside. Now a stupendous column of crimson fire would be rising into the sky. The noise of rushing winds and the feeling of pressure eased, subsided, and for an eerie moment we lay crouched in an oasis of unnatural calm.

The three angles of the cave had saved us. The full force had been broken. I sincerely believe that had that not occurred we would have been done for.

Also, I recognized why this strange peace descended.

Now the immense pillar of fire tearing up into the heavens would be pulling air into its shaft. Instead of being crushed to death we stood in peril of being sucked out and over the precipice.

Breathing became difficult with the amount of dust choking everywhere and the loss of atmospheric pressure. I hoicked Partagus up and started resolutely for the central opening at the back of the cave. A few paces inside that black hole a dim blue light grew.

The Eye lay smashed on the ground and no turquoise gleam shone from the glassy fragments.

As I watched the blue oval of light grew and a dear form became clear. Delia! Once before W'Watchun had sent an apparition of Delia of Delphond, Delia of the Blue Mountains, when I was running from the Tchekedos. Then he'd entrapped me. Now—now the phantom of Delia raised her hand, palm out.

About to rush forward into that central opening, I checked.

Imperiously, Delia signaled with that upraised palm for me to stop, to go back, not to enter the tunnel.

Instantly I grasped her meaning.

W'Watchun was warning me. Gripping Partagus, and panting a trifle, I looked left and right and then back to the center.

The noise rolled up like thunder on a clear day. The roof trembled. With deceptively slow movements cracks appeared. The rock split. In a smothering sheet of destruction, rocks and dust rained down. They fell in a sheet across the entrance, fell between the apparition of Delia and myself.

The crimson light was fading. Dust obscured vision. I spat grit and wanted to wipe my streaming eyes; but did not.

Left or right?

The central opening was now thoroughly blocked by debris. Hauling Partagus along with a fist in his hair I started for the left hand tunnel entrance.

Slowly the ground beneath our feet stopped acting like a swifter in a rashoon. Groping forward blindly I felt stone beneath my fingers and faintly, like a spectral glimmer, a spot of white light appeared ahead.

Well, after all my experiences with the Illusionist, I could still think: "Good old San W'Watchun!"

The lamps were dim and badly needed to be trimmed. But they illuminated enough for us to see more and more as we ventured deeper along the tunnel. The way proved tortuous and tricky. Eventually I slashed Partagus's bonds free from his ankles, stood him up, snarled into his ear: "Now you march, sorcerer!"

W'Watchun had been clever. He knew that I would take instant notice of any command from Delia. He was well able to project her glorious face and form by his subtle arts. In a very real sense she had saved me. Without that crucial intervention I'd be lying back there in the central opening, squashed as flat and bloody as a flea beneath a calloused thumb.

Partagus stumbled along ahead. After our ordeal he was in reasonable shape. Mind you, I felt as though I'd been dealt with by ol' snake. The enormity of the luck we'd had back there remained still difficult to grasp.

The Wall would no doubt have gone up again the moment we were through. What was going on in Khon the Mak's siege camp now?

Certainly the sorcerers would have regained their senses.

By removing their chief they'd been deprived of sufficient kharrna to overpower the occult defense inside the mountain. They would not break the Wall down now, thank Zair.

We came to a narrow-gutted and jagged section where the lamps glowed dimly. Partagus hit his head on a low-thrusting piece of stone and yelped gurgling through the gag. He fell down.

Sink me! I said, and put a hand under his armpit and lifted him up. As we progressed he stumbled along slowly and more slowly. In the end I slung him over my shoulder, telling him to behave himself, or else, and went on at a better pace.

A scuttering sound from up ahead brought me up all standing. The noise grew louder. A myriad tiny feet were scampering along the dark tunnel towards us.

From the dimness into the vague glow of a single lamp they swarmed like just what they were, a horde of rat-like beasties with sharp snouts and red eyes and bristling whiskers.

A tide of them flooded about my ankles. They did not stop to bite. They just ran madly on like a pack of lemmings heading for the sea.

The last of them vanished into the gloom at our backs and I faced forward to see just what was chasing them.

He wasn't a tralk, but looked somewhat like that ferocious animal although on a smaller scale, and his armored bulk almost filled the tunnel. His two pincers waved before his scooped jaw, his four eyes looked as mean as they come and his six legs bunched as he readied himself for the charge that would add me and Partagus to his dinner.

In these confined quarters the Krozair brand would have no room to swing. A thrust might not prove decisive. So I drew the drexer, poised and then, not waiting for the mini-tralk to reach me, charged full tilt at him.

The blade swept left and then left again on the reverse cut. Both hits scored—luckily, by Krun! His two left-hand eyes burst. His ferocious uproar changed to a high shrilling. A damned great claw almost had me, leaving a bloody gash down my side. I skipped back, balanced lightly, ready to take out his right-hand eyes.

He swayed on those six legs which were now widely braced.

You could feel deep sympathy for him, for he was doing what he had been designed by nature to do. I waved the sword. I hoped he would not try to charge again but just run off.

He hesitated, swaying, his claws opening and shutting with a clashing sound. He turned his head to see from his right side, for the left eyes oozed blood and mucus. And he kept up that nerve-wracking shrilling which echoed and bounced between the craggy walls.

The smell gushing from him nauseated me. Partagus, on the ground where I'd dropped him, made terrified gargling noises. I felt glad I hadn't removed his gag.

Shaking the sword again, I advanced a step.

The mini-tralk clashed his pincers. His armored body swayed back on the six legs. I shouted, high, incomprehensible, stupid words. He backed away. His claws scrabbled on the stone. He stopped and then backed away again. I followed and slashed the blade through the air in front of him.

He gave a screech like a bursting boiler and scuttled back.

The light just showed me his squat body turning about in a widening of the way and then he was off. The last of him was a long-drawn wailing screech echoing along the tunnel.

I let out a breath.

After that little encounter I felt much more at home.

After all, this was Kregen, and a fellow cannot expect to stroll down a tunnel without meeting a monster or two, now can he, by Vox!

Some oily rags snugged in a pouch on my belt. Not wishing to waste one, perforce I marched along with the sorcerer slung over my left shoulder and the drexer naked in my right fist, the blood congealing to blackness on the blade.

We passed a goodly number of side passages and cracks where I kept alert for more attacks. None came. Some of these sub-tunnels were of a reasonable size, confirming what I'd been told that the whole place was honeycombed with runnels. The lamps marked our course. As we left them to the rear they died after a time.

This way proved to be longer than the center tunnel; but eventually we hove up against a lenken, brass-bound door with an Eye positioned in the lintel above. Putting Partagus down—and surprisingly gently, too, by Krun!—I banged the sword hilt on the door.

The door opened with a theatrical creak and grey cobwebs pulled apart until they broke. Lifting the sorcerer, for he was far past walking, I carried him into mellow lamplight. Ronun greeted me with a wry, lop-sided twist of his beak.

"Lahal, jis," he said, very formally. Then, cheerfully: "By Rhapaporgolam the Reiver of Souls! I scarcely expected to see you again. You are heartily welcome."

"Aye. Carry this lump for me, will you?"

Ronun motioned a couple of his juruk forward who took the Illusionist as though he were a sack of corn. We went through to the main chamber. Everything was as before, the people in their lotus positions immobile, the auras of their mental force almost tangible.

Chekaran came in, his yellow Chulik face with the upthrust tusks very fierce. "The master is asleep—" He saw Partagus and checked himself. His fierce expression turned into one of absolute hatred. "By Likshu the Treacherous!" Before anyone realized what was happening he whipped out his sword and slashed it cleanly across the Illusionist's throat. His blow was delivered with such intemperate savagery that the head leaped from the shoulders.

Blood spouted from the stump of the neck.

"Down to the Ice Floes with him, the blintz!"

Violence of this kind, whilst endemic in some parts of Kregen, does not leave me unaffected. I felt outraged.

"I've dragged that fellow all the way up here!" I fairly bellowed. "Now look!" I felt disgusted. "What a waste of effort!"

"Better to have finished him before, majister." Chekaran sounded completely unrepentant. The two guards dropped the headless corpse, and the Chulik bent and wiped his blade on Partagus's scraps of remaining black clothing.

"What'll San W'Watchun say?"

"That I shall find out when he awakes. Now, majister—"

"Now I need a drink, some food, and then I shall sleep."

"Quidang!"

Shortly after that, with a glass of full-bodied red in one hand and a bunch of palines in the other, I sought the bed put at my disposal. I'd been active for a day and a night and because no fatigue had been allowed to inconvenience me, I hadn't felt tired. Now I could relax. There was a quick stab of guilt at the memory of the way I'd nearly dozed off in the cave entrance before disposing of the Prism of Power.

Then I felt amusement. Disposing! That titanic explosion had been felt right in the heart of the mountain, here in the chamber where the Wall was maintained. The people at their desks, of course, had been shifted by the shock; not one had moved. Not, that is, by her or his volition.

As always my last thought before sleep is the same. On this night I could luxuriate in the vision W'Watchun had used to warn me of the rockfall. How marvelous she looked! Clad in her russet hunting leathers, rapier and main gauche strapped on separate belts around that lissom waist, her Claw in its carrying bag, her whip neatly coiled, oh, yes, my Delia looked what she was—the most perfect woman in two worlds!

A little Och girl woke me and I rolled out, knuckling my eyes, and after the necessary ablutions went off to find breakfast.

Breakfast, like most meals here, consisted of a variety of different dishes spread upon the table. Helping myself I ate well. Some time into the meal W'Watchun came in. He filled his plate and came over and sat down by me, and we exchanged the morning greetings.

"You did extraordinarily well, majister."

When I questioned that, evidencing my efforts with Partagus and his summary fate at the hands of Chekaran, he said he had no quarrel at all with the Chulik. He gave his opinion that I should have disposed of the traitorous Illusionist. "Then, majister, you could have dragged this Hyr Kov up here since he bears you so much malice."

"His wings have been plucked for him. Now the Prism of Power is destroyed—what will he do?"

"There are others—"

"Oh, aye. Nothing is perfect in an imperfect world."

"That is true. Luckily you knocked loudly on the door and Jiktar Ronun was within earshot."

I felt a little surprise. "There was an Eye over the door."

He shook his head and said that that Eye was out of commission and not watched.

"But there were lamps in the tunnel."

Now he looked surprised. "You are sure? Well, majister, of course you are. But there have been no lights in that tunnel for some time. It is sealed against the tralkniks."

Curiouser and curiouser. We took palines and munched for a time in silence. Then, feeling the gratitude proper to a fellow whose life has been saved by the person with whom he is eating breakfast, I said: "The first time you sent an apparition of Delia you entrapped me in nets. I felt anger at that. This time, well you were extremely clever to send a phantom of Delia to warn me that the roof was about to fall in." I spoke clearly. "I give you thanks, san."

He stopped munching on the palines.

He stared at me, his eyes opening wide. Surprise made his mouth open and his head tilt a little to the side.

"I sent a projection to warn you?"

"Aye."

He shook his head. "No, majister."

I felt as though the whole mass of rock above had fallen on my head.

This had to be got straight. My voice husked.

"San. You did not send a phantom of Delia to warn me?"

"I did not, majister."

I was drowning. I was falling into a pit of fire. I felt as though molten lava was eating my body away. I tried to swallow and could not. The palines in my hand sprayed out in a fountain and rolled across the floor.

It was clear. It was hideously clear what had happened.

I had seen Delia. There was no mistaking her dear form.

But if W'Watchun had not sent a phantom, then who had sent it? There was only one answer to that.

231

The Star Lords had sent her. The Everoinye had sent a very special kregoinya. She had arrived and warned me and the rock had fallen... fallen...

Delia had been no apparition.

She was real and alive and vibrant, warning me, and the roof had fallen...

I felt very strange. I stood up. Somehow I was running like a crazy man for the entrance to the center tunnel. No, I was not like a crazy man—I was a crazy man.

I ran for the center tunnel and what I would find at the end.

Wrath of Antares

Dray Prescot

The planet Kregen under the twin star Antares four hundred light years from Earth offers fantastic opportunities to those willing to risk all, to stake their lives against the chances of disaster to gain fame, fortune, glory and love. On that beautiful and terrible, savage and exotic world, passions run high, deeds are valiant, and under the streaming mingled ruby and emerald lights of the Suns of Scorpio all a man or woman desires may be theirs.

Dray Prescot has been taken to Kregen many times to carry out the mysterious designs of the Star Lords. Now they want him to become the Emperor of Emperors, the Emperor of All Paz. At the moment he is attempting to unify the sub-continent of Balintol against the overweening ambitions of local rulers, so that a united front can be presented to the predatory reivers from over the curve of the world—the dreaded Fish-heads, the Shanks. Prescot is skeptical of the whole concept of an Emperor of All Paz; but the Star Lords will it. These rulers of various countries of Balintol, and the people trying to usurp them, appear to care only for their own ambitions.

Prescot is a man above middle height, with enormously broad shoulders and a magnificent physique. He has brown hair and brown eyes that are level and dominating. There is an air about him of abrasive honesty and indomitable courage. He walks like a savage hunting cat, silent and deadly. Yet his humanity has not been calloused by his extraordinary adventures on Kregen, rather the reverse.

Having saved the Illusionist of Winlan and preserved the Wall that retains the demon monsters created by Khon the Mak's Dokerty priests, Prescot now realizes to his profound horror that the phantom of his wife Delia he saw buried by falling rock was no apparition.

Alan Burt Akers

One

A madman clawed at the debris with torn and bleeding fingers. The close confines of the tunnel echoed to a hoarse and desperate gasping. The detritus spilled in a heap as massive to a distraught imagination as the whole of the Stratemsk, daunting, heartbreaking, agonizingly slow to clear. Dust choked everywhere distorting the weak light of the torch wedged into a cleft. A maniac tore at the jumbled rock. A fellow bereft of his senses cursed and choked and ripped at the sarcophagus that entombed all he loved dear on two worlds.

That poor demented creature was me, Dray Prescot.

Delia had stood here to warn me, the real, wonderful Delia and no weird phantom conjured by Illusionist magic. She had warned me—and the roof had fallen on her.

The jagged chunks of rock lacerated my fingers, scored my palms. There was blood—so what did that matter? Nothing! The insensate mass aroused such hate within me I choked with bile and dust. I had to break through! I must see what horror there was to see.

The aftershock of the explosion of the Prism of Power had brought the roof down and among my retching gaspings the roof creaked above. I ignored it. Nothing mattered in all of Kregen save my Delia... nothing!

The picture of Delia with the roof falling in shards and sharp-edged shatterings all about her burned itself past my retinas into my brain. That ghastly picture would torture me past remorse—for at the time I'd dismissed Delia as a mere apparition sent by San W'Watchun to warn me. The roof creaked again; or was that my diseased imagination demanding retribution?

A large jagged boulder resisted my efforts. I bent and pulled and hauled and shook the thing, trying to prise it away. That stupid piece of rock was ugly, hateful, despicable, disgusting. It lay there with rivulets of dust trickling from its edges and in my rage and despair I swore the nauseating thing leered back at me and mocked me.

In this waking nightmare gripping me I imagined I heard above my frantic pantings a distant shout. I distinctly felt the floor tremble—or was that me, trembling in fear and terror for my Delia?

Dust smoked into my face. The torch tumbled down and was

extinguished. For a moment, a moment only, a ray of light struck past my shoulder. The rumblings in my head sounded distant and vague. But they were not in my head. For a single instant I glanced up in the darkness and saw the roof splitting apart.

The roof fell on me and the black cloak of Notor Zan enveloped me in the embrace of oblivion.

When I woke up for the first time I let out such a yell of pain I thought it would bring down this roof on me, too.

I felt the needle's little prick, then another, and most of the pain faded away. My eyes appeared to be surrounded by yellow so I knew my head was heavily bound up with clean yellow bandages. Another needle pricked into my skin and off I went again into unconsciousness.

The second time I woke up the pain had dulled to a throbbing that permeated just about all of my body. I heard the murmur of voices at my back and tried to turn my head. At once a hand restrained me. The ceiling was completely covered with intricate paintings. The colors and shapes charmed. This Kregan philosophy of occupying the mind of a recumbent and helpless patient is capital therapy. I could look at those pictures all day quite happily—

Like the cruel blade of an axe smashing down a door another and altogether dreadful picture flashed before my eyes.

Delia! Delia of Delphond, Delia of the Blue Mountains, smashed and mangled and bloodily destroyed under tons of mountain debris. That picture tortured me so that I cried out in agony of spirit.

The acupuncture needle brought blissful emptiness.

On my third awakening I knew that, as I was Dray Prescot, I had to overcome this nightmare. Delia was gone. Therefore I had to come to terms with the horror. Delia would desire—would command!—me to go on with life. Were there not our children to cherish? Were there not our comrades? Were there not all the happy memories of our times together? Well, then, fambly, she'd say. Get on with it!

A spoon touched my lips and soothing syrup spilled over my tongue. I did not open my eyes. I took the nourishment placidly.

Then I was dispatched off to sleep again. What I dreamed I do not know. I remember nothing—and perhaps that is best. My dreams must have been agonizing.

The next time I awoke I opened my eyes to study the room, not with any interest in my surroundings or desire to know what was going on; but simply because that was what was expected. Apart from that amazing and therapeutic ceiling the room was totally unremarkable. Beige painted walls, yellow curtains, a low table with a bowl of flowers and the bed—that was the sum total of what I could see. The door must be outside my range of vision and I just couldn't be bothered to turn my head to look.

Now, for an old and wily fighting man not to ascertain where the door in a room was located was completely unheard of in the warrior circles in which I moved. That glaring omission just goes to show how far down in apathy I was sunk.

Oh, yes, because I knew Delia would command me in her most formidable tone of voice to go on with life I would obey her and do so. But there would be no joy in it.

Thus deep in depression an idle thought occurred to me. The voices I imagined I heard at my back in the tunnel and the fresh light must have been real. Someone must have pulled me out. At once I felt impelled to action—dolt! Something I should have thought of right away, staring me in the face, half-blinded by pain though I was, something I must know immediately. A question I must ask—now!

I yelled

I shouted, I bellowed, I created an uproar they could have heard under the Pilza waterfall smashing down between its crags.

A round, frightened face appeared beside the bed, as it were hovering in the air. Two bright blue eyes opened and the little pink mouth started to stretch into a frightened scream.

I forced myself to remain calm and sober. I couldn't smile but when I spoke I hoped I sounded like a normal man.

"Please do not scream. I am perfectly well." That, of course, was a downright lie. "Who pulled me out? I must see them at once, right now."

"Of course, majister." She whisked off at once in a rustle of starched bodice and I flopped back on the bed.

My shouts must have brought everyone running and they must have been waiting outside the door. It didn't matter how fast they were; the wait stretched and stretched for me. My old heart went clatter bang like a calsany cart over cobbles. I felt my fingers curling into fists. I yelled again: "Hurry it up there!" and on the instant heard the door open and they crowded in. They formed a ring about the foot of the bed and gazed at me.

San W'Watchun with his amazing glassy eyes favored me with a look like that of a disappointed schoolteacher regarding a backward child. The Chulik, Chekaran the Balass, slapped his half-drawn sword back into the scabbard, an action paralleled by the cadade, Ronun ti Bjorfling. The others of the Illusionist's personal guard wore various expressions, mostly of relief that I wasn't being murdered in my bed.

As for Mistress H'Havalini, her serene Venahim face showed no emotion save that of perfect peace. Her astonishing talents as a practitioner of the mystic healing process known as schonibium must have been practiced on me, to restore the balance of the spirit.

"Majister—" began the Illusionist.

"Who pulled me out!" I bellowed it so the words rang in the bedroom.

Then, a tithe of polite conduct occurring to me, I rapped out: "My thanks, my deepest thanks. What did you see in that confounded tunnel? Did you find—?" I was astonished to discover I couldn't speak the words. They crescendoed in my old vosk skull of a head like the famous Bells of Beng Kishi. But I couldn't say them aloud.

Chekaran said at once: "The tunnel was cleared completely. Nothing—no one—was discovered."

My eyes closed. I felt dizzy. My head felt as though it was coming off, spinning.

"Nothing—no one?"

"The tunnel was cleared after you were taken out. Every palm's width of it. Nothing, majister."

I closed my eyes. Delia had been there. W'Watchun had not sent an illusion to warn me the roof was caving in. So the Star Lords had sent Delia. Could I hope the giant Blue Scorpion had whisked her away in time? That was the agonizing point of which I could not be sure. Had she been taken up to the Star Lords a mangled corpse?

Staring upon these men of W'Watchun's guard I reflected that I'd not known them for very long. In that time, though, we'd fought together, come a little to understand one another, lost a comrade. Not one of them was a Pachak with that race of diff's strict code of nikobi in service. They'd given their word to obey the orders of the captain of the guard and those set under him in the mercenary form, which varied from region to region in the nature of these things. I felt that I could trust them.

All the same—all the same, I had to see for myself.

When I went to swing my legs out of the bed I found they were most reluctant to move. With a petty gesture of annoyance I swept the sheet aside. From ankle to thigh, each leg was encased in windings of yellow bandages. Most of my body was similarly wrapped. The head bandage slipped a trifle just like dear old Deb-Lu's wobbly turban. To say I looked like a mummy was patently obvious.

In a kind of low, growly, hoarse voice, I said: "You'll have to carry me between you. I must see."

Well, of course, they tried to dissuade me. They failed.

By the time I'd been carried, pushed, pulled, and finally dragged to the end of the tunnel past where I'd so frantically dug at the debris, I had to admit it. Not a single sign that Delia had been there could be discovered.

My brain was not working aright, I was sure of that. A thought struck me which, simple though it was, appeared to me with stunning force. The Illusionist W'Watchun had not sent a phantom of Delia to warn me; suppose the Everoinye had not sent a flesh and blood woman but had dispatched an apparition of Delia? Well?

The thought tormented me.

After that futile tunnel expedition and the dreadful thoughts invading my brain accompanied by the incessant clanging of those famous Bells, I withdrew into myself. I drew a cocoon about me. Oh, yes, I obeyed the Puncture Lady and the needleman and Mistress H'Havalini and stayed in bed and drank my broth and slept and recovered my strength day by day.

The day came when I could actually walk unaided from one side of the room to t'other. Yellow bandages still wrapped me. Apparently this was a part of a technique practiced by the needleman, Doctor Drewinger, which he called The Clonset Jibr'chun. I called it a bloody nuisance.

This information was given me by the little round-faced, blue-eyed maiden who had popped into view when I'd yelled. Her name was Shalli, an apim lass, and with her two little colleagues, Thansi, a Fristle fifi, and Solana, an Och maiden, nursed me. They were brisk, efficient, pert and utterly charming. When the time for a pungent medicine came around, or the time to change the acupuncture needles, they were strictness itself. No jumped-up hairy Clansman who had become an Emperor of Emperors could awe them or halt their firmness.

These three maidens, although from a Nursing College and not a refined ladies' school, were well worth Gilbert and Sullivan writing songs about them.

To be honest, they were about the only cheer I had at that ghastly time.

Orders restricting ale and wine consumption were rigidly observed. When Ronun tried to sneak in a bottle of a fine yellow, it was removed from his person with the alacrity of a devotee of Diproo the Nimble-Fingered. The three lasses kept on refilling the water jug. This, they informed me, more than a little primly, was a strict injunction from Mistress H'Havalini. "Water will help purify your ib."

Now although in many manufacturing processes there will be unpleasant wastes, on Kregen the amounts were so small that Mother Nature could deal with them without trouble. Kregan water is not filled with impurities. Still, Kregans use a simple and effective method of water purification. Water from source is run through beds of heather. This needs to be old heather with hairy stalks so that the solids are trapped and pure water flows through. I can tell you without a shadow of a doubt that Kregan water is a superb drink on its own. Mind you, Beng Dikkane and his ales do have a salutary effect on the original liquid!

Still wrapped in bright yellow bandages I grew stronger each day. When I asked for a sword so that practice could be taken I admit I was surprised when Shalli trotted in holding my drexer in its scabbard as though it were infected with some deadly disease.

She held it out, her snub nose wrinkling in distaste.

All her reactions to a weapon were perfectly understood by me. Gravely, I said: "Thank you, Shalli." Then, unable to keep my black-fanged winespout shut, quite unnecessarily, I added: "A weapon is merely an object. The person wielding it is—" Then I stopped myself from this preachy babbling, and turned away, and sat on the bed.

So, after that, I was able to go through the exercises of a sword. My muscles objected at first; very quickly suppleness and speed returned. Because of my dip in the Sacred Pool in far Aphrasöe wounds healed quickly. The calamitous rock fall had broken bones, cut and lacerated me, given me a fine old headache. But I mended so rapidly that the three little nurses pursed up their lips in surprise.

All the same, Doctor Drewinger kept on with his damned Clonset Jibr'chun. Bound about like a mummy I stretched and thrust, parried and riposted against shadows.

There was no denying I'd get better far faster than Doctor Drewinger and Mistress H'Havalini could imagine. There was no real need for the close-wrapped bandages. They began to interfere with my sword exercises. Surreptitiously, I loosened the yellow cloth here and there at vital places to allow easier movement. After that the drexer turned into the familiar blur of silver as it hissed through the air.

Still, by the Black Chunkrah, I was not up to standard yet!

Whatever damage had been done to my head must be getting better for pain struck only now and then and the Bells of Beng-Kishi donged and dinged away to blessed silence.

All this made me realize that I'd been cooped up for goodness knows how long. I needed a good long walk in the fresh air.

The only problem with that ambition was that I was located in the heart of a mountain. Still, a brisk stroll through the various chambers and passages ought to start the blood pumping. Accordingly, when the little Och nurse came in with a bowl of gunk that, to be sure, tasted very fine, I drank it off, said thank you nicely, and then went on: "And now, Solana, I am going for a walk." I handed her the bowl and set off for the door.

Her alarm became at once visible. "Majister—" She stammered something about it being far too early for me to venture out. "What Doctor Drewinger will say I daren't imagine."

Assuring her that she would not get into trouble on my account I went out and stalked along the carpeted passage under the glow of lamps held in the hands of statues of various interesting kinds. The window in the bedroom, of course, had been merely decorative. There were more fake windows with painted vistas beyond. At least, I assumed they were pictures. With an Illusionist of W'Watchun's skill they could be real phantom fields and trees out there.

By the time I turned the corner at the end I was already feeling more cheerful, although nothing would lift the blackness of spirit that permanently engulfed me. One just had to go on.

The belt supporting the sword cinched tight around my waist. Sheer habit impelled me to take the weapon. Oh, and, yes, this was Kregen and on that tremendous and dangerous world having a handy weapon is more often than not a vital item of survival.

Inevitably, my steps took me in the direction of the three tunnels. No one appeared to be about, and I guessed Solana had run off to tell the good doctor of my misdeeds. Entering the center tunnel and starting along it I walked in a most sober, most grave, most despairing way. Had Delia been a phantom? Had she been snatched to safety in time?

The end of the tunnel, past the place where the debris from the fall had been cleared away, took me out onto that narrow, wind-blown ledge. The colossal scale of the chasm below impressed me all over again. Standing with my back pressed against the stone I could see the clouds writhing down there as the wind blew. A few birds wheeled and cavorted. The place struck me suddenly as entirely abhorrent.

I began to turn away to re-enter the cave leading to the tunnels. A glint of silver at the corner of my eye brought me back to stare out once more. The silver was no illusion, no trick of the eye.

Starting from the lip of the precipice, just beyond my feet, a silvery bridge extended out across the gulf. I gaped at it. Pretty silver lamps were strung above the walkway. High clouds dissipated the red and green lights of the twin suns. The lamps burned brighter even as I watched.

The bridge was there. There could be no doubt among all my troubled doubts about that statement of fact.

Now the Illusionist, San W'Watchun, and I had been getting along capitally during the recent events surrounding the protection of his famous Wall and my destruction of the Prism of Power. But it was still fresh in my memory how he had tricked me into believing I had never been to Kregen, that I was still stuck in the Royal Navy back on the Earth of my birth, four hundred light years away. He'd stopped pestering me to learn the secret of gunpowder. He appeared genuine.

Tentatively I put a foot on the slats of the bridge. If W'Watchun wanted to get rid of me, seeing me of no further use to him, he might guess I'd accept this challenge. Then, halfway across, he'd fold the bridge and I'd plummet down there into the gulf.

The bridge felt firm. It did not sway as it ought, given its construction and the strength of the breeze. With one foot on the silvery bridge and the other on the precipice lip, I pondered. This reminded me of having one foot on shore and the other in the boat. When the boat moved away with the current, then, splash! in you went.

A breath sucked deeply into my lungs, chest out, head up, I put the other foot onto the bridge and took a couple of steps forward.

With a jolt that staggered me so that I grabbed at the handrail, the slats underfoot began to move smoothly on. The handrail kept pace. Holding on, balanced, I was carried forward over the abyss.

"Sink me!" I said, aloud, both annoyed and relieved. "Old W'Watchun has really scrambled my brains with all his illusions."

Of course! I should have realized at once. I was being summoned by the Star Lords.

With that established I could anticipate what would come. I would ask. The Everoinye would reply. But—would they? Might they not as they so often did fob me off? 'That is not for you to know.' How many damned times had they said that in their lofty way?

Well, this time the occasion was far more important—nothing else was even remotely comparable in importance—so I'd keep on asking. I'd lose my temper. I'd rant and rave. What I determined was that I'd not lift a finger ever again to assist the Star Lords. Never!

That was settled. Queyd-arn-tung! No more need be said.

Over the seasons since my arrival upon Kregen the Star Lords had used a number of different ways to transport me into their august presence. There had been a variety of locations in which they'd interviewed me. The sheer awesomeness of this being taken up—or it could as easily be down—to face superhuman people continued to make me feel a trifle queasy as to the guts. Oh, yes, by Krun, I'd yelled at their spy and messenger, the Gdoinye. It was nowhere as easy to rant and rave at them.

The bridge continued to slide smoothly on towards the distant cloud bank. Beyond there I'd probably find an impressive golden gateway, or a series of passages along which chairs hissed rapidly. Whatever lay ahead, I hoped the Everoinye would provide a welcome glass of wine. By Mother Zinzu the Blessed—I would welcome that!

The blueness struck with supernatural swiftness. Cold and wind and penetrating blueness everywhere enveloped me. I glanced up. Yes, there he was, the Giant Blue Scorpion, leering down on me, snatching me away from the bridge, hurling me—somewhere.

Even as I tumbled head over heels through the blue void, I snarled to myself: "By Vox! Can't they make up their confounded minds which way they want to summon me?"

Only when my shoulder blades thumped onto hard ground did the realization hit me that the Blue Scorpion really did come from the Everoinye. They'd snatched me off the silvery bridge. Perhaps, after all, that bridge *was* a product of W'Watchun's sorcery.

There was no time to ponder anything other than to take in the scene before me and to act. My job for the Star Lords involved being hurled into perilous situations to rescue somebody. I took that seriously; the Emperor of All Paz bit I still found difficult to swallow. So I just ripped out the sword and charged.

If the truth be told, I suppose that after all my trials and tribulations and frustrations, the sheer act of laying about me with a blade vented the bad humors. This would get the blood flowing. I trusted to Kurin that the internal blood would be mine. As for the external, well, these were a pack of villains for sure. In this attitude I own to the shame of it—but, remember, this was Kregen.

A rutted and dusty road ran through a little glade among overhanging trees. The temperature felt much as it had been in Winlan, from which I'd been transported. A farm wagon stood with a broken front wheel, tilted over to the side. There was no sign of draught animals, mytzers, probably. The traces were cut and the animals had fled, frightened by the clamor of battle.

Dead bodies encumbered the ground as I ran swiftly on.

The mercenaries guarding the wagon had fought well and earned their hire. Their dead lay intermingled with the bodies of the men attacking them—fighting men who wore short red capes.

There was therefore no problem over whose side I was to assist. Two guards were left, being attacked by four of the red-caped men. Then I checked. Directly before me a fellow whose right arm had been cut off and which lay at his side, reared up despairingly. He was close to death.

His face was a mere mask of blood over ashen features. His eyes were pits of blackness. He tried to shout and blood gushed from his mouth. His armor was riven. He coughed blood and as I reached him he lifted his left hand imploringly. He must have seen me arrive. He husked out words all blood-spattered.

"Kregoinye! In the—wagon—"

He fell back, exhausted to death.

I shouted as I raced past. "Kregoinye, dom. May you traverse the Ice Floes of Sicce safely!"

One of the guards was down. The other swept his blade one way and a return thrust skewered him. He toppled over, shrieking.

So there were four of these Dokerty-lovers for me to deal with. Something caught at my legs and I almost tripped over. Dragging myself upright I roared on. Two swift cuts, left and right, and there were only two opponents left. As I swirled around to accept the onslaught I felt once more something clutch at my legs.

Red cape flaring, the first leaped at me. He raised his sword. Moving smoothly to deflect the blow and riposte, I felt my legs as though caught in a vice. I spared a swift glance down.

Yellow bandages! By Zair, the damned bandages had unraveled and now they were entwined about my legs like a man-trap. A yellow trail abaft me showed how they'd undone and straggled free to trip me up. I fell over.

The fellow's face was contorted with hatred and the desire to kill me. His mouth ricked open in a murderous snarl. He started to swing the blade down at my head.

With startling suddenness a throwing-knife sprouted from his eye. It made that typical sound—ter-chick!—as it went in. He screamed and fell away.

A light, silvery, altogether wonderful voice at my back called: "And now what mess have you dropped yourself into, Dray Prescot?"

Two

A live enemy armed with a sword remained ahead of me. I did not turn to stare back at the owner of that mocking, laughter-filled, marvelous voice. Generally speaking it is not wise to turn your back on your foe. This fellow, a somewhat larger than smaller specimen of a Varang, with monkey-like features, fringe of hair over his eyes, round cupped ears and a moustache down to the first buckle on his armor, carried a longsword, a clantzer of the pattern favored in north Balintol.

Fully expecting him to screech maniacally after the fashion of Varangs, and charge down on me to hack off my head before I was up, I dealt four swift blows at the entangling bandages.

He did not charge. His eyes appeared to glitter through the fringe of hair. He swung the sword over his head. But he did not charge.

Any warrior who wishes to stay alive on Kregen keeps his weapons sharp. The drexer bit cleanly through the yellow cloth. I stood up. Gulping a huge breath I turned my head back to indulge in the most luxurious sight on two worlds.

"You hairy old graint," she said, quite conversationally. "What kind of a fambly are you?"

The sweet air of Kregen, scented by the trees and blossoms, came to me in an extraordinarily refreshing wave of scent that bound up my emotions. I felt—what did I feel? Uplifted, expanded, joyous, so vastly relieved that my old heart seemed to be going like those trip-hammers the tumps use in their underground forges.

She looked absolutely incredible. If I said divine, I would exaggerate only in a spiritual sense, not in a material.

The trim russet leathers were cinctured by the diagonal belts around her waist, slender as an aspen tree, and the rapier and main gauche remained in their scabbards. Her tall boots shone. Her right hand was in the act of drawing another terchick from the battery strapped abaft her right shoulder. Over her left hand the Claw glinted with razor-sharp power. The black whip lay coiled against her thigh.

As for her hair—that shone as I always remembered, the outrageous auburn tints gleaming through the mellow brown, free and open to the air and the Suns. Her mouth parted in a smile so—so—all I knew was that I could drown forever in the glory of her smile.

That gorgeous face abruptly changed. Her eyebrows drew down. The red mouth snapped shut. I whirled about.

So this was why the Varang had not charged at once!

From beyond the stationary cart three of his bully-boy comrades emerged. Like him, each wore the short red cape that proclaimed them all as fighting men employed by the priests of Dokerty.

Their blades reeked with blood. They must have been busy at the loathsome task of killing the servitors and driver of the cart. Now, the three of them, a Fristle and two apims, together with the Varang, would finish off these two new arrivals as everyone else had been slain. So they thought.

Already in this brief spurt of action I had recognized with considerable dismay that I was still not fully fighting fit. Oh, yes, I'd seen off those first two smartly enough. But I'd felt the pull on my muscles, the extra effort required. The rockfall had punished me severely. All that meant, of course, was that I must make further efforts, that I must drive everything that was Dray Prescot into a single force that overcame opposition. These four cramphs needn't think they were going to slay Delia, Delia of Delphond, Delia of the Blue Mountains. No, by the Blade of Kurin, no!

The Fristle's cat-like features wrinkled up in a leer. His whiskers bristled. In his feline hissing voice, he said: "By the lady Tilly of the Golden Fur! What a prize!" His scimitar lifted.

One of the apims, a blocky fellow with a scar from eye to chin, shouted: "Put your sword down, tikshim. We'll let you run away."

The other apim, tall, with yellow hair poking out from under his helmet, simply laughed. His red cape, I noticed, was very tattered about the hem. In fact, all of them looked somewhat travel-worn.

"Wary of the girl!" snapped the Varang. "She threw a terchick straight into Nath the Sullen's eye. She's a she leem."

I, Dray Prescot, admit to the sins of boasting and bravura showing off. I didn't laugh; but I spat out: "Believe it!"

That gave me an idea. Shifting my sword to my left hand I bent and dragged the bloody terchick from Nath the Sullen's eye. I waggled it between my fingers, pretending to throw it at the Red Capes.

Their reactions amused me. They became instantly more alert, switching their weapons up, clearly apprehensive.

"Which one of you wants it?" I called—casually.

Judging by the ribbon-knot on his shoulder, the Varang appeared to be in command. He shouted: "Fan out! Charge the blintzes!"

The wonderfully luxurious and relieved feelings in me that Delia lived and that, moreover, we were together, shriveled. Now she stood in imminent peril of dying—permanently. At that moment of inward terror I forgot that Delia was nowadays employed by the Star Lords as a kregoinya, as I was employed as a kregoinye. She was trusted by them to carry out hazardous missions. Deliberately, out of fear for her safety, I had blotted those dreadful realizations from my mind.

Even as the four Red Capes spread out and rushed upon us I determined that when I next saw the Everoinye I'd tell them—implore, rather—beg them to release Delia from this work. Of course, she'd told me she loved it. Well, she would, wouldn't she, being Delia? She'd said it so carried forward the work she carried out for the Sisters of the Rose. Now, by Vox, we were to see the truth!

The Varang bored straight on towards me as his fellows spread to the flanks. I hurled the terchick. He dodged and rushed on. I cursed myself. So much for talking and bombasting! I should have chucked the thing straight into his eye the moment I ripped it out of Nath the Sullen's bloody orbit.

What I then did surprised him. Instead of fronting his charge, I bolted off to the rear where Delia stood, Claw over left hand, rapier in right fist. She glared at me. "What would Seg say?"

"Ah," I replied, heavily. "What would Hap Loder say?"

So, together, shoulder to shoulder, we faced them.

In the fight that ensued the six combatants possessed between them only twelve arms.

The Varang wielded a longsword, the Fristle his scimitar, the two apims swung braxters. I used the drexer. Delia employed her rapier, the Jiktar, and her Claw, her jikvar. Of all those weapons I supposed, soberly, the Claw was the most deadly.

Certainly, the first of the fighters to go, one of the apims, had no time to scream but span away with a face like a mere red pudding. The Fristle, trying to get at Delia, screeched: "She is a devil!"

I was experiencing some difficulty with the Varang's damned clantzer, for he kept smashing it down with what he considered overpowering force. My drexer deflected and slid the blows as at the same time the second apim tried to slice me with his braxter.

The blades screeched as they slid past one another rather than clanged. The Varang was mighty quick for his size and the apim kept dancing about like a hovering insect trying to stick his sting into me. And, mind you, like any green young coy I kept half my mind on something other than the combat in which I was involved. Needless to say, that preoccupation was the fight Delia was waging.

A sudden sweep of the drexer across the Varang's face which missed his nose by a hair's breadth—unfortunately, by Krun!—and I stepped back three paces, swiveled, and went after the apim.

He let out a great squawk and brought his sword around in a horizontal parry. "Help me, Hardo, you rast!"

The Varang roared and jumped after me so that I was forced to let the apim's parry work. The blades chingled together with more force. All the time I was hoping that my opponents' blades would snap. They ought, if all the Swordsmen Beyond the Clouds bore down on the side of justice, they ought to be made from the inferior steel of these parts. "Come on," I snarled to myself. "Snap, blast you, snap!"

As we swirled about on the grass, smiting and parrying, thrusting and dodging, I tried to see what Delia was up to.

The damned longsword crashed down on my sword and I felt the jar shoot clear up my arm and shoulder and jolt my skull. I was most certainly not on top form, by Vox! No, I was a long long way down the scale of competence in this confounded scrap!

Delia, in a flashing glimpse from the corner of my eye, swept her Claw across in what would have been a deadly scything blow. The Fristle jumped back, slashed his scimitar in a cunning counter, and Delia took it along her rapier in a sweet parry and instantly riposted. The Fristle swayed back and the narrow blade hissed past his side.

She followed up at once with another attack and the catman gave ground. In that swift glance I saw the black terror on his whiskery face, and knew with an uplift of joy that Delia was all right.

With that comfort I could turn my full attention to the two confronting me. Now I could allow my body and senses to flow into the sword, to wipe away sluggish thought, to let long-ingrained habits of sword fighting using what skill I had learned to take over. Instinct and skill and sheer downright cunning now dominated my actions.

And, on that, the longsword swept in as it were from nowhere and chunked down my side. Strips of yellow bandage flew.

"Ha!" yelped this Varang, Hardo. "Now I have you, blintz."

The apim took courage and bore in as I skipped away. The drexer parried his first blow, whistled around and deflected the second strike from the longsword, twisted back as I ducked, and went point first into the apim's throat.

He tried to gargle something as he span away, dropping his sword, hands to mangled throat. He fell.

The Varang snarled, a deep, guttural curse utterly incomprehensible, and leaped at me.

My drexer seemed to act on its own initiative. Every massively powerful attack of the longsword was met, checked, slipped, driven back. The monkey-faced Varang took a slicing cut along his left arm, at which he let rip with a screech like that of a hyrowof caught in the jaws of a leem. His blade slashed in again.

As I parried I heard a shocking scream at my back, so that I leaped sideways, imagining a back-stabbing thrust. The Varang pressed on hard. I couldn't see directly behind me, not having the eyes of a scaly Branliner who has two in front and two abaft, so was forced to deal with monkey-face on the instant.

My fears for Delia returned with a rush so powerful I almost let the longsword through. But instinct persisted, the blow narrowly missed and once again I leaped back. The Varang did not pursue. He stood motionlessly, sword cocked. Drops of sweat rolled down his hairy face. The hair over his eyes hung in matted strings. He panted, creaking the buckles of his armor.

In that brief pause, not at all uncommon in a hand-to-hand fight, I had the chance to confirm my fears for Delia. I looked.

Sink me! There she stood, glorious, glorious, the bloodied Claw gracefully turned so that she could rest her left hand on her hip without the blood fouling her russets. Her rapier bore a long smear of dark blood along the blade. She looked at me from under down-drawn brows.

"You are not feeling well, my love?"

"Ha!"

"He does have a great big sword."

By Lucilli the Radiant! She mocked me with that deep humor that so enraptured me. What marvelous good fortune in all of two worlds had enabled me, plain sailorman Dray Prescot, to win so great a prize? For her I would do anything. Nothing else mattered.

Hardo the Varang abruptly swept up his longsword over his head. He let out a screech that he intended to be blood-curdling. He sprang full at me, hair flying, eyes wild, mouth contorted.

Although he relied primarily on his strength to bash and break down an enemy, he was not without a certain skill. He had kept my blade out competently enough—up to now.

In a flurry of blows and counters, we fought. The blades slid and screeched, and then a rolling twist and a delicate thrust pinned his left arm below the fringe of armor. He staggered back. Blood began to drip.

He stared malevolently at me. Even so, I was minded to let him go, not to kill him, respectful of his prowess.

He was a Varang. Hairy and monkey-faced he might be; he would not quit the field. He ripped his short red cape off and flung it away. He flexed his muscles, unmindful of the dripping blood.

He charged.

In a few quick passes it was over. He reeled back, gasping, dropping his sword, toppling, spinning on tangled feet. He fell.

"Messy," was my Delia's verdict. "Not at all pretty."

She smiled, only a small, half-hesitant smile. I knew for all her words and her proud, brave attitude, she was deeply affected by scenes like this. She fought superbly when she had to. She detested that. She would far prefer to be at our home in Esser Rarioch in the garden. And, with a thump of blood around the heart, I knew she longed for us both to be there, together, happy, forever having had done with this detestable blood-letting.

We looked one upon the other, standing among the corpses and the blood. We moved forward towards each other. Silently, we embraced, breast to breast. If we were not at home, then in each other's arms we were as near to our spiritual home as we could be.

Three

There was much to tell.

As we cleaned our weapons companionably together she told me what she'd been up to—at some of which I trembled clear down to the soles of my feet—and I related my doings.

At one point she interrupted to say: "During that fight, my love, you kept looking over at me."

"Aye."

"You great fambly! You onker! That way you'll get yourself killed."

"Well—" I began, very lamely.

"I have my Claw."

"Oh, aye. Still—"

"If I need you I will call."

"Yes, and well," I said, somewhat hotly. "I can remember more than one occasion when you did not!"

She tossed her head at that, and scrubbed fiercely at her rapier. "That was because—"

"I know," I said in a voice suddenly soft. So to stop further discussion of this sore subject I kissed her, whereat she kissed me back so ardently it fair took my breath away. Parting is the very devil, as they say. Meeting—ah, well, that is another story!

She said: "I met up with a great golden Kildoi. At first I thought he was dear Korero—but—"

I could not feel jealousy. With Delia, after one fraught experience, that was impossible. I broke in: "Ha! That confoundedly clever fellow Fweygo, a calsany for a zorca!"

"Yes, my love."

She told me they'd sorted out a peck of problems for the Star Lords. The silvery bridge she knew about, for the Everoinye had taken her up in similar fashion. The poor devil of a kregoinye with his arm cut off had been sent here on orders. When he succumbed the Star Lords had simply sent the Giant Blue Scorpion to snatch me from their bridge and hurl me down here to get on with the job. They had no idea I was wounded and not fighting fit. Delia had witnessed that, and had given the Star Lords a piece of her mind.

At that I laughed. I could imagine it. There was no daunting Delia of Delphond!

So she'd come striding onto the scene in the nick of time to rescue me. What a girl! She insisted on giving my whole body a thorough inspection, tut-tutting at the bruises and welts and wounds.

She re-wrapped the bandages, this time not in some quack's fandangled ideas of therapy but in a business-like way to do their proper task.

She mentioned the Sacred Pool of far Aphrasöe. She, thank Opaz, was not hurt at all.

Just why the dead kregoinye, Louis Pelong, and ourselves had been dispatched to this place at the moment remained unclear. Obviously the paktuns had been guarding the wagon. We both stared at it as it stood so inoffensively on the dusty road.

"Still inside," said Delia.

"Aye."

We were a team. How marvelous, how absolutely wonderful, to be adventuring again with Delia! Nothing in two worlds can equal it!

Before we went over to the wagon I picked up Hardo's longsword. The clantzer was well made and must have been built over the northern mountains, where they made steel of better quality than here in Balintol. Of course, the weapon was nowhere in the same class as a great Krozair longsword. Still, it was serviceable and any Kregan fighting man prefers to have more than one weapon on which to rely in the heat of combat.

After wiping off the blood—my damned blood!—I strapped the scabbard on and slid the sword home. It felt quite good.

Then we walked cautiously over to the wagon.

As I'd suspected when the Fristle and the two apims had appeared, there were bodies of servitors sprawled in their own blood on the other side of the cart. Delia wrinkled up her nose. But these horrific scenes are part and parcel of life on Kregen. We had to get on with the mission on which the Star Lords had sent us.

The trees hemmed in each side of the glade. The dusty road bore ruts from past rains and consequent mud. Neither of us cared to venture an opinion as to exactly where we were. I was convinced we were still in

Balintol, by reason of the red capes of the attackers, mercenaries degraded into serving the priests of Dokerty. Delia concurred in that opinion. Although, carefully, she did say that the religion of Dokerty could have spread further afield.

By the disgusting diseased left earlobe and putrescent warts of Makki Grodno! I said, to myself, I hope not!

As we approached the cart the light dimmed. The streaming mingled radiance of the Suns of Scorpio gradually faded to deep ruby and emerald. The twin shadows dropped down about us and the first heavy spots of rain fell. Above us the clouds gathered darker and darker. Soon the rain began to kick spurts from the dust.

Delia smiled at me. "Do you remember walking through the Hostile Territories with Seg and Thelda?"

"Aye. Poor old Thelda!"

"Now, now, you hairy old graint!"

Whereat I laughed. Oh, yes, I can laugh when I am with Delia. "Now if Seg were here, and Inch—and the others—"

"Then we would not be alone together."

I let out a sigh. You could not gather all happiness together in one place.

Delia pulled her russet leathers more closely over her mail. She wore a particularly fine mesh of link steel, manufactured in the Dawn Lands. Each link was lacquered carefully, either with lac from an insect or the sap of the lac tree. This hard coating was impervious to water. All the same, no professional Jikai Vuvushi, as no competent fighting man, likes to get their metal armor wet. I remembered the amount of time required to clean the mail of the Inner Sea, the Eye of the World. Spit we had in abundance after a libation to Beng Dikkane; brick dust had to be used in miserly fashion when at sea for long voyages. As for my bandages, in no time they were soaking wet.

The wagon proved to be a sturdy affair, with bronze rims to the wheels of a good thickness. At the moment it lay open although there were fastenings for a tilt. The rain spattered on a tarpaulin untidily flung upon the bed. The cart's angle, by reason of the broken wheel, had toppled the contents into the corner. Barrels, a spade and pick, loose coils of rope, boxes and sacks—nothing appeared remarkably out of place in there.

A bulge in the tarpaulin moved.

Delia's rapier leaped into her fist before my drexer cleared scabbard.

She leaned over and gently poked the bulge.

A frightened voice squealed: "No! No! Help! Help!"

Briskly, Delia said: "Come on out, dom, and show yourself."

"Don't kill me!"

"We won't harm you. Now come on out." Delia's calm voice brooked no opposition in its firmness.

Gravely, I said: "You're safe now. I believe we are here to assist you."

A plump white hand, much beringed, appeared over the flap of canvas and pulled hesitantly. A flat red cap with a broken feather popped into view followed by the face of its wearer. That countenance was pale with shock, dark-eyed, the mouth shaking, the ears protruding. The fellow climbed out stiffly, trembling with anticipation of the dreadful fate awaiting him. He had heard what had gone on around the cart. His hired mercenaries had failed and all been slain.

Now he must consider that he had been discovered and it was his turn to die.

As Delia gripped his arm and assisted him over the side of the cart and onto the wet grass I stared. I felt a sick sensation in my guts. Had we got this all wrong? Had we charged in on the wrong side? Should we have assisted the attackers? I didn't know.

For this man wore the red robes of a priest of Dokerty.

Delia took all this in, and then, being of the female persuasion, asked the first practical question: "Are you wounded?"

"N-No. No. Who are you? Are you sorcerers, a wizard and a witch." He stared on us and then on the bloody scene around.

"No." Delia was sharp. "Who may you be?"

He was a plump, well-nourished fellow, not overly tall, and an apim. I wondered if it was in his mind to lie. But he was in such a state of funk—to give his condition its correct appellation—that he couldn't dissimulate.

"I am San Cuisar, High Priest of Dokerty, known as the Oblifex. That is my use name. Who are you?"

Before Delia could speak, I said: "I am Drajak the Sudden."

Delia said: "I am Alyss—"

Out of some deep-rooted deviltry and love of her, I put in sharply: "Known as the She-Leem."

Delia gave me such a look as warmed the cockles of my heart! Well, and hadn't that poor devil back there given her the soubriquet?

"Then you will address me as proper to my rank!"

So he was getting his courage back. If we had been sent here to save him from his enemies then we needed him to function with all his apples still on the branch, as they say on Kregen.

An abrupt shock of remorse hit me. No, not about this poor specimen; but about Delia. She-Leem indeed! Rather, she should be called a zhantilla, one of those pre-eminent glorious wild animals that grace Kregen with their presence.

A look of devilment superior to my disastrous effort stole over Delia's face. She glowed.

In a sweet voice she said: "You say that is your use name. What is your real name?"

I groaned.I suspected we were in for half a bur's nonsense of multi-syllabled naming that would bore the bristles off a porcupine. By Krun, I was right!

He started off with the Double. Well, he would, wouldn't he? C'Cuisar followed by an interminable string of syllables. He finished by saying: "Vad of Igverli."

"Vad?" A Vad is the second highest rank of nobility.

The rain drooped his broken feather down most forlornly.

"Yes. Although I gave it up for my son when the call came from Dokerty." He lifted a plump hand. "Now will you find me some shelter? At once!"

I didn't care about shelter. I knew what I should do. I knew what I should do, instantly, without remorse or pity. He was a priest—a High Priest!—of the debased and degenerate cult of Dokerty. I should lift the longsword, for given the choice I'd prefer not to soil the clean drexer, and cut him down where he stood.

No doubt about that, by Krun!

But, of course, I couldn't top him in cold blood.

Delia saved me from my uneasy and fractious thoughts. There was a mystery here. There was a question that needed to be asked. Delia favored me with a sidelong look. With the rapport between us I sensed she was seeking a subtle and diplomatic way of posing that intriguing question. The answer should be highly interesting, too!

The rain dropped down now straight and hard between the trees. This slightly pompous and faintly ridiculous figure of a hated Dokerty priest blurted out: "Will you find some shelter! Bring me my cloak, at least, you pair of drikingers."

Fetching out the fellow's cloak, red and ornate, I saw that this slighting remark gave us the opening for our question.

Mind you, he must have thought me an odd kind of bandit to be trussed up in yellow bandages. I'd have to sort out some armor. The fresh scent of rain on leaves and grass began to wash away the raw stink of spilled blood. I'd let Delia ask the questions. And this red-robed ninny hadn't even offered us a thank you!

This whole situation might be—probably was, as this was Kregen—fraught with enormous peril. It was raining. I was beginning to feel sharp set. In the absence of a needleman some of my wounds began to sting a trifle. And I could do with a good long draught of the finest. All these trifles meant nothing beside the overwhelming fact that once more Delia and I were together.

Delia of Delphond is undoubtedly a most charming lady. She is also as devious as they come. The sweet curve of eyelashes over her superb brown eyes gave a picture of young innocence.

"I am surprised," she said in that mellifluous voice that can melt an iceberg at fifty paces, "most surprised that a person of your high rank should ride in a mere farm cart."

You could see the hook go in and the line tauten and the victim come clean out of the water into the net.

"My lifter unfortunately crashed. The people of the nearest village were only too anxious to assist me—"

"Well, of course!"

He shook his shoulders under the rain-shining cloak.

Now my Delia was not naive enough to suppose that a person who had reached the position of High Priest—no matter in what religion—was not possessed of intelligence and a forceful personality. This Cuisar had been badly shaken by the attack and knocked off balance. Over indulgence in gentle mockery would not go down too well. Of course, if the fellow became obnoxious then Delia would, regretfully, show him the error of his ways. Still, just for the moment, he was a ripe target.

"These people who slew your guards—" Delia gestured gracefully. "I see they wear red capes very much like your robes."

"Ingrates!" he spluttered out. He clutched the hood of the cloak over his head, knocking his cap askew. The feather was long past redemption. "Miserable assassins! Sent by those I once trusted. Blintzes! Ingrates! Doomed and damned to Dokerty's wrath!

This was interesting. If there was dissension among the Dokerty lovers that could only be a benefit to honest folk. If he continued to support those of Oltomek, then we were very remiss in seeing off the Red Capes. This was a line of thought most uncomfortable. And it troubled me—and Delia, who was probably seven steps ahead of me, anyway. So far there had been no intervention from the Star Lords. Because of that I trusted we had done the right thing and that in some way the Red Capes were acting for Dokerty.

I said: "These red caped folk betrayed you?"

"They are mere hired minions. They have their orders to kill me. Well, I am the Oblifex! They will regret their treachery!"

The dimness grew as Zim and Genodras, hidden above massy clouds of an ominous darkness, slid down to the horizon. Delia was the first to spot the new arrival. She cocked that imperious head up.

"Vollers!"

They were there, scudding beneath the clouds, swooping down towards a landing along the muddy road.

Cuisar let out a strangled screech. "They have found me! The blintzes will kill us all!"

I was starting to shout: "Get into the trees!" I opened my mouth and Delia simply grabbed Cuisar and hustled him smartly towards the forest. Action and not words—that is my Delia!

Perforce I ran helter-skelter after them among the trees.

Four

Under the trees the wet undergrowth, the dripping leaves, the gloom that enveloped everything in a pall, gave an eerie feeling. The only sounds were the rain pattering down, the swish as we pressed on through damp undergrowth and the hoarse and heavy gasping of Cuisar.

Once we were in for twenty paces or so Delia struck off at an angle. I nodded sagely to myself. She was quite right. She wanted to take a look at these new arrivals and that would best be done by sneaking along parallel to the road and then peeking out.

"P'raps we'd better leave him hidden back a bit before we make our recce." The moment I spoke I felt an onker. Delia would never miss an obvious point like that.

She was very sweet about her reply. "Yes. Best."

"Don't leave me!" he squeaked. Delia hefted him along with one slim hand under his armpit. His feet touched the damp ground now and again.

We were making tracks that could be trailed. I trusted the rain might obliterate them before the fellows, whoever they were, got onto us. If not, well, my new longsword might drink a trifle. Then, very soberly, I had to rethink that bombastic thought. I was very definitely not up to scratch. I'd felt my strength leaching away during the fight.

With her remarkable acuity of eye, just how much of my fragility had Delia noticed? She'd commented caustically on my slowness. The dreadful thing that would inevitably follow from that alarmed me. She'd peremptorily order me to stay with Cuisar whilst she risked the recce alone.

This was precisely what she did.

"And no arguments, Drak the Not So Sudden!"

Saying futile words and warnings to take care I watched her as she glided like a wraith between the trees and vanished into the gloom. I felt as though my skin was on fire. I couldn't keep still. I fidgeted and chafed and worried. Oh, there was no use my telling myself that she was an accomplished adventurer. She went off at the behest of the Sisters of the Rose, or of the Star Lords, and got into all kinds of horrendous scrapes. She'd come through like a cork bouncing on water. She knew what she was doing.

And I, natheless, worried myself frantic.

What the hell were two people, supposed to be an Empress and an Emperor of All Paz doing gallivanting about in peril like this? Certainly, we'd chosen this life when we'd renounced the crown and throne of Vallia. But when the stark reality drove me half insane with worry, I longed for our home in Esser Rarioch.

Cuisar just sat huddled up under a tree. Every now and again he'd rock slowly backwards and forwards, mumbling to himself.

My mission for the Everoinye in which, this time, I fully agreed, was to destroy the demons created by such a man as this. No doubt he was deeply embroiled in the ghastly tortures that prepared a normal young man or woman into an infecto, a sublime, ready for the dread word of command which, to be honest, I didn't care to repeat. I should simply have his head off, here and now.

Presently he stopped making those soft whimpering sounds. He'd had a hard day, that was a certainty. He drifted off to sleep.

Then he started to snore.

By Krun! What a window-rattler he had! His snores blasted out in a huge succession of gargles and blubberings and gurglings like water running down the plughole. Everybody knows what snoring does to the unfortunates who have to listen.

I tell you, quite frankly, this fellow Cuisar the Oblifex came closer to having his head chopped off over his damned snoring than because he was a thrice-condemned and Opaz-forsaken priest of Dokerty!

About to grab him by the throat and choke him awake—or into silence—I took my gripping hands away as though they were twin snakes that had struck and missed their mark. I rolled over and sat up, the drexer in my fist.

"You were late, my love, late and slow."

I'd neither heard nor seen her as she'd approached. Only at the last moment had that sixth sense possessed by Clansmen and old sailor-men—and Krozairs of Zy!—warned me.

"Who could hear anything through this fellow's noise?"

"You sound disgruntled."

"By Vox! I am!"

She laughed a small, diminutive little laugh, and told me the vollers had flown off. The fresh Red Capes had rooted around among the contents of the wagon, throwing the things every which way. They'd not taken anything with them. "So they didn't find what they were looking for. Good. Bad cess to 'em!"

Then, being Dray Prescot with a tithe of that rough and ready fellow's recklessness left, I said: "Pity we couldn't have snaffled a voller. Now we have to walk."

"Not for the first time."

Delia wanted to know, if they'd found Cuisar, would they have slain him out of hand or would they have taken him prisoner. The rain eased and stopped and we moved out into the open to avoid the continual drips from the trees.

Using the tarpaulin and the softer sacks, we made bedding and covered ourselves up. Delia and I took turns on watch. Cuisar slept and he took a considerable quantity of prods in the ribs to shut up his infernal snoring.

There were provisions in some of the sacks and boxes. These we devoured, and finding a high-class wine, a Roubail from Enderli, in a straw-wrapped flask, we quaffed that off in fine style.

By the time the streaming mingled lights of Zim and Genodras flushed the morning in apple green and palest pink, we felt much more on terms with the world.

With the most delicate of touches and the utmost tact, Delia began to worm his story out of Cuisar. First off, he wanted to go to Winlan. He intended to throw himself on the mercy of the great Illusionist, San W'Watchun, of whom he had heard much.

This surprised me. Until I'd come to a kind of rapprochement with W'Watchun, I'd heard only evil of him. Of course, if Cuisar was a villain, then he no doubt imagined there would be two of them, birds of a feather, congregating together in their wickedness.

Then he told us why he'd fled from Enderli and my surprise collapsed at once. Of course! It all fitted!

Cuisar the Oblifex, High Priest of Dokerty in Enderli, the country to the north east of Balintol, had been ousted by—

"A Dokerty-forsaken blintz of a noble from Tolindrin!" Cuisar mouthed the words in a self-consuming fury. "And his tame High Priest, Nath G'Goldark, who is not fit to clean the ablutions of the temples of the High and Mighty Dokerty, have brought Oltomek into disrepute!" He babbled on about these great blintzes wanting to torture people so that they could become demons. Ibmanzies! Cuisar would have none of it and they'd tried to arrest him, have him killed to further their dark plans.

"Hyr Kov Khonstanton," I said. "Khon the Mak."

Cuisar showed his shock. "You know him?"

"Oh, aye. He and I have crossed swords before."

Now it was clear Khon the Mak had cleared off to Enderli where he knew another Flutubium concealed a Prism of Power. He needed that so that the priests of Dokerty could turn decent young folk into ibmanzies. So that meant some time must have elapsed, although by flying in a lifter he could reach Enderli in short order. I frowned.

My next move was obvious. I must go to Enderli and destroy the Prism of Power there, as I'd destroyed those from Tolindrin and Caneldrin. My kregoinye comrade Fweygo had dealt with the Prism of Power from Kildrin.

Delia was looking at me with a long brooding stare.

"It has to be, my love," I said, somewhat hopelessly.

"Of course."

When I asked her what we should do with Cuisar, she made a little gesture that, whilst not hopeless, was perilously close.

"Your duty," piped up the Oblifex, "is to escort me to San W'Watchun."

I gave him such a glare he flinched back. "And if you so detested what they wanted to do, why did you not destroy—"

"You know too much, Drajak! I could not destroy the symbol of authority, the divine gift from Oltomek! You must be mad!"

The quandary in which I found myself tore at my emotions. My duty was plain. The Star Lords ordained that, and if I refused to obey they'd callously toss me back four hundred lights years to Earth. That, I could not, would not, have.

But at the same time my duty was to Delia. I could not, would not, leave her to wander alone through the perils of Kregen. She might wish to escort this Cuisar the Oblifex to Winlan and deliver him safely into the care of W'Watchun. Then, I must go with her.

Pondering this apparently insoluble problem, I went grimly about the task to hand. There was enough reasonably fitting armor to give me some protection. Clothes were easier. We buried the unfortunate kregoinye, Louis Pelong, and the other corpses were left to the birds of the air to digest back into the food chain. Cuisar spoke a few Dokerty-laden words over the bodies of his guard. I am well aware of the callousness of that action; but time pressed. If I, having obtained this vital information, did not act upon it instanter, the Everoinye would pounce.

As though on the signal of my thoughts we heard a raucous squawk above. We looked up; Cuisar heard and saw nothing.

Up there floated not one but two magnificent golden and scarlet hunting birds. Their feathers shone in the early suns light. Gdoinya and Gdoinye, they circled above us, wide-winged, intolerant, gazing down with beady eyes sharp with meaning.

They squawked again, said nothing, and spiraled higher and higher until they vanished into the blue.

Delia wanted to know what the two spies and messengers were reporting to the Star Lords. I said I didn't know, and, by Krun, I didn't care. Oh, yes, foolish, I know. But then, Delia...

On her insistence some of the yellow bandages remained, poulticed to the worst of my wounds. I'd soon be better and fighting fit. Kitted up, with a splendid second breakfast consumed, I still was completely unsure of what I ought to do for the best.

Having heard my account, Delia was fully aware of what was going on and of the importance of dealing with the ibmanzies. If they were allowed to spread over Balintol they would completely wreck the vital plans for combination of the nations to resist the Shanks. The way to stop the ibmanzies was to destroy the power that created them—to exterminate the Prisms of Power.

And yet—and yet—Delia would be marching through hostile Kregen, shepherding this bleating High Priest. That was a dread I couldn't allow.

"If our comrade Fweygo turned up," she said, and stopped.

"Aye." I grunted it out, grudgingly. "Well, let's get started."

Shouldering a sack of provisions, armored and weaponed, I set out along the drying road. Delia let fall a low cry. I marched along stubbornly. They would follow.

I set my face towards the south west—towards Winlan.

Well, I should have known, shouldn't I? The blueness dropped about me with savage suddenness. The Giant Blue Scorpion hovered above me. Coldness, rushing winds, falling, I dropped away into the infinite blueness.

Five

Even as I tumbled head over heels through the blustering wind and the palpitating blueness I felt absolute frustrated fury.

I'd gambled and I'd lost.

Previously when the Star Lords sent me on a mission to rescue someone in pursuance of their own inscrutable plans, I'd known that I had to save that person, or persons, and stick with them until either they were safe or the Everoinye released me.

Delia and I had been sent to rescue Cuisar the Oblifex. We'd done that; but he still wasn't safe as witness the pursuit of the Red Capes' vollers. So, the natural ensuing thought was that we had to see him safe to where he wanted to go. The Prism of Power in Enderli, vital though it was, I'd gambled was second to saving Cuisar.

Now the damned great Blue Scorpion grasped me up and tossed me hither and yon, blasted me with cold and biting winds. To a Herrelldrin Hell with 'em! Delia concerned me. Yet, as you will readily see, I was blind in my concern for Delia. She could take care of herself. She'd done so. She'd proved how tough and resourceful an adventurer she was. If anyone could get Cuisar through to W'Watchun, Delia of Delphond, Delia of the Blue Mountains, could, without doubt.

The transit through the shining cold of the blue emptiness lasted and lasted. By now I ought to be at my destination. Now this casual snatching up of a fellow from one part of the world and dumping him down in another could never be taken familiarly. Oh, sure, I bombasted and put on a brave face confronting the Everoinye; the truth was that I felt sick right down into my guts. This feeling was not quite terror. Apprehension at what they could do to me if they chose, certainly, concerned me

These people—for they had once been human—were now superhuman, possessed of powers far beyond those of the greatest mages of Kregen, surpassing the superhuman but mortal Savanti of Aphrasöe.

However often I was called by the Everoinye, the experience remained chastening, eerie, a part of my life I could view only with the greatest awe. So, because of that, and because I am by nature a rebellious soul, I bellowed up into that blue infinity.

"Come on, Star Lords! Sort yourselves out! Where away are you sending me now? Are you going to drop me again?"

For, remember, they'd bungled before. I often hazarded the guess they were growing senile in their enormous life span.

Again I shouted into the void: "And while you're at it you can patch me up!" This they had done before. "My bruises ache and my wounds sting! You say you do not wish me to be damaged in your service—well, I damned well am right now!"

Through the echoing blueness an abrupt tongue of red fire shot up over to my left. That was more promising. That red hue announced the personal arrival of the Star Lords. I opened my mouth to let them know I was really damaged and a lance of acrid green fire speared up on my right. I knew who that was, the rast!

Ahrinye! The Star Lord who might by a few hundred thousand years be younger than his colleagues! The rebel, the super-human who wanted to do things his own way in defiance of the rest of the Everoinye, he'd hungered to run me, as he called it, to the fullest possible extent of my capacities. After that, when I collapsed, he'd discard me.

The green swelled into a shape resembling a broad-bladed spear. Alarmed, I looked around in somewhat of a desperate frame of mind for the comforting golden-yellow glow that would herald the arrival of Zena Iztar. She would defend me from this maniac Ahrinye. No yellow light shone through the blue between the red and green. Zena Iztar must be off on her wide-ranging travels, sorting out problems that mere mortal man could never comprehend.

The green swept over and around me. I lost all sight of the red. My fall through emptiness persisted; but I felt the wrench all through me as I went tumbling head over heels into that ominous green fire.

Jagged bolts of lightning struck in coruscating fury all about me. Gargantuan explosions of supernal thunder rattled the very bones in my body. Up and down I went, around and around. The acrid greenness wormed its way into every pore of my skin, chiseled into my very being. Gasping for breaths of air that scorched my lungs, I felt as though the life was being squeezed out of me.

With a jolting thump far harder than my usual arrival, I hit something that resisted. The greenness coiled about me still. I stared about, struggling to stand up, and could not move.

I realized I was securely held on a flat surface, pinned there by invisible forces, completely helpless.

Pain struck in with leem's fangs. Agony so intense gripped me so that I tried to shriek but could not utter a sound. For what seemed like half-a-dozen lifetimes that horrific suffering continued.

It ceased, suddenly and as abruptly as it had begun.

The voice spoke like the kiss of a scalpel.

"I am Ahrinye! I have repaired your damage. You should be grateful, Dray Prescot, and pay homage."

Trying to speak, I found to my amazement that my mouth shook so much that only garblings came out. Yet, I shouldn't be surprised. Super-humans could carry on like this. All the same, I knew I was repaired, in Ahrinye's terminology. As a mere human of flesh and blood, I was a thing to be used and discarded when the use was over. So, like the other Everoinye, he wanted his tool to be fit and up to the task set to his hands.

Lying there on the slab I felt the change as my bruises and cuts vanished. I'd been feeling like a leem's lunch; now, slowly, I regained the normal use of my limbs and muscles, felt the blood pumping evenly, felt my breathing steady. So, that cramph Ahrinye was good for something, then, by Krun!

Yet I sensed his healing was not as efficient as that of the other Everoinye. They'd hurt me; but nowhere near as much. He'd taken longer. And I regained my full fitness more slowly.

The acidic voice sliced with authority: "Now, Dray Prescot, you will obey the commands of Ahrinye."

The transition began at once and continued unevenly as the slab disappeared and I felt myself floating up with the greenness flickering all about. That color faded; no redness asserted itself, and imperceptibly I found myself at length floating in mid-air with the flooding tangled radiance of Zim and Genodras shedding their beams of emerald and ruby upon the land.

Only—that land stretched out far beneath me as I drifted unsupported through a fluffy bank of cloud.

Below me a vast encampment reached from a white-foaming shore back to the trees at the foot of an escarpment. Tents covered wide areas, there were picket lines for animals. The radiance of the Suns struck glints from metal and everywhere fighting men marched and drilled and paraded.

A great army prepared itself. When I managed to distinguish just who those soldiers were I felt the chill, a dread premonition of disaster to come. Carefully, as I drifted along with the breeze, I took stock of the damned Opaz-forsaken Shanks below. There were Schtarkins and Shants and others of those fish-headed and snake-headed people who persisted in sailing up over the curve of the world and raiding the lands of Paz.

There were no ships and no fliers in sight.

Fiercely I hungered to know just where this enormous camp was on Kregen. This was an invasion force of a magnitude that would tax the nations of Paz, tax them to the limit, for the blind idiots still fought among themselves.

Quite automatically after the fashion of any experienced and professional Kapt, any general worthy of his salt, I wedged into my head the layout of the camp, where the chief tents were, the lines, the cooking facilities, the armories. The list impressed me.

One doleful sight did not impress me in the slightest. All it brought was memories of horror. They were there, a considerable number of them, probably reeking to high heaven. The slave bagnios filled me with revulsion, and anger, and the unappetizing knowledge that drifting about in the upper air I could do nothing to rectify their blasphemous existence.

Despite the enormous importance of this Shank concentration I studied so attentively, do not imagine that for one moment I forgot what had just happened. Oh, I don't mean Ahrinye and the real threat he posed for my future welfare. For those of you who have so faithfully followed this narrative of my adventures upon Kregen—and I say with a full heart how much I appreciate that fidelity which comes with my gratitude to you all—you chosen ones will know what stirred my emotions now. You will assuredly understand what filled me with bitterness, with sorrow, with a futile anger, was my parting with Delia.

How agonizingly the ripping away of my heart's desire struck into me. Keen, keen—keener than the slicing cut of a Krozair brand! I felt that parting congeal around my heart like the chilly grasp of the Ice Floes of Sicce.

Yet, as you also know, I had to go on. Delia had been brought gloriously back into my hectic life; now she was gone. The girl for whom I cared most on two worlds was gone again, absent, away, somewhere I could not share the warmth of her presence.

My thoughts were brutally chopped off as the biting, acidic voice of Ahrinye echoed in my ears.

"Remember, Dray Prescot! This is Schinbalasch. This is but one cesspool among many."

With that my free-floating buoyancy evaporated. Weight slogged back into my body. I fell. Pitching down I became conscious that this was not a helpless, head-over-heels, uncontrolled descent that would smash me into a bloody pulp when I hit the ground. Then, and my breath checked at the enormity of it, I saw the reason for that and where I was heading.

Straight, Ahrinye aimed me, dead straight at a stinking slave bagnio.

Already, it seemed in my heightened state of imagination, already I could hear the long suffering wails, smell the stench of the place. Closer and closer the hell-hole neared. In only moments I'd be thumped down into a blood-stained purgatory, into an all-embracing torture chamber, into the worst kinds of horror mortal man can inflict upon his sisters and brothers.

Ahrinye, you great shint! That evocative Lohvian expression of revilement and contempt fitted the scene. But I said it to myself. I was confident—well, almost confident—that the Star Lords could not read my mind. Still, you never knew. Ahrinye, I thus bellowed soundlessly again, to myself, reverting to the Balintolian. You nasty little blintz!

Down and down I plummeted and there appeared no way out of this mess. So, I made up my mind to tackle what might come with what I could muster of courage and fortitude. As San Blarnoi says: "When your head is about to be chopped, then bend the neck gracefully."

Whilst I acknowledge that it is ludicrous to imagine that San W'Watchun could take from my head enough details to arrange a highly convincing, nay, a totally convincing, representation of the Royal Navy of Earth, yet Ahrinye could not read my mind. The fact remained I treasured this idea. This acrid little stinker did not have the same powers as the other Star Lords.

Now the wind of my plunge buffeted me, swirled my hair, stung my eyes, and all the time the ground leaped up hungrily.

"Star Lords!" I bellowed it out, now, in my old foretop hailing voice, as loudly as I could against the wind bluster. "Everoinye! I'll be damaged in a few moments! Are you going to allow a—"

About to say something to the effect of a little, jumped up squirt, I shut my black-fanged winespout. A faint wash of red seeped up and penetrated the enveloping green. A weird resulting color never came out of a mortal paint pot. That ghastly hue spread across the heavens. As the two colors intertwined so black clouds smoked at the interface. Lightning bolts slashed across the sky with such brilliance my eyelids snapped shut, and still the brilliance smote through. The thunder took me up and rattled the bones in my body. I felt the taut dragging sensations, as though my arms and legs were being wrenched out of their sockets.

The Star Lords struggled with Ahrinye, and he with them, and the supernatural forces, colliding and battling, filled the firmament with clamor. Like a chip in a millrace I swept hither and thither, helplessly. This proved to me that I was still really and truly the pawn in the greater schemes of these supernatural beings I'd denied and attempted to resist.

So, being a stubborn old vosk-skull, I tried to will myself away from both red and green. What my efforts were worth in the maelstrom of occult powers I'd no way of knowing—save, perhaps, just perhaps, save that I felt the easing of the tearing sensations.

Voices echoed between the rumbles of thunder. Words I could not grasp—the acid of Ahrinye and the sonorousness of the Star Lords—seemed to fill the sky from horizon to horizon.

Tossed about hither and yon, one moment upside down and the next whooshing upwards headfirst, only to be flung down again, I growled out words to the effect of: "Make your bloody minds up!"

Although, I could not wish Ahrinye to emerge victorious from this occult contest. Jeehum! If that happened then I was finally done for. That green bastard would have no mercy.

Just how long all this lasted I didn't know. I was vaguely conscious of movement, apparently of the whole world, pulling me to the side. My eyes ached with looking—was the red prevailing?

Through the turmoil of colors and wind and shafts of lightning and enormous crashes of thunder, I saw a rift in the clouds below. The masses of vapor—be they real clouds or supernatural manifestations—parted like curtains in a theatre. I stared down.

A green land, then, this, with rivers and rounded hills and forests and meadows. A few red-tiled roofs showed and white roads running in idle curves with few straight lines.

The riot of combat now hullabalooed away above me. Red and green writhed up there, drawing away, convoluting one into the other, dissipating—vanishing. The Star Lords and Ahrinye carried on their fight intent on that. They must have tucked me away into some supernal file for later attention.

With that comprehension came another and altogether more devastating understanding.

My direction of travel continued downwards. There was no more being swept up and over and over. Down I was going, groundwards.

Flailing my arms, thrashing about with my legs, all that was totally useless. Yellowness blossomed beneath me. A beautiful golden yellow, spreading into the shape of a gigantic hand, cupped palm upwards, stretched between my hurtling body and the unyielding ground.

When I hit, the sensation was akin to dropping into a four-poster feather bed. I sank down and down, caught a distorted glimpse of trees over my head, and in a last lucid thought realized that Zena Iztar had caught and saved me. But I'd been spat out of the Everoinye's fight with venomous force. Zena Iztar's feathers checked my full-scale impact; but I still slogged into the ground so that the enveloping cloak of Notor Zan came as no surprise.

Six

The chirrupy babble of many light voices woke me. For an instant I lay still, relishing the warm air and the marvelous scents that wafted over me. The voices chattered on, mixed with nervous giggling. I opened my eyes and sat up.

The young voices turned into screaming and shrieking and a pack of children burst away from me like pollen being shed from a bloom.

The children halted in a nervous ring about ten paces off and their huge eyes regarded me as though I'd fallen from one of Kregen's moons. What, I wondered, had they seen of my arrival? A quick scrutiny of my surroundings showed that I'd landed in a garden packed tightly with all manner of the most gorgeous flowers. Yet, whilst the flowers indicated the garden status of this place, its size tended toward that of a farm. If I'd tumbled down out of nowhere here, then no wonder the youngsters were wary.

Standing up I was satisfied to feel no shooting pain, no quick stab of agony from some sorely used part of my anatomy. As I moved the swords at my side clanked.

All the children jumped as though goosed.

I nodded sagely to myself, reasoning I had solved the puzzle of my location and why the children were so scared. They would not have seen my arrival. I fancied I knew the name of this land—the clues were the pleasant warmth, the pitched red roofs indicating adequate rainfall, the children's attire, for some wore some clothes, their abhorrence of the swords, and, most indicative of all, the large scale production of flowers.

This was Vaiwadrin, the Flower Country.

Many mysteries clung to the land, situated where the borders of Winlan and Enderli met and touched the border of Caneldrin. From time immemorial those three countries respected Vaiwadrin's frontiers, any potential invasion being countered by the other two nations' reactions. Everything that was bright and beautiful belonged to the Flower Country. Yet there existed their darker side when a citizen went astray and needed to be disciplined. The outside world knew little; the rumors were that punishment, never physical, was a damn sight worse in its psychological rigor.

Still, the Suns were shining, the scent of flowers filled the air, I felt good—why meditate on gloom and doom?

Also—I needed a wet and food, in that order.

I called out in the gentlest voice I could manage, which I don't doubt sounded like a wild beast growl to these lads and lasses.

"Llahal, doms!" Oh, yes, it is always wisest to treat kiddies with proper respect and not to kiddiewink them—at least, when they can hear you.

"I just dropped in." Well, by Zair, that was true! "I'm a poor traveler in need of your assistance."

A tremendous amount of agitated talk among them followed this first attempt at diplomatic relations. A prodigious quantity of arms waved in the air. A young girl, bolder than the rest, stepped out closer to me. One foot kept wiping the calf of the other leg. She must have been the equivalent in age to an Earthly girl of twelve or thirteen. She wore a lap-lap and a pretty string of beads.

When she spoke her voice quavered; but she aroused my admiration by the way she persisted in carrying on, even more than what she said—which was pretty dire, by Krun!

"You're no poor traveler. We know who you are. We don't like you. You are a nasty horrid aragorn. Please go away and do not come back—ever!"

With that she switched about and dived helter-skelter back into the ranks. A hum of agreement from the children swelled rapidly into a chorus. They did not like the aragorn, that was for sure! But, then, who apart from fellow bandits did like 'em!

I don't think the youngsters would have thrown stones at me, for the folk of the Flower Country do not resort to violence. But their shouting, which grew stronger mur by mur, rattled me severely.

Salvation came in the shape of a party of adults, all dressed in light airy multi-colored clothes. Some of them wore shamlaks with wide openings. The fellow in charge carried a shepherd's crook which, here in a flower farm, would be his symbol of office.

Now was the time to use this famous yrium I possess, the super charisma that impresses profoundly and was the reason the Star Lords chose me for this Emperor of All Paz nonsense in the first place.

So I exerted my power and charm and in no time we were all chatting away like old chums.

This was, indeed, the renowned Flower Country of Balintol. Everything was sweetness and light, I was told, until the aragorn came along in their usual fashion and set up a fortress nearby. Then they spread out over the neighboring countryside exacting their tolls.

Once this area had been drained they'd move on. As the people of Vaiwadrin renounced violence no one was going to help the folk of this farm complex. Even the traders from the surrounding nations were forced to deal with the aragorn. Because most Kregans enjoy flowers about them, there is always a brisk trade in blooms. Quite apart from the beauty and scent side, flick-flick plants were grown and potted on and sold all over the place. Kregans also like to keep their houses free of flies, and the flick-flick dotes on flies.

Hieron, the leader, told me that the current crop was just about ready for seed collection. These seeds found their way all over Balintol and beyond. He went worpling on.* Now, mock and deride the Emperor of

---

* worpling: A word of indeterminate meaning which I take in general to indicate

Emperors bit though I did, the moral fact remained that I owed these gentle folk assistance. Were they not part of Paz?

Once the Star Lords and Ahrinye had sorted out their quarrel—and I trusted the Star Lords would sort out Ahrinye—they'd bethink themselves of me and the pressing problem of destroying the Prism of Power. In view of that I decided I'd give the good folk of the Blue Lily, as the farm was known, the benefit of a few days aid before setting off for Enderli.

The flaw there was that I had no form of transport and my story, which had been accepted, that I was a lone traveler seeing the world, gave me no chance of acquiring transport. Therefore it looked like the Everoinye must send their Blue Scorpion for me, or walking.

Once I'd finished this little imbroglio somehow and walked clear of the Blue Lily I'd have to hire whatever was available. Being a good paktun, I think you will by now understand that when I dressed myself in those Red Capes' gear I'd also emptied their purses and pockets.

Hard training dies hard, as Beng Wilkiy of the Birch said a good number of centuries ago. I could afford something better than a freymul.

The authority of my yrium put these people at peace, yet still they could not stop themselves from exhibiting unease over my swords. Of course, they were perfectly correct. Still, this was Kregen and I am Dray Prescot, and so this is the way fate ordains.

They did not confine their skills with plants only to flowers. Oh, no! By Zair, the vegetables they raised, properly cooked, tasted heavenly. Their husbandry was just as dedicated and they were not vegetarians. I tell you, during my short stay at the Blue Lily I ate right royally. Of course, I must add that for all the excellence of their cuisine, they were not quite as good as my people of Esser Rarioch. And, too, their wines were of the first cru; but, again, not quite up to the fantastic excellence of the wines of Jholaix. But, then, naturally, few vintners are!

Now you have to remember in all this wallowing of eating and drinking and good fellowship, I gave thought to my next step. When a fellow goes adventuring about Kregen, getting into scrapes and earning a living as a paktun, he must expect to be injured from time to time.

At the moment I was in top form. I felt, as famous people have said, two hundred percent. So these Opaz-forsaken aragorn had to be dealt with.

Well, I had a Plan. Oh, yes, by Vox, I know, I know! All the same, this time the plan was really a Plan, all neatly thought out.

The bold girl who had first accosted me, Rita the Bodacious—for she'd

---

someone talking on at length, maundering or jabbering, perhaps, whilst the auditor barely listens, wrapped in his or her own thoughts. Kregish is, obviously, a language of subtlety where simple words cloak a variety of shades of meaning and where they are joined together to form other expressions without the benefit of linking syllables. *A.B.A.*

acquired a soubriquet early in life—turned out to be a voracious reader. By this time I could accept the sight of a pretty lass poring over a book which declaimed in glowing colors the wonderful, marvelous, superb (etc., etc., etc.,) adventures of Dray Prescot.

Just who wrote the damn things and who manufactured the lurid stories I didn't know and had made no attempt to find out. They were true works of the imagination for ninety percent of the narrative, for they detailed imbroglios I'd never experienced. Some of the weird monsters I was supposed to have slain rescuing beautiful damsels in distress were so revolting I wondered the pages didn't melt or burst into flame.

Rita sat absorbed in a tome entitled: 'Dray Prescot and Delia fight the Giant Octopus for the Pearls of Tancrophor.'

That did startle me. Now they'd put Delia into their confounded fairy tales! And as for the Pearl fisheries of Tancrophor, well, if I ever thought Delia dived there I'd sweat blood and call out the entire army of Vallia to bring her back!

Brothers had killed each other rather than dive for those infamous Pearls from Tancrophor.

Bright and early the following morning after a fine first breakfast, with Zim and Genodras, here called Balron and Balig, shining splendidly away, off I set. The Flower Country was in truth cut off from the rest of Balintol, for they used the ancient names for the Suns. The farm folk had pointed out the way and given directions and begged me not to stir up the aragorn. Retribution would be fierce. In addition, I did not care to dwell on the unwelcome thought that perhaps they fancied I was going off to join up with the drikingers.

Striding along through massed banks of flowers, tasting the scented breeze, opening up my lungs, I realized again the wonder of Kregen. What a world of contrasts the place is! Well, I was off to pitch myself headlong into trouble of formidable dimensions. This I had chosen out of my guilty feelings that, if I were supposed to be an emperor, then I'd better try to act like one. There was no damsel in distress to rescue—at least, as far as I was aware. Mind you, as this was Kregen, as I have said before, rescuing princesses was all in the day's work for an adventurer. That gallant activity happened with considerable frequency under the mingled lights of the Suns of Scorpio.

This gang of aragorn had arrived relatively recently in the district and because the Flower People would not be troublesome a wooden fort had been built atop a small hill. There were many rounded hills with streams flowing between them, and what with the rain the country was well-watered. Surveying the fort calculatingly, I came to the obvious conclusion that these depraved drikingers might not welcome a stranger.

The yrium would help, clearly; but I had more than my fair share of knowledge of how these packs of bandits operated. All would depend on boldness and panache. "By the distended abdomen and tree trunk thighs of the Divine Madam of Belschutz!" I hitched up my swords and marched on. "There'll be a way!"

They rode out from the front gate of the fort to meet me as I slogged up along the dusty road. The hill might be low and rounded; its gradient together with the wooden stockade would deter all but the hardiest of attackers. I waved in a special way. When I'd spent that raucous time with the Flutsmen in my rough and tumble career on Kregen I'd learned the secrets of the bandits' trade. Just as the paktuns had their secret societies, so too had drikingers, flutsmen, aragorn.*

After my wave I sat down, plonk, in the dust at the side of the track. Their zorcas' legs trampled all about me; but I just sat, a hand over my heart.

"Llahal, doms!" I said, at last, brightly. "This damned hill is the right devil."

A lance point jabbed towards me. I caught it in my fist and twitched it sideways and hauled. The fellow, he was a furry Fristle, pitched headlong over his mount's nose.

"All right! All right!" I spoke briskly. "Hold on!" They milled about, and zorcas do not take kindly to heavy handling. And, anyway, it was a crying shame that beautiful animals like zorcas should have to descend to carrying bloodthirsty bastards like aragorn. "I come in friendship bearing a message from Red Rackan the Reducer to your leader, Portlo the Render." I stood up and I put the snap of yrium-carried authority into my words. "You are here only on Red Rackan's forbearance, never forget. Escort me to your leader—now!"

Given that they were who they were—unhanged villains the lot of 'em, by Krun!—they should have stuck their lances clean through me. They did not. You can thank—or blame—the yrium for that.

Still, after that, as I bluffed my way through to speak to this Portlo the Render, success came probably not so much from this insubstantial yrium but from my own ugly forceful manner that brooked no opposition. This Portlo fellow wore a red kerchief bound about his head and a gold ear-ring. I wondered if he'd grown tired of the life on the ocean wave. Naturally, I thought of Viridia. Going through the flung-open doors I advanced into this mephitic den.

Most of these gangs when they set up their base of operations like to live in style. Mostly they run to a large open baronial-style hall, complete with rafters and roaring fire and solid wooden tables and benches. They go in for childish games involving taking risks with knives and fire. They do

---

* Prescot has mentioned these episodes in his career before but we do not have any cassettes containing these adventures. A.B.A.

not seem able to pass a day without indulging in fighting amongst them-selves. As for drunkenness, well they make a—well, I was going to say a pitiable lot; but pity for these cramphs is far more often than not mis-placed. Although I had shared in many exploits with flutsmen, and a few with drikingers, I found it extraordinarily difficult to tolerate aragorn.

Portlo the Render leaned forward in his carved chair at the head of the table. He rested his chin on his fist. He regarded me loweringly. Naturally, he was well-built, an apim, girded with swords.

"Well, blintz!" His voice grated. "A message? I've never heard of this onker Red Rackan—what?—the Reducer! Ha!"

"You are new hereabouts. Red Rackan has taken that into account. He will, of course, require tribute from—"

"What!" Portlo bounded from his chair. His face, purple normally from the good life, congested even further. "What! Tribute!"

"You are trespassing."

He started to flail one of his swords about. "Let him come and tell me that—face to face!"

"You will regret it if he does."

He'd worked himself into a right royal rage now. His gang clustered in the hall, watching and listening. Portlo's authority lay on the line. He knew it. He pointed the sword at me.

"Take this jackanapes down to the dungeons while I think what to do." He wiped his lips with a stiff forefinger. "Tribute! Ha! Drag him off, now!"

Seven

I felt no surprise whatsoever at this turn of events. The fate of envoys bear-ing overweening and unwelcome demands very often involves having their heads served up on plates for Return To Sender.

In this case there was no sender to whom my old vosk-skull of a head could be returned. They took my two swords away. They didn't chain me up. Portlo stowed my weapons away under his chair and then waved me off.

In a voice far more gravelly than his, I said: "You will come to your senses soon, Render. Red Rackan will have no mercy on you if you make an unwise decision. Think well on this—Render."

With that off we went. My guard, four hefty fellows, were clearly much put out that they'd drawn this duty. They wanted to start the evening's drinking and entertainments.

Waiting in the passage were half a dozen plump girls wearing the layers of multi-colored clothes favored by women in some parts of Balintol. They wore brass ankle-bells, many chains that looked like gold but were not, bangles, and carried cymbals. I gave them a look as we passed; they lowered their eyelids in a fashion I thought not so much demure as exhausted. They'd dance, I supposed, for as long as these rasts of aragorn required. I felt sympathy for these girls.

The dungeons of which Portlo had appeared so proud turned out to be merely a passage and cell dug out of the hill. Some timbers here and there retained the earth. The cell door consisted of tree trunks not over a finger-length in width lashed together and swung on leather hinges. An Angerim, all sharp teeth and spikey hair, gave me a kick to help me into the cell. I allowed myself to stagger forward in the gloom relieved only by one torch. "And stay there and rot, blintz!"

My fake stagger abruptly turned into a genuine toppling crash as my legs tangled up with a bundle sprawled on the dirt floor.

The bundle let out a wail and scrabbled away clutching trailing garments about it. I managed to break the fall and so turned and sat up. "Well, now," I said in a voice I tried to gentle. "Now who might you be, dom, and what have you been up to?"

This uncharacteristic flow of words was wrenched from me, I supposed, because of the very startlement of the tumble. So I tried to cover that lapse by saying: "Llahal."

The quaver in his voice revealed the depths of his terror; but he tried to control himself. With a snap, he said: "You do not address me as dom; I will not tolerate this familiarity." He gulped a breath. "Llahal. I am San Quenlo, and you will speak to me with due deference."

"Lahal, san. Of course."

He sniffed to indicate his importance and for a space relapsed into silence so that I could take stock of him. The torch was a poor thing and smoked vilely but it gave enough light for me to make out his remnants of ornate clothes. Once they'd glittered with gems and embroideries. The aragorn had ripped everything of value from the poor fellow. The heavy gold chain was gone from around his waist. The amulet no longer swung from the gold chain about his neck, and the chain was gone too, naturally. He was a Sorcerer of the Cult of Almuensis. Without his great book, his thaumaturgical hyr lif, which had once been locked to the chain about his waist, his powers were gone, too. His face showed abject dejection. Yet the lines of accustomed authority remained, giving him a most pathetic appearance.

This San Quenlo hadn't even bothered to require my name. That could be because he was sunk in apathy, it could be because he still considered himself too important to worry over riff-raff like me.

To Portlo the Render I'd given an old name I've used before. I said I was

Chaadur the Ripper. That, therefore, would be the name this Almuensis mage would hear—if he bothered to ask.

After a time, I asked him when we were fed. He snorted and replied that the last meal of the day was done, and that we'd get breakfast, if we were lucky and everyone up there wasn't drunk. This seemed to open him up, for he began, in the way people under tremendous pressure do, to tell me about his very important person.

I listened, for information, however apparently useless, is worth learning. He said his lifter had failed and crashed and the aragorn had taken him when he was unconscious. "Had I had my book—!" They'd found out about him and were holding him for ransom, which, he was confident, would be paid. "The great Oblifex, Cuisar, will ransom me, I know, for he is a man of honor. Particularly after all my labors for him."

So I shut my black-fanged winespout and closed my goggling eyes. My advent here had in no way been at random. No, by Krun! Zena Iztar's beautiful golden hand had snatched me from the occult fight and placed me here deliberately.

The next step was obvious. I had to win this sorcerer's confidence. The very first item on the agenda, though, was to discover if he was a damned Dokerty lover.

A few carefully chosen questions, casually posed with all possible respect, elicited the information that he belonged to a cult within the Sorcerers of Almuensis. I kept everything low key, as though merely making conversation and being respectfully polite.

He was clearly terrified for his life, ransom or no ransom. Some pointed guesses as to our fate, dropped into the conversation here and there, stoked up his fears. I felt sorry for him. But Zena Iztar hadn't dropped me down here without a very good reason. When I mentioned that the aragorn took pleasure in drawing out their victims' insides, he whimpered and cowered down within himself. I went on about this Oblifex Cuisar. "If he is as powerful as you say, san, and with all due respect, would he not have asked a Wizard of Loh to—"

"Them!"

"Yes, well, san, or perhaps a Sorcerer of Balintol."

"Those he did not trust." He wiped his lips.

I wondered why he hadn't blown my head off for impertinence. He went on to say that he was an expert in the arcane art of Traps, both the setting and the cancelling of them.

To say that I felt like a person who has been given pieces of a puzzle to fit together was quite apt. There were clues hanging about, darting insects to be caught in the net—in this case the net of reason and resolution.

The moment I asked him where the aragorn had put his magic book, the answer popped into my head. Under Portlo's chair, of course!

Time was a'passing and still lots to do, as they say in Clishdrin. I stretched my arms and stood up. "What—?" he quavered.

"They should most of 'em be the worse for drink by now." I looked up at the roof, which had been simply built by stretching timbers across the hole they'd dug to make their famous dungeon. "H'm. Roof or door?" Either would succumb to a determined onslaught.

This place had been dubbed mephitic by me when I'd gone in and in truth it did smell ripe. The quicker I was gone the better. From the idea of the layout I fancied the roof would open up into the hall whereas the ladder and passage we'd used to arrive here lay just beyond the inner entrance. Door, then. I lay hold of the timber.

"What are you doing?" San Quenlo squeaked out as he tottered to his feet, one hand outstretched. "What? What—?"

"Why, san, I've had enough of the stinks. I'm breaking out."

"I'm not coming with you—they're all makib up there—"

"Oh, don't fret. I'll return for you. You are a most important personage and I shall need you later on."

"Need? Need?" He liked to repeat himself, evidently.

Ignoring the poor old fellow I pulled tentatively. The door remained firm. So I put my foot against the place opposite the bolt outside, and shoved. Two brisk thrusts and the door broke open with the bolt flying off, just as though a swifter had rammed it.

All the aragorn were not blind drunk.

That hairy and unpleasant Angerim ran up the short passage dragging out his sword and spluttering his wrath.

He took a swipe at me, which I avoided. I reached in past his blade, seized him by the neck, and choked him a trifle. At the same time my other hand took his sword away.

Not enough noise was made, I judged, to be heard aloft. San Quenlo heard it, though. He screeched out: "It's not me! Not me! I'm not trying to escape!"

Turning my head back I started to snarl: "Shut—" and then changed it to the more decorous: "Be quiet, san!"

The limp form of the Angerim dragged along abaft me like a sack of momolams. Back in the cell his ripped up clothing served to bind and gag him. San Quenlo looked on goggle-eyed. "Soon as you get your book back, san, you'll be all right."

He just made squelchy noises and huddled in the corner.

Moving silently I negotiated the passage and, after checking no one stood at the top of the ladder, climbed up swiftly. The space before the door leading into the hall now contained a hooded watch chair made from cane, very similar to those made in the Misty Mountains. The Fristle sitting in the chair on guard was not too drunk; he was far enough gone to be able to do nothing to stop me from putting him to sleep. Adding his braxter to the Angerim's, I carefully opened the door.

What a sight! Bodies lay strewn all over the place, draped across benches, sprawled wide-armed under tables, with Portlo the Render slumped in his chair. The noises of snoring and broken mutterings formed a non-musical accompaniment as I walked across.

Under his chair, concealed by a dirty blue velvet cloth, lay quite a little treasure trove. Well, some of the gold would be useful, and that was stowed away in my borrowed pouch. The drexer felt good in my fist after the local braxters. The hyr lif had been roughly wrapped in a yellow towel, together with the chain and lock, and these I took up, wondering just how wise I'd be to return them to San Quenlo, the renowned Sorcerer of the Cult of Almuensis.

What remained certain sure was that Zena Iztar had sent me here to hoick Quenlo out of it. Clearly, he figured prominently in our future plans. So be it, then.

A tap on the head made sure the Render slept more profoundly. With swords and book stowed away I slung the aragorn's body over my shoulder and retraced my steps through the hall. I dumped him at the front door and went down the ladder to the cell.

"Come on, san. Time to go."

Now you will notice with what exquisite politeness I treated the sorcerer. I helped him up solicitously, brushed dust from his tattered clothes, supported him as he tottered out. "But—but—" he stuttered, shaking his head in disbelief. His whole body shuddered.

He had to be carried up the ladder. At the top I put him down and said: "You'll have to walk, san. I've this rast to carry."

As I put him onto his feet the book slid out and fell to the floor. He looked down stupidly. Abruptly he let out a cry like the gargle from a freshly cleared blocked pipe and bent to the hyr lif. His actions were shatteringly swift. He took the chain into his fingers and all their tremble had vanished.

"No time for that now." I spoke more harshly than I intended. "We must get clear away. Come on."

He stood stock still, clutching the book. Then, still with these new swift actions, he opened the front cover. He let out a sigh of relief. The amulet was there, tucked into its recess in the binding. I recalled down the Moder how San Yagno had used the amulet to detect traps and a spell from his book to smash open a chest of gold.*

San Quenlo was a changed man. Oh, yes, his magnificent robes were torn and filthy, his gems were gone; but he radiated the authority habitual to him. He seemed to shine.

---

* See *A Fortune for Kregen*, Dray Prescot volume 21, Book 3 of the Jikaida Cycle. A.B.A.

"Yes," he said, and his voice had changed and become fuller and rounder, richer. "Yes, you are right."

Then he said a few words to thank me. Nothing effusive; but I felt he meant them.

Outside in the warm night air with the scents of moonblooms wafting about us a high overcast shut off the stars and the Moons.

With those few words Quenlo had changed my opinion of him. Oh, I didn't doubt he was a formidable mage. He did have powers. But now he had shown that he still had proper decent human instincts, quite apart, of course, from his perfectly understandable fear.

"Do you require a sword? If not I'll leave these two."

No hesitation whatsoever checked his reply. "No, thank you."

The two braxters went into a bush. Probably they'd have broken across at the first blow of real strength, anyway. With the clantzer and drexer I felt reasonably well-provided with weaponry.

Quenlo's amulet was considerably smaller than the one Yagno wore. Without knowing exactly, I felt convinced this meant that Quenlo possessed higher powers than the Almuensis cultist lost down the Moder. Mind you, it could mean the opposite; I didn't think so. Whatever Cuisar the Oblifex had hired Quenlo for, the Dokerty priest was a man of power and influence who would pick the best he could get.

What Cuisar's purpose intended I couldn't know. Quenlo would have to be carefully handled to find out. His babbling phase had passed but as we walked on in the pleasant night I learned that he hailed from Huringa and was currently travelling the world to improve his thaumaturgical knowledge. He'd been on his way to Prebaya to meet up with a famous mage, San K'Kardo, there.

"These Sorcerers of Balintol are most impressive," I said. "Especially the Illusionists."

"You speak sooth. Still, I do have some powers."

Making a polite reply, I reflected that this modesty was most uncharacteristic of an Almuensian, for there was no irony here. Perhaps he'd taken better stock of me than I appreciated.

Portlo the Render started to wriggle on my shoulder and make an outcry, so I dumped him down, hard. I told him some home truths. His befuddlement subsided as the truth sank in. "And the whole pack of you had better be gone before the Suns sink tomorrow night. He made one attempt to argue. One only. "The mage here will see to it that you go." I cocked an eye at Quenlo. He smiled. He was going to enjoy this. Now, he'd get some of his own back.

He made Portlo hop about with fireballs bursting around his feet. He sizzled him up a trifle. He put the fear of Cottmer's Caverns into the aragorn chief. Portlo, shaking, agreed to depart.

"And now take your degenerate self off to that drunken scum you call comrades. Remember! Before tomorrow night!"

Portlo the Render slunk away. Quenlo said: "I will burn their fort about their ears if they do not go."

"Burn it anyway, after they've gone."

"Aye."

With that business satisfactorily concluded, we went on to the Blue Lily farm where our news was received with joy. Young Rita the Bodacious even went so far as to reach up and give me a peck on the cheek. "It is like a story about Dray Prescot!" she exclaimed, all rosy with happiness. "Although, of course, he would have done it on his own." For I'd given full credit to Quenlo and his Gramarye antics.

"Silence, you impudent shishi!" said Hieron, concerned.

So I, Dray Prescot, laughed.

Eight

Fweygo said: "If you keep looking at the blintz, Dray— ah— Drajak, he'll blow our cover for sure."

"There's a little Fristle fifi just beyond him. I'm looking at her. At least, that's what he'll think."

Fweygo twisted around casually to look. The tavern was filled with noise and laughter and the smells of ale and cooking. He nodded. "Very tasty. We'll have to knock him over soon."

I supped on my ale, which was a reasonable local brew here in Nerlinium, the capital city of Enderli. Over the past few sennights the Star Lords had hoisted me out of the Blue Lily farm and dumped me down here with Fweygo. We were slated to go after the Prism of Power belonging to the priests of Dokerty in Enderli. San Quenlo had been happily accepted by the folk of the Blue Lily and he told me he'd stay until they shipped out the seeds, when he'd go on to Prebaya.

The fellow we watched in this relatively reasonable tavern, The Crowser and Molp, rejoiced in the name of F'Farhan the Unctuous. He had been pointed out to us as an important priest of Dokerty. Through him we sought to gain access to the inner secrets of the local temple. We'd worm our way in, seize the Flutubium containing the Prism of Power, fight our way out, and destroy the pestiferous thing.

Enderli, in the short time I'd been here, proved to be an interesting country. Sharing many of the same artifacts and architecture of the other lands of Balintol, it had its own very special character which marked it as alien. Well, cultures, races of diffs, customs, have been so well muddled over Paz in Kregen that you sometimes find yourself brought up short by shock at something entirely unexpected as thoroughly everyday.

The first question I'd asked Fweygo when we met up was answered by him in a voice I found startlingly soft. "Yes, I do know. She was summoned up to the Everoinye with me. She is still with them."

"Thank Opaz for that."

Fweygo, my kregoinye comrade, a splendid golden Kildoi, was festooned with the weapons proper to a fellow with four arms and a tail hand. As for me, the Star Lords had condescended to leave me with my clantzer and drexer and the best bits of armor I'd gleaned from the Red Capes. Fweygo knew about them. He was dismissive. "Once they were paktuns of honor. Now they serve these blintzes of Dokerty priests."

"Maybe. We'll still have to go up against them." I did not want to sound defeatist; but my good comrade Fweygo tended to dismiss the opposition with the lightness born of his own prowess. I'd told him all about San Quenlo and San Cuisar the Oblifex. He agreed there was a puzzle here. I'd not mentioned Zena Iztar, implicating the Star Lords, and he'd nodded sagely. "Don't worry, Drajak. I'll take good care of you. After all, you have to be the Emperor of Emperors, the Emperor of All Paz. The Everoinye command. So it will be accomplished."

That load of old nonsense had to be ignored, it goes without saying. What was annoying was the fact that the Star Lords had whisked me up out of the Blue Lily before I'd progressed very much further with my investigations into the mystery of San Quenlo and San Cuisar the Oblifex.

"We should think this conundrum through." Fweygo took a swig at his ale and went on: "You said Quenlo visited a Sorcerer of Balintol before carrying out his task for Cuisar?"

"Aye. Somewhere in Enderli. He was not specific."

"Another of these Illusionists, I'll warrant."

"No. Quenlo said San L'Lengul was a Necromancer."

"One of the grave-diggers brigade? Unwholesome, them."

I finished my ale, plonked the pot on the table, stood up. Without even looking around, Fweygo did the same. Together, shoulder to shoulder, we walked to the door and out into the evening following this important priest F'Farhan the Unctuous.

This Dokerty cultist walked along very upright, head erect with squared shoulders. In his red robes he made a striking figure and passersby kept respectfully out of his way. Of heavy build, he had one of those massive chins that always appear blue and in need of a shave. He carried a shortish gold-knobbed balass cane, which I took to be one of his little affectations here in Nerlinium.

Twinned shadows dropped long and longer across the road. From the air, I did not doubt, this city would look a mad jumble of buildings all squashed up higgledy-piggledy fashion. Their roofs were of a variety of styles and colors, their walls either nearly all open window spaces or sheer blank edifices of brick or lath and plaster. Most of the streets and alleys merely wended around the buildings from long use. There were a few larger roads slashed through in reasonably straight lines. Baron Haussmann would have rubbed his hands with glee.

F'Farhan walked on at some distance. Our brave shoulder to shoulder stride to the door finished on the threshold. Fweygo went ahead and I tagged along in the rear. Both of us had tailed suspects before this and knew the drill.

The whisper our informant, a little twisted Polsim, Nath the Gnarled, had given us included the rumor that F'Farhan, although undeniably important, lay under something of a cloud. Naturally, the main gossip of the city was the disappearance of the Oblifex. The Chief Priest had simply gone missing. Dark rumors abounded. F'Farhan had not been in Nerlinium when Cuisar's evanishment became known.

Well, I knew very well that someone knew where he'd gone, and sent those unpleasant Red Capes after him. By now he should be well onto conducting his business with W'Watchun, as Delia had met Fweygo and now she'd gone up to have a little chat with the Everoinye.

Fweygo flitted ahead, and for all his four arms and tail he blended in with the twin shadows like a wraith. Lights were coming on all over the city now, and as with the buildings, lighting up at random, here and there. Fweygo's plan—which I ought to dub The Plan—involved catching F'Farhan in a conveniently murky spot, knocking him gently on the head, wrapping him up in the voluminous blue cape Fweygo carried for that purpose, and of asking him the very necessary questions.

Among the many temples and shrines to various deities here the building devoted to Dokerty lumped hugely. The structure was ugly and vulgar, as one would expect. It stood in a sizeable kyro of its own with the surrounding houses forming as it were a frieze. F'Farhan skirted the kyro in the shadows and, to my surprise, headed off down a most dolorous alleyway between nondescript buildings housing Opaz knew what villainy and chicanery. Fweygo was a mere moving shadow among the other shadows as he followed. I padded along silently after.

In the unplanned and untidy layout buildings jutted out forcing the street to twist around them. A narrow, three-storeyed house pushed a gable end across the direct route and the street bent to conform. F'Farhan flung a swift look over his shoulder and then darted for the door, which was contained in an overhanging archway.

Fweygo speeded up to keep in touch. I followed.

The swiftness of F'Farhan's dash for the doorway availed him nothing. Silent and deadly in the shadows of the arch, they waited for him.

Four black-clad wraith-like figures pounced on the priest.

The gold-knobbed balass cane whirred. F'Farhan wasn't going down without a fight. All the same, these four stikitches, hired assassins, would have him, aye, by Krun, and spit out the pips.

For a moment I lost sight of Fweygo. As I started to run I confess I was supremely angry with the situation. "By the Bloated Belly of the Divine Belschutz! You stikitches won't have him!" My feet slapped soundlessly on the ground as I hurled myself forward. "He's ours!"

A whirl of movement erupted from the shadows of the gated archway. Two assassins were down already. Like a Catherine wheel of destruction, Fweygo ripped the stikitches to pieces. In only a handful of heartbeats it was all over. Four stikitches lay on the cobbles. Their blood smoked black in the light. Fweygo composed himself.

He turned to me as I sprinted up, already cleaning his blades. "You really will have to learn to be quicker. There were only four of them. Had there been more, well—"

"You'd have seen 'em off—" I started to say.

F'Farhan had his breath back now. "Drag them inside, and be quick about it!" His voice, as expected, was full and fruity.

Seeing the sense of that, Fweygo and I complied. Before the Kildoi bent down, I bent first and grabbed a leg from two of the corpses and backed away into the archway. Fweygo said: "Ha!" and dragged his two in. He fully recognized my bravado. He could have hauled the whole four of them in—and have a hand for another.

F'Farhan slammed the door shut. He let out a breath. We stood in a narrow passage lighted by a mineral oil lamp; the smell of dampness thickened the atmosphere and the general appearance of the house was drab and dingy. "They would have killed me, for sure, if—" He stopped and shook his head. The fact of someone trying to kill you remains highly salutary. Still, he was recovering well.

Exchanging a quick glance with Fweygo I saw he shared my thoughts. For the moment no need existed for us to thump this Dokerty priest on the head. Gratitude could be put to good use.

"Through here."

We dumped the stikitches by the door and followed F'Farhan into the second doorway on the right. He stopped and let out a cry. That sound echoed with a scream of horror, a wail of disbelief, a sob of despair. That cry was wrenched right from the priest's guts.

We pushed into the room and by the slanting rays of an ornate lamp saw the shambles.

Fweygo caught F'Farhan as he collapsed. My kregoine comrade was very practical. He shoved a corpse off a chair and put the priest down carefully. F'Farhan's face looked like green cheese. There were six dead priests of Dokerty strewn about the room.

"We'd better bring the assassins in. Put 'em all together." Fweygo straightened up from F'Farhan. "A mutual destruction."

"Aye."

By the time we'd done that F'Farhan had so far recovered to ask our names, to thank us, and then to shudder back into revulsion. The Kildoi found a wine flagon and some goblets, and we fed the shaken man with a mellow red. Redness dribbled down his chin. He motioned to the corpses. "My friends. All dead. And it would have been me, too. I know." He drank again as Fweygo supported the goblet. "I know whose handiwork this is! May Dokerty strike him down!"

I looked straight into F'Farhan's face. He stared back.

Speaking with my old gravel-shifting voice and putting some of the yrium-born authority into my words, I said: "Hyr Kov Khonstanton. Khon the Mak."

For a moment I thought I had miscalculated. He gave no particular reaction but sat hunched, with one of Fweygo's hands holding the goblet under his chin. Then I saw he was still sunk in the apathy and agony of shock and despair. He shivered. "Yes, him and that despicable toad he calls a High Priest, Nath G'Goldark, who isn't fit to be a stable-hand, let alone an Oblifex."

Fweygo's subtlety frayed a trifle then as he said: "Why should a priest of Dokerty kill other priests?"

F'Farhan jerked up, knocking the goblet askew so that red drops spouted up. "Because he is evil!" Then he swung a shocked face towards us, his mouth trembling. His eyes widened. "What do you know of this? Khon the Mak! You are paid by him to kill me!"

"No, no." Fweygo soothed the frightened fellow down. Only a moment's reflection showed the priest that had we wished to kill him we wouldn't have saved him. Whether or not he recognized the real reason for saving him, I didn't know. As an important priest he had to be a person of some intellect. Fweygo drew him out at this time when he was still in his dazed condition. F'Farhan was loyal to San Cuisar. Out of the city at the time the coup took place; when he returned he wisely kept his head down. Lately he'd been recruiting those still secretly loyal with the intention of reversing the situation. "I was supposed to meet Narlin tonight. He did not appear."

"You think he is the traitor?" Fweygo wanted to know.

The raw smell of blood, always unpleasant, began to be most unsavory in the close confines. I stood up, "They know the whereabouts of this house. A Safe House, I suppose it was. We'd better move off sharpish."

F'Farhan flared up at once. He gestured around to the gruesome scene in the blood-soaked room. "Look! I cannot leave my brothers! It is unthinkable! They must have proper burial—"

Fweygo put a hand under his armpit and lifted him. "Come on, san. It's a pity; but there it is." F'Farhan struggled uselessly. "But—But—" He tried to thrash about and Fweygo simply slung him over his top shoulder. Thankfully, we left that scene of horror.

"Come on, now, san." Fweygo spoke briskly in the passage just before we went out into the street. "No more fuss."

They don't have many fluttrells in Balintol; but the correct expression here was: "You have to come to the fluttrell's vane."

Following on at the back I couldn't stop myself from bumping into the priest draped over Fweygo's top shoulder. I looked out.

A party of a dozen or so Red Capes came marching along the street carrying torches on poles. They looked an ugly lot.

Kildois do not use oaths to any great extent. I'd been surprised that Fweygo had used the word blintz. Now he said something deep in his throat I didn't catch. He swung about.

"We'll have to run for it! Out the back! Come on, Drajak! Put some grease on your axles! Leg it!"

In a wild scamper we rushed for the passage leading to the back door.

Nine

Annoyed with myself, I stopped stock-still. By the rotting fangs and diseased earlobes of Makki Grodno! What was I about, being panicked like a young coy? Swiftly I returned to the front door and slamming it shut shot the bolts, top and bottom. There was no chain, whereat I scowled. Let 'em break in, bad cess to 'em!

With that, off I galloped after Fweygo and his burden.

My kregoinye comrade enveloped the Dokerty priest in the voluminous blue cloak. We paced swiftly among the jumbled houses along the twisting streets. Talk about a maze! All the same, it was all too easy to dwell on those poor damned dead folk back there, and the tortuous alleyways fitted our somber mood.

Fweygo told F'Farhan that if he intended going to another safe house he would prefer it to be somewhat safer than the last.

Although not particularly tired I'd welcome a slap up meal and a comfortable bed for the night. This desire would not, I felt, conflict with my wish to get on into the Dokerty temple. With the assistance of F'Farhan we ought to be able to crack that little nut.

Moving swiftly through the evening with lamps dotting the darkness erratically, we left the vicinity of the temple. The sky lay dull and overcast although no rain fell. The priest made a little gesture with his fingers crooked and joined. He muttered under his breath. I caught most of the rattled-off rote words. There were no moons or stars in the sky. Like many people of Kregen he did not feel comfortable unless there were shafts and shards of pinkish light falling upon the land, or the steely glitter of stars in the heavens. His words were no doubt a condensation and distortion of a prayer sent up by ancient peoples to mitigate the disasters that would befall them without the comfort of the moons and stars. He would know this little folk saying was sheer superstition; but being a good Kregan he liked to bet both ways. This applied, I realized with an inner smile, even to an important priest of a wide-spread religion.

For men and women with this eccentric belief, Nights of Notor Zan must be exquisite torments, by Vox!

Of course, with the inevitability of vaol-paol, it began to rain. Flitting through the puddled lights between pools of darkness we hunched up our collars and padded on. I reflected that in these our later dealings with the cramphs of Dokerty I'd already come across one priest who seemed a decent sort. Maybe in F'Farhan we had another.

Truly, the world was being turned upside down!

A clump of brilliant lights drifted slowly across the sky above with the lines of rain scintillating in a halo about the vessel. These ovverers which used canvas and wind for propulsion were relatively new to Balintol and Persinia. We in Vallia had been forced to develop the type because of our lack of some of the vital ingredients of the silver boxes that lifted and propelled airboats. I shook water off my hood with a gesture petty in the extreme. Here I was prancing around in Balintol when I should be—then I checked myself. Confound it! Drak and Silda were Emperor and Empress of Vallia. They wrestled with the inscrutable problems of supplying the Air Service. My job was and remained getting rid of these pestiferous Prisms of Power and the monstrous ibmanzies they created.

Once that had been done other tasks awaited my attention. Mind you, I wondered how we could be sure that all the Prisms of Power were destroyed. This one in Enderli that Khon the Mak was in the process of taking over might not be the last. Opaz forfend!

F'Farhan turned abruptly into an alley angling off between anonymous structures which toppled against the rain-drenched sky. A single lamp burned feebly on the corner. "Where," I said to Fweygo, "is he taking us?"

"To someone who will conduct us to a Safe House."

Well, yes and all right. I could do with a meal and sleep; but my guilt over pursuing Khon the Mak pressed on me. Just as the future tasks of taking the Regent C'Chermina, King Tom and San W'Watchun and putting them in a room together and not letting them out until they'd agreed to co-operate against the Shanks, remained to be done. Also, I'd have to drag in this King N'Norgad the Belly of Enderli. I stepped in a puddle and didn't even bother to curse.

F'Farhan led us to a nondescript building and a large Rapa barred his way with a scowl. The rain pattered down outside and I caught only some of the words that passed. "Only fighters allowed now."

"But I must see Nath the Nose."

The surly answer: "Only fighters."

F'Farhan swallowed down. "Here is one..." Fweygo was pushed forward. The entrance was lit rudimentarily and the lamplight and the shadows and the rain and the closeness of it all created a powerful sense of unease. The Rapa was curt. "No one with more than two arms." F'Farhan was clearly desperate. "All right. Then here."

The Rapa looked at me, his beak condescending. "Yeh, dom. Take him through. May Paranka the Biceps help him, the poor fambly."

The dank, coarse smell of wet clothing enveloped us as we trailed along the passageway. Lurid pictures on the walls showed impossibly-muscled men and women knocking seven kinds of brickdust out of one another. Their knuckles were bare. The discordant hum from ahead grew into the sounds of a crowd aroused into excited shouts.

A gallery led us past above the heads of the crowd below in the pit. There were all kinds of folk down there enjoying the show; yet a single glance revealed they shared one thing in common. All were wealthy. This was no common mob of folk from the warrens out for rough and ready fisticuffs. These dilettantes required blood to be shed, yes; they wanted to be entertained by their so-called sport.

In the ring marked off by three parallel red ropes two women slugged it out. I took a single look; my mouth twisted in disgust, and I walked on. This was nothing like the fights between Jikai Vuvushis, Battle Maidens, who fought for other reasons than merely earning gold.

"In here."

The room contained tables on which men and women were being ministered to with oils and massage. The aromas smoked in the atmosphere. A Hytak whose face was a mere red splodge obviously caused concern to the needleman attending him. A Chulik stood by, rolling his hands over and over, rubbing his knuckles. He was not marked. He was large. No—he was big. No—he was a giant. He overtopped everyone in the room. F'Farhan looked around nervously. The Rapa disappeared back to his post at the door after speaking to a dapper apim in full evening dress—Enderlish evening dress, that is. He came over.

"You'll do." His face, red and full-fleshed though it was, looked tired. Before he could go on, F'Farhan said: "I must speak to Nath the Nose—"

"Him! Oh, he's taking bets right now. Be in later."

"But—"

The apim, evidently the promoter, turned away. "Naghan! Over here. New boy for you." With that he went to talk to the Chulik.

Naghan rolled over, broken-nose, cauliflower ear, rolling shoulders and all. He twitched his head now and again. He sized me up.

"Fists only, dom. Done a bit, have we?"

Fweygo said sharply: "This is not a good idea."

"Gotta wait for Nath the Nose." I found to my amusement that I spoke with this pseudo-tough huskiness these lads love to adopt.

The priest started to say something, stopped himself, started over. "I'll go and—" He turned quickly and moved away among the people.

"Here comes Horter R'Raneed." Naghan moved deferentially aside for the promoter. He looked tireder than ever. Truth to tell, I'd not been on Earth just recently, but this evening-dressed boxing promoter lacked one essential adjunct to his trade. He did not have a big cigar stuck between his pudgy lips.

"You'll fight Chandrur." He waved a beringed hand.

Naghan said: "He's just fought, horter—"

"Yes. He did rather mangle that Hytak. That's what the clients want. He's ready to go again. So jump to it."

Fweygo said: "That's it. You're not going to—"

"Have to, if the priest wants to see this Nath the Nose."

"But look at the Chulik! He'll pulverize you."

"I agree that fists alone present a problem. A crafty kick in the where-withals would do him a world of no good."

The current fight finished with a wild-beast howl from the crowd and the mangled remnants were carted in and laid out on the tables. You'd have great difficulty deciding who'd won. The giant Chulik came over and looked down on me. I cocked my head up to stare back. He said nothing; just grunted, and, wrapping a magnificently-patterned robe about his muscular body, went off with his handlers. I judged he was enormously strong and possibly slow; he was certainly muscle-bound.

Fweygo used his tail hand to scratch his nose. "You're determined to fight him, then?"

"Aye."

"Very well. I'll go and put a bet on." He gave me a calculating stare and went off, gliding like a golden ghost among the throng of handlers and masseurs and boxers.

After that the event went off with the professional boredom of these people, who'd seen it all. Naghan, known as the Ear, put me into the charge of an apim who was almost as broken-down. This Llangro the Alumsetter slapped me on a slab and rubbed oils in with the casual skilled way one expects from a masseur. He didn't say much, except to say he'd do his best to patch me up if I lived.

Keeping my brave old scarlet breechclout as the only item of clothing, I was led out when the time came. The mob howled, I disdained them and clambered through the red ropes. There was no referee. I do not believe there were any rules, either, except that fists only were to be used.

The Chulik, Chandrur, entered to tumultuous applause. He played to his audience, flexing his muscles, doing a few knee bends, polishing up his tusks. These were banded three times in gold.

The starting gong blattered into the noise, ringing in what should prove a bout of pleasant entertainment to these refined people.

With startling speed Chandrur danced over to me and gave me such a buffet that I went sprawling backwards on the sanded earth. The instant I clawed up he clouted me over the ear and I went all whichways.

He stood over me, his enormous chest bulging, ready to hit me again. Dray Prescot, I said to myself, you're in for it now!

Ten

Oddly enough, considering my circumstances, the thought that popped into my head concerned the girls fighting in the ring when we'd passed by. Perhaps I'd been too hard on them in my oh-so-righteous-judgment. Maybe they needed the cash. When you are desperate with poverty gnawing an empty belly a few punches might not seem so terrible.

At that instant, before I scrambled up, the Chulik hit me again. Flat, bang, wallop, I went across the sand.

So the Marquess of Queensberry would find short shrift here.

In an undignified scramble across the ring I managed to put some distance between me and Chandrur. The fellow was very very strong. I knew that. He was also quite quick, and this was an unwelcome surprise. I stood up and faced him and this time when he hit out with his right, I blocked the blow with my left forearm. Instantly, like a piledriver, his left whistled around to bury his fist in my guts.

I whoofled. By Krun, I sounded like a burst steam boiler!

So this meant he had skill in boxing. Just how much remained to be ascertained, if I could stay on my feet that long.

The Disciplines of the Krozairs of Zy were, naturally, of limited use.

They enabled me to block the pain and use it. Turko's Khamorro tricks, too, could not be fully used. It was fists only.

So perhaps some of the rough and tumble of my days in the Royal Navy of Nelson's time would prove efficacious. That being settled, when Chandrur bored in again, this time with a succession of punches, I ducked and weaved and let him go past. As he went I gave him a good one in the side under his ribs. He span about immediately. He roared. He jumped in with fists flailing.

Over I went, sprawling on the sand. Half up, I saw him bend down with every intention of striking me. I rolled away rapidly. I jumped up. I backed off. By Vox! This would not do, not do at all!

He stalked me around the ring. Naturally ignoring what this unhealthy crowd were yelling I still caught the noise of their displeasure. As I back-pedalled I found myself hoping that F'Farhan would find Nath the Nose damned quickly and finish his business with him.

Chandrur showed the gleam of gold of his tusks. "Stand still, you blintz!"

Just how skilled a boxer was he, then? By Vox, now was the time to find out. So I boxed him. I feinted, and ducked and weaved, danced with feet forward and back, played him. He did not hit me as frequently as he had. But he still contrived to get through. The pain of these blows, all neatly filed and docketed away and used to power my own return strikes, was still bearable. For how long?

No, I said to myself. This would not do! By the diseased liver and lights of Makki Grodno, this hulking great Chulik must be shown the error of his ways.

By this time he was more wary of me. I'd hit him, too.

He cocked his fists and moved sideways, shuffling, tucking his chin down into his shoulder. Blood shone greasily on his knuckles.

That, by Krun, was my blood! I felt an irritating trickle down my left temple. I just hoped my eyebrows would perform the function for which nature had designed them. No doubt my face was gory, too. Chandrur sidled around and then jumped in, both fists flailing.

A straight left which would have stopped, would have knocked over, your ordinary fellow made no difference. He roared in like a runaway vove. Our bodies collided and I flapped my arms about his gross form to stop myself from being run over. We clinched.

For a moment we stood in the center of the room, locked together. The beast howl of the crowd smote in suddenly. My head was sticking out from under his armpit as I clung on for dear life. Straight ahead in the front row of the audience the face of a man sprang out from all the rest. He abruptly appeared isolated, hanging in a cloud-shrouded limbo. He was shouting and waving his fists like the others. But he was not like the others, oh, no! I knew him, the cramph.

The corpse-pallid face, the blue-black hair, the thin, almost bloodless lips, the sharp chin, the piercing eyes, oh, yes, all these characteristics added up to the countenance of Hyr Kov Khonstanton, Mak Khon, known as Khon the Mak. So the rast had decided to take an evening off from his torturing preparation of youngsters to turn them into infectos. He wore evening clothes that were, as usual with him, black with gold lace and a trimming of red. That instant appeared to stretch and stretch as I stared.

Like any buffoon I stood there and Chandrur gave his arm a nasty twist and my head jumped so that I thought it was coming off my shoulders. I was in a fight. There was no time to stand about gawping.

My fists thudded meatily into the small of his back and he grunted and his grip relaxed. Ducking out to free myself, I once again was shocked by this massive Chulik's speed. He seized me up again and this time his head bent just above mine as his arms grasped me.

"Give in now, apim, before it goes worse for you."

"So you're feeling the pain, hey, Yellow Tusker." More often than not there is no sense in talking to an opponent. Now I went on in a hard metallic voice: "I am surprised you're still in Balintol. All the Chuliks down south have gone back to your islands. The Shanks are attacking you there. Perhaps you do not fancy a real war?"

Well, of course, no one with any sense fancies a war. But this suggestion of cowardice on his part got to him. The crowd yelled insults and demands that we get on with the combat. "Shanks?"

"Aye." The momentary distraction undid him. His bear hug relaxed. I stepped back to get set. His head was still down as he digested this news. My first blow really did the business. That punch landed full on the point of his chin. Sure, I hit him again; but he began to buckle at the knees. He went down to the sand and then flopped over.

So this giant Chulik, Chandrur, had a glass chin!

The uproar of the crowd abruptly fell to complete silence.

For perhaps three heartbeats this unnatural quietness held; then the place erupted. Supposing I'd better act like a victorious boxer I lifted both arms above my head. By Krun, I felt the pull of the damn bruises then, I can tell you!

Staring arrogantly around as the handlers ducked into the ring I saw a commotion by the door. Men were hurrying to leave and others were stopping them. Briefly the whirlwind form of a golden Kildoi showed and then vanished as men piled in. Welshers, I supposed.

Casually and carefully I looked to see what Khon the Mak was up to. His thin pallid face looked disgusted. Great! He'd lost, too. At his right side sat a bulky Malfsim wearing obvious armor under his evening clothes. A Malfsim's head gives the impression of being all face with tiny features. Button nose, pinched mouth, pig-like eyes are surrounded by what seems like acres of skin. A Malfsim always makes me think of him as a ginger-bread man. This fellow wore three swords and three daggers but I saw no glint of gold or silver at his throat.

On Khon the Mak's left sat a rat-faced polsim in gaudy finery. He was busily working with a writing stick and pad, no doubt assessing what his master had just lost. Bad cess to the lot of 'em!

Ochs came into the ring to sand and rake the floor and I departed and went back to lie on a table and let the handlers do what they could for my cuts and bruises. The howl from the crowd lifted again so the next bout had started.

Fweygo came in looking pleased and jingling a bag.

"They started to run," he said and added with some satisfaction: "but we caught them and made them pay up."

"You bet on me?"

"Well, naturally."

So then I told him that Khon the Mak was out there and that our next step would be to follow the rast. Fweygo wanted to know about F'Farhan and Nath the Nose and the Safe House and food and sleep.

"We strike, as they say in Clishdrin, while the iron is hot."

I went on to say that, anyway, we did not look as though we'd get much sleep tonight, so the Safe House was superseded in our plans. Fweygo favored me with an odd look, and I realized I'd been speaking far more forcefully than I usually did with him. Like a number of my kregoinye comrades, he felt he was leading us, and this was agreeable to me.

Swinging myself off the table, not without a twinge or two, I pulled on the borrowed clothes and armor. I'd have to clean the bronze Real Soon Now to prevent corrosion. At least the togs were dry.

Remembering my encounter with the Oblifex Cuisar, I spoke in a low voice to Fweygo as I finished buckling up. "We must not let F'Farhan know what we intend to do with his precious Flutubium and the Prism of Power." I explained Cuisar's reaction of horror at the thought that the divine gift of Oltomek would come to harm. Fweygo nodded. He suggested that my con-viction that the Prism of Power reposed with Khon the Mak was erroneous. Far more likely, he thought, that it was still with the priests in the temple. Mind you, Fweygo had little if any experience of Khon the Mak. I couldn't see the fellow, having disposed of the chief priest, not laying his hands on the Prism of Power, the magical artifact he'd travelled many dwaburs to find.

As for this king of Enderli, Khon the Mak would have him wrapped around his little finger by now—tied by his whiskers, as they say on Kregen.

"I'll play F'Farhan along." Fweygo spoke confidently.

"In no time at all he'll get us into the temple, and then—"

"Here he is," I interrupted. Fweygo turned. F'Farhan gave us both a look that if it wasn't so annoyed would have been comical. "Nath the Nose. The hulu. He welshed on his bets and ran off."

Fweygo let a small smile broaden his lips. "One crafty little polsim did get away before we caught the others. Ha!"

"Fweygo," I said with a certain bite in my words. "Do you go with the priest here. You'll find somewhere to go."

"Yes, but—"

I hitched up my swords. "Oh, I've some unfinished business to attend to. Remberee." With that, off I went, through the passageway, out into the street. The last boxing bouts should be over in short order. Then, why, then, I'd see what Khon the Mak did. A little chat was well overdue with that black-hearted rast.

Eleven

Thankfully the rain had stopped. Occasionally a few palely pink shafts of radiance from the Maiden with the Many Smiles shone down, so that meant the clouds were slowly clearing. This was going to be a capital night for undercover work and a trifle of skullduggery.

A scene of busy activity developed as the patrons turned out. Shouts of: "Loxo! Loxo!" went up and the link men hurried to bring their lanterns on poles to light the way of the revelers. As the rain had ceased some link fellows brought torches. The lights reflected in long streaks across the wet pavements. Riding animals were brought round from the stables at the rear of the premises. Some two-wheeled carriages were being used; these bloods wouldn't dream of riding in a four-wheeler. Among all this I looked for my target.

The devotees of Diproo the Nimble-fingered plied their trade. Hawkers shouted their wares, mostly fruits and sweets and candies, cheerful comestibles to moisten the mouth after the hoarse shouting at the boxing bouts. All in all, to the normal easy-going young fellows about town, this presented a charming picture of the good life for those who wanted that. For a fellow like me with a mission in life at odds with easy-going, the pleasure of it all came from the ease with which it offered me concealment.

Among the myriad smells the delicious aroma of squish pie wafted into my nostrils. At once I thought of my comrade Inch. Well, as that long streak would say, there's no time like the present for fortifying the inner man. Of course, shortly thereafter he'd have to stand on his head, or perform some other ridiculous action called for by his precious taboos.

A couple of coppers secured me a handsome wedge of squish pie and keeping watch on the crowds I downed the delicacy gratefully.

This transaction brought the state of my finances to mind. The cash I'd secured from the Red Capes would be enough for me to hire a public vehicle should Khon the Mak ride or drive away. A strapping young Gon with sparsely buttered bald head looked likely. He pulled a light two-wheeled cart, a kind of jalopy, with wicker seat and frayed cushions. A very short period of hagglement saw me hand over four silver bhins as a down payment to secure the vehicle for my use.

During all this the nagging feeling kept on in my old vosk-skull of a head that it was far more probable that the Flutubium would be housed within the safety of the temple. Probably Fweygo was right. All the same, this yetch Khon the Mak had a mighty persuasive way with him. Drawing a breath after the last of the squish pie, I decided to stay with my original course of action.

He came out with his cronies at last, strutting a trifle, pausing to sniff the night air, the big important man among clients. I'd no apprehension that he'd recognized me in the ring. Truth to tell, I was surprised that so cold and ascetic-seeming a person would attend a boxing match. Ostlers brought round zorcas, pushing their way through the last of the throngs. Khon the Mak put his hand on the muzzle of his zorca, stroking. He moved closer to whisper in the animal's ear.

Oh, yes. He did have another side to him. Mind you, any person of sensibility likes zorcas. His home life might be idyllic, although there were rumors to the contrary. People aren't dyed evil black all through. No, the trouble with Hyr Kov Khonstanton was his gnawing hunger to dominate and rule all of Tolindrin, to which end he would murder and bring down cities to ruin.

And—he created demons from hell to serve his desires.

The group stood by their mounts, talking. The young Gon I'd hired, Gurnley the Wheels, might be in for a breathless run this night.

Khon the Mak's tame priests of Dokerty didn't actually create the ibmanzies; they summoned them from the nether pits. Create or summon, I didn't give a bent copper ob. The fact remained they had to be stopped.

Presently the group left their mounts in the care of their grooms and began to stroll along under the stars and moons which shone erratically as the clouds rolled away.

Half a dozen of them walked along in Khon's group, all self-important men, self-satisfied with their life style. There was no sign of the Malfsim with his gingerbread-man face and half-concealed armor. The ferrety little polsim was missing too. Probably he'd been dispatched to pay Khon's debts; assuming, that was, that the Hyr Kov would pay up promptly.

They sauntered along, in no hurry, taking the air. I hesitated, pondering my next step. The little jalopy cart would be useful as cover; equally, it was now an embarrassment. So much for planning ahead!

"Here, Gurnley the Wheels." I spoke briskly. "Another four silvers. That should pay you. You are dismissed."

He rubbed a hand over the smooth buttered scalp. He looked both puzzled and amused. He took the money. "Payment for work not done. Well, as San Blarnoi says, I do not mind saving my sweat." He spat on the coins and tucked them away. "My thanks, horter. Bright moons."

"Bright moons," I replied automatically, and turned to see where Khon and his cronies had gone in the dappled moon shadows.

Although Llangro the Alumsetter had slapped a sticky ointment on my bruises, my ribs still ached more than somewhat from the pounding they'd taken from Chandrur's massive Chulik fists. Moving set my pains up again. Perhaps I should have retained the services of Gurnley the Wheels and his little jalopy cart.

No time for this shillyshallying now. The group I trailed, one among the many small groups in the throng, turned down a street to the right. Not without a wince or two I trotted along to the corner and put an eyeball around the damp wood. There they were, strutting along and gesticulating. Shadows dropped about them as a cloud passed overhead. I made shift to dart along from the corner, keeping close to the uneven walls.

When the Maiden with the Many Smiles cast down her fuzzy pink light again I gave a quick breath of relief. They were still in sight a little further on.

Dodging to the corner of this building I waited a moment before crossing the open space to the next. A sudden, soft, pain-filled cry sounded off to the left. I swiveled to look. Down this alley a contortion of shadows writhed.

The cries spurted up again, and I made out the dim figures of a man grasping a woman against the wall, and two other men beating a woman on the ground.

I didn't think. I just ran down the alley shouting angrily and dragging out my sword.

"Get off her, you damned double-dyed kleeshes!"

A stray beam of pink light splintered into a star off the sword blade as I ran. Opaz knows what kind of figure I presented to these cramphs. They span about, straightened up, let go of the women and scampered off. They ran fleetly into the deeper shadows.

The woman against the wall, an apim lass, just stood there dragging gulps of air through flared nostrils. One hand clutched her multi-colored garments about her breast. The girl on the ground, a Sylvie, flopped over onto her back, sobbing.

Galloping up and waving the drexer after the departing villains, I skidded to a halt. The Sylvie's crying was most distressing.

"You're all right now." I bent to her. "It's all—"

The rustle of clothes, the flicker of an unexpected shadow above me, and I jerked back. Too late! The club smashed into my head with the full force of a young girl's muscled arm. Over I went, feeling as though Chandrur was still at me. Sparks and comets flared across my vision. A damned great spike of pain lanced from the crown of my head to the soles of my feet.

Here in the shadows the ground was still damp, smelling of ancient foods and unnameable objects. My nose went squash into the muck. Trying to roll over with as much speed as I could muster, I was aware of the club striking into the ground past my ear with a most evil thwunking sound.

"Stay down, you blintz!" The girl was panting above me.

Now the Sylvie erupted into action. She leaped on me. The sword was trapped beneath her body. I felt another confounded blow and more sparks shattered into my eyes.

A voice as incisive as a blade made from ice said:

"Enough! Let him up."

Yellow lamplight spilled across the ground. I rolled over. The girls stood up and drew back. The light showed their faces inflamed, excited. They panted. The light illuminated this pretty scene and I knew what an onker I'd been, what an onker of onkers, a get onker. Among his retinue, Khon the Mak gazed down at me with his corpse-pale face drawn into a ghastly smile of satisfaction.

The Bells of Beng-Kishi started up their merry carillon again, bouncing in my head from ear to ear. I'd just about finished with them from Chandrur; now these two hussies—

"So you imagined I would not recognize you!"

I didn't bother to answer him. I'd been gulled. I'd been completely hoodwinked. I felt like a well-chewed slipper.

"After what you have done I want to know much more about you, Drajak the Sudden. Oh, much more! Drag him along!"

I put a fist in one of the men's eyes and got a foot into another's guts. But they tapped me again and I sagged and when I was once more compos mentis they'd bound my wrists. What Khon said was quite true. The bonds were not lesten hide, so he needed to learn more about me. They carted me off along the higgledy-piggledy streets. As best I could I took note of which way we went, locating myself with the alley of the entrapment as the locus point.

All the same, by Krun, I felt the biggest idiot in all of Kregen!

After an unpleasant travel time we reached a bronze bound gate with watchtowers either side. Torches burned luridly against the darkness. The gates were thrown open and, with Khon in the lead, we all went through into a courtyard. Many-windowed walls with flowerless balconies enclosed the space. The yard bore in with a chill, a dire presentiment of what was to come.

The grooms brought in the zorcas, who tossed their manes and scraped their hooves. The trip here had not taken a long time. Khon the Mak would have mounted up to ride otherwise. He vanished through an arched opening, shouting orders. People bustled about and shortly thereafter I was conducted to a chamber with narrow windows, a coved ceiling, furnished with two chairs and a table. A small red and blue carpet which was not Walfarg weave covered a scrap of the stone floor.

The door was slammed behind me as I was pitched in on my nose. Picking myself up and feeling the bruises pulling, I tested the bonds. Well, by Beng H'Lavini, renowned in the knot trade, they should come loose readily enough.

Not doubting that spyholes secreted in the walls were filled with eyeballs watching what I did, I made a grimace, as though finding the bonds too tough to break.

Now this situation was far more dangerous an incarceration than my brief sojourn in the so-called dungeon of the aragorn. This place was probably a palace belonging to a noble friendly to Khon. Or, more likely, a fortress-palace belonging to some inveigled wight Khon the Mak had won over with promises. I judged he wouldn't be using threats just at the moment. After all, as a noble from Tolindrin, down south, he was in a foreign country here in Enderli.

The somber lesson I had just learned was that the Hyr Kov was a more accomplished plotter than I'd hitherto believed.

Sitting on one of the chains, I rested my head on my arms on the table and closed my eyes. If I slept they'd wake me up when they wished to begin their interrogation.

Just before I drifted off to sleep, but before my never-failing last thought, I marveled at my behavior. Where was the Dray Prescot who only a handful of seasons ago would have gone roaring and raging about the chamber, maniacally striking at the door, rampaging like a demon at his incarceration? Why did I not burst the bonds about my wrists? Well, they'd be broken when the time was right. I'd changed wonderfully in later seasons upon Kregen. Yet, despite this alarmingly meek reaction, I was sadly aware that I could still erupt into an unholy demon of rage and fury against oppressors. Oh, yes, may Opaz forgive me, I was still that same Dray Prescot who burst upon the world like the wild Clansman he was.

Sleep claimed me for a short respite; but I heard them as they tramped up to the door. Men in armor, guards come to protect the sacred person of their master. I stirred myself and sat up.

The door smashed open and in they trampled. Well, they made a bonny sight to a fellow in the undertaker's trade.

The malfsim jumped forward and hoisted me out of the chair.

"Easy with him—at first, Nangro."

"At first, notor!" And this Nangro giggled. His hair down that ginger-bread countenance was black and coarse, hanging in strings.

The puissant hyr kov strode forward and sat in the chair. He was flanked by four guards. Between them, though, they shared only a single bronze chavonth head. The polsim stood a little to the rear and side, which seems to sum up many polsim characteristics. His rat-like face and sharp eyes studied me intently, so that I wondered if he was a cut above the rest. Then, by Krun! I noticed he was wearing my drexer scabbarded to a gilt belt around his narrow waist.

Khon the Mak wiped his lips with a yellow cloth. So the black-hearted rast had partaken of a meal whilst I languished down here. I hoped the palines were off. He gestured. "Pilnor—mind you take every sentence down. Miss nothing."

"Yes, notor, yes." The polsim produced his writing kit.

By Zair! I rather fancied this snotty little polsim, Pilnor, would have precious little to write down. Nothing, in fact!

"Put him back in the chair, Nangro."

"At once, notor!" The malfsim grabbed my arm to jerk me forward. With a single ripping wrench the bonds parted around my wrists. Swiveling, I put my foot into Nangro's guts and without stopping leaped at the polsim. He squeaked—just the once—before I clouted him around the ear. He started to fall down but I grabbed him up with my left fist and with my right dragged my drexer free.

In the instant I turned with the brand ready the four guards rushed at me, getting in one another's way, shouting, waving their swords. Savagery possessed me. I cannot excuse my actions. The horrid chingle and scrape of steel in the small room echoed like the screeches of the doomed Witches of Tricina, who are let out for one day a season from their eternal incarceration in the Furnace Fires of Inshurfraz. In an instant my blade reeked with red blood.

"Get him! Kill him!" Khon the Mak's shouts had lost all their icy calmness. The first guard went down minus an arm. In that flashing instant I caught a glimpse of Khon the Mak scampering for the door. A guard stepped in boldly and by the time a feint and a thrust had disposed of him, the hyr kov had vanished. With him went his lackeys, Pilnor the polsim stylor, and Nangro the malfsim bodyguard and torturer. The remaining two guards hesitated. I waved the sword at them—and they fled.

So, total savagery had not possessed me utterly, to the thanks and praise of Opaz!

Now the vital necessity was not to escape but to go prowling in search of the Prism of Power. Enough primordial anger remained seething within me to make life very difficult for anyone who sought to stop me.

Poking my head out into the corridor I realized that the very suddenness and barbarity of my onslaught had carried me through so far. The polsim would probably have run in any case. The gingerbread man was supposed to be a fighter; but his first duty was the protection of his employer. Now, mark me, I did not think Khon the Mak was any kind of coward. Quite the contrary, from his reputation. He'd scuttled off so abjectly because of my abrupt and primeval savagery.

Opaz alone knew what my face must have looked like!

The corridor lay empty. Padding along, sword snouting, I felt the after tremors of that mad passion still vibrating through my blood. A parcel of fresh guards came running up, bronze-clad, brandishing swords and spears. After the first couple of blows I had to regain my self-control. Two heads rolled on the floor. The others came on bravely. Trying to measure my blows, trying to make the well-trusted Disciplines of the Krozairs of Zy steady my sword arm, I still saw my blade cleave through helmet and skull and burst in a shower of blood and bone out under the poor wight's chin.

The remainder hesitated. I did not. I charged.

Two more went down, left and right, and the right one had his own sword forced back remorselessly until his blade snapped. The others turned to flee. I leaped on them. Striking with utter barbaric fury I chased them along that gory passage. The last one threw up his arms and let out such a screech as echoed in the nethermost pits of hell.

Pausing in this reckless slaughter I drew in a shuddery breath. I was not panting from these exertions. Rather, the devil in my brain that drove me on drew sustenance from every blow. Blood smothered me and the raw stink, usually so distasteful, now smelled with no more offence than a butcher's shop.

Moving on along the next passageway, I turned at right angles to be confronted by a closed door in an arched opening. The corridor continued on to the left. The door had been covered in blue velvet at some time in the past; the cloth was now faded and tattered.

A well-run palace would not condone this worn-out appearance in any but the least important places. Time to move on, then.

A furtive movement beyond the door brought my instant attention back to what lay beyond the blue velvet. The door moved inwards for a hand's-breadth, and stopped. Faintly, I could make out a person breathing there, deep purposeful breaths. I knew what that kind of breathing portended. By Krun, did I not!

Stepping back and bracing my legs, I lifted the sword.

The first unholy guard who stepped through there would inspect the ceiling and walls as his head rolled along the floor.

The door swung open and a sword snouted through.

I brought my drexer down in a slicing slash.

In the next instant I was frantically trying to deflect the blade.

"I see you're in trouble again, Drajak," said Fweygo, stepping through the doorway.

Twelve

"All that blood is not yours? You are unharmed? I am amazed."

"I nearly took your head off!"

"Ah, well, in that I think you were a trifle slow."

He carried swords in two of his hands. Blood gleamed wetly upon the blades. I thought to needle him a little, gee him up as they say in Clishdrin. I made my voice neutral.

"You were going to the temple. Find the Prism of Power?"

"F'Farhan—" he began. He stopped himself, breathed in, breathed out, started over. He made me hide a smile. He told me that the priest had been very circumspect, very suspicious; but in the end Fweygo wheedled it out of him. Halfway to the temple F'Farhan at last revealed that the Flutubium had been taken by a priest called San Schakaro. He intended to use it for a purpose which Oblifex Cuisar and F'Farhan could not condone. Fweygo said that F'Farhan would not say what that purpose was. That was a secret far too vile to be disclosed.

Schakaro found a ready ally in Khon the Mak and a certain Trylon T'Taxkrin in whose palace we now were. "So I came looking."

"If it's here we must find it." The words sounded banal. I went on: "Khon the Mak is here. He wanted to question me and he called me Drajak the Sudden." This continued to puzzle me, for in the tent on the bleak mountainside of W'Watchun's hideaway he'd shouted to his tame priest G'Goldark: "You know who he is!"

"It's no matter," quoth Fweygo. "If we have to chop him, then we chop him. Now let us get on."

He swung off along the corridor and then halted and turned to give me a typical Kildoi quizzical look. "He gulled you with those two girls you mentioned. Maybe he has a scheme to hoodwink you again. From all you say he is an adroit adversary. I'll have to make sure—"

"Yes, Fweygo," I cut across. "I'm sure you will."

With that settled off we went along the passage. The trophy we sought should be safely secreted where its location would be difficult, to say the least. Fweygo remained supremely confident we'd locate the pestiferous thing in short order.

As San Blarnoi says, in certain circumstances one or two determined men will succeed where armies fail. I just hoped the certain circumstances were with us now. Some of that terrible fury that had burned through me remained so that immediately after that weakling thought I found myself striding along as superbly confident as my kregoinye comrade.

An irritating thought kept nagging away at the back of my mind like a pestiferous fly. We negotiated more passageways. The Flutubium must be in a place of security and, given the mentality of these people, it would no doubt be ornately decorated with the arcane runes of their religion. I checked at a corner and asked Fweygo how the temple managed without their great symbol.

Apparently the temple services could be conducted with other symbols than the Flutubium. I'd seen some of these grandiose golden idols atop their gilded poles before. Khon could keep and use the upflung conjoined wings that contained the Prism of Power at his pleasure. From time to time it would have to be taken to the temple for great occasions. Khon would make damned sure he took it right back again.

The palace would become like an overturned ants' nest shortly. We had a little breathing space yet. Just beyond the edge of masonry of this corner two eidolons supported the architrave over a doorway. The door was closed and a tiny line of dust at its foot where the slaves hadn't quite cleaned properly indicated it was seldom used. The eidolons were of an odd race of diffs called chransters who from the waist up were splendid specimens, and from the waist down were shaggy and gnarled. So the eidolon could just represent the upper half. The females were as well-endowed as Sylvies. I stared narrowly.

Palace architects, it seemed to me, always had this penchant for putting the knobs and levers to open doors to secret passages in the more rounded parts of their sculptures. The configuration of walls here indicated to me through knowledge and experience that a secret passageway lay just beyond.

Stepping up to the eidolon and pressing the button I heard the sudden swift sounds of a scuffle at my back.

Turning about sharply, sword in fist, I saw Fweygo just stepping back from the third guard who was falling to join his two companions in their common pool of blood.

He shook his sword. "Come on, Drajak! Do try to keep up!"

Nodding to the black opening just being revealed as the door in the wall slid aside, I suggested, politely, that this way would be better.

Fweygo used his tail hand to rub his nose. "How did—?" he started, and stopped, and said: "Yes. Capital notion."

I didn't smile—at least, not outwardly—and allowed my kregoinye comrade to go into the opening first.

Like most palaces and temples of Kregen, this place had its secret runnels between the walls. Slits here and there afforded light and ventilation. Dust lay heaped against the walls, so there had been some traffic. Flang skins drooped from projections and spider webs created gossamer screens. We went along quietly.

Of course, the dust started to get up my hooter and I was forced to bury my nose into my neck cloth to stifle a sneeze.

"Do keep quiet, Drajak." Fweygo's words pierced as thinly as a stiletto. "Somebody is in this room beyond the wall."

He applied an eye to a slit, waited unmoving for a couple of heartbeats, and then moved back and went along the passage silently. Not even bothering to peer into the room I followed on. The state in which I found myself struck me as uncanny. On the surface I was going along quietly with my comrade through the secret ways. Within me, ah, well, I was aware of the furnace of rage that choked up, stoked by frustration and the need to get on. In a strange way I dreaded the time when that fury would explode.

Now Fweygo was as well aware as I that we had not entered this hidden world to hide from the guards. On the contrary, we could inspect the denizens of the various chambers and select our man.

The Kildoi did the selecting. We had mounted a flight of flang infested steps and when Fweygo peered through a slit, he nodded and beckoned me to look.

The room on the other side of the wall was handsomely furnished. Samphron oil lamps burned with a mellow yellow. An amphora stood in its gilt tripod near the sofa on which sat a rubicund, jolly fellow in an evening robe. His robe was a deep red. On the facing wall a gilt-framed picture showed a cleverly-painted representation of the winged symbol of the Flutubium, sacred to Dokerty.

I stepped back and regarded Fweygo and for a moment our eyes met. So that was settled.

This long-dead palace architect provided prominent levers within the secret ways to open the doors which were concealed on the outside. Fweygo put one hand on the lever, two other hands held swords, his fourth hand rested on the door. His tail hand was empty.

With a brisk and decisive motion he hauled on the lever and thrust on the door. It swung open and in the next instant he bounded into the room and a sword kissed the startled fellow's throat.

"Not a sound, dom!"

After that the questions were answered fluently. Most of these grand residences have their own chapels, often quite a number when the lord is of a religious bent. We had penetrated into the wing given over to living rooms for the resident priests. This fellow, San Taston, who ministered before Dokerty, proved only too happy to show us the way to the shrine.

In his fear he managed to stutter out: "There are guards. Onkers—they'll not wait—they'll kill us all!"

Neither Fweygo nor myself dignified that with a reply.

I picked up the priest's goblet from the small side table and tasted the wine. "Quite reasonable. Small-bodied, but fruity."

Fweygo gave me such a comical look I took another sip to cover my mouth. He lifted San Taston up by the neck of his robe and plunked him down on his feet, hard. "You will take us, now! We are newly employed and you are showing us what our duties will be. Dernun?"

"Yes—yes," he quavered

Fweygo told him to strut ahead importantly. We had scabbarded our swords; but the Kildoi assured Taston that they could leap out and bury themselves beside his backbone in no time at all if he acted foolishly. "No, no! I won't! Please be careful of my arm. It's been sore for a sennight now—"

He stopped at what Fweygo said and let out a little squeak. "The soreness will be cured if I chop your arm off, won't it?"

The palace was now in a turmoil. Dead guards had been discovered littering the place, and no one knew what was going on. We marched on after Taston. He was a devotee of Dokerty and therefore by definition he had to be evil, hadn't he? Well, I was no longer sure of that simple reading of the situation. The example of Cuisar and F'Farhan rankled. Perhaps the idea of creating ibmanzies made the practitioners of that despicable custom mad, the greed for power drawing them ever deeper into the monsters' mire.

Along the plushly carpeted corridors slaves were fairly running about their business. Guards, not all wearing the red cape, marched about with drawn swords. No one offered to stop us. Taston clearly was about religious matters and the guards had other duties.

Probably, too, the expressions on Fweygo's and my face deterred questioning.

This frightening fury within me had to be controlled. There seemed no particular reason for it, apart from my general sense of impatience at the continual frustrations impeding what I had to do.

Perhaps, too, after my recent and fleeting encounter with Delia, my agonizing worries over her welfare beat more forcefully.

Whatever the reasons which in this cold way I could try to analyze, and fail, the fury boiled within me waiting to burst forth.

Two groups of guards at the center of a wide chamber were obviously in the middle of an argument that grew more heated with every moment that passed. No weapons had so far been drawn; but fists waved menacingly. One group wore the short red capes, the other was composed of hired paktuns. An interesting fact here was that whilst the mercenaries were of different races of diffs, all the Dokerty guards were apims. We skirted around what promised to be an entertaining brawl.

This tension between the Red Capes and the regular guards might be entertaining, yes. We were now penetrating into the temple area proper with its shrine to Dokerty and could expect to run across more and more Red Capes. We did not wear red capes.

"How much further?" growled Fweygo.

"Not far, not far!" squeaked Taston.

Expecting a modest sized chapel that one would find in a palace, as we went on I realized I'd have to revise that opinion. The decorations became more and more grandiloquent. Statuary, paintings, wall hangings, even the chandeliers, all existed to praise Dokerty. The standard of artistry was high and the expense enormous. Quite clearly Trylon T'Taxkrin was a passion-ately devoted believer in Dokerty.

The entrance to the chapel reared up, flanked by marble wings, crowned with golden clouds. The carpet writhed with patterns. The four Red Capes on guard stood aside respectfully as Taston strode on. His habitual strut of authority stood him in good stead then. A failure on his part would have seen Fweygo explode into action.

Because of the lavishness outside, I was not surprised by the enormity of the Dokerty-inspired interior. The place blazed with red, oppressive, lowering. Gold flashed everywhere. The altar lifted beneath a canopy of gold-ribbed crystal. Stinking incense burned to make my nostrils curl. Symbols of Dokerty and Oltomek stood in rows down each side leading up to the altar. On the slab of crystal reposed the two main symbols of the reli-gion. We were interested only in the two conjoined wings of the Flutubium.

A shuffling step heralded the arrival of an ancient fellow with a beard to his waist. I wouldn't care to hazard how old he was. He wore the red robe and carried a staff on which he leaned.

His cracked old voice carried no strength. "San Taston! You are not... I am on duty here."

Taston made a vague gesture. He did not know why we had forced him to guide us here; he understood we were trouble. "No, San L'Livero, I— uh—"

Fweygo started to say: "You are relieved, san—" when six Red Capes marched from the shadows beyond the altar. Their leader, a pugnacious, red-faced fellow who wore the insignia of a Hikdar, snapped: "You!" He pointed his stick at Fweygo. "Out! Out!"

"Please—" Taston said. He swallowed down. "Help! Help!" He scuttled like a woflo away from Fweygo towards the Hikdar.

In the next split-second swords scraped as they cleared scabbards and the Kildoi catapulted into action.

The drexer leaped into my fist. The next split-second saw me alongside Fweygo and knocking away a blade and slicing in the backhand to take out the Deldar of the guards. My troubled anxiety over the storm of violence waiting to break out had to be thrust aside. Perhaps the very act of violence might purge the violence within me.

The Red Capes fought. They fought hard and viciously for their lives. After the Deldar the following man seemed to run in on my sword of his own volition. Of course, he only seemed to do this; the drexer sought him out with its own fluidity directed by my sword arm.

As I swung about to tackle the next one Fweygo whistled one of his blades down and the man dropped spouting blood.

He said: "You took two and I four. Evens, I'd say."

I shook blood drops off my blade. I grunted something surly. Banter at this moment appeared to me out of place.

The doors at our backs smashed open and more guards rushed in. The four on duty outside had been reinforced by a dozen or so.

They let out menacing yells and charged, their weapons high.

"I'll hold them off." Fweygo spoke just as calmly as before. "Do you go and get the Prism."

"Aye."

No point in arguing it with him. A few bounds took me up the steps to the altar. The Flutubium came up into my grasp with a sudden and surprising shock of familiarity. I smashed the thing open and dragged out the engraved box containing the Prism of Power.

If that was smashed now we'd all be blown to the Ice Floes of Sicce without time to touch the enfolding Mists.

Fweygo was hard at it and bodies went flying as he raged around in a circle of death.

Before leaping down to join him I tucked the box safely away. Then I gave a quick scrutiny to the shadows beyond the altar. A crimson velvet curtain half draped a dark door set deeply in the wall.

The distance was not far. A flashing glance back at the Kildoi showed him like a golden Catherine wheel, spinning with the sparks of blood as guards toppled away. He'd brought his tail hand into the action now, and was striking with force enough to wound and disable. He husbanded his strength. He really was rather splendid.

The door had to be checked before we committed ourselves. A golden cartouche of the two joined wings gleamed dully on the lenken surface. The bronze handle felt cold. I pushed and the door gave, to reveal darkness illuminated vaguely by a dim red radiance in the distance.

The coldness of the bronze handle shattered my illusion that we were succeeding. I felt a distinct prickle run over my skin. "Fool!" I snarled to myself. "Onker!" Of course, in the instant in which I picked up the box containing the Prism of Power I should have known.

With a gesture as much of despair as fury I hauled the box out. It felt lumpy in my hand. No warmth emanated from it.

If I cracked the lid a tiny fraction open, would the red glare of hell break out?

Savagely I snapped the lid back. A brown and black scorpion reared up, tail high, slashing at me.

With an involuntary yell I couldn't stop I hurled the thing away. "Fweygo!" I roared it out. "Come on!"

Moving down to assist him I felt the pangs of despair fasten on my guts like leeches. The Prism of Power was not in this Flutubium. We had failed. And now half the palace guard were out to part our heads from our shoulders.

Thirteen

Fweygo's circle of death meant that I could not stand shoulder to shoulder with him. As he whirled creating a spray of blood about him so he retreated slowly. I ran down and instantly was engaged in a savage combat with four of them, four ugly fellows with their short red capes flying as they pranced about.

They had to be dealt with sharply. One of their braxters was grabbed up and I swung that into action at once, only to see it snap across at the second blow.

The broken hilt went hurling across to mangle a man's face.

Fweygo snapped out: "You have it?"

I chopped a fellow left, ducked and sliced his companion before I snarled back: "No. The box held a scorpion only."

The Kildoi said nothing; but his skilled swordcraft sharpened up. We reached the open door with the Red Capes like a pack of hungry werstings struggling to drag us down.

"Go on!"

There was no time for argument so I did as Fweygo bid and backed into the opening. I moved back to give him room and took a good grip on the edge of the door.

His form contorted like a marionette silhouetted against the lamplight of the temple. His swords flashed red. "Come on!" He continued to fight. "Get set! I'm hauling you in!"

With that I grabbed the thick upper part of his tail as it coiled back for a killing thrust up between his legs, and pulled.

He went back past me so fast a Red Cape had the misfortune to follow.

I clouted him on the back of the neck and slammed the door shut in the face of the next guard. Probably the force pulped his nose.

Pulling the beam down into the brackets to bar the door I judged it strong enough to resist for some time.

Fweygo yelled out: "You pulled my tail!"

"Aye." Naturally enough I was well aware that races of diffs with tails do not like their nether appendages pulled. It stands to reason. It is an indignity. It demands instant retribution.

So, quietly for all my inner fury, I added: "I crave your pardon, Fweygo. It was necessary."

He shook his shoulders, the golden gleam muted by the dim red radiance. "Well." He spoke a mite grudgingly. "You did warn me."

"And the damned box contained no Prism of Power but an Opaz-forsaken scorpion."

"The Everoinye—" He shook his head. "No. Impossible."

"I agree. The scorpion was put there as a guard. So?"

By this time we were marching smartly along the corridor. The light brightened. No doubt this was a way used by the priests.

"So where is it?" The answer to that was obvious, and also unknown.

"San Cuisar escaped and he took the Prism of Power with him. That's why the Red Capes were after him."

"Aye." Fweygo went on wiping his swords as we marched. "You said he was going to W'Watchun."

"So he said."

"I'll have to think about this. Look, there's a door up ahead." The Kildoi in his bewildering fashion went on wiping a sword, opened the door and stuck another sword through. "Just an anteroom."

Pegs along the wall held red robes.

"No," I said. I spoke heavily. "It'll never work."

"A pity. Come on."

The most obvious expectations we must face were more confrontations. Yet I had the feeling that the guards, who would want to go around by another route to catch us as we left here, might not be readily allowed in these quarters. This was priestly territory. All the same, after a period of haggling, the guards would be let in. Self-importance is a mortal sin. Sometimes its pettiness can work in your favor. We prowled on, ready for that next confrontation.

A spark of light caught in my eye. I blinked. Fweygo strode on ahead, swords snouting. The silvery spark persisted, and expanded, and turned into a many-spiked star glittering in my eye.

What in Zair's name was all this, then? I turned my head and the star of sparkling light turned with me, so that confirmed it was really in my eye and not an outside apparition.

The center of the star shape writhed with smokey vagueness. The cardinal points were certainly more pronounced than the others; but just how many rays extended between the main points I couldn't make out. They altered in size and length and number bewilderingly. I tried shutting my eyes and the star remained, sparkling silver.

Fweygo turned to beckon me on through a doorway. He said, very sharply: "What's the matter?"

"Nothing. Go on."

"You look—"

"Nothing!"

"Very well."

We went on. In my limited experience almost all Kildois are smart. As they say in Clishdrin, they're smart cookies. This splendid specimen of the Kildoi race of diffs wouldn't let drop whatever it was he'd seen in my face. No by Krun!

This enigmatic star sparked and glittered in my eye as we marched on through chambers where some disarray showed the haste with which the inhabitants had left. Leaving the area dedicated to the work of the temple, and going cautiously—mighty cautiously, by Vox!—we entered a series of rooms given over to the domestic work of the palace.

The star abruptly expanded to three times its size. In the same instant I heard—or I imagined I heard—a silvery laugh, like the tinkle of water in a fountain. The laughter changed to words; but they were quite indecipherable. Like a calloused finger and thumb snuffing a candle, a black star shape obliterated the silver. I blinked. Star and sound were gone.

My comrade's voice roused me. "Ah!" Fweygo sounded most satisfied. "I think we're in business."

Pushing the conundrum of silvery stars that winked into existence in a fellow's eye aside, I saw what caused the Kildoi's pleasure. Two Red Capes stalked cautiously ahead of us. Quite clearly the palace had been emptied of people so that the search could turn up the intruders easily.

These two Dokerty guards did not know what hit them.

We donned the red capes and draped them tastefully. We checked each other's appearance. Fweygo kept his two lower arms inside and tucked his tail up.

He'd pass as an apim unless a busybody nosed too closely. Marching with the stiff arrogance expected, we strode boldly forth. I happened to have donned the kit of a swod; Fweygo had taken the Deldar.

When we were stopped by a Hikdar and his men Fweygo reported in fine style. He was brisk and military. The Hikdar nodded and gave orders, at which Fweygo saluted with a smart: "Quidang, Hik!"

We marched off to do the Hikdar's bidding until we were out of his sight. Then we resumed our way towards the exit.

The unpleasant yard through which I'd been dragged with my hands bound was not the way Fweygo chose to leave the palace.

Oh, no, by Krun! That wasn't his style! The silence of the palace struck me as strange, even eerie. Normally the passageways and chambers echoed to the chatter of voices, the sounds of work being done, the slip-slop of sandals on marble pavements. Fweygo's style turned out to involve using a small although still ornate side door. Through the last deserted corridors we passed like wraiths. The door opened on oiled hinges. The sentry boxes outside were empty.

"He brings his favorites in this way," commented Fweygo and led off smoothly across the road. The night struck fresh and the high glitter of stars between clouds shone reassuringly.

A shout lifted at our backs. Taking no notice we walked swiftly on into the shadows of the house opposite, set at an odd angle to the palace walls. The bellow rose again. Unmistakably that was the regimental roar of a Deldar. We ducked into the shadows and vanished from his sight.

"If they chase us, they don't stand a chance." Fweygo sounded amused.

The fury constrained within me had been a trifle assuaged by these recent gory events. The resentment at my fate remained pent up and simmering. Walking swiftly on I knew what must be the next step.

In a voice I tried to control and make neutral and which came out with a hard metallic ring, I said: "You're always telling me I'm this Emperor of All Paz. Very well then. You say the Everoinye charged you with the task of helping make me this proper emperor—"

He tried to interrupt; but I went strongly on. "So be it. I'll act like a damned emperor. Come on!"

The Emperor of Vallia had recently upgraded his representatives in Balintol to the status of ambassadors. Here in Nerlinium the new ambassador was Strazab Erlinen, known as Erlinney the Dour. He was a straight up and down kind of fellow who had done well in the Time of Troubles and made money providing riding animals to the army. Filbarrka advised me that this Erlinen charged honest prices. Thither I led Fweygo, brooking no argument.

The embassy stood in its own grounds with the walls at odd angles to the streets outside. The guard—I did not recognize any of them—smart in their Vallian kit, let me in on the password. As you know, all the Vallian embassies had been stocked with goodies such as an adventurer might need, all paid for by me.

Strazab Erlinen was politeness itself, scrupulous in his observance of protocol and order. He greeted Fweygo formally. Then in his study we got down to the business at hand.

"An airboat, majister? Certainly—how large?"

"Speed is the criterion. A four-seater at most."

In no time at all this was arranged. I believe his chief stylor went out to a lifter drome to buy the craft. She was a likely looking article, sleek, and with highly polished varnish. She was new. Her name was *Scent of Palines*.

"Hmph!" said Fweygo to that piece of information.

We took our leave of the ambassador after a huge meal, a bath and a welcome change of clothes. We intended to sleep by turns. A dagger was tossed and the first turn fell to the Kildoi.

As I turned into the flying silks and furs, I told him to sort out a new name if he wanted to. By the time he roused me to take my watch he'd come up with a blinder. "*Red Ruin*. Aye, that's her name."

I just thought to myself: "Zair look down on me now!"

Fweygo went to sleep. The lifter soared on as the morning broke in a glory of emerald and ruby striking in broad rays past the clouds. Night rushed away before us. The air stung with the zest of life. Looking down on my kregoinye comrade I realized that for all his peculiar Kildoi ways he held a place in my affections along with all my blade comrades.

When push came to shove, or as Seg Segutorio would say, when the shaft nocks the string, Fweygo the Kildoi would be there in the front rank with the best of us.

The ground rushed past beneath. A lake appeared, glittering silver like a star. When I looked around the lake sped past to the rear; the star remained sparking and spiking in my eye.

"Confound the thing!" I shook my head, closed my eyes. The star remained. Again I heard the tinkling laugh and the unintelligible words. Once again, after a time, the black star blotted out the apparition. Was I losing my eyesight? Was I losing my mind?

The journey continued. Fweygo woke up and we ate and talked—hugely and sparsely—and felt refreshed. *Red Ruin* proved a rapid flier and we devoured the dwaburs.

All the same, we wasted time flying to the Cave of the Wall by that gigantic precipice. San W'Watchun was not there and we were very smartly ordered to clear off by the guards. So we turned south west for Winbium.

A certain delay occurred, first in discovering where the Illusionist was staying, and then of gaining admittance. The time we should have taken, just under a terrestrial day and night, took somewhat longer because of the dogleg in our flight path. Eventually the Chulik Chekaran ushered us into that same damned chamber where I'd first gazed into W'Watchun's eerie glassy eyes.

Without any idea of the kind of reception I'd receive, I was pleasantly surprised when the sorcerer welcomed us in warmly. We did not beat about the bush. We told W'Watchun. His face took on an expression of fear, quickly controlled. "San Cuisar is here. He sought my protection. But another Prism of Power! This could be disaster!"

San Cuisar was summoned. Just as white and plump as before, he looked as contented with his lot as one could suppose he'd be.

"Horter Drajak," he said, plumply. "I owe you my life. And the Lady Alyss is a marvel among all women. But there is no cause for your questions. I believe you know more than is good for you."

"Khon the Mak is after the Flutubium." I spoke harshly. The time for shillyshallying was gone. "If he lays hands on it—"

"But he cannot!"

"Why not?"

He blinked at my rudeness, and said: "It is hidden in a place where it is safe. It is well-guarded." He sniggered. "Very well guarded, by Dokerty!"

Cajole and threaten as we would, he insisted the dreadful thing was safe and secure. He said he understood these arcane matters far better than we. Eventually W'Watchun gave his opinion that he believed Cuisar. The Flutubium and the horror it contained would not be found by Khon the Mak. With that we had to be content.

"In that case," I said. "I have other matters to concern me touching the welfare of all Balintol."

Fourteen

The sword blade hissed past my ear and smashed into the grimy brickwork. The blade did not break. The four warriors trying to kill me in the street imagined they had me cornered, backed up to a brick pillar.

Their attack had been so swift and sudden they'd almost had me—but almost is not good enough when dealing with a Krozair of Zy.

A smooth sideways movement, checked, and my drexer sank into the warrior's throat above the corselet rim. He'd gone with my sideways action, and so paid the penalty of not paying attention in the middle of a fight.

The other three yelled all kinds of threats and dire promises of retribution and bore in with their swords seeking a more intimate acquaintance with my guts. Springing away from the pillar I swirled my brand before their eyes, darted three quick short thrusts at the trio, and danced away. The shadows of the house perched on the pillars above us fell about me. I shouted back at the Tchekedos.

"Clear off, you bunch of no-good hulus! And take your fansho with you—he's not dead yet."

A quantity of profanity filled the air as they hesitated. They swashed their swords about. If they'd carried shields then they'd be swashbuckling. They looked ugly, and angry, and—dare I say it?—a trifle scared.

There was no doubt this attack was motivated by one or other of the Tchekedos I'd alienated before. They'd caught me in the street as I was returning from a pleasant thankyou visit to the Lamnian merchant Dorval ham Hesting and his cadade, Jiktar Larghos Frenden the Quick. They'd been kind when I'd crawled out of the sewers. Quite clearly they'd not expected to see me again. Turning up with a Dunder porter carrying a wicker case of bottles of fine vintage on his flat head surprised them.

We'd spent a pleasant evening and now, on the way back, these moronic Tchekedos wanted to ship me off to the Ice Floes of Sicce.

They shifted about, looking both mean and furious. They flourished their blades. The wounded fellow groaned away, holding his fingers to his neck where the dark blood ran down over his ridiculously fanciful neckerchief. This lot wore neckcloths almost as enormous as Elizabethan ruffs, "Go on!" I snarled at them. "Schtump!"

Strange the way authority operates! Once I'd climbed through the hawsehole onto the quarterdeck in the Royal Navy back on Earth I understood authority being administered as well as received.

Of course, this damned yrium of mine had a hand in it. These Tchekedos all fired up to do me mischief had seen one of their number wounded. Should that have stopped them dead in their tracks? Not likely! But it did. Stopped them stone cold. They scuffed their feet. They brandished their swords. They spat on the ground. Then they ran off.

I stared after them balefully. I could do without this kind of nonsensical interruption to my plans. Mind you, that latent fury within me had not burst out. Perhaps unconsciously I'd recognized that these Tchekedos were just not worth the effort.

Wiping the drexer clean I slapped the blade away. That would receive a proper clean and oiling later. My armory left up in the Cave of the Wall when the Star Lords called had been brought with the Illusionist to Winbium. As you know, I always relish strapping on my arsenal of weapons. The Krozair brand snugged sweetly and the rapier and main gauche had been cared for by Ronun's juruk.

A flicker of silver started up in my left eye.

"By the pestiferous tripes and bilious bowels of Makki Grodno!" I snarled aloud into the warm evening. "Whoever you are! Either make yourself known or get out of my head!"

The silvery tinkle of a voice spoke. Again, the words were unintelligible. In their cadences, though, I detected no note of menace. Rather, by Krun, the words sounded entreatingly, trying to force their meaning past what occult barrier stood between us. The voice pleaded to be understood.

This time the obliteration descended more slowly. The star slowly turned brown until all the silver was obscured. Then the whole kit and caboodle vanished. By Vox! As if I didn't have enough to contend with, without puzzling over mysterious silver stars in my eyes!

Walking quietly back through the streets past the strange top-heavy houses, I ruminated on the problems facing me. For one thing, had I been too bombastic and boastful to Fweygo? I'd promised to act like an emperor. He'd certainly given me one of his quizzical Kildoi looks. Well, as to that part of the puzzle, to achieve what I now intended to do would require me to exert all the yrium and act like an emperor who knew what he wanted and was determined to have it.

San W'Watchun provided first class hospitality and joined us for the evening meal. Again we went over Cuisar's promises. The Flutubium was safely secreted somewhere. My actions now depended on that situation remaining intacta. W'Watchun's Wall continued in being, serving its vital purpose. "I'm off south to Tolindrin," I said. "First thing in the morning."

The alacrity with which Fweygo agreed to accompany me suggested he took his role about this emperor nonsense as ordered by the Everoinye with the utmost seriousness.

Straight after the first breakfast we set off in *Red Ruin*. The remberees were shouted up as we rose from the flat roof. I pushed the control levers hard over and we soared away into the brilliance of a fine morning on Kregen with Zim and Genodras shining in ruby and emerald glory all about us.

Inscrutable Kildoi Fweygo! He was clearly becoming more than a trifle unsettled about his relationship with me. On the one hand there was this directive he'd received from the Star Lords to assist me in any way possible to ensure I was accepted as the Emperor of All Paz, the Emperor of Emperors. On the other was this feeling he so strongly held that he was the fellow in charge of our partnership.

As to the latter, I held warm and comradely feelings about the loveable way my kregoinye comrades Pompino and Mevancy had treated me. By Vox! What would it be to have them here now to adventure along with Fweygo and myself! And then I shuddered at the prospect!

In due course we reached Oxonium. That marvelous city perched on its fantastic islands with the deep runnels between still looked forlorn. The damage wrought showed as ugly scars among the buildings. Many of the towers supporting the cableways between the hills had been rebuilt and the cars journeyed from hill to hill. But many black areas of desolation made the heart ache for so much wanton destruction! Here the ibmanzies had done their dastardly work.

"We see the Hyr Kov Brannomar first," I told Fweygo. "Then we tell King Tom what time of day it is."

"They know this Khon the Mak, then?"

"Oh, aye. They ken him well."

More lifters and ovverers than I'd expected soared above the city. Evidences of rebuilding showed in scaffolding clothing many of the buildings. By Krun! I'd had my fill of scaffolding!

"I shall need to go to the Shrine of Cymbaro." I didn't tell Fweygo why this was necessary. "The Vallian Ambassador here is a good friend. He'll help us."

How, I wondered with a strange sense of levity intruding on my somber thoughts, was the worthy ambassador getting along with our Veda?

A soft blueness washed up within the lifter. I stared. Fweygo's form dimmed and wavered in the obscuring blue. Automatically I looked up. The Giant Blue Scorpion of the Star Lords had stolen surreptitiously upon us. In a twinkling everything turned blue. Fweygo vanished. The cold rush of ghostly winds blustered about me.

In the next instant, up I went. The Scorpion enfolded me.

The blueness drained away into total darkness. My feet hit an uncarpeted floor and I staggered forward for a moment before catching my balance. The sweet smell of flowers filled the air.

A voice spoke. "Dray Prescot! What are you about?"

The moment was fraught with danger. The absolute necessity of keeping my temper and not allowing fury to overwhelm me must govern my actions and words. "Sorting out Balintol."

"There is a Prism of Power unresolved." The whispering voice of the Star Lord penetrated the darkness like a rapier blade.

"It is hidden, I am told, so safely that no one can find it."

"You are told. That remains to be seen."

One of those ominous silences followed. If the Star Lords had hauled me up here, wherever here was this time, to check on my progress, then let them ask outright. They could be devious and they could be forthright. Let them realize the implications—if they could.

They asked in the end and I spelled it out carefully. To my astonishment they answered at once. "But, Dray Prescot, be quick!"

The transition followed swiftly. Blueness snatched me up, whirled me headlong through coldness, slapped me down on cobbles. The streaming mingled lights of the Suns of Scorpio brightened all about. I knew instantly where I was.

On one side the waters of the Great Northern Cut sparkled in the light. On the other the inn and posting house, The Rose of Valka, stood with its doors open to welcome me back. Young Bargom, still called young despite he no longer was, stepped outside his inn door, saw me, opened eyes and mouth incredibly wide, started in a-yelling, and rushed at me with open arms.

"Strom! Lahal and Lahal!"

He pumped my hand as though drawing water for a city's inns. "Jen! Strom!"

Well, after all this uproar other Valkan patrons tumbled out all agape. The fresh air filled with excitement. One new and ugly factor intruded on this happy scene. I said: "The Flags of Death are flying on all the masts. Who?"

They sobered at once. "The Lord Farris."

This news struck me cruelly. Farris! Utterly loyal to Delia, a friend over many and many a season, he ran the Vallian Air Service with crisp and humane efficiency. And now the kaotreshes flew.

All over Vondium the Proud City the kaotreshes flew for the Lord Farris.

After a suitable time of talking and drinking with these Valkans I went up to the palace. I was dressed decently and I gave my face a twist on the way so as not to be delayed. The place was quiet. Even when Inch and Sasha greeted me we spoke in low tones. Delia was there. She had been crying. I clasped her and we could not speak.

"Well, my old dom, I am glad to see you, especially at so unhappy a time."

"Seg!"

They were all there. All these splendid friends I'd made during my time on Kregen. The family were there. Even Zeg and Miam had flown in from Zandikar. Lela and Tyfar had come from Hamal. Lildra accompanied Jaidur from Hyrklana; but Delia said sadly that things were not as right as they might be with them. Velia and Didi were now strapping maidens, Sisters of the Rose, dedicated. And, of course, Dayra, Ros the Claw, arrived late and in full fighting kit of the Sisters of the Rose: rapier, main gauche, whip and Claw in its bag.

Turko and Korero joined us. When I greeted Korero I saw how alike and yet different he was from Fweygo. In truth we made a somber party.

Our comrade Wizards of Loh, apart from Rollo, were fully occupied in their arcane otherworlds. They'd put in an appearance at the funeral as apparitions.

At last the Emperor and Empress of Vallia arrived.

Silda, too, had been crying. I said to Drak: "I did not know Farris was dead. I came to Vondium to see you on a matter of urgent policy. We'll discuss it after the funeral."

The funeral of the Lord Farris was a most impressive ceremony.

The avenues were thronged with folk. The procession stretched a good dwabur in length. The canals were choked with boats. The air blackened with the fliers and flyers of Farris's Air Service. Every aspect of the day of mourning went through impeccably.*

Because Farris had been a warrior, afterwards we held a proper noumjiksirn for him. We sent him off on his journey through the clinging Mists

---

* Here Prescot gives long detailed lists of everyone who was at the funeral. Lord Farris, remember, was one of the early converts to Prescot through his loyalty to Delia. Farris was taken up in the newly constructed skyship *Empress Silda* because he'd been a sailor before he'd become an airman and ceremoniously dropped from the skyship over the ocean for a burial at sea. *A.B.A.*

and through the Ice Floes of Sicce, and trusted to Opaz he would reach the Sunny Uplands beyond.

Now, of course, the various regiments of the emperor's juruk featured in a special way in all this. You know the lads. You know how they would greet their Kendur. Mind you, Drak as the current emperor received their total loyalty. All the same...

When, at last, I was able to be closeted with Drak and Delia and Seg and a few other close comrades, Drak told me that he'd been running the army down. "Well," I grunted. "I may have work for some of my—I mean our—choice regiments."

I told him what I planned and he nodded gravely. In that instant he was the emperor and I a supplicant; not son and father.

He agreed, as I knew he would. He knew how to mend his neighbor's fence, as they say on Kregen. Of course, Seg as the King of Croxdrin and Emperor of Pandahem, wasn't going to be left out. So Inch, as the King of Hyr-Thoth-Ghat-Loh, stoutly declared neither would he. Zeg, regretfully, shook his head. Jaidur couldn't contain his impatience and promised that Hyrklana would be represented.

"Y'know," said Inch at some point in the discussion. "Much as I enjoy going off adventuring with you, Dray, I really don't like leaving Sasha."

At this, Jaidur made a little kecking sound in his throat.

Seg said: "Milsi—" and stopped. Then he added: "It is so odd that I've long since given up trying to fathom it out. I detest every minute that I'm not with Milsi. Yet I joy in going off adventuring with you, my old dom. Strange."

Yes, I said to myself. Dear old Seg! It must clearly be far more difficult for him than me. I had no choice in being parted from Delia. When the Everoinye send their Giant Blue Scorpion, well, dom, it's up you go and no argument!

Agreements being reached it was completely inevitable that I spend an uproarious evening with my lads of the guard corps. These great kampeons drank to moderation and sang inordinately. We had 'The Maid with the Single Veil' and 'The Last Portion of Pie.' For some of the chiefs of the Phalanx who'd joined us we had: "The Brumbyte in the Ranks.' Of course and naturally, we had "No Idea At All, At All, No Idea At All"—accompanied by gales of laughter.

Walking quietly back to the palace and bidding them all remberee, I went up the private stairs and entered what was a familiar room, to find it smothered in blueness.

The Star Lords had given me my time. Now they called me back to Balintol and to work.

Fifteen

From the chill and confusion of whatever otherwhere it was that the Star Lords sent me through, I saw the outlines of *Red Ruin* form about me. Fweygo had arrived first and now he straightened up as the last of the blue vanished. His strong Kildoi face took on a look first of surprise, then of questioning, and finally of alarm.

"It's all right," I said, very quickly. "You did not know him. He was a very old and dear friend." For, of course, I still wore the mourning clothes proper to the time of death. And, equally of course, I carried my arsenal of weapons girded about me.

After I'd sketched out my doings in Vallia, saying that it had been extraordinarily pleasant to see the family again despite the sadness of the occasion, Fweygo said he'd seen his family too. They did well and prospered up there in Kildrin, which pleased me. We both saw that he'd been thus occupied whilst I finalized the business.

The lifter swung over the runneled city of Oxonium. Much rebuilding had been carried on and many of the cable cars were running again. We touched down in the courtyard of the Vallian embassy.

After the ultra-efficient guards passed us Elten Larghos Invordun bustled up, smiling, holding out his hand. "Lahal, Drajak!" Then, abruptly, he checked himself. "You went to the funeral?"

"Aye."

"A sad loss, a sad loss." He looked at Fweygo.

So I made the pappattu and the next instant a girl glowing with health and beauty ran across the grass managing to shed most of her shamlak in her haste. She hauled the garment over one rounded shoulder. "Drajak!"

"Lahal, Veda. You are well now?"

She did not fling herself into my arms, because that was not Veda's way with men for whom, I believed, she still had a distaste and a distrust. But I gathered she was pleased to see me again.

Fweygo stared at her and the pappattu was made and we all went up into the embassy for a slap up meal. There was news to impart.

During the course of the conversation I told Elten Larghos what I intended to do. He nodded sagely giving it as his opinion that fighting men needed to be employed and that Vallia seemed to be acquiring the burden of responsibility. When I said I'd require the little juruk I'd brought here the last time, he agreed. I'd been paying them so that the general directive that Vallia did not employ mercenaries was not breached.

Truth to tell, he went on, his own cook, Master Ornol the Roasts, did not get on with Master Nath the Ham. "You cannot have two cooks sharing the same kitchen," and he shook his head.

After the meal and a trifle of rest I shifted into new simple clothes, a dark blue shamlak, and declared I was off to see Hyr Kov Brannomar. Instantly the Vallian ambassador said he would go too.

Fweygo, evidently not wishing to be seen to be left out, agreed to the suggestion. Veda pouted, pulled up a shoulder strap, and bade Elten Larghos be careful. I hid a smile. These two, then, against all odds, it might appear, were approaching an understanding.

Well, by Vox, and the best of Vallian luck to the pair of 'em!

We did not make the journey by cable car but flew across in *Red Ruin*. I told Fweygo that Elten Larghos and Hyr Kov Brannomar both knew my identity but used Drajak. I added: "I may have to sound more like a pompous and overbearing emperor than I like. But I do not anticipate any resistance from Brannomar. He runs all Tolindrin for King Tom, and is a fine man of sense."

We were ushered into one of Brannomar's smaller reception rooms with due protocol. King Tom was there visiting Brannomar, so that was useful. Refreshments were brought, privacy secured, and I told the Tolindrinese what I intended.

Still a novice in the matters of kingship, Tom glanced at Brannomar. He nodded and said: "I thank you, majister. I am sure the king will agree without hesitation. The treaty, as you know only too well, was held up. Hyr Kov Khonstanton—"

"Him!" broke in Fweygo, and immediately fell to silence.

King Tom laughed. "I see your friend has met Khon the Mak."

We explained the situation of the Prisms of Power. Yet, despite the protestations of Cuisar, I still felt uneasy.

With many good wishes the little meeting closed. Little it might well be; it held tremendous significance for the future of Balintol. That meant, by Krun, it held significance for the future life of a poor wight called Dray Prescot upon the marvelous world of Kregen. If this scheme was not accepted, the Star Lords would be most unhappy, most, by the dripping nose and mucus-clogged eyeballs of Makki Grodno!

The ambassador said he'd have the necessary papers drawn up at once for the signatures of King Tom and the Emperor Drak. Feeling we had accomplished something of importance, we took our leave. As we parted I reminded the Tolindrinese that the agreements cut both ways. They nodded. They understood that well enough.

So *Red Ruin* took to the air once more. I dropped Fweygo and Larghos at the embassy and then flew off for the Shrine to Cymbaro.

The twin suns shone pleasantly and I fancied the priests of Cymbaro might offer some light refreshments. They were what is called a Good Bunch and if all the damned Dokerty lovers could be converted then Balintol would be a far happier place.

A swift shadow—the two shadows of Kregen, red and green—fleeted across the voller.

Now what did the Gdoinye want, for the sweet sake of Sana Fayroa? I glanced up. The surprise I felt was genuine. Up there, turning its head from side to side to observe me as it planed in lazy circles, soared a bird black as midnight. Only its beak and claws relieved that somber darkness. They gleamed sharply with the metallic sheen of gold.

As I gaped up at this strange raptor, a fleeting flash of scarlet and gold streaked through the air. The Gdoinye drove with obvious utter determination into the dark intruder. For a moment a wild melee of flapping wings and shattering squawks cavorted above my head. The two powerful birds were of a size and they were fighting with the utmost savagery.

"Come on, Gdoinye! Come on, you great onker! Get him!" I yelled with all the fervor of a spectator in the Jikhorkdun, urging on his favorite kaidur. "Slice the cramph up! Hack 'n' Slay!"

If the Gdoinye heard I knew not. If he took any notice I didn't know. But a swift passage was followed by a shower of black feathers. Shades of the Black Chyyan! The screeching shrilled viciously into the bright air. The wings whirled, claws struck, beaks stabbed.

Immediately the black bird broke free and rose on heavily beating pinions. It glared down with its head on one side. The beats strengthened, the tail whisked around, and the bird soared high and higher against the twin suns. The Gdoinye did not follow. He twitched his head to regard me, then he, too, soared away and vanished in the blue.

"By the stupendous belly and monumental thighs of the Divine Madam of Belschutz! What was all that about?"

Bending, I picked up a dull black feather from the deck of *Red Ruin*. I regarded it blankly and turned it over in my fingers. So the damned bird was real, then, and not another illusion.

Rather soberly after this strange and unsettling occurrence I continued my flight over the Hills of Oxonium to the Shrine of Cymbaro.

When I stepped out of the lifter in the flower-bordered courtyard a priest I didn't know greeted me with a grave Llahal. In the middle of my reply I was aware of a hurtling shape in the corner of my eye. A canny old leem-hunter reacts first and possibly thinks afterwards. I dodged sideways and span around. A lithe vigorous form all arms and legs leaped on me, shrilling: "Drajak! Drajak!"

Disentangling myself and holding him off at arm's length, I said: "Dimpy! You imp from Sicce's Gates!"

Well, we had a right old reunion. He'd grown and fleshed out; he was still a lively young scamp. Naturally, I asked after Tiri. Young Lady Tirivenswatha remained at the mysterious seminary of Farinsee. Her studies went along apace and her tutor, Mistress Janetha, confided privately to Dimpy that her powers within the religion of Cymbaro were becoming more formidable every day.

A delicate question about their relationship elicited the information that Tiri was devoted to Cymbaro and was highly unlikely ever to marry. As for Dimpy, he'd parted company with Princess Nandisha on the friendliest of terms and thought of becoming a priest of Cymbaro. At this I expressed complete surprise. He laughed and said he'd rather changed his opinion of religions and some people since leaving the gang-infested runnels between the Hills. However, he was not cut out for the task, the acolyte's ways too restricting. Anyway, the priests said he was too rumbustious a youngster. So, he was looking—

"Well, now," I said, trying to look judicial. "We'll see."

He smiled, completely confident in his young raffish ways.

The priest, San Drefendo, offered the expected refreshments, and we walked cheerfully through the cloisters in animated conversation. An abrupt flicker of silver in my eye broadened swiftly into this vibrating silver star that so plagued me of late.

I brushed an annoyed hand over my eyes, shaking my head.

A quick, puzzled expression flitted over Dimpy's young mischievous face. "What—?"

"Nothing," I spoke sharply.

The change in Dimpy was startling. He swiveled to regard me. His eyes opened. "Yes," he said, on a breath. "He's here."

He stared at me. "Tiri says you look well." He paused and smiled and went on: "She says you have the most complicated and devious mind she has yet run across."

"Tiri!" I spoke like a loon. "The silver star! That is Tiri—"

"Yes. She's working on it. She'll get through one day."

In the wonderful and terrible world of Kregen apparently impossible things happen. Magic is not a matter of party tricks. Here, though, young Tiri was using the power of religion to contact us. Did she, I wondered, use the same otherworldly place through which her messages travelled as the sorcerers. Perhaps each discipline or religion utilized its own little piece of occultism?

As though echoing my thoughts, San Drefendo told me that the means Tiri used were quite different from the kharrna of a mage. As we sat in the airy refectory enjoying homely and satisfying refreshments, I could not help but reflect how this contrasted with the deep mysteries of Kregen. I suppose I had grown a little used to magic during my time here; but these sorcerers and divines could never be taken for granted. The sheer uncanniness of it all, the unease felt subconsciously, the very deeds they could so eerily perform—oh, no, life on Kregen was very definitely not like life on Earth!

Eventually Dimpy got his way and when I said the remberees he shouldered his kit wrapped in a blanket at the end of a stick and boarded the lifter. He remembered to perform the fantamyrrh when he climbed in, and that pleased me.

After the catastrophes that had swept Oxonium, flying craft of any description were hard to come by. The Vallian Ambassador had a considerable amount of what the folk in Clishdrin would call clout. He obtained a fine lifter for us capable of taking a pastang of swods—of course he had to pay considerably over the odds, that was understood.

The lads of the little guard I'd created were glad to see me and even more glad to be flying off to do something—even if they had no idea what that something might be. We flew off the next day. *Red Ruin* led with Fweygo, Dimpy and myself aboard. The new voller, *Dani's Delight*, followed carrying the guard.

The silver star did not put in an appearance. Tiri might well categorize my mind as complicated and devious. The plan I was now engaged upon was simple-minded. What I was doing was so obvious I understood only too well why I hadn't done it before. This was a matter of pride in reverse. Because I so detest all this pomp surrounding the trade of being an emperor I'd shrunk from using the paraphernalia of a ruler's resources. Telling Fweygo I was damn well going to be an emperor and to be seen being an emperor was all very well. Now, by Vox, I was actually doing that. I was in it up to my neck!

These morose reflections actuated my actions when we reached the outskirts of Prebaya, capital of Caneldrin.

Orders were given to the lads to find a comfortable inn. Fweygo and Dimpy would wait with them. There were protests. These I quashed with the arrogance of your dyed-in-the-wool emperor.

Then, dressed smartly and with my weaponry about me, I went off to see the Lady Quensella.

Oh, yes! She might very well wish to claw my eyes out. One ugly fact remained very certain. This was going to be a most awkward and uncomfortable interview. She'd offered herself and her position and been refused. Her fury at being scorned, as she saw it, might render my plan utterly useless the moment we met.

Well, by the pustular pendulous backside and diseased deformed nose of Makki Grodno! I'd damned well go and find out!

Sixteen

I, Dray Prescot, Vovedeer, Lord of Strombor and Krozair of Zy, do not now and never have professed to be superior to any of my fellows. Oh, sure, I've accomplished many fanciful things; but then, I've failed many times, as you know. Going up to her palace to meet the Lady Quensella my mind drifted off to other subjects. Quensella and her twin sister, the regent, Lady C'Chermina, did not get on.

There was absolutely no doubt in my mind that in my friends I'd been blessed above all the riches of Kregen. Seg Segutorio was the finest blade comrade a fellow could ever hope for. Considering the enmity between Quensella and C'Chermina here reminded me how beautifully Seg's wife, Milsi, Queen of Croxdrin and Empress of Pandahem, got on with her step-daughter, Silda, Empress of Vallia, Drak's wife. They loved each other as mother and daughter should. Yet I knew Silda did not forget her real mother, Thelda—ah, Thelda who always meant well!

This then recalled painfully to me what Delia hinted at regarding The King and Queen of Hyrklana. Jaidur, my youngest lad, and Lildra were experiencing difficulties in their marriage. All I could do was hope that this ugly situation would sort itself out. I knew only too well how he, Vax Neemusbane, would resent any word from me and flare up like an exploding volcano.

In that situation I felt helpless. Here, with the feuding twin sisters to deal with I had an altogether different situation to face. A sigh escaped my lips, to my surprise. I'd just have to be this big, arrogant, overbearing emperor I'd promised Fweygo.

Mind you, whilst I was fully aware that one should hate the crime and not the criminal, as so often I'd tried to do in the past, with some of the so-called evil characters I'd met on Kregen that task was all-fired difficult. The problem, as San Blarnoi says, is rather like carrying a block of ice through the Furnace Fires of Inshurfraz.

Before reaching the modish villas and palaces along the river one had to pass through poorer areas. How many of these poor folk had fallen on hard times through the villainy of others? Further on the beggars congregated at corners, bowls at the ready, pitiful arms outstretched. One could never become hardened to these unpleasant sights; yet I felt there were less beggars than I'd seen before. In addition, there were fewer soldiers moving about their business in the city. Quensella's palace appeared ahead and, mentally hitching up my sword, I strode straight for the main gate.

A powerful Hytak in the fancy armor provided by the Lady Quensella standing guard grounded his halberd and said: "Hai, Jik! Lahal! You are well met!"

"Lahal, Ornol," I replied. "Good to see you."

So—there was no difficulty in actually getting into the palace. The lady's new guard had been recruited by the chiefs of her old guard, which was now mine. Lucky chance dictated that one of the few new swods I knew stood sentry duty at the right time.

Word went ahead and in no time at all I stood in the antechamber to Quensella's private apartments. Through those ornate doors, the last distressing time I'd seen her, had taken place a ludicrous yet distasteful scene I did not care to dwell on.

The major domo, Tral the Strict, even more fat and waddling, showed me in with a look of contempt he did little to conceal.

Well, she looked healthy. She did not rise from the couch as I entered. She was the great lady, languid, a silken scarf trailing from slender fingers, her whole attitude one of graciousness and nobility. She would listen to what lesser people had to say.

She wore a blue lounging shamlak of dazzling cut. Her features remained calm; but two straight dark lines cut her forehead between her eyebrows. Oh, yes, by Vox; she was a coiled spring ready to unleash all her fury and resentment.

We spoke politely with the lahals and she offered refreshments. Pointedly, she did not ask me to sit down.

"I am surprised you have the—that you have come back."

Her breast remained calm; but as we spoke two spots of fire rose in her cheeks. Then, because, I suppose, poor girl, she couldn't help it, she said on a breath: "You have come back to me!"

Very gravely, I disillusioned her. Now, at any moment she could yell for her guards and order my head off. She had that power. The situation, despite its polite icing, was fraught in the extreme. "I am here on political matters."

She slumped back on the couch. Her lower lip thrust forward and up, overlapping her upper lip. She twisted the silk in her fingers. Then: "Politics! You—you know what you did to me!"

That, of course, was the trouble, by Krun! I'd done nothing to her when she'd panted, begging, at my feet. "You know my position. I would value you as a friend—"

"Friend!" Abruptly she sat up and now the movement of her breast became agitated. Her face glowed. In the next instant she'd yell for the guards. She waved her hand before her face, the silk trailing like a comet's tail. "You—you beast! I offered you—Now you come here prattling about politics!"

"Many dangers exist—"

"True! Too true! You refuse me—why should I not have them take your head off, and mount it on my bedroom wall? Hey?"

Patiently, I went on: "The needs of Caneldrin—"

"Oh, do stop this nonsense!" She stood up and began to pace about. Yes, she did look like a great cat, feline and deadly. "What do you know of politics? A paktun. One I made my cadade! You would do well to leave to your betters things that do not concern you."

That, of course, was the way these great ones of the world considered their inferiors. She saw nothing ill in that.

In a voice as sharp as I intended I began to spell out the situation. All the time I was fully aware of this dark fury within me waiting to flare out in destructive wrath. I had to control that!

I told her that I bore a diplomatic message for the regent. I needed safe conduct in to see C'Chermina. She, the Lady Quensella, would provide me with that.

She tossed her head and that petty gesture heartened me for I took it as a sign that she was listening. "Why should I?"

"Simply, for the good of all Balintol."

"A diplomatic message?" She stopped pacing about. "Who sends this message? And why should you carry it?"

"I carry it because I am trusted."

She sniffed at that. "Well? Go on, you hulu, who?"

"The Emperor of Vallia."

"Ah!"

She caught the silken scarf to her throat. "Vallia!"

"You knew I was Vallian? Surely?"

She brushed that away with a vague gesture. "Since you prate about politics—you must know—The Vallese wanted to ally with the Tolindrinese—but that failed." She turned on me swiftly. "You know what the message is? You must tell me, Drajak!"

"Oh, it's no secret. If you invade any lands of Balintol the Vallians will support them. Equally, if you are invaded, we will support you."

Her eyes were wide. She licked her lips. "Yes, yes. I see that. That will make my dear sister writhe in torment. Ha!"

With a sudden shift of mood she eyed me as a leem might stare at a ponsho. Again she licked her lips. "Why should I believe you? It doesn't make sense. The Vallian ambassador would—he'd go to C'Chermina—why you? All this secrecy? Well?"

I made a small dismissive gesture. "That was the way it worked out. The ambassador will present the full treaty in due course."

There was no doubt about her state of mind. She was a simmering volcano ready to blow everything apart. Yet I sensed a change in her. All her desires had been set on passion: now she began to scheme in different avenues of ambition. What I had told her made a difference. The look she gave me now was more like a usurer sizing up a prospective victim with a tidy calculation of interest to charge.

"You are privy to Vallia?"

She'd wrapped it up; what she meant was—was I aware of Vallian secrets, was I in the know. I told her I was merely acting for the emperor. She bit her lip at this and went on another tack.

Flinging herself on the couch she bade me sit down. The little gilt over-stuffed chair was not comfortable; but I sat down.

Remember, she was a great lady. Her twin sister was the regent. Certainly, ambition flowered in her breast.

In the end she got down to brass tacks. She could offer me nothing more than she already had, and which I had refused. But would I assist her? It could be done. There were many fighting men ready to serve her. The plot, if familiar, could be useful, mightily useful by Krun!

What she did not know was that if I failed in all these intrigues my punishment would be to be hurled back to Earth, four hundred light years away. There I'd rot until the Star Lords decided they needed me again in their unfathomable schemes.

Saying that I'd have to think on this, as it touched on honor, I managed to satisfy her that, at the least, I remained a friend.

"If your sister is foolish enough—should she—well, then perhaps it would be better for all Balintol, and therefore all Paz."

"I trust you with grave matters, Drajak."

Sink me! I felt very sorry for her. Extremely sorry.

She was besotted with me, which caused me to feel highly uncomfortable, by Krun. Here was I, as she thought, a mere paktun, yet she wanted me to assist her in the highest affairs of state. Clever and manipulative as she was, only a woman blinded by passion could be so foolhardy.

Naturally, as an old leem hunter, I wasn't that gullible. I'd have to be doubly on guard. This could all be her little scheme to get even with me, for a woman scorned is very very dangerous. She could involve me in her plot and then denounce me as a treasonous rogue. Her sadistic triumph would be complete in my degradation and execution.

After all, here was a lady who had hired Schrepims as assassins to wreak her vengeance on those who had offended her.

We talked some more. Our conversation so far had been peppered with non-sequiturs; now and with growing freedom Quensella spelled out her ambitions. They had been stifled in her younger days. Now they broke out overweeningly.

As for arranging the meeting between C'Chermina and me, well, that figured largely in her schemes. The arrangements would take time, as they always do in courts caught up in the fog of intrigues, but Quensella saw the meeting as the starting point of her plot.

She did not fling herself at me again, with her clothes half off draggling along the carpets. She held out her hand, which I shook instead of kissing.

She assumed a regal pose of icy hauteur when Tral the Strict was summoned to show me out. He didn't like me, remembering a certain lesson in politeness I'd given him—free of charge.

"Until tomorrow, Drajak the Sudden! Remberee."

"Remberee, my lady."

Outside in the streets the town was buzzing. People ran and shouted the news. The excitement smoked on the air. The great day had dawned. The glorious regent, the Lady C'Chermina, had struck.

The news chilled and gripped me as though the Ice Winds of Gundarlo blew piercingly through to my heart, lacerating hope.

C'Chermina had at last given the order. The troops of Caneldrin were now marching south, a great army invading Tolindrin, a mighty host sweeping on to victory.

What price treaties now?

Seventeen

I said to the Emperor of Vallia: "It's pointless you coming over here yourself. That's what you have generals for." I looked at the Empress of Vallia. "Tell him, Silda, for the sweet sake of the Lady Dulshini!"

My lad Drak set his jaws firmly. He was as stubborn as a calsany when he set his mind to it. Silda knew this well enough, so she approached the problem from a different direction. We sat in the Vallian embassy in Oxonium, capital of Tolindrin, with our armies camped outside and the aerial forces taking on stores. Brannomar welcomed us with open arms and put his own forces in order.

"C'Chermina has lost the services of Prince Ortyg. She has no ibmanzies. The business should not take long." Thus spake Drak.

Now in the normal course of affairs when kings and emperors travel about they do so with colossal pomp and circumstance. Think of some of the high and mighty rulers I've known on Kregen. My Val! They took with them on their journeys people, tents and equipment to make up a whole city.

My lad Drak took after me, at least, in this one aspect. He wasn't exactly incognito; but he had only a small staff and lived with military frugality. Silda matched him in this. And, of course, there was another aspect in which he took after me, the desire to go off adventuring. For all his gravity he loved to get away from the protocol of court life. Silda, therefore, was torn between two desires.

"Jaidur and Inch will arrive in a few days—" Silda broke off what she was saying, shook her head, and relapsed to silence.

"Precisely!" said Drak with a growl. "I'm staying!"

"In that case," I said. "I might return to Prebaya."

"That's a capital notion, my old dom! I'd like to see what these two fractious sisters are like."

"Oh, aye, Seg. They're a right pair, by Vox!"

My blade comrade rubbed his hands together and gave it as his opinion that he would be able to collect many first rate songs up in the central and northern parts of Balintol. His latest project was the compilation of a hyr lif containing the local songs of many regions about Kregen. A remarkable man, Seg Segutorio, and no mistake!

We did not prattle idly. Decisions had to be taken, and they were. Messengers came in with reports and went out with orders.

In the accepted pattern of opening a campaign, C'Chermina's generals sent off their flying elements to scout forward. We replied and checked them here and there, and there and here they broke through. The likely routes of their advances were calculated and plotted onto the campaign maps. When the forces drew nearer then we'd mark up the battle maps. In all this busy activity I tried to hold aloof.*

As the emperor, Drak must run affairs, in conjunction with the Hyr Kov Brannomar of Tolindrin.

Preparations continued and contingents marched out with bands playing and banners waving. On a bright morning I wanted to show young Dimpy a few more sword tricks, for he was learning apace. The young scamp was nowhere to be found. Exasperated, I wondered if he'd gone off with the troops for what he might consider an adventure. Like any youngster of spirit he thirsted for renown.

Later that day, towards the setting of the suns, he turned up. In answer to my somewhat intemperate question he told me he'd been down in the warrens between the Hills, revisiting old friends.

"Hmph," I grumped. "Well, fetch your rudis and I will knock a few lessons into you."

As agile as an eel, quicksilver fast, he proved an apt pupil. When I'd let him pink me with his wooden point, we flopped down to partake of ale, and a thought occurred to me. "Nagzalla's Nasty Neemus," I said. "I ran with that gang for a time, as you know. I think I'll pay 'em a visit. By Reder, yes!"

Dimpy merely said that was a good idea and that he'd come down with me. He was puzzled by my position within the embassy, although having

---

* Prescot gives a comprehensive Battle Order for all the forces. The lists of names are impressive. He indicates that the old guard corps regiments like ESW, EYJ, EFB, ELC, etc. were reserved under his hand. *A.B.A.*

no knowledge of the high level meetings. He just accepted me at face value, as Drajak the Sudden, who was a good friend and mentor.

When I asked Silda for news of Delia she told me that the Sisters of the Rose were involved. So, salut! I could ask no more.

The combined armies were undoubtedly an impressive force. Everybody had something to do. Without Delia, I felt very much out of it all. Inch had gone off north as part of the forward strategy.

The long sunny days of Kregen appeared to me longer than ever and less sunny. Down with the gangs in the warrens would tone up my spirit.

"Come on, my old dom! You look as though you've lost a zorca and found a calsany."

"Aye, Seg, aye."

At my information that I intended to go down and revisit Nagzalla's Nasty Neemus, Seg brightened up. He'd heard me speak of them and now nothing would satisfy him but that he must come along too.

After the earthquakes and the ibmanzies and the fires, the city of Oxonium was still in poor case. Yes, the ruins were being cleared away and fresh buildings rose to replace the destroyed; still, the place had a long way to go yet. Food and provisions of all sorts had to be brought in by the services of Vallia and Hamal and Hyrklana. The warrens, then, opined Seg, couldn't be much worse. "Ha!" I said. "You wait!"

We were sitting in a private snug and Seg went on polishing up a new bowstave. Well, that remark is totally unnecessary. When was Seg not building a new bow? Now, though, there were these songs. "They do sing down there, don't they?"

"Aye."

Seg rubbed contentedly. "Excellent!"

Interestingly enough, whilst Dimpy treated me as a kind of uncle figure, a friendly furry fellow, he held Seg Segutorio in undoubted awe. Seg was a king and emperor along with the other rulers here. In the way of young feckless rascals he didn't bother his head over things beyond his immediate purlieus. What pleased me more was to see that Dimpy's respect for my blade comrade originated more from Seg's prowess with the Great Lohvian Longbow than for the regal side of him.

So, suitably kitted out in dark colored tunics and with our Kregish arsenal of weapons about us, we descended into the warrens. After the riots when the gangs had pillaged the upper city, order had been restored and the relationship between the Hills and the warrens was more or less back to what it had been. There was no need to traipse through the secret tunnels. Keeping clear of the restored Kataki Watch would be our major problem.

"By Erthyr the Bow!" declared Seg, hands on hips, staring about on the lurid scenes, "this place is ripe!"

Now of course Seg had much the same trouble as myself in avoiding the best intentions of his people. We'd both had to sneak off. A bet I wouldn't take was that no one of our various guards followed us.

Looking about warily just in case, I found myself reflecting oddly enough, just why I was doing this instead of going off to see the Lady Quensella. Not without a mention of Makki Grodno, I came to the somber conclusion that this was preferable to skullduggery with the lady who could prove she was no lady—with the point of an assassin's dagger. Talk about frying pan and fire, by Krun!

Seg's descriptive of the runnels was accurate—they were ripe to a richness of ripeness that filled the nostrils and scorched the back of the throat. "Remember," I told my companions. "Down here I am Kadar the Hammer."

Evidences of the aftermath of the catastrophic earthquake engineered by Khon the Mak's incompetent Wizard of Loh still encumbered the alleyways. Kov Brannomar had stepped in to assist the poor folk down here. That was as much political as humanitarian, naturally; it had the result of quietening things down considerably.

Still, down in the warrens cramped between the Hills quietness was a relative term. The place smoked with activity of all manner of dubious, mercenary and plain cupidity manifestations. We went on through these dens of iniquity ready to resist the seeking blade and the thrusting dagger.

Since Dimpy and my last visit to Nagzalla's Nasty Neemus there had been changes. People had been crushed in the earthquake and others had succumbed to the hectically lethal way of life and death down here. Brory the Bold still lived and he greeted us with a tankard in one hand and a dagger in the other. The pappattu was made with Seg who accepted the offered jar with relish. Before we settled down to a night's entertainment I tried to find out the state of play here. Brory would have none of that. His new wife had produced twins and he was inordinately proud of them—and of her. He'd given her a new name: Basalma the Beautiful and Bounteous.

We duly wetted the babies' heads. Since the time of the earthquake when the gangs had labored side by side, much enmity had evaporated between them. Not that, by Krun, they didn't still steal from one another and try to invade territory. But Brory said that, by Reder, the old viciousness had gone.

Sitting comfortably with a jar in my fist and getting ready for the singing session that would follow, I saw with concealed amusement and admiration Seg taking his writing tablet out. He was all ready to record any songs new to him.

A tiny flash of light splintered into the corner of my eye. The light gleamed turquoise.

Instantly, I turned my head. The turquoise light vanished.

Lopy the Lame produced a flute and Nath the Bellows strummed on his banjo-type instrument, a hummummba. A few chords introduced

"The Pits of Hell are Sweet because of my Loved One." Breaths were taken, mouths opened, everyone was ready to come in on the bar. A breeze passed silently across the assemblage. Absolute silence fell. A black-cloaked figure wearing a tall cylindrical black hat walked in through the door. Through the door.

At once, instantly, I guessed what dire news San W'Watchun brought. Our anticipation of disaster had become reality and now we faced absolute catastrophe.

Eighteen

Nath Javed—Nath the Impenitent, Old Hack 'n' Slay—said: "By Vox, Jak! Going adventuring again! Diashum! Indubitably magnificent!"

Seg bent a look on him that stopped the Impenitent in his tracks. "Ah—" he said, "Jak—I mean Drajak—"

"Quite." Seg turned that powerful handsome face of his away and went on as though there had been no interruption. "I agree entirely, my old Impenitent. But we do have more bodies with us now."

What my blade comrade said was perfectly true. The flier provided by the Vallian Air Service cut sweetly through the fresh Kregan air. With her flew a little armada of vollers scraped up from here and there carrying the volunteers. These folk came from a number of different sources and I had to hope they'd all get on, one lot with another. If they didn't, well, then, by Krun! I promised myself I'd sort 'em sharpish.

Dimpy clutched the rail and stared at the countryside rolling past beneath. He was still new enough to travel by lifter to relish the experience with all the thrills of a young lad. Still, to soar through the sweet Kregan air with Zim and Genodras shining away above casting down their streaming mingled lights of ruby and emerald is something to be savored—as I may have mentioned before.

Even at the height we were flying the intoxicating scents of flowers reached up and drenched the air with perfume. We'd left the Yellow Deserts of Caneldrin to the rear and now flew over Vaiwadrin, the Flower Country of Balintol. The Abley Mountains ahead would soon be in sight. Among those peaks and valleys lay our goal—Skull Crag.

When W'Watchun made his dramatic and ghostly appearance down in the warrens of Oxonium, our worst fears were realized. Now time was not on our side. Brory the Bold could not be dissuaded from coming with us. With him he brought a few choice members of the gang, Nagzalla's Nasty

Neemus. They thought it fashionable to call themselves the Three N's in these latter days. You could almost see their rascally fingers twitching at the thought of expected loot.

The twin suns slanted across the sky and Seg gave his opinion that we wouldn't make Skull Crag before nightfall.

Fweygo said: "That'll make no difference."

He was, of course, absolutely right. We were well equipped with the tools necessary for the task ahead. We flew in *Eregoin's Answer*, a fine roomy voller with powerful artillery. One of the following Vallian airboats was *Wenhartdrin's Cheer*, a perfectly appropriate name for her passengers. Oh, yes, by Vox! For she carried elements of my Guard Corps, volunteers from various regiments. Naturally, as everyone volunteered, the lucky swods were chosen by lot.

A somber reflection made me frown. Lucky? When we flew into dangers as dire as any that had plagued Kregen?

Well, by the Blade of Kurin, the lads would feel themselves supremely fortunate to be flying off to adventures with their Kendur! And to a Herrelldrin Hell with any thoughts of danger!

Nath Javed shared those sentiments to the full. He was now climbing the ranks within the Chuktar grade, yet he'd been overjoyed when my summons brought him away from his units up there in the forces challenging the regent C'Chermina's advance. He remembered the Coup Blag. That, of course, was why I'd invited him along.

As for the little juruk I'd created for Quensella and who now served me, they kept very quiet among themselves. My incognito wouldn't last at this rate, no, by Krun!

The directions given us by W'Watchun were, I'd assumed, specific enough. The suns sank in sheets of glory as the mountains came fully into view, their flanks lit luridly in deepest rose and glittering green. Only the few highest peaks carried caps of snow. Our target, we understood, lay on the flank of a lesser mountain. We should spot it because it jutted out, like a skull, hence its name, Skull Crag.

The last filaments of color washed from the sky. For a space before The Maiden with the Many Smiles rose a vague darkness shrouded the land. Stars pricked the vault above, their constellations very familiar to me now. Four hundred light years away the world of my birth rolled around its little yellow sun, and towed along its single silver moon. That speck of light in the galaxy was far too far away to be discerned.

"By the Resplendent Bridzilkelsh!" Brory gave vent to all his vigorous Brokelsh annoyance. "Where is the benighted place?"

"Benighted is right," observed Fweygo in his dry way.

Everyone peered into the pall of darkness. The place had to be down there somewhere, benighted or not.

Dimpy exclaimed: "There it is!" He pointed. Then, at once, yelped: "No! It isn't—that mountain's no skull."

A refulgent pink glow rose above the peaks and The Maiden with the Many Smiles beamed down, the moon's light picking out crevices and fissures, throwing the slopes of the mountains into high relief.

Old Hack 'n' Slay's face, staring out into the russet and vermilion stained shadows, looked as though cast from bronze. He spoke quietly to young Dimpy hanging on the rail. "To go off again with Jak the Bogandur and Seg the Horkandur! By Vox! I've prayed for the day!"

Dimpy said: "But Drajak, who you call Jak, is—"

"Tush, young fellow! He gives the orders. We act!" Nath Javed's tones were surprisingly gentle. "That is all you need to know."

"Well, I suppose so, by Ferzakl. But then, why have you got three names?"

Nath Javed heaved up a sigh full of mockery. "That, youngster, is another story!"

Other low-toned conversations went on aboard *Eregoin's Answer*; but every pair of eyes—except for Ob-Eye Larghos—stared hungrily overside at the wild peaks and mysterious valleys. I mentioned to myself the anatomical peculiarities of Makki Grodno, and immediately followed that by a fervid illumination of the massively grotesque bits and pieces of the Divine Madam of Belschutz. By All the Names! Skull Crag had to be down there somewhere, and we must find it instanter!

The time-honored custom of offering a gold piece to the first person to spot what we sought I'd considered and then rejected. That scheme smacked of the petty. Everyone was looking as hard as they could. All the same— So, just about to holler out that a fat gold piece was on offer for the first to spot Skull Crag, I shut my black-fanged winespout.

A roar from up for'ard—"There she is!" was followed by a whole chorus of folk bellowing that there, indeed, reared Skull Crag.

I did not breathe a sigh of relief. I'd been absolutely cold certain we'd find the damned place—and now we had.

A gossamer wisp of cloud passed across the face of the moon followed by thicker strands. The erratic lighting played games with the shadows of the mountain and gouged deep pits of blackness in the eyes of Skull Crag. Seg said in his non-committal voice: "Be tricky to land down there, my old dom." He took a breath. "If Delia were here, she'd do it with one hand in the air."

"Aye. But she's not." Silently, I added: "Thank Zair!"

Now your fussy and unpleasant kind of emperor might well have summoned the captain of *Eregoin's Answer*—Tyr Naghan ti Fromion—and apostrophized him on his duty to put us down safely. Questions would be asked about the competence of the pilot at the controls. Well, by Krun, I was an unpleasant enough fellow at times, although I suggest not a fussy one, so I took a turn down to the control cabin and poked my head in.

"Majister!" barked Tyr Naghan ti Fromion, and saluted in a casually smart fashion.

"Captain," I said, equably. "Please carry on."

"Quidang!"

So that dealt with that. We'd get down in one piece.

Then, of course, the old doubting Dray Prescot made me surmise that my appearance at the control cabin might well have given the pilot the jitters. Perhaps, trying to be subtle, I'd messed up. Oh, well, now we were in Ernithor the Quick's experienced hands on the control levers and, also, in the compassionate hands of Opaz.

As we descended cautiously the Maiden with the Many Smiles lifted in the star-spattered sky. The angles of shadows changed. The serrated mass of rock formed into the shape of a skull altered so that the stark outlines took on an appearance of heart-chilling malevolence.

"Ferzakl!" said Dimpy, on a breath.

The breeze died as we dropped lower shielded by the bulk of the mountain above. A strange silence wrapped us all. That eerie absence of normal sound continued until Seg in his powerful voice called out: "That skinny object reminds me I need a square meal."

The spell was broken. Chatter started about the decks. People looked almost shame-faced that they'd been so affected by a mere lump of unusually shaped rock. I said to myself: "Good old Seg!"

He was right, too. A good stuffing of grub before we set off—plus, a wet or three—would sustain us against the hardships and perils we were about to encounter within the catacombs.

We dropped lower and lower into the ominous shadows of the valley. The skull face towered over us as the pilot sought for a possible landing site. Looking at the scraped barrenness pitted by the eyesockets and nose cavity I felt the dark coil of black fury within me. That wrath must be contained; but the hateful skull brought return hatred so that I grasped the rail with clenched fists.

Conscious suddenly of Seg's quizzical gaze upon me, I tried to break the thrall of anger. We ought, I told my blade comrade, to take up his suggestion and have ourselves a sumptuous meal.

I refused to think the obvious—that this might be our last meal together upon the terrible if beautiful world of Kregen.

Eregoin's Answer hit with a rolling crash sending us swaying from our grips on the rail. One or two unlucky wights fell and toppled along the decks, to the raucous comments of their fellows. The lads were over their primeval fears and were back in good heart. The rest of the little armada touched down. Food and drink were taken. Weapons were checked. The delving equipment was brought out. We were ready—or as ready as we'd ever be—to face the horrors of Skull Crag.

The way in lay through the opened jaws.

Well, what else would you expect?

Also to be expected were the words carved above.

DESECRATION IS DEATH

This was not the flowery ritualistic curse so often found inscribed as warnings and threats to protect tombs. A dark chill emanated from those words. They meant what they said.

Because I was Dray Prescot I hitched up my swords, stuck out my chest, and stalked first into the opening. There was no bravado in this action. It was done because it was necessary to be done and seen to be done.

Quite a jostle for position took place at my back as the lads sought to be next into what many of them considered to be a hellish opening into destruction.

A light voice at my back, saying: "Keep your rotten torch out of my eyes, Nath!" made me whirl about in astonishment.

"What the blue blazes are you doing here, Veda?"

She laughed mischievously and hauled up a slipping strap. "I stowed away! D'you think I wasn't coming, then, Drajak?"

I shook my head. Women! Still, she'd been a Jikai Vuvushi and a good comrade. And she had a better reason to be here than most. She'd been a part of the ibmanzy programme.

Big Balla came across and nodded to Veda. "We'll do well."

I sighed. I wondered just how long it would take for the delectable Veda's clothes to fall off.

This little hiatus in our entry gave Brory the Bold and his rogues of Nagzalla's Nasty Neemus their chance. They were after loot. Like werstings on the trail they shot off along the tunnel leading in from the skeletal jaws. They did not rush on blindly. Every one of these scamps was a hardened gang member from the warrens. They did their job swiftly; they did it professionally. We followed.

The place smelled. As our lights picked out the crudely cut walls they revealed dancing motes in the close atmosphere, flecks which seemed to our heightened senses to carry odors. The prevailing smell was of grave dirt. Musky, tickling the throat, yet not over offensive, it was hardly a charnel stink. That appeared to us to smoke everywhere. Torches flaring and lamps swinging, we went on.

Quite a crowd of folk pushing along the tunnel meant some congestion ensued. Members of different groups felt it their right to walk along close to me, up front. About to halt and sort this stupid nonsense out, I halted all right, because Fweygo pointed, saying harshly: "There! That's the first!"

The headless body of a fighting man lay crumpled against the wall.

Torches picked out the gruesome details. Blood shone blackly.

The walls contained slots from which a blade had swung across, decapitating the unfortunate swod. "A Headclutcher!" Fweygo said. "Cut it off and snapped it away."

The throng milling around at my back now made too much noise. This was hardly the way to conduct a perilous adventure into catacombs, by Krun! A vigorous body pushed through, two massive shields held aloft above head height. The glorious golden Kildoi looked ferociously displeased. He wore armor, bristled with weapons, and he thumped the shields down with a crash. He stared at me meanly. "Here you are! I really can't have you creeping off like this, Dray—ah—Jak—! It's bad for my nerves."

"It's news to me you had any nerves, Korero."

In that moment the feeling in the atmosphere changed from comradely banter to a potentially apocalyptic conflict. The two Kildois stared one at the other. They stilled and stood as though graven. Slowly their tails lifted up, the hands clenched above their heads. As this ritual went on members of the various groups passed along, going past with curious glances, but pressing on into the mountain.

With slow deliberate movements the Kildois tail hands made gestures. Still with the same meaningful deliberation, carefully, the two hands came together, and clasped, and shook. Words were spoken, arcane phrases from long ago. Finally, two right hands extended and clasped. "Lahal, Korero." "Lahal, Fweygo."

So, that was all right, then, thank Zair!

Letting out a breath I managed to stop myself from saying with the utmost sarcasm: "Can we get on now, then?" What had passed between the two Kildois was part of their culture. That had to be respected.

Having Korero the Shield at my back is quite clearly a reassuring situation. If that hellish contraption, the Headclutcher, swished down to decapitate me it would be stopped slam-bang in its disgusting tracks by one or other of Korero's shields. All the same, by Vox! Didn't this just show up the difficulties my comrades made me suffer when I wanted to go adventuring on my own?

Fweygo said: "We'd best get on now." He glanced at the pitiful swod's body. "Khon will be having his difficulties getting through the catacombs."

Quite so. When San Cuisar the Oblifex gave San Quenlo the Sorcerer of the Cult of Almuensis the commission to protect the hidden Flutubium and its Prism of Power, the mage had stuffed this Skull Crag with traps, traps and more traps. Khon the Mak was having to fight through them up ahead. We stood a good chance of catching him before he could complete the task to ensure his life's ambition.

Contorted shadows fleeted along the walls as we went on. Echoes bounced. W'Watchun had said he thought the traitor was Narlin, the Dokerty priest who'd not been where he should have been. I did not think the who mattered. The damage had been done. Khon was deeper into Skull Crag than we were, battling his way through sorcery to reach the Prism of Power. I could only hope the traps would slow him up enough for us to catch him, the black cramph.

Whether or not San Quenlo's traps were affecting Khon I didn't know. They were certainly doing us no good. The tunnel opened into a chamber where torchlights pricked the gloom. At the entrance lay a body in a torn tunic, his insides outside, clasped in a steel fist.

At my expression Seg said: "D'you know him?"

"Aye. Naghan the Reckless. One of the Three N's."

"Why," put in Nath Javed, "wasn't this trap sprung before?"

As we went on that question assumed greater and greater importance. We lost men—good men. Through gloomy halls and dusty corridors in the flickering lights of torches and the swinging shadows thrown by lanterns, we made our tortuous way through the catacombs.

Through Skull Crag and its parent mountain many mazy tunnels had been dug ages ago. The whole place was a series of mausolea. Tombs stood in serried ranks. Stacked shelves held coffins unending. Some folk said the place had been constructed by followers of Enemath, reputed to have eight arms and four eyes, blessed with the gift of frenzy. His cult was long dead, like his devotees lined up down here.

Of course, a curse lay on the place, quite apart from traps.

Dimpy, no respecter of authority, piped up: "I thought this great blintz Khon the Mak was springing all the traps? Well?"

Nath Javed in his bluff army way began to rumble: "Mind your manners—" but he checked himself. Then: "By Vox, the youngster poses a question. Indubitably so!"

"My name's Dimpy," the scallywag protested vigorously, "not youngster—" His words were drowned in an eruption of noise that belched from the wall opposite. The whole wall bulged and showered bricks and mortar outwards in a lethal fan. Frantically we dived for the floor. Dust and smother enveloped us and sharp cries of pain rose as men were hit. Peering through the haze of brick dust I made out dark forms leaping at us, agile, lethal, predatory—the bodies of men wrapped in grave shrouds, decaying bodies of men long dead.

Instantly a confused struggle began as our lads fronted this necromantic attack. Hooked, blackened claws and chipped yellow fangs sought to rip our throats out. Swords flashed and cut. A wild melee rampaged among the shattered detritus of the wall.

The fight was not long in duration; it was hard and intense.

"Hack 'n' Slay!" The ferocious bellow reverberated through the uproar.

A savage blow disposed of the leprous-looking undead creature raving at me, all teeth and claws, and I was able to fling a quick glance across. Dimpy was flailing away with his knife. Towering above him and whirling two swords, old Nath the Impenitent protected Dimpy as he chopped the horrors to pieces. Dimpy and Old Hack 'n' Slay working together as a team. Heartened, I threw myself into the task of clearing away this necromantic rabble. We had to push on!

When at last the final horror had been banished back to whatever hell it had crawled out of, we took deep breaths of the still-polluted air. "Erthyr the Bow!" said Seg, wiping sweaty brickdust from his face. "We must get on faster than this!"

Big Balla finished wiping her short sword and said rather crossly to Veda: "Oh, for the sweet sake of Ferzakl, Veda! Do put some clothes back on, at least!"

Veda slapped her cleaned sword back into its scabbard, tossed her head, made a half-hearted attempt to pull the remnants of her clothes about her, and said: "It's easier to fight like this!"

Very shortly we were all pressing on again through the labyrinth, shadows fleeting eerily along the walls ahead of us.

From the corner of my eye I caught a single fleeting glimpse of a flash of turquoise. In the next instant the eye disappeared and the form of San W'Watchun appeared. There were a number of hurried movements, and secret signs made by the members of the expedition. The tall cylindrical black hat, the black robes, all looked the same. But the Illusionist's face bore an expression of deepest alarm.

No one spoke, we all waited. W'Watchun took a breath—he was not breathing our tainted air but that of wherever he was now.

"The news I bring is very grave. Khon the Mak took San Quenlo with him, into Skull Crag." W'Watchun made a small, hopeless gesture. "He has forced the Almuensian. Quenlo disarms the traps, so that Khon the Mak's people may pass without hindrance—"

"And then the sorcerer sets them again!" I bellowed. "And we trigger the damned devilish contraptions!"

Nineteen

The black wrath seething within me drove those passionate words bouncing against the walls. Before the echoes died Seg, good old practical, fey, Seg snapped out: "San! Can your sorcery affect this mage Quenlo?"

The tall black hat swayed as W'Watchun shook his head.

"I bring bad news, I know, and there is more. Khon the Mak discharged that incompetent Wizard of Loh who caused the earthquakes. He hired a new Wizard of Loh, more competent, more powerful—who blocks my magic."

"So thaumaturgy is useless!"

A shocked yell screeched from ahead followed immediately by a smashing roar drowning thin screams. A wall of dust rolled down towards us. W'Watchun vanished. Pushing on through the dust trying to hold our breaths and wipe our eyes, we stumbled onto the scene of tragedy.

A lumpen great statue of some mythical beast carved from the virgin rock of the mountain lay across the passage. The dust cleared to reveal more. Arms and legs stuck out from under the grotesque statue. Blood ran across the dusty floor and puddled darkly.

"More good men lost." Fweygo sounded savage. "The traps—"

"Aye. But we must press on!" As I spoke I felt the grief for good men gone tangled up with bitter wrath.

Our brave bold expedition was rapidly turning into a shambles.

Testing most rigorously for traps we found some in time; most we did not. A swod carefully negotiated what was clearly a loose flagstone. His comrade nodded, for they worked as a team, and pressed the flagstone with his spear. Nothing happened on the floor—but a damned great steel fist whistled out of the wall and degutted him.

Very seriously, I began to wonder if this torture was worth enduring. So Black Khon would take the Prism of Power. We would ambush him as he emerged flushed with his temporary victory.

A moment's reflection showed me the futility of that!

In situations of stress and extreme danger, men and women tend to call on their gods. They may have forgotten their particular deity for the preceding decade; in times of troubles religion comforts.

So it was that many and varied were the exhortations to the many and varied Gods and Spirits of Kregen echoing in that dolorous catacomb. Some of the deities called upon I'd never heard of before.

As was to be expected there was an abundance of Tolaars. There was not, as I expected, a single call upon Dokerty. One virile young fellow, who'd already been wounded, held his shoulder, marching stoutly on. His name was Chankaree the Ash. He called on Cymbaro.

Moving steadily forward in that fetid atmosphere with the shelves of corpses lining the way, I kept my senses alert for the here and now. But I began to turn over an outrageous idea in my old vosk skull of a head. What if—? Suppose—? Could it?

Khon the Mak's confounded adept Wizard of Loh had properly scuppered San W'Watchun. Sorcery had failed us. We needed to think this through from a different direction. I recalled the alternative magic I'd taken an interest in over in Loh. There had to be a way!

With the screeching roar of an avalanche the section of ground directly before me lifted straight up into the air. A brownish-yellow skeleton leaped up from the revealed gap, clawed over the lip and waving a monstrous sword charged straight at me.

The jar of the boney thing's blow against my blade jolted up my arm. A quick deflection and return cut was met by the skeleton's immediate skillful parry. Whoever he'd been in life, in death he was a first rate swordsman, by Krun!

Other skeletons swarmed out of the hole. The expected roar shattered over the scrape of steel. "Hack 'n' Slay! I just love skelebones!" Nath Javed's blade cut and bit as he surged on.

The first skeleton must be the leader and he checked my next attack, although with some difficulty. Instinctively after the twinkle of steel was followed by the opening I prepared to thrust home. That nonsense had to be stifled. Instead I slashed the brand at his neck and the thing managed to prance away in the tiny moment of hesitation.

At once I followed up. I heard the faintest of whooshes past my ear. A broad-bladed arrowhead struck the skeleton's neckbones and shattered them into fivestones. In the next instant another arrow smashed the skeleton's right knee so that it toppled over with a crash.

Seg at my back didn't say a word and neither did I. Folks said arrows were useless against skeletons and in the normal way that is so. Once the same folks saw Seg Segutorio shoot they would revise their informed opinions.

Everyone appeared to be in there fighting now, whirling this way and that. Big Balla and Veda worked as a team. Both ladies' costumes were distinctly décolleté; they fought like zhantillas. Fweygo went calmly and remorselessly on taking skeletons to pieces. At my back Korero shifted about in a way I knew, so that I called: "Go on!" Instantly he was away like a zorca from the start line, swords bright.

Now Seg stowed his bow away at these close quarters and used his sword to deadly effect. Bits and pieces of splintered bone flew everywhere. In this wild confusion there was just time to notice no more boney horrors came climbing out of the hole. Gradually we overcame them. We overcame and demolished them—but not without loss and wounds to ourselves.

We had to go on, we had to overcome Quenlo's traps. As we walked cautiously along the next series of corpse-lined passages, I said to Seg and Fweygo: "These Opaz-forsaken skelebones. I do not believe they are the work of Quenlo."

They agreed, and gave their opinions that the necromantic horrors through which we fought were the products of the geas laid on this haunted place by the builders. They wished to protect their dead from delvers and treasure hunters. That seemed to us a perfectly proper and reverent attitude. Unfortunately, it hampered us in the pursuance of an aim far greater than merely seeking for gold.

Veda, who had a wild, hair-swirling look about her, said then the Undead should be holding up Khon the Mak and his party—which, she added somewhat venomously, was A Very Good Thing, by Wanchun the Vile!

We expressed our approval of the thought. Then I was able to revert to the fanciful notion buzzing in my head before the last lot of skeletons attacked so suddenly.

Calling Dimpy over, I spoke to him in a low voice. "Can you ask Tiri to—"

He shook his tousled head, stopping what I was saying stone dead. "Can't, Drajak. She has the power, not me."

Makki Grodno flooded into my echoing head with all the violence of the repressed black wrath pent within me.

"Devil take it!"

"She speaks to me every day, though. Wants to know what I'm doing—and what you're up to now."

"Ah! Has she—?"

"Not today, so far."

Perforce, then, I had to wait on the curiosity of the lady Tirivenswatha in distant Farinsee. "The moment she does, Dimpy, tell me. I must talk to her urgently through you."

More tricks and traps followed. Larghos the Fracter, a stout jovial fellow whose spear was notched with many victories, went yelling down the maw of some waxy disgusting plant that struck from a crevice. Poor old Larghos went down in one gulp, just like a fly swallowed by a flick-flick plant on the windowsill.

In a gesture I knew was petty, I sliced my blade down and struck the lethal flower head from its stalk. Juice oozed—red juice.

That disgusting flower was probably Quenlo's handiwork. It stank abominably. The skeletons and Undead must almost certainly be a part of the original protection of Skull Crag. Quenlo had been down here before to secrete the Prism of Power. I had the dull feeling that Veda's sanguine appraisal of Khon's situation might not be accurate.

We just had to get on!

After more horrors and lost people, at last—at long persevering last!—Dimpy called: "It's Tiri!"

I swallowed down and then licked my lips. "Right! No idle gossip. Tell her our position. See if she can spy on Khon the Mak up front. Sharpish, now, Dimpy!" Then I added: "Please."

His taut young face concentrated. The magic of this communication was not lost on me. If I gambled aright— This was not sorcery. This apparently occult signaling was possible through the power of Cymbaro, the intense power of that religion.

Dimpy nodded, coughed, and said that Tiri reported that she was using her silver star to peer through the eyes of a fellow in Khon's party. His head was strangely simple of thought, as though all his own desires had been flushed away. I knew what that meant.

"Ask her if there are many young people—lads and lassies—wearing white gowns and whose minds are uncomplicated."

Immediately Dimpy reported that Tiri could see half a dozen people who fitted that description. There were guards in bulky armor, many wounded. There was poor old San Quenlo, roped up like a calsany. There was a highly impressive fellow in magnificent robes. Tiri said his aura breathed kharrna. She added a trifle impishly, so Dimpy said, that for all his sorcerous powers he could not detect her presence looking through the eyes of the young girl in white.

The two sources of power operated as it were side by side. The mage had no idea that a devotee of Cymbaro spied on him, that religious eyes and ears saw and heard what he was doing.

There was no way of telling how far ahead of us Khon's party had progressed. Tiri said that the old fellow—by whom she meant Quenlo—was very shaky on his feet and could not walk very fast.

He also had a rope between his ankles which allowed short steps only.

This information I regarded most favorably—save for being sorry for the Almuensian. With him to hold them up and the ancient defenses of Skull Crag, Khon's people might yet be caught before it was too late.

The fetid, close-pressing atmosphere of the catacombs came not so much as a result of thousands of dead bodies but as a psychological realization of their presence. The smells came from more earthy sources, like the rotting remains of the man-devouring blooms.

Dimpy said Tiri kept jumping from one vantage point to another within the bodies of the sublimes ahead. My own concerns over this confounded Wizard of Loh were mixed up with puzzlement about him. That enigma would have to be dealt with later. Now I asked Tiri, through Dimpy, to watch most carefully what happened when a trap was reached.

The answer was not long in coming—she reported the party halted at the entrance to a lofty chamber lined with coffins. Shadows congealed in the ceiling spaces and bats flew, their wings flickering between the torches' illumination. Quenlo was roughly hauled forward. Carvings of gargoylish beings from an underworld no one would wish to visit covered the entranceway. Quenlo carefully looked and then pressed two fangs, two eyes, and the forked tail in the representation of something that existed only in nightmare—and on this damned wall.

Khon the Mak, arrogance personified, stalked on as Quenlo quavered out that the way was now clear. Now Black Khon had not reached his eminent position, or even the age he was, by not being clever. He motioned to a swod from his guard, who swallowed down, and marched on, head high, spear raised, straight through the gargoyle-covered entrance.

He walked on unharmed.

Dimpy said: "Tiri, despite her sweet nature, has taken a thorough dislike to this Khon the Mak blintz."

I didn't laugh. But the comment deserved that.

The infecto girl through whose eyes Tiri spied walked on with the others. Quenlo halted and waited. We knew with absolute certainty that he would now be busy resetting the trap.

I asked Dimpy to make his way forward and tell the lads up the sharp end to watch out for the cavern as described by Tiri. The folk on duty at the front at that time happened to be from 1EYJ. They were to report back and then wait at the entrance for further orders.

"Quidang!" was their instant response. Capital lads!

What to me was a most gratifyingly short time later word came down that the lads were at the gargoyle entrance. When I reached them I saw their smart yellow jackets bore the marks of our perilous journey through this necromantic subterranean realm. Oh, yes, the time between Khon the Mak and us was, as I said, gratifyingly short; that did not mean we hadn't suffered further casualties on our way here. Even more conscious of the black suppressed rage within me I pressed the two fangs, the two eyes and the forked tail. Everyone watched intently.

"Sink me!" I said. "In for a ponsho, in for a leem!"

Without further ado I marched into that coffin-lined chamber.

For what seemed to me a century of heartbeats I marched on with my fist wrapped around the hilt of the Krozair brand—just in case!

Nothing happened. All remained silent and still.

I called back in quite a mild voice. "Forward."

More than once I'd made the attempt to lead off myself and whilst the paktuns of my small private juruk had no objections, my lads of the guard corps would have none of that. They were here to protect their Kendur, and protect him they would. Queyd-arn-tung!

In the interim three more reports winged back from Tiri. Quenlo, she reported, looked exhausted and was being dragged along.

Seg fancied we could not be too far in the rear. Fweygo measured out the next distance between traps, and thought we were catching up.

If Quenlo was in this pitiable state, others might also be. Through Dimpy I asked Tiri the condition of Nath G'Goldark, Khon's tame priest of Dokerty. She said he was bearing up well, and was clearly buoyed by the excitement of finally putting his hands on the Flutubium. He'd have to be dealt with sharpish.

"Seg," I said as we walked along. "This damned Wizard of Loh is the primary. G'Goldark the secondary. Unless—"

"Pity I can't shaft this Erthyr-forsaken Prism!"

You could imagine the whole of the mountain and Skull Crag exploding and fountaining into the air like a volcano, and then collapsing and falling with the finality of death upon us all.

"Pity."

"Aye."

Fweygo gave Seg an odd look at the vehemence of my comrade's words. But then, Fweygo knew little of Seg then. Seg flexed his broad archer's shoulders and said: "Why this disgusting object Khon the Mak is consumed with ambition escapes me. By the Veiled Froyvil! Doesn't the cramph know where ambition will get him?"

Now Seg had begun life without prospects and was now king and emperor. I knew—and to my shame and concern—that he'd only agreed to these arrangements because he knew they pleased me. Like myself, he'd give the lot up tomorrow without regret.

For a time we went along in silence after that. Quenlo's traps might have been circumvented by us and our use of religion to thwart magic; the Opaz-forsaken masters of the Undead still struck.

A raving mass of zombies charged us, all dripping flesh and dangling eyeballs. They stank most powerfully. They wielded axes and swords. Shades of dear old Makki Grodno! We got stuck into them with a vehemence to match and overpower their own berserk carryings on.

That turned into a desperate fight. Steel glinted silver and then fouled with dark stains. Contorted shadows danced madly along the walls. The grunts of combat, the panting, mingled hideously with the screams of the wounded. Oddly enough, even as I whirled my blade, I was surprised by the shrieks spurting up from the zombies as they fell in pieces before the steel. I didn't much care to use the Krozair brand on them as demeaning the magnificent sword. When it was done and we paused, collecting our senses together, I wiped the Krozair blade, reflecting that it had been used in a noble cause.

"We must be nearly on 'em by now," I said, fretfully.

"From now on we keep silence."

So, a noiseless band, we prowled on along the gloomy ways.

One item of my thoughts I'd not passed on to my comrades.

I was severely disappointed in San W'Watchun's performance. Oh, surely, he'd warned us and been of assistance. But he admitted he was powerless against the Wizard of Loh. I suppose I should have realized something of the truth when W'Watchun had gone to such lengths to discover the secret of gunpowder. He evidently could not hurl fireballs. This confounded mage up ahead could—and, by Vox, would!

Tiri reported back then that Khon had reached his goal.

The black-hearted cramph stood with his people in a wide chamber where many sconces blazed vivid lights. Here the chiefs of the ancient religion were stored away, tier after tier along the walls. Tiri said even at second hand she felt the creepiness of the place.

Fweygo said: "We are two traps away."

"Then let us go forward!"

Reaching a convenient pausing place within a miserable-looking room where two dead swods from Khon's party lay in scattered pieces, I called the leaders of each unit in our party together. I held what Kregen fighting men call a Quidang Group. This is not an Order or Operations Group where ideas are discussed before the orders are given. A Quidang Group—QD—obviously from the name, means a meeting where the leader tells the troops what he—or she—wants done without argument or objection. Naturally, my lads of the guard corps were having none of that, particularly 1EFB, until I overrode them.

Simply saying that we all couldn't rush into the final chamber because of the narrowness of the doorway I finished: "It is settled. Queyd-arn-tung!"

Tiri's reports were accurate, for which I gave thanks to Cymbaro. This whole horrific experience was bad enough. Had Tiri failed in her use of those very special powers and attributes she had learned at Farinsee, then everything would have been much much worse.

Fittingly enough, Dimpy pressed the correct places on the wall to de-activate the last trap set by Quenlo.

Now all that lay between us and Khon the Mak and his mob must be traversed in absolute silence. One hint of our presence and Khon's Wizard of Loh would pounce.

Acting under the instructions he'd received in the QD, Dimpy whispered directly into my ear when Tiri reported in. Around the next bend in the corridor, where an eight-armed Talu pranced carved in a marble that glinted as though the image was alive, stretched the final passage to the entrance.

We sorted ourselves out. Seg, of course. Fweygo, Korero. Nath Javed, who commanded churgurs, sword and shield troops, just plucked a crossbow from an eager swod of 1EFB and stood with us. I gave him a look, said nothing, nodded my head. If we were to work our bows efficiently, that was the maximum number we could cram abreast in the corridor. Old Hack 'n' Slay's crossbow was a drawback, of course; I couldn't find it in me to deny him. A second and a third row of lads from 1EFB formed up abaft. The Sword Watch and the Yellow Jackets might complain; they couldn't out-argue the Foot Bows.

Now armored men moving forward over stone floors cannot help make some noise, however much they try to avoid it. We'd have just enough time to reach the entrance and catch those inside the chamber in the same positions that Tiri informed us. There ought to be one clear shot. One each, from the five in the front rank.

All orders were given by hand signals. There were few. Everyone knew what had to be done and their part in the attack.

Mind you, when I say one shot from each, there would inevitably be two from Seg Segutorio.

Those two shafts, equally inevitably, would be the most accurate—by Erthyr the Bow!

This silent approach suited me in other ways. I know I am naturally and by training a taciturn sort of fellow. Yet, as you know, I suppose as a counter to that I so often run off at the mouth, my old black-fanged winespout turning into a real blabbermouth. Now I could concentrate every fiber on what was to come in the next few seconds.

A dim blue radiance wavered into indistinct movement before me. It coiled and writhed, blue streaks dulling and then shining out, coalescing into a phantom blue shape. Instantly I held up my hand and we halted our forward movement.

The whisper reached only my ears, that I knew.

"Jak! I trust I do not intrude. But I bring news—"

Deb-Lu-Quienyin's words stopped and I saw his familiar form become stronger. His magnificent old turban hung over one ear. His patient, wise face looked this way and that and then back to me. "Where are you?"

I put my finger to my lips. The tensed up lads at my back would start to fidget about in a minute. Deb-Lu understood at once.

"I have spoken to San W'Watchun, a delightful fellow, quite unlike what we had been led to believe the Sorcerers of Balintol were like. The Wizard of Loh with this dreadful person Black Khon is Nag-Rin-Chandon. He's known to us. I am disappointed in his choice. However—" Here Deb-Lu pushed his turban straight. "My news is that Drak has reached an understanding with the regent C'Chermina. The war is over."

I mouthed words silently: "Thank Opaz for that." Then I pointed imperiously down towards the door, right through Deb-Lu's sorcerously projected form. "We can not wait!"

"Of course, of course! Absolutely!" Deb-Lu vanished.

A savage thrust of my sword to order us on again was followed instantly by the unmistakable sound of armored men moving.

Much as I welcomed my comrade Wizard of Loh's news about the peace breaking out in Balintol, Deb-Lu couldn't have brought it at a much worse time, by Krun! The halt and subsequent movement on betrayed us. The group within the chamber heard us, that was for sure.

The lighted opening before us seemed to our heightened sense to come no nearer as we pressed on. Everything became as though etched in acid on our brains. Straining muscles, pumping hearts, stretched sinews drove us on. We followed our plan—our pitiful, doomed plan—and erupted from the tunnel into the chamber.

The scene was as Tiri had described. The sconces shot shards of light into every recess. Guards turned to face us. Khon the Mak and G'Goldark were busy in a corner, their backs turned. The resplendent figure of the Wizard of Loh, Nag-Rin-Chandon, began to lift his arms. The sleeves of his robe sparkled with mystic sigils.

All five of us in the front rank loosed. The shafts sped.

Light formed a lance of fire from the Wizard of Loh. It coruscated towards us, dripping flames. The brilliance took the flying arrows into its embrace and devoured them utterly.

In an enormous crashing thunder, spitting flames, the lance of fire struck directly for us.

Twenty

Nothing existed in the world save for that coruscating bolt of fire lancing directly for my chest. A single agonizing thought of Delia pierced through my mind.

With fingers that felt like lumps of dough I reached for the next arrow. The shaft came out sweetly and nocked to the string. All the universe concentrated into a blaze of scorching fire burning into my eyes.

The light brightened incredibly. The noise as of cataracts of fire increased. The brilliance became unendurable and the heat smoked over my skin. My eyes squeezed wetly closed.

The light lessened! Astonishingly the brilliance faded. Fighting pain I forced my streaming eyes open.

A second lance of fire struck from the side, roaring. It clamored in gouts of fire and flame against the first. The two spears of raw energy fought.

Every nook and cranny of the chamber with its tiers of corpse-laden coffins lit up as though a sun burned at the center. Seeing remained difficult. Shading my eyes I could just make out the form of the Wizard of Loh in his ornate robes standing tall and stiff, arms outstretched, radiance filling his face with color. Reaching for the bowstring again I realized the futility of trying to shoot the Wizard of Loh. The far side of the chamber was concealed by the two bolts of fire. By all the foulness of Makki Grodno! I knew what the priest G'Goldark was doing right now. About to spring up and run around the side I was halted by the abrupt disappearance of the first sorcerous shaft of fire. It blinked out like a blown candle.

Elation filled me at that and I levered myself up—

A crackling noise as though the world split asunder, and a spear of flame leaped from Nag-Rin-Chandon. It swirled in gobbets of radiance towards the ghostly form of Deb-Lu. His own energy beam slewed and the two forces of raw energy struck head on.

They struggled. Spitting sparks and smashing the air of the cavern with thunderous noise, the two forces strove one against the other. They collided with enormous discharges of sorcerous power.

Quickly at the point where they met a disc began to form. Spinning and shooting out sparks like a Catherine wheel it swayed back and forth. Now it groped towards Deb-Lu, then it halted and swayed back towards Chandon. The light and heat and noise drowned the senses.

I knew what that magic disc of light was. That was the famous Quern of Gramarye. Eventually, it would crunch down one or other of the mages' projections of power and eliminate him utterly.

Because Deb-Lu was not here in person I fancied he could not utilize all his kharrna to bolster his attack. Obviously some had to be used to sustain his thaumaturgical presence. This gave Chandon a chance that, otherwise, I suspected he would not enjoy.

Roaring and shrilling the Quern of Gramarye filled the chamber with brilliance and confusion. Shadows moved indistinctly. Absolutely no prizes are offered for correctly guessing who of our party shot first.

Seg's shaft found a target among those shifting shadows. It fell away with a screech unheard in the din. High, clearly audible, cutting through all the uproar, a single word spat like a white-hot stone spouting from a volcano.

"Dokomek!"

We were too late! Now we were in for horror!

Khon the Mak had won through. He'd found the Flutubium and Quenlo had de-activated the traps so that now the Dokerty priest could swing it up in triumph. The poor, damned, doomed infectos, sublimes totally unaware of their fate, would understand for their very last intelligent thought that the chief priest called them to the greater glory of Dokerty. Poor devils!

And—devils was correct! Through the brilliance gouting in the chamber and bouncing in shards of light from the serried coffins, shadowed forms moved like ghosts glimpsed through evening mist.

The swift thought struck me that I trusted fervently that Tiri had withdrawn from the empty mind of the infecto before the poor lass became so hideously transformed.

Our people fanned out from the entrance and those with bows shot with the steady rhythm taught in the Academy by Seg Segutorio. He tried to pick individual targets through the blaze of brilliance and the maddeningly shifting shadows. He shook his head in annoyance.

"Missed!"

I suppose, once or twice a century, Seg misses his shot.

Now the indistinct forms lumbered closer. A fresh roaring broke like the clamor of caged leems above the confusion.

"Ibmanzies!" I called. "Spread out!"

My heart felt like a lump of lead. My own brave lads, all the folk with us, remained. Not a one ran off. Now I was asking them to surround these demons from hell, to fight, to throw their lives into the scales. By the dripping eyeballs and mucus-clogged nostrils of Makki Grodno! Those scales were weighted most diabolically against us!

Every now and then a shard of incandescent light span from the Quern of Gramarye and struck randomly. Coffins burst into flames. A long scorched groove cut through the marble by my feet. If the damned ibmanzies didn't get us, we stood to be incinerated by the occult conflict waged by the two sorcerers.

What was happening to those young innocent lads and lassies in their neat white robes didn't bear thinking of. They believed in Dokerty. They'd embraced the religion whole-heartedly. Veda had done so. She'd discovered the horrendous truth in time, thank—well, certainly not thank Dokerty! She knew what was going on.

Those pretty young girls and those strapping youths having gone through the enormity of agony to make them sublimes ready to receive a demon of hell into their very beings, had been given the dire command: "Dokomek!"

The Prism of Power hidden in the Flutubium exerted its malignant force through the youngsters' heartbreaking honesty of faith.

Through the smoke and brilliance of the chamber the ibmanzies continued to be difficult to distinguish. We did not surround the demons, rather we formed a semi-circle with its apex at the tunnel entrance. Bows lifted and shafts winged through the turmoil.

Those doomed young folk were going through the transformation. Their bodies swelled, shredding their white robes. Black bristle hairs sprouted. Their teeth elongated into yellow fangs, dripping with ichor. Their feet splayed and talons thrust forward, razor sharp. Monstrous demons from a blasphemous hell, they shrieked their insensate rage and charged.

The smokey air filled with flying shafts. The first demon to appear clearly bristled like a pin-cushion or a hedgehog. He was foaming, shrieking, bleeding, and he rampaged on clawing and grasping caught in the maniacal passion of his desire to kill and go on killing.

Seg shot one eye out and I shot the other.

The thing didn't stop, of course. Unable to see where it was going it swiveled, striking blindly, and collided with the second ibmanzy who screeched from the smoke. The two fought.

"Capital!" exclaimed Seg.

"That's more like it," observed Fweygo in his dry way.

The situation was fraught with primeval horror, yet my comrades went calmly about their business. Oh, yes, I began to feel a trifle less leaden about the heart region. More ibmanzies appeared.

The cruelty of the barbed arrow and bolt heads as they bit deeply was not lost on me. Khon the Mak and his crazy ambitions was the prime architect of all this suffering. The black wrath pent within me for so long at last burst out.

Shooting no longer satisfied the dreadful blood lust that gripped me. You know how I detest this so-called red curtain that is reputed to fall over a fighting man's eyes in the heat of battle. I threw down the bow. I ripped out the splendid Krozair brand. Without thought, driven by the passionate wrath vibrating through all my being, I hurled myself at the ibmanzies. The Krozair blade flamed.

As I struck and struck again I was only vaguely aware of clothyard shafts piercing past my shoulders and spitting into the monsters.

Deep, vengeful cuts hacked bristly legs and arms. The Krozair sword fouled with blood and ichor. The stenches in the chamber sickened. The noise spurted in with the rolling surf-beat of a typhoon beating against a rocky shore. One single dominating purpose animated my frantic actions. The purpose was hardly thought. It stemmed from a profound primordial lust to rid the bright world of Kregen of these damned doomed ibmanzies once and for all.

How long the nightmare lasted I have no way of telling.

Rips and cuts scored blood tracks across my skin. Yellow talons gashed across my arms. I felt no pain—not then. Wrath for all the dark injustices of the world dominated everything.

The brilliance of light in the chamber abruptly dimmed to the radiance of the many lamps and candles. The noise changed from a series of clashing concussions to a shrilling hissing. The demon against whom I struggled, hacking and slashing, bore down with talon-armed hands seeking to rip me apart. The Krozair brand snicked up over my shoulder ready to slash with every ounce of vicious wrath in me—and the thing's head vanished in a gust of lightning-vivid infernal power.

I sagged back, trembling, all my limbs shaking. I shook my head. I knew what had happened. Dear, mild, gentle old Deb-Lu-Quienyin had overcome the other Wizard of Loh. The Quern of Gramarye had smashed back and consumed Nag-Rin-Chandon utterly.

Raw power delicately controlled by Deb-Lu's kharrna reached about the chamber and demolished the remaining ibmanzies.

Just a few paces from me the headless body of an ibmanzy twitched in the last electrical throes of death. Soon he would shrivel back to the youth the demon inhabited. In his hairy protruding stomach a stux lodged, with blood and ichor flowing about the shaft. At the hideous thing's feet lay the pathetically torn body of Velino the Lark, a jolly, cheerful fellow liked by everyone. I could, again, only mourn for him.

When I was myself again I looked about on the carnage. There was no blue ghostly form, no friendly face crowned with its toppling turban. Deb-Lu had gone. Wrapped up as he was in the arcane pursuits demanded of him as a practicing Wizard of Loh, he had looked in on us summoned by W'Watchun, done what was necessary, and departed.

He had grave news for us, that I knew. He'd be back. Unfinished business lay to my hand in Skull Crag, yet I could take joy already from what Deb-Lu told us. If peace was breaking out over Balintol as a result of the intervention of Vallia and her allies, then that was, by Vox, an outcome devoutly to be thankful for!

The scene in the chiefs' burial chamber bore the macabre appearance of grand guignol; bodies sprawled everywhere, blood congealing on the marble, burst coffins spilling their ages-old corpses to mingle with the carnage. The most pathetic dead were the limp and torn bodies of the young folk now returned to—almost—their normal forms after their hideous transformations to demons from hell.

Inevitably some of our lads took longer to recover from the horror through which they'd just been than others. After experiences of this order of terror it is difficult, to say the least, to pick oneself up, whistle a tune, and stride off for the next adventure.

What had to be done, and done damned sharpish, was to find Khon the Mak.

Many of his guards were piled up in a miniature hecatomb at the far side of the chamber. They'd died in various ways. Some were torn into pieces, so the ibmanzies had got in a little practice on the home team before starting on us. A few guards with arrow wounds were still alive, crawled off into a shadowy crevice. Now the ibmanzies were gone, the wounded were calling out for water.

We had to minister to them, of course. Seg called across: "Here's the Dokerty priest feller." Nath G'Goldark lay crumpled with a long arrow through him. Seg took out his knife. "One of mine. I'll just have it back. Unbroken, thanks to Erthyr the Bow."

Seg shifted the high priest's body to get more comfortably at his arrow and a sharp, high-pitched scream spurted up.

Hauling the priest away from the wall with savage energy, Seg exclaimed: "Ha!"

"Oh, aye," I said. Then, grimly: "Come on out!"

From the crevice concealed by G'Goldark's body Khon the Mak crept out like a whipped cur dog. He looked ghastly. He shook.

"Please—" he stammered, and licked his lips, and fell silent.

The men who'd fought through horror with me came up and stood regarding the Hyr Kov. Veda stepped forward and put her hard toes into his ribs. Seg hauled her back. Nobody was talking—odd!

Now I experienced a new fear, a terror of myself. The black wrath that burned so darkly in me must explode now. Here was this miserable creature, cowering before me, the author of so much agony. I feared my rage would tear forth and I would commit an act for which afterwards I'd be mortally sorry.

I, Dray Prescot, glared down on Khon the Mak. The blood thumped around my body, and some leaked out of sundry wounds. My head rang not with the Bells of Beng Kishi but with resonant echoes of all that this person had wrought in Balintol. He deserved his sentence.

My sword lifted. Like blood running into the scuppers from an autopsy table, the wrath in me flowed away.

Calmness descended on me so that I stopped trembling. I lowered the sword. The time for wrath had passed.

Without turning around I spoke in a hard level voice.

"Take him away. Look after him and keep him fit to stand his trial."

Somebody at my back snapped out: "Quidang!"

Veda and Dimpy were looking at me—staring at me. Big Balla left off cleaning her short sword to stare. If they knew who the fellow they called Drajak the Sudden really was, if by this time they must realize I was Dray Prescot, I really didn't care. All Veda's romancing about the stories of Dray Prescot had to be seen in its true comic light. In all probability she'd take a long time to get over this shattering revelation and in the interim she'd be mighty hoity-toity, by Krun, an absolute devil-lady in her own right!

The sin of tiredness stole over me with subtle power. The chamber of corpses stank. The place was an abhorrence and an abomination. We had to get our dead and wounded out—and go!

Then what was to do?

I put a bloody hand to my head. My lad Drak would see the peace held for now. I supposed, dully, that I'd have to parade a trifle in my grand capacity as Emperor of All Paz. The hollow title must be used to make sure the various rulers of Balintol abided by the treaties. We must all then bend our energies to confronting the Shanks. I stepped forward and picked up the Flutubium.

For the moment, here and now in this place of horror, it was over. My comrades were waiting for me to speak.

"By Mother Zinzu the Blessed! I need a wet!" I looked around on the men who'd fought so devotedly. "Then it's home!"

"Aye, majister!" Then, surprising me, shocking me, they lifted their swords in a glitter of blades. "Hai Jikai!"

I shook my head, amazed. Was this a jikai, then? I did know that on the way to Esser Rarioch the Prism of Power could be tossed contemptuously into the deepest ocean. The confounded thing would no longer be used to wreak its horror upon young folk. Wrath was satiated.

"Home!" I shouted. Then, to myself, added: "Home to Delia!"

A Glossary to the Balintol Cycle

Compiled by Els Withers

References to the six books of the cycle are given as:

INA: *Intrigue of Antares*
GGA: *Gangs of Antares*
DMA: *Demons of Antares*
SCA: *Scourge of Antares*
CHA: *Challenge of Antares*
WRA: *Wrath of Antares*

NB: Previous glossaries covering items not included here can be found in Volume 5: *Prince of Scorpio,* Volume 7: *Arena of Antares,* Volume 11: *Armada of Antares,* Volume 14: *Krozair of Kregen,* Volume 18: *Golden Scorpio,* Volume 22: *A Victory for Kregen,* Volume 26: *Allies of Antares,* Volume 32: *Seg the Bowman,* Volume 37: *Warlord of Antares,* and Volume 43: *Scorpio Triumph.*

abscess-covered and veined legs of the Lady Dulshini, by the: oath used by Prescot.
Aaran: a small and select religion of the utmost dedication.
Abley Mountains: mountains north of Caneldrin.
advang: race of diffs with porcine features.
Aephar: race of diffs whose women are incredibly beautiful.
Affleck the Wine: Gon servitor of Strom Korden. INA
Akhchutz rot it!: Oath used by Perempto the Shorn.
Alley Leems: a street gang in Oxonium.
Alyss: alias used by Delia.
Amintin: town on the west coast of Balintol.
Angerim: race of diffs with sharp teeth and spiky hair.
Autarch's Stakes: a prestigious chariot-racing event of Emgidu.
Autmoil Hall: a room in the temple of Dokerty in Prebaya.
Aventure: British Navy ship of which Prescot dreamed of being Second Lieutenant.

Baldur: father of Nath Seegfreedhan.

Baldur: one of the zorcas driven by Prescot in the chariot races of Emgidu. SCA

Balintol longsword: a variety of longsword smaller than and inferior to the Krozair longsword.

Balrey the Pretty: nephew of Bolgo the Rapacious. DMA

baltrix: a saddle animal of Balintol. INA

Balig: a Balintolese name for the green sun of Kregen.

Balron: a Balintolese name for the red sun of Kregen.

Bancur the Bansun: Brokelsh sentry in the citadel of Santoro. SCA

Bandi: mili-milu kept as a pet by Tirivenswatha.

Barca L'Lambton na Freydin, Kov: retainer of San W'Watchun. CHA

Barter Hill: another name for the Hill of Dancing Ghosts.

Basalma the Beautiful and Glorious: wife of Brory the Bold. WRA

Beng Trunter the Nosher, by: an oath used by Prescot.

Besti, Lady: sister of Kov Brannomar, a witch. INA, GGA, DMA

Bharang: stromnate west of Amintin; also the capital city of the same.

bhin: a silver coin of Balintol.

Big Balla: Hytak member of the Hellraisers. GGA, WRA

Black Library: library of arcane knowledge in the shrine of Cymbaro.

bloodhounds: the Kregan variety features six legs and long fangs.

Blue Lily, the: a farm in Vaiwadrin.

Bolgo the Rapacious: manager of a lifterdrome in Lakensmot. DMA

Brace: bosun of *Roscommon*. CHA

Brango the Toriner: member of the Roaring Fifties. GGA

Branliner: Scaly race of diffs with two eyes in front and two behind.

Brannomar, Hyr Kov: a noble of Oxonium. INA, GGA, DMA, WRA

Brass Lily, the: a tavern in Oxonium.

braxter: variety of sword generally found in the eastern regions of Paz, nominally a straight cut and thruster but with a slight and cunning curve to the blade.

Brighton: ship's doctor of *Rockingham*. CHA

Brory the Bold: Brokelsh member of Nagzalla's Nasty Neemus. GGA, WRA

Bruk-en-im, by: a Brokelsh oath.

Byrom: son of Princess Nandisha, rescued by Prescot and Fweygo in Amintin. INA, GGA

Cabbage Alley: a street in Oxonium.

calimer: cable car.

Caneldrin: country in the north of Balintol.

Cave of the Wall: a cavern in a remote mountain location used as a sorcerous retreat.

C'Chermina: regent in Caneldrin, aunt of King Yando. DMA, WRA

C'Cronal, San: chief priest of Dokerty. GGA

C'Cuisar, San: Vad of Igverli and high priest of Dokerty in Enderli. WRA

Chaadur the Ripper: alias used by Prescot in Vaiwadrin.

Chained Veesons, Avenue of: a street in Prebaya.

Chandrur: a Chulik boxer of Nerlinium. WRA

Chankaree the Ash: a devotee of Cymbaro who assisted Prescot in retrieving a Prism of Power. WRA

"Chariot with One Wheel, The": a drinking song.

Charwis: a yellow wine.

chavpaktun: term for a paktun who wears the bronze chavonth-head at his throat.

Chekaran the Balass: Chulik guard in the retinue of San W'Watchun. CHA, WRA

Cherry Chavonths: a street gang in Oxonium.

Chezra-Gon-Kranak, by: a Kataki oath.

chranster: race of diffs who from the waist up are splendid specimens, and from the waist down are shaggy and gnarled.

Chulgar ti Daster: guard commander of a young Lord in Oxonium, a Hytak. INA

clanscreetz, or clantzer: name for the Balintol longsword.

Clipped Rhok, the: an unsavory hostelry in Oxonium.

The Clonset Jibr'chun: a rehabilitation technique practiced by Dr. Drewinger, involving wrapping the body in yellow bandages.

Cloud Scamper: lifter used by Prescot in Caneldrin.

Combat Cutie: nickname for a Jikai Vuvushi, not always appreciated.

Como the Hump: Deldar who worked as a guard under Prescot in the palace of Prebaya. DMA

compib: literal meaning "life-spirit," technique of applying nerve pressure to bring a person to consciousness.

crawzer: beast like a brown and black man-size centipede.

Croken of the Rainbow: a deity of Balintol.

Crowser and Molp, the: a tavern in Nerlinium.

Crystal Griffon, the: a high-class tavern in Oxonium.

Cymbaro the Just: a minor deity of Tolindrin, revered by San Padria na Fermintin.

Dagert of Paylen: Amak of Paylen, a gentleman rogue with whom Prescot crossed paths in Oxonium. INA, GGA, DMA

Dancing Ghosts, Hill of: a hill in Oxonium.

Dancing Nun of Schweyenza, by the hairy armpit of the: an oath used by Prescot.

Dani's Delight: an airboat which carried the Vallian guard from Oxonium to the Cave of the Wall.

Delnik: a subordinate rank, similar to the Matoc of Hamal.

Diamond Tribe: one of the ancient nine tribes of Caneldrin.

dillope fruit: a juicy form of satsuma.

Dimpy: member of the Hellraisers Gang, rescued by Prescot in Oxonium. GGA, WRA

Djondalar of the Twisted Staff, by: oath used by Prescot.

Dokerty: a deity of Tolindrin.

Dokomek!: command triggering the transformation of an ibmanzy.

Donggi: the old amak of Paylen, father of Dagert.

Dorval ham Hesting: a Lamnia merchant of Winbium. CHA, WRA

Drajak the Daxer: alias used by Prescot in Prebaya.

Drajak the Sudden: alias used by Prescot.

Dray Prescot and the Castle of Doom: a Kregan book.

Dray Prescot and Delia fight the Giant Octopus for the Pearls of Tancrophor: a Kregan book.

Drefendo, San: a priest of Cymbaro in Oxonium. WRA

Drendi: twin brother of Duven, who went off to become a mercenary.

Drewinger: a needleman in the retinue of San W'Watchun. WRA

Drino: Xaffer stylor in the retinue of Lady Quensella. DMA

Dromang, by: oath used by Dimpy.

Lady Dulshini, by the pendulous belly and massive thighs of the: oath used by Prescot.

Duven: attendant in the shrine of Cymbaro in Oxonium. GGA

E'Eolana: a venahim healer of Prebaya. SCA

Emgidu: a city of Kildrin.

Enderli: country to the north-east of Balintol.

Enemath: god of an extinct cult, reputed to have eight arms and four eyes, blessed with the gift of frenzy.

Eregoin's Answer: a fine roomy voller with powerful artillery.

Erlinen, Strazab: known as Erlinney the Dour, Vallian ambassador to Enderli. WRA

Ernithor the Quick: captain of *Eregoin's Answer*. WRA

Erwin: Valkan who worked under Prescot as a guard in the palace of Prebaya, also known as the Waggler. DMA, SCA

Extrans: black-skinned island race given to weaving flowers into their flowing black hair.

Fall of the Suns, The: an ancient pub of a very grim nature.

Fanciers, Kyro of the: public square in Oxonium.

Fando: father of Fweygo. SCA

Fandon: village leader of the Fleurese. DMA

Farinsee: stronghold perched atop a mountain resembling Ayers Rock.

Fat Lardo: a cook in the palace of Oxonium. GGA

Fat Nath: deceased member of the Roaring Fifties.

Feast of Beng T'Tolin: a festival in Oxonium.

Felice: a Fristle fifi attendant in Kov Barca's villa. CHA

Fergie: beloved of Mimi. INA

Ferndown Street: a street in Oxonium.

Ferzakl, by: an oath used in Oxonium.

F'Farhan the Unctuous: proprietor of the Crowser and Molp. WRA

Finul: a young, carefree Fleurese man. DMA

Finzy the Oracular: Quensella's chief servant girl. DMA

Firben, Mother: Princess Nandisha's puncture lady. GGA

Flanko the Fish: Fristle trumpeter in the retinue of Quensella. DMA

Fleurese: a vegetarian people who live along a secluded tributary of the great river in Caneldrin.

Fluted Hen, the: an inn in Bharang.

Flutubium: sacred winged symbol of the cult of Dokerty, containing within a Prism of Power.

Flying Vosk, the: a middling tavern in Oxonium.

Fonnell the Fractious: Fristle bandit, in the hire of Prince Ortyg, who stole Strom Korden's sword from Prescot. INA

Fortro N'Norgoil: high-ranking priest of Dokerty, whom Prescot interrogated in Santoro. SCA

frazzer: dish consisting of a bed of imported rice loaded with meats of indeterminate origin, a variety of vegetables, peppers, all mixed into a violently red sauce.

Froisier: a passenger on *Gleaming Thunder*. DMA

Furney: an illusionist working for Kov Barca. CHA

Fweygo: a kregoinye, a Kildoi, who worked with Prescot in Amintin. INA, GGA, SCA, CHA, WRA

Fweygo: grandfather of Fweygo, and former teacher of Mefto the Kazzur. SCA

Galloping Zorca: lifter commandeered by Prescot in Winbium.

Garlash the Lips: a Gon gang member of Oxonium who plays the trumpet. GGA

Garnath the Stout: crewman of *Galloping Zorca*. CHA

Gildrim: grumpy race of diffs with long baboon-like noses, close-set eyes and unruly mops of hair, two arms and a tail. Unlike other movable Kregen tails, that of a Gildrim is relatively thick but flexible in an almost miraculous way, to which the average Gildrim secures a great club, a skull crusher, with six protruding triangular blades.

Gleaming Thunder: a flyer on which Prescot was a passenger. DMA

Glima the Pie: Gon cook aboard *Galloping Zorca*. CHA

Golden Zorca, the: a private and high-class tavern in Oxonium.

Goron: pilot of a flyer taken by Prescot. DMA

Gralufon: twin brother of Granumin, who runs security for the temple of Dokerty.

Grand Central: largest hill in Oxonium, containing the palace of the king, temples and courts, grandiose buildings serving a busy and important capital city.

Granumin: senior adviser to C'Chermina, killed by Schrepim assassins. DMA

Great Jikai of Tacgide the Meek, the: title of a play attended by Prescot in Prebaya.

Green Rushes, river of: tributary flowing into the Largesse in Prebaya.

Grogan G'Gulandor, Kov: a noble of Winlan, who considers himself the leader of the Tchekedos. SCA

Gron-Arm-Chenlang: a wizard of Loh working for Khon the Mak.

Gurnley the Wheels: a Gon rickshaw puller of Nerlinium. WRA

Hans: Grenadier aboard *Roscommon*. CHA

Harcourt: ship's carpenter of *Roscommon*. CHA

Harland Lifter, the: a middlish tavern in Prebaya.

Harpion the Sallow: worked as a palace guard under Prescot in Prebaya. SCA

Hartagas the Marvel: oath used by Jiktar Zonder ti Rannellden.

Hastings, Dr.: ship's doctor of *Roscommon*. CHA

Hellraisers: a street gang in Oxonium.

Herpato Froth: a guard in the retinue of Princess Nandisha. SCA

H'Havalini: a Venahim healing woman. CHA, WRA

Hieron: a tribe leader in Vaiwadrin. WRA

Hindrod Gate: leads onto the wayfarer's drinnik just outside the walls of Emgidu.

H'Lavini, Beng: patron saint of knots.

Holy Golden Sash of Tolaar, by the: oath used in Oxonium.

Homespun: name of a street in Oxonium.

hummummba: a banjo-type instrument.

hyrscreetzim: master swordsman.

Hyslop Nath ti Vernaloin: a sub-priest of Dokerty in Prebaya, who lent Prescot some clothing. SCA

ibma: a type of soul, distinct from the ib.

ibmanzy: a demon, a mutated human being with engorged, bloated, distorted face, eyes like branding irons, jagged, fang-like teeth, radiating an aura of immanent evil, hands twisted into obscene claws, obsessed with the maniacal desire to kill and go on killing.

Ibserrail Chamber: chamber in the Shrine of Cymbaro in Oxonium, where the spirit might find resuscitation.

Illargo: needleman who treated Prescot in Prebaya. DMA

Impolimar: deity called upon by Lingurd.

Imps of Khabriana, by the: oath used by Perempto the Shorn.

Indros the Stout: a paunchy little Och, the landlord of The Pronto and Risslaca. SCA

infecto: person who has been infected with the spell to become an ibmanzy, the transformation to be triggered by a word of command.

Inglos Brandmal, by: oath used by Prescot.

Itemo: race of diffs with grayish hair and down-drooping dew-lapped faces.

"It is futile to argue against a Krozair longsword": saying among the Krozairs of Zy.

Jakar, by: oath used by Bancur the Bansun.

Janetha, Mistress: tutor of Lady Tirivenswatha. WRA

Jazipur, Lord: chief advisor to Hyr Kov Brannomar. INA, GGA, DMA

Jenni Farlang: young girl, working in a Ruby Alley jeweler's shop, discovered murdered and dismembered. GGA

Kaodrin: district of tombs outside Oxonium.

Kaonik: Krozair technique of applying nerve pressure to render a person unconscious.

kaotresh: "flag of death", flag flown during time of mourning in Tolindrin, white, with a white center surrounded by a black ring.

Karibar, by the Belly of: oath used by Bancur.

Khon the Mak: nickname given to Hyr Kov Khonstanton.

Khonstanton, Hyr Kov: a claimant to the throne of Tolindrin. INA, GGA, CHA, WRA

Kildrin: country of Balintol on the west coast north of Tolindrin and south of Winlan, barred off by mountains on the east, birthplace of most Kildois.

knot of the Kovneva Sinkie: a legend similar to that of the Gordian knot, but this everlasting knot held closed the night robe of the Kovneva Sinkie, to be loosened by Kyr Nath, well known from many stories and songs.

"Kovneva Sophie's Wardrobe, The": a drinking song.

Korden, Strom: killed by assassins while attempting to deliver a sword to Kov Brannomar. INA

Krando: a Kataki who made a slaving raid on the Fleurese. DMA

kunsan: short spear very like a Zulu assegai, very like the similar weapons used by Clansmen of Felschraung.

Laces, Souk of: a market in Oxonium.

Lady Fayreen the Abandoned, by: oath used by Prescot.

Lakensmot: city of Caneldrin.

Lally, Sana: priestess in the shrine of Cymbaro. GGA

Landi: chavpaktun working in the palace of Prebaya. DMA

Lardo: Fat.

Largesse: river on whose banks Prebaya is located.

Larghos Deft-Fingers: a street thief of Prebaya. SCA

Larghos the Fracter: Vallian soldier killed attempting to retrieve a Prism of Power. WRA

Larghos Frenden, Jiktar: known as the Quick, cadade to Dorval ham Hesting. CHA

Larghos Invordun na Thothsturboin, Elten: Vallian ambassador in Oxonium. INA, GGA, SCA, WRA

Larghos Kraneyzendo: mythical figure who drove a chariot through thunder clouds and amidst the lightning shafts.

Larghos Nath H'Harmen: alias used by Prescot in Prebaya.

Larghos S'Snaffding: a second-hand lifter merchant in Prebaya. SCA

Lart's Chavonths: a chariot-racing team of Emgidu. SCA

larvan: "layer on of hands"—someone who heals by touch.

"Last Portion of Pie": a drinking song.

Lawrence: First Lieutenant of *Aventure*. CHA

Lazlo: young Fleurese man. DMA

leygromak: unnatural creature created by sorcery; one example is described as looking like a cross. One arm was that of the head of a beautiful girl, blonde hair swirling, blue eyes wide, red lips moist and full. Opposite her the head was that of a monster from nightmare, squamous, dripping with ichor, three red eyes glaring in mad passion. Its fangs lapped its lower and upper jaws to form a vice of death. The crosspiece's arms were those of a reptilian monstrosity with lashing barbed tail and a gigantic hairy spider, all legs and antennae, writhing uncontrollably. The creature floated head-high, dribbling puss onto the ground and drifting along leaving a trail like a snail's.

lifter: term used in Balintol for vollers.

Liftu: agent employed by Naghan Raerdu in Oxonium. INA

Lingurd: polsim resident of Oxonium. INA

linomin: hooved beast with bristling fur and curved tusks.

L'Lallistafuros, Vadni: former identity of Sana Lally.

Llanili the Stout: captain of a lifter taken by Prescot. DMA

Llangro the Alumsetter: a boxing coach of Nerlinium. WRA

L'Lengul, San: a Necromancer of Enderli. WRA

L'Livero, San: a priest of Dokerty in Nerlinium. WRA

L'Luminophrontesia, Kov: a noble of Caneldrin. DMA

Lochrivarn, Avenue of: a street in Oxonium.

Logan: a young priest in the shrine of Cymbaro. INA, GGA

Logan, Strom: a noble of Oxonium, a portly Hytak, an old paktun who'd served his time and saved his money and been rewarded with a small stromnate. GGA

Logan Umpitor: alias used by Prescot in Prebaya.

"Lola the Fair and the Door Handle": a song ever so, ever so, sad right up to the last line, which is so raucous it reduces listeners every time to helpless laughter.

Lolalee: a member of the Hellraisers. GGA

lopy: a small animal.

Lopy the Lame: a member of Nagzalla's Nasty Neemus. WRA

Lora the Leemkin: deceased member of the Roaring Fifties.

Lorgan ti Mindlo: a friend of the cadade in the palace of Oxonium. DMA

Louis Pelong: a kregoinye.

Lucilli the Radiant: a Kildoi goddess.

Lurking Shadows, Hill of: a hill in Oxonium.

Lycon the Standard: an Yvonnim hired as a guard in the palace of Oxonium, who was transformed into an Ibmanzy. DMA

Mabal: a name used in Balintol for the red sun of Kregen.

Madam Moly Mushtaq, for the sweet sake of: oath used by Prescot.

"Maiden with the Single Veil, The": a song current over most of Paz.

malfsim: race of diffs whose heads give the impression of being all face with tiny features. Button nose, pinched mouth, pig-like eyes are surrounded by what seems like acres of skin.

Margayla Street: name of a street in Oxonium.

Marlo M'Maringo na Schull, Strom: nephew of Kov Barca L'Lambton na Freydin. CHA

Marsippo the Melancholy: tailless Hytak lookout aboard *Galloping Zorca*. CHA

Matol: a name used in Balintol for the green sun of Kregen.

mazarnil: unruly.

Melly: sister of Dimpy.

Milius: ship's doctor of *Roscommon*. CHA

Milsi the Slinky: a Vallian agent in Oxonium. GGA

mili-milu: small friendly monkey-like creature kept as pets.

Mimi: rather large woman whose room Prescot entered by mistake. INA

Miriam's Zhantils: a chariot-racing team of Emgidu. SCA

M'Marmor, San: Khibil advisor to C'Chermina, following the death of Granumin. DMA

Mogper, Jiktar: captain of the city guard of Bharang, an apim. INA

Molar Na-Fre: Pachak who worked under Prescot as a guard in the palace of Prebaya. DMA, SCA

Momolam Street: a street in Oxonium.

"Moonbright": "Goodnight" in Kildrin.

morntarch: a rattling scepter used in sorcery.

mutfer: short for mutrowferim.

mutrowfer: chariot.

mutrowferim: charioteer.

muzzilla: fierce beast, all hair and fangs and claws, with a whiplash tail.

Naghan the Barrel: Prescot's spymaster in Oxonium. INA, GGA

Naghan's Droombs: a chariot-racing team of Emgidu. SCA

Naghan the Ear: a boxing manager in Nerlinium. WRA

Naghan the Flabby: Och water carrier taken on by Prescot in Prebaya. DMA

Naghan the Flea: polsim who worked as a palace guard under Prescot in Prebaya. SCA

Naghan ti Fromion, Tyr: captain of *Eregoin's Answer*. WRA

Naghan ti Indrin: Advang who plotted to kill Quensella in Prebaya. DMA

Naghan the Leaves: an herbalist of Prebaya. SCA

Naghan the Ordsetter: follower of Lord Jazipur who accompanied Prescot to recover Strom Korden's sword. INA

Naghan the Rash: pilot aboard *Galloping Zorca*. CHA

Naghan the Stout: another name for Garnath the Stout.

Naghan the Twist: Gon retainer of Princess Nandisha. GGA

Naghan Vindo, Elten: Vallian ambassador to Caneldrin. DMA, SCA

Nag-Rin-Chandon: Wizard of Loh who assisted Khon the Mak. WRA

Nagzalla's Nasty Neemus: a street gang in Oxonium.

Nalan C'Cardieth, Hikdar: handler of a pack of werstings hired by Ranaj. GGA

Nalan ti Perming: Hytak who worked under Prescot as a guard in the palace of Prebaya. DMA

Nalgre Froi's Deren: a tavern in Prebaya.

Nalgre the Planks, Deldar: a member of the guard in Prebaya. DMA

Nalgre ti Poventer: a Vallian diplomat in Oxonium, a Gon, who wears a red eyepatch. GGA

Nalgre the Ron: red-headed agent employed by Naghan Raerdu in Oxonium. INA

Nalgre S'Scholian: a retainer of San W'Watchun. CHA

Nalgre the Unster: alias used by Prescot when arrested in Oxonium.

Nalgre ti Poventer: a soldier of Vallia acting as a messenger of the Vallian ambassador in Oxonium. GGA, DMA

Nalimer's Iridescent Faerling: venue for animal-fighting shows in Oxonium.

Nandisha: a princess rescued by Prescot and Fweygo in Amintin. INA, GGA

"Nandy Nath's Blind Pilgrimage": title of a song.

Nangro: Malfsim retainer of Khon the Mak. WRA

Narlin: a priest of Dokerty.

Nath B'Bensarm: Strom of Bharang. INA

Nath the Bellows: a member of Nagzalla's Nasty Neemus. WRA

Nath's Cake and Bun Emporium: a cake shop in Oxonium.

Nath the Chanter: another name for Nath the Singer.

Nath ti Fangenun: Jiktar in the service of Prince Ortyg, killed in an attack on the palace of Princess Nandisha. GGA

Nath the Frogenstal: a guard in the retinue of Princess Nandisha. GGA

Nath the Gnarled: a Polsim informant in Nerlinium. WRA

Nath G'Goldark: new chief priest of Dokerty in Oxonium. SCA, WRA

Nath the Haggler, Kyro of: a public square in Oxonium.

Nath's Hammerers: a chariot-racing team of Emgidu. SCA

"Nath the Iarvin among the Clouds": a comical song of Tolindrin, which tells of how Nath the Iarvin, a simple candle-maker's son, sought his fortune in Caneldrin, the nation immediately to the north of Tolindrin. He found himself one day on one of the volgendrins that circle in the air in that country and by calling upon Tolaar the Mighty sailed the flying island all the way south to Tolindrin. The song finishes with Nath the Iarvin's joyous reception at home.

Nath ti Lernerzun: a passenger on *Gleaming Thunder*, an Och. DMA

Nath L'Llonge: a chariot-racing manager in Emgidu. SCA

Nath Market Street: a street in Oxonium.

Nath the Nose: Gon arrested along with Prescot in Oxonium. INA

Nath Seegfreedhan: owner of Vando's Lilies, to whose aid Prescot came in Emgidu. SCA

Nath the Seeing: member of Nagzalla's Nasty Neemus. GGA

Nath Shivenham, Lord: alias used by Naghan Raerdu in Tolindrin.

Nath the Singer: a member of Quensella's guard. DMA, SCA

Nath the Solarkey: gauffrer arrested along with Prescot in Oxonium. INA

Nath the Sullen: a Dokerty warrior slain by Delia. WRA

Nath the Swagger: Brokelsh underling to Chekaran. CHA

Nath T'Tolin: deceased husband of Princess Nandisha.

Nath the Vosk: proprietor of the Spotted Gyp. CHA

Nazrak, Prince: deceased brother of Prince Vanner.

Neap the Traiky: retainer of Princess Nandisha. GGA

Nelacion, by: oath used by Kov L'Luminophrontesia.

Nerlinium: capital city of Enderli.

Nessve: Hytak physician and larvan in Oxonium. GGA

Net and Stickling, the: a tavern in Amintin.

Nethized, Most Puissant: a minor cult of Oxonium.

Nine Autarchs: the ruling council of Kildrin.

Nisha: daughter of Princess Nandisha, rescued by Prescot and Fweygo in Amintin. INA, GGA

N'Norgad the Belly: king of Enderli. WRA

Noni Seng: young girl, a seamstress, murdered and mutilated in Oxonium. GGA

Norun: twin brother of Ronun ti Bjorfling.

noumjiksirn: a wake.

obachnin: large savage beast which walks on four clawed legs and waves four clawed forelimbs about, with a nightmarish head where three eyes glow.

Oblifex: title of the high priest of Dokerty.

Oelefer: a deity of Winlan.

Oily Nath: fry-cook in the palace of Oxonium. GGA

Olabal: an Och, landlord of the Fluted Hen. INA

Oltomek: deity of the cult of Dokerty, considered the hand of Dokerty upon the face of Kregen.

Opus: name of a mountain in Balintol.

Ornol the Roasts: cook in the retinue of Elten Larghos.

Ortyg: alias used by Prescot in Santoro.

Ortyg: a Hikdar in the constabulary of Oxonium. INA

Ortyg, Prince: a claimant to the throne of Tolindrin. INA, DMA

Outer Pannoilia: mythical country beyond the lake of fire where zombies sleep.

ovverer: type of flying craft capable of ethereal levitation but lacking forward propulsion except for wind power.

Oxonium: capital city of Tolindrin The inhabitants live in some luxury and splendor on the flat tops of a number of steep-sided hills. In the runnels between the hills, some marshy, some drained and filled with the hovels of the poor and slaves, some allowing the rivers to flow to their conjunction by the grand central hill, the suns strike only around the hour of mid. The plateaus are linked to each other by a system of cable cars.

Padria na Fermintin, San: pilgrim on the road to Farinsee encountered by Prescot. INA

"Paktun's Promenade": a drinking song.

Palfrey the Pfiffer: body servant of Dagert of Paylen. INA, DMA

Paline Lanto: shop girl killed and mutilated in Oxonium.

Pansy: a young Fleurese girl. DMA

Papishin: a variety of tree.

Parsons, Captain: captain of *Roscommon*. CHA

Partagus, San: once apprenticed to San W'Watchun, traveled to Loh for mysterious purposes.

Passion: one of the zorcas driven by Prescot in the chariot races of Emgidu. SCA

Paynor, San: a priest of Cymbaro in Oxonium. INA

Penitence Alley: street which runs alongside the Temple of Tolaar in Oxonium.

Perempto the Shorn: Khibil who worked under Prescot as a guard in the palace of Prebaya. DMA, SCA

Perfume Patrol: public servants in Oxonium, who spray scents and disinfectants to suppress unpleasant smells.

Perseverance: one of the zorcas driven by Prescot in the chariot races of Emgidu. SCA

Petegland: uncle of Dimpy. GGA

Pilnor: polsim scribe in the retinue of Khon the Mak. WRA

Pin Street: name of a street in Oxonium.

"Pits of Hell are Sweet because of my Loved One, The": a song title.

Pixirr: god of mischief.

Pleasant Rest: a tavern in Prebaya.

polsim: tailless race of diffs with pointed ears, narrow devil's faces, deep vee-shaped mouths, and leathery skin.

Portlo the Render: leader of a band of aragorn in Vaiwadrin. WRA

potbelly and generous ladle of the master chef Ramdiz of the Recipes, by the: an oath used by Dagert.

Power: one of the zorcas driven by Prescot in the chariot races of Emgidu. SCA

P'Pernorath, Vad: a local official in Lakensmot. DMA

P'Pinxi, Kovneva: a noble of Caneldrin. DMA

praxul: nasty, squamous, scuttling beast, about waist-high, warty of scaled hide, with claws and three stalked eyes.

Prebaya: capital of Caneldrin.

Pride: one of the zorcas driven by Prescot in the chariot races of Emgidu. SCA

Prodacta: a patron saint of sandal makers.

Prodigal: a trident of good Lohvian quality used by Prescot in Oxonium. GGA

Pronto and Risslaca: a tavern in Prebaya.

purple eyes and cherry-red lips of the Princess Luciliah Debliah from the mystical woods, by the: oath used by Prescot.

purtle: a cheap variety of wood.

Quail and Cypher: inn in Prebaya.

Quarnus: Hytak Hikdar in the guard of Dorval ham Hesting. CHA

Quavens: diffs with apim-looking faces but bodies of strange configuration.

Quenlo, San: a sage of Almuensis who works for C'Cuisar. WRA

queyfor: seal ring.

Q'Quensella, Lady: a passenger on *Gleaming Thunder.* DMA, WRA

Radiant Light: a tributary which flows into the Largesse in Prebaya.

Ragaran the Ordsetter: a passenger on *Gleaming Thunder,* a Rapa. DMA

Raging Volcanoes, the: a street gang in Oxonium.

Rakif: a Kataki who made a slaving raid on the Fleurese. DMA

Ramley: a Lord and Tchekedo of Winbium. CHA

Ranaj: an attendant of Princess Nandisha, a numim. INA, GGA

Ranto: a guard in the retinue of Princess Nandisha. GGA

Ravelstan Street: a street in Oxonium.

Red Ruin: airboat used by Prescot and Fweygo.

Relentless Regret, Bridge of: a bridge in Prebaya convenient for suicides.

Remor Street: a street in Prebaya.

Rena: name used by a young girl rescued by Prescot in Winbium. CHA

Renata: Hytak girl aided by Prescot in Prebaya. SCA

Renko: Hikdar guard in the palace of Prebaya. DMA

rhok: a golden coin of Balintol.

Rinaldrin: country of origin of Ronun ti Bjorfling.

Rindle: one-eared Rapa with straggly green feathers who bought a zorca from Prescot. INA

Rita the Bodacious: a farm girl of Vaiwadrin. WRA

Roaring Fifties: a street gang of Oxonium.

Rockingham: British Navy ship of which Prescot dreamed of being First Lieutenant.

Rofi: a child of Ranaj, rescued by Prescot and Fweygo in Amintin. INA, GGA

Rolan: a child of Ranaj, rescued by Prescot and Fweygo in Amintin. INA, GGA

Rolico's Strigicaws: a chariot-racing team of Emgidu.

Rondjas's Hill: a plateau in Oxonium.

Ronun ti Bjorfling, Jiktar: captain of San W'Watchun's guard. CHA

Roscommon: British Navy ship of which Prescot dreamed of being First Lieutenant.

Roubail: a high-class wine from Enderli.

R'Raneed: a boxing promoter of Nerlinium. WRA

Rushi of the Puddings and Cakes, by Mother: oath used by Prescot.

Salinchez, by: oath used in Oxonium.

Sammle the Erkanstater: a guard in the retinue of Princess Nandisha. GGA

Samphron: sister of Dimpy. GGA

Sando: beloved of Renata. SCA

Santoro: town located atop a mountainous outcrop in the desert.

San Vester's Challenge: a gambling game, named after the sage who'd invented it some thousand or so seasons ago, a matter of placing numbered squares down in such a way as to complete the winning sequence and deny the opposition that favor.

Scent of Palines: previous name of Red Ruin.

Schakaro, San: a priest of Dokerty in Nerlinium. WRA

Schinbalasch: a Shank encampment.

schonibium: an ancient spiritual healing technique.

Screaming Leems: a street gang of Oxonium.

Serinka: wife of Ranaj. INA, GGA

Shalli: apim girl who nursed Prescot in Winbium. WRA

shamlak: tunic-like vestment worn with a gap of at least a hand's breadth down the front, fastened across the front with cords stretching from button to button.

Shansi: the Sprite of Love, who sends her loop of flowers down to entwine lovers.

Shensi: a type of play, all puppets and buffoonery.

Shirree: sister of Prince Vanner. INA

Sijilo the Oivon: Hytak who worked as a palace guard under Prescot in Prebaya. SCA

Simpkins: midshipman aboard *Roscommon*. CHA

Skull Crag: a peak in the Abley mountains.

Skullbiters: subgroup of the Hellraisers.

Sleed the Slick: Khibil member of the Hellraisers. GGA

slikker: a blade in length between a shortsword and a braxter, favored where steel is expensive.

sliptinger paste: a tasty dish cooked in a pot.

Smitoll, by: a polsim oath.

Solana: Och maiden who nursed Prescot in Winbium. WRA

Spotted Gyp, the: a tavern in Winbium.

Staky: a member of the Hellraisers. GGA

Stancher, Captain: captain of *Aventure*. CHA

stryle: obstinate.

Sturgies, Hill of: a plateau in Oxonium.

stylox: a beast with graceful slender legs and curly horns.

Suzy the Surcease: a puncture lady of Prebaya. SCA

Swan Street: street in Winbium, so named for an ancient fountain graced with stone swans.

Tafnu: a servitor of Princess Nandisha. INA

Tansi the Lily: young girl of Oxonium, murdered on the steps of the temple of Dokerty in Oxonium. GGA

Tansy: name used by a young girl rescued by Prescot in Winbium. CHA

Tarbak the Sohan: Brokelsh resident of Oxonium, who took in Lingurd when he was injured. INA

Taston, San: a priest of Dokerty in Nerlinium. WRA

Tchekedo: neckerchief-wearing warriors who swept out of the northern mountains to conquer Winlan.

Thansi: Fristle fifi who nursed Prescot in Winbium. WRA

"That the governance of a country should be left to blind heredity!": saying attributed to San Blarnoi.

Thrushness, Lakes of: lakes located in the north of Tolindrin.

Tilly: mistress of Fweygo's family farm, among many other talents. SCA

Tilly of the Golden Fur, by the Lady: a Fristle oath.

Tiri: See T'Tirivenswatha.

Tjorus: name of a mountain in Oxonium.

Tolaar: chief deity of Tolindrin.

Tolindrese: inhabitants of Tolindrin.

Tomendishto: a prince of Tolindrin, later king. INA

traiky: lucky.

Trako Ironbelly: Kataki Captain of the City Watch in Oxonium. INA

Tral the Strict: Quensella's major-domo. DMA

Tricina, Witches of: doomed witches who are let out for one day a season from their eternal incarceration in the Furnace Fires of Inshurfraz.

Trinkim: race of diffs with thick bald heads, bulging eyes, and stubby fangs.

T'Taxkrin, Trylon: an ally of Khon the Mak owning a palace in Nerlinium. WRA

T'Tirivenswatha: nicknamed Tiri, temple dancer from the retinue of Strom Korden, rescued by Prescot. INA, GGA, WRA

T'Tolin: ruling family of Tolindrin.

Tygnam ti Fralen: Hikdar in the guard of Hyr Kov Brannomar. INA

Ulak the Eye: Undurker crew member of *Galloping Zorca*. CHA

Umpitor Kyro: a public square in Oxonium.

Umrigg: an isolated village with an inn of satisfactory quality.

Vaiwadrin: "the Flower Country"; mysterious land located where the borders of Winlan, Enderli, and Caneldrin meet.

Vando's Lilies: a Chariot-racing team of Emgidu. SCA

Vanner, Prince: father of Princess Nandisha.

Varang: race of diffs with monkey-like features, a fringe of hair over the eyes, round cupped ears, and mustachioed, prone to screech maniacally.

Varghan na Vernheim: code name used by Prescot in Caneldrin.

Veda: sometimes known as the Mazarnil, a young girl rescued by Prescot in the temple of Dokerty. DMA, SCA, WRA

veeson: wild animal of Balintol not unlike a leem.

Velino the Lark: Vallian soldier killed attempting to retrieve a Prism of Power. WRA

Velda: mother of Dimpy. GGA

venahim: a race of diffs with two arms and no tail, corpulent of frame, heavy ridges over the forehead and around the eyes, which are piercing, renowned for their mysterious healing powers.

Villodrin: country in Loh with golden-haired apim inhabitants.

Vita, Lady: manipulative wife of Lord Jazpur. INA

Vo'drin and Buckets: a passable inn in Lakensmot.

Voidal twins: Vallian spies in Oxonium. INA

Volarminanster, San: nicknamed San Volar, the chief priest of the cult of Tolaar. GGA

voryachin: ugly fish, consisting mostly of jaws and teeth that can separate a person into two halves.

Wanchun the Vile, by: an oath used by Veda.

Wenhartdrin's Cheer: airboat which carried Vallian soldiers to retrieve a Prism of Power.

Wheesh-amakler: Balintol spirit of the winds.

Winbium: capitol city of Winlan.

Winlan: country in the north of Balintol.

Wocut: a sorcerer who serves Hyr Kov Khonstanton. INA

worpling: a word of indeterminate meaning which Akers takes in general to indicate someone talking on at length, maundering or jabbering, perhaps, whilst the auditor barely listens. wrapped in his or her own thoughts.

Worthing: ship's doctor of *Aventure*. CHA

W'Watchun: a renowned Illusionist of Winlan, Sorcerer of Balintol. SCA, CHA, WRA

Xalanx: a perfumed vintage out of Xuntal.

Yando: young king of Caneldrin. DMA

Yellow Deserts: deserts located in Caneldrin.

Yunivils: a race of diffs startlingly unlike apims but nice people. They believe that they must be buried with their arms behind their backs and their hands grasping their heels; otherwise they will not be received into their heaven, but instead will be hurled down to their hell, Makchun.

Yvonnim: race of diffs with no tail and only two arms, who have particularly sharp hearing through their floppy ears. Their noses are broad and flat, reaching from cheek to cheek, and their eyes are deep under a wide, protruding forehead.

"Zakryst's Great War Horse": a song current over most of Paz.

zerzy: a mountain-dwelling animal.

Zonder ti Rannellden, Jiktar: a Hytak cadade in the retinue of Strom Logan. GGA

Zorca Heart, the: a famous inn in Umrigg frequently used for assignations.

Alan Burt Akers

Alan Burt Akers was a pen name of the prolific British author Kenneth Bulmer, who died in December 2005 aged eighty-four.

Bulmer wrote over 160 novels and countless short stories, predominantly science fiction, both under his real name and numerous pseudonyms, including Alan Burt Akers, Frank Brandon, Rupert Clinton, Ernest Corley, Peter Green, Adam Hardy, Philip Kent, Bruno Krauss, Karl Maras, Manning Norvil, Chesman Scot, Nelson Sherwood, Richard Silver, H. Philip Stratford, and Tully Zetford. Kenneth Johns was a collective pseudonym used for a collaboration with author John Newman. Some of Bulmer's works were published along with the works of other authors under "house names" (collective pseudonyms) such as Ken Blake (for a series of tie-ins with the 1970s television programme The Professionals), Arthur Frazier, Neil Langholm, Charles R. Pike, and Andrew Quiller.

Bulmer was also active in science fiction fandom, and in the 1970s he edited nine issues of the New Writings in Science Fiction anthology series in succession to John Carnell, who originated the series.

www.ingramcontent.com/pod-product-compliance
Lightning Source LLC
Chambersburg PA
CBHW022002050726
47499CB00002BA/269